LIVING CHINA

FLYING CHINA

LU HSÜN
Swan Studio

LIVING CHINA

Modern Chinese Short Stories

COMPILED AND EDITED BY
EDGAR SNOW

WITH AN INTRODUCTION BY THE EDITOR
AND AN ESSAY ON MODERN CHINESE
LITERATURE BY NYM WALES

a JOHN DAY book

REYNAL & HITCHCOCK: *NEW YORK*

Published by
JOHN DAY
in association with
REYNAL & HITCHCOCK

*Made in Great Britain. Printed by Western Printing Services, Ltd.,
Bristol*

ACKNOWLEDGMENT

ACKNOWLEDGMENT is made to the editors and publishers of *Asia*, *Forum*, *Life and Letters To-day*, *China To-day*, and *Voice of China* for permission to reprint certain stories which have already appeared in those magazines. Thanks are also expressed to Agnes Smedley, to Messrs Lawrence and Wishart, Ltd., and to the International Publishers, New York City, U.S.A., for permission to reprint *Slave Mother* from *Short Stories from China*. The editor is further indebted to the publishers of *Asia* for allowing him to reprint his article on Lu Hsün in this volume.

CONTENTS

INTRODUCTION

By the EDITOR

SOME explanation should be offered of why this book came to be compiled, and how. The processes behind the work range over a period of five years. The motivation for it derives from a mixture of curiosity and experiment, but chiefly an intense interest on my part both to find out and to make available to Western readers the answer to the question, "What is happening to the creative mind of modern China?"

No one can stay long in this country without realizing that he is living in a *milieu* disturbed and enriched by the materials of dynamic art. The break-up of the world's oldest continuous culture, the collapse of a many-walled fortress of old values, and the struggle internally and externally to impose something new to replace them; the focusing of a sharp critical lens on ideas, things, and institutions that for centuries have been accepted as moral, virtuous, and normal, with the consequent rejection of whole series of beliefs; the discovery of new dimensions in time and space judgments; the kind of healthy chaos everywhere in which are being fermented the germs of mighty and meaningful economic, political, and cultural transitions over the whole of Eastern Asia—these are the broad arenas of conflict and contrast and revaluation in which the flood of human life beats turbulently in China to-day. And they are the conditions of mutation which have hitherto made the earth fecund and stirred with new life the womb of great art.

Anyone at all sensitive to his environment cannot help

wondering in China about the intellectual activity around him, and wanting to pry into it. That is what happened to me. The hundreds of 'interpretative' books on China written by Occidentals, and even those by Chinese for Western readers, did not satisfy. Their emphasis was nearly all on the past, and concerned with problems and culture-patterns already interred. Alien writers know very little about the mind of China, and the sinologue, generally encrusted with conservatism and horror of all pulsations indicative of change, scrupulously avoided investigating it. Most of the Chinese writers either disparaged modern China or presented it with a false façade to suit the suscepti-bilities of a foreign audience. This was, of course, before the appearance of Lin Yü-t'ang's *My Country and My People*.

I wanted to know what the Chinese intellectual really thinks about himself, what he talks and writes about himself in Chinese. How do the present-day upper- and lower-class Chinese, among themselves, really work, act, love, play, and rationalize their *rôle* in the design of things? What moves and interests them, and why? What is significant to them, what provides them with purpose in life, now that Confucius and Mencius and Hsun Tzü and Mo Ti and other once-sacred names no longer invoke piety in them? What intellectual imprint has China's violent contact with Japan and the Western world left upon the artist, and how does he express it? More especially, how does he articulate it in the imaginative literature he writes for others like himself—exclusively for Chinese eyes and appreciation, and not with the notion of pleasing foreign readers, or of cater-ing to foreign prejudices, or of feeding the Western avidity for the 'exotic,' the 'quaint,' and the 'picturesque'?

But when I turned to look for literature of this kind I was astonished to find that there was virtually none of it in English. No important modern Chinese novels had been translated, and only a few short stories had appeared obscurely in short-lived or little-read sectarian papers. That

was in 1931, and little even of the classical fiction of China
had yet been converted into English, including the epic
Shui Hu Chuan, which Pearl Buck later brilliantly translated
as *All Men Are Brothers*. The translation of *Hung Lou Mêng*,
or *Dream of the Red Chamber*, had just been made, Herbert
Giles' *Strange Stories from a Chinese Studio*, an English
version of the ancient *Liao Tsai*, had also been published,
and Brewitt-Taylor's rendering of the *San Kuo*, or the
Three Kingdoms, had been out since 1929. But of modern
pai-hua, or vernacular literature, of writing of the revolutionary period, only a few scattered fragments had
appeared in English.

I asked many Chinese and foreign friends why this was
so. Most of the foreigners, even those who knew the
language, thought it was because there was nothing of much
value. But, I argued, even if contemporary China has
produced no great literature, there must be much of
scientific and sociological interest, and for utilitarian purposes alone it ought to be made available to us. With
millions of words of creative writing pouring from the
rapidly growing Press of China, appearing and being avidly
read in increasing numbers of newspapers, weekly magazines, periodicals, and books, there was, I felt, certain to be
material of importance for an understanding of the spiritual
and material and cultural forces at work in reshaping
Chinese thought. Most Chinese agreed with me, and
referred me to the domain of the short story, where literary
creativity has largely centred since the renaissance of 1917.
But who would travel across its vast spaces, a literary *terra
incognita* to the Western world? Who would select and
translate and edit?

It was meeting Lu Hsün and Lin Yü-t'ang that finally
decided me to undertake the task myself. Lu Hsün as a
personality so impressed me with his breadth of humanity,
his warmth of sympathy, and his keen perceptivity of the
life around him that I felt sure his writing would provide

interpretations of interest. And Lin Yü-t'ang's wit and a facile way with words in English, his skilful and mature and penetrating satire and good-humoured 'old-roguism' (to borrow Lin's own phrase), were a promise that equally important talent must lie hidden in recent writing in the Chinese language, and be worth bringing into English.

I knew little Chinese then (and make no claims to sinology now), but I found an able collaborator in Yao Hsin-nung, a talented young critic, playwright, and essayist, and a close friend of Lu Hsün. Together we first explored Lu Hsün's *Na Han*, universally acknowledged to be the most important native influence on the development of the modern short-story form in China. The work of Lu Hsün included in this volume is the fruit of that collaboration.

Later on I sought and secured the co-operation of a number of China's leading writers in the choice of representative stories of their well-known contemporaries. Among those to whom I owe thanks for this kind of assistance are: Lu Hsün, whose social and political *rôle* in China is remarkably similar to that of Gorki in Russia, and whose writing has won him the name of "China's Chekhov"; Mao Tun, perhaps China's best-known novelist; Hsiao Ch'ien, editor of the *Ta Kung Pao Literary Supplement*; Chêng Chên-to, editor of *Literature*; Lin Yü-t'ang, editor of *The Analects*; Ku Chieh-kang, one of China's outstanding scholars; Yao Hsin-nung, mentioned above; Miss Shih Ming, two of whose stories are included here; and—through the medium of Hsiao Ch'ien—Shên Ts'ung-wên and Pa Chin, both of whom have powerfully influenced the growth of modern Chinese literature.

But none of these writers is to be held individually responsible either for the volume itself or for the translations, for I did not always accept their advice. In the end what critical judgment I possess was the criterion of selection, and I am prepared to be assailed for this as much as it pleases you. However, there is wide disagreement among

Chinese authors, and it is just as wide among readers, concerning 'best stories,' as is shown by various Chinese collections. Most of these were consulted, of course. Although this volume copies none of them, nevertheless it contains the authors, and many of the stories, found in representative collections. A list of these is included in Appendix B.

For assistance with the translations other than those of Lu Hsün I am indebted to various Chinese writers, including Ku T'ung-chih, Hsiao Ch'ien, and Shih Ming—as well as to my old scholar-teacher, who speaks no English, loathes modern writing, and gladly washes his hands of the whole business.

Sinologists, should any care to peruse these tales and compare them with the originals, are advised to have strong stimulants near by, for in some cases they will be needed to minimize the shocks over liberties taken in the functions of editing. Let it here be candidly emphasized that these stories are not offered as 'literal' translations, if by literal is meant that for every Chinese character must be found a precise equivalent, and that every idiom must be rendered into exact (however unintelligible) English.

What I have endeavoured to do is to convey the spirit of a piece of work, to interpret it rather than to photostat it, and to put it into English that would transmit the emotional as well as the intellectual conviction behind it. It is often quite impossible to do that in a 'literal' translation of Chinese. I have retained original idioms wherever possible, and this is in the majority of instances, but I have sometimes refused to keep a simple pun or historical or classical allusion that would require a half-page footnote to make it comprehensible, and thereby contribute further to the legend that the Chinese are 'queer' people.

Altogether it has been no easy task. Indeed, had I divined a fuller notion of the sheer fatigue and tiresome manual labour attached to such a work I should never have 'rushed in.' I assure anyone interested that I would much prefer to

write three books of my own rather than have to repeat the operations that have gone into the making of
this one.

I found, for one thing, that some of the 'best' Chinese
stories were too long for inclusion in a collection. Many of
them might be considered full-length novels or at least
novelettes, yet their materials and themes, their range of
action and incident and whole compass of development, are
essentially those of short stories. Lu Hsün's *Ah Q Chêng
Chuan* is such a story, as are Mao Tun's *Spring Silkworms*
and Shên Ts'ung-wên's popular *Frontier City*. Others are
found in the works of Lao Shê, Kuo Mo-jo, Chang Tzü-
p'ing, and Wang T'ung-chao.

It may be stated that with few exceptions nearly all such
long stories would be much improved by drastic condensa-
tion, and many Chinese critics have agreed with me in this
opinion. Chinese writers are miserably paid. The average
rate is from $3 to $4 (Chinese) per thousand words, and it
rarely exceeds $5[1] per thousand. Hence there is a temptation
for all but the best authors to string beads on the necklace
of their stories indefinitely. There is often padding with
essentially meaningless though usually pretty enough dialogue and narrative, which contributes nothing to the
development of the story, thus sacrificing interest, coherence,
and compactness of style and form in order to pay the
rice-vendor—a practice by no means unknown in the
West.

Curiously enough, this defect has appeared in some of the
finest stories written, and becomes decidedly marked in the
English translation. Chinese do not seem to mind such
purposeless rambling, for it is an old trick of the oral story-
teller—who, however, is licensed to spin out his yarn
because he deals in the formless epic. But the Western reader
is sure to find it irritating in the short story, so that in several
included in this volume I have made so bold as to omit

[1] The Chinese dollar is worth about 1s. 3d.

certain passages and episodes. In the cases of *Ah Ao* and *Suicide* this surgery had the authors' consent; in that of *Mutation* the author was consulted, but without result.

But the sins of the editor do not stop there. I have, besides, made it a practice to embody in the text, in the few places where required, explanatory words or phrases or sentences, in order to avoid extensive footnotes which the terseness and obscurity of the Chinese language might otherwise have made necessary. In three or four or perhaps more instances—for example, in *Voyage beyond Law*—I have added clarifying terms to describe people or situations which, in the original, had to be left ambiguous to please the censors. Here and there, when the full richness of the image evoked by the combination of Chinese characters could not be conveyed by a mere translation, I have deepened the colour, or expanded a phrase, to achieve a closer resemblance to the contour of thought or feeling or implication inherent in the original.

With all this, therefore, let no one trouble to inform me that the translations are not always 'literal' or even 'accurate.' They would be even worse than they are if that were the case. I am not, however, as bad as George Bernard Shaw, who, in converting Siegfried Trebitsch's *Jitta's Atonement* into English, considered the translation "a quite minor matter," and turned the play from an Austrian tragedy into a Shavian farce. For the stories here are in their spirit and inner content faithfully handled. Their materials, their fundamental point of view, the problems they pose in Chinese destiny, are presented with integrity. The reader may safely believe that through them he is getting, if not literary works of imposing genius, at least a wholly fresh and authentic expression of a decisive new cultural stage, attained by a process of history in its march of centuries across the vast and wonderful country within whose borders dwells a fifth of the family of men. Here, as through a giant eye thrown over its rivers and plains and valleys and peaks,

B

is an organic view of the heart and the mind, and perhaps once or twice the soul, of living China.

Something of that historic process, and the *rôle* in it of writers excluded from as well as included in this book, is essential background for a sympathetic reading of the pages that follow. For this purpose there is included in an appendix an outline of modern Chinese literary development, written by Nym Wales, an authority on modern Chinese art and literature. Based on extensive original research and painstaking study, and prepared after consultation with several of China's foremost literary critics, it is, I believe, the first full-bodied analysis and discussion of this kind to appear in English.

PEKING
July 1936

PART I
STORIES BY LU HSÜN

LU HSÜN
(1881–)

LU HSÜN (also transliterated Lu Shun, Lu Hsin, or Lusin) is a *nom de plume*. The real name of this celebrated Chinese writer is Chou Shu-jên, and he was born in 1881 in the city of Shaohsing, in Chekiang Province. His family had for generations produced scholars. His grandfather had the degree of *Han-lin*, which was the highest honour a scholar could attain under the Manchu dynasty. His father, who died while still young, was a *Hsiu-ts'ai*, the rank given to successful candidates at first imperial examinations.

As a child in such a family Chou Shu-jên naturally received a thorough tutoring in the classics, but after his father's death troubles began. It appears that not all the old scholars were squeezing rascals, for literary distinctions had not made the Chous wealthy, and the boy and his mother were left penniless. He was never a 'beggar,' as exaggerated tales relate, but his mother had to accept charity for some time, and it was only after great difficulty that she got him to Nanking and into the Government schools. There he entered the imperial naval academy, and later on he transferred to the school of mining and engineering, where he graduated. He managed to get himself sent to Japan for further study, at the Government's expense.

In Tokyo he studied medicine, and, having completed his course, returned to China in 1909. He was bitterly disappointed because he had been unable to continue his education in Europe, and refused to practise medicine, of which he knew "just enough to be a menace." Instead, he began to teach in his native province. Hopeful and enthusiastic when the revolution triumphed in 1911, he went at once to Peking, where he was drawn into the intellectual life which was then beginning to stir China.

For fifteen years he led a life of diverse and vigorous activity. He accepted a position with the Ministry of Education, and concurrently taught at three different universities. Among these was the famous Peking National University, cradle of the Chinese literary renaissance, and as centre of student-union politics the source of no small trouble for officials. Meanwhile Lu Hsün edited the *Man Yuan* and the *Yu Shih*, literary periodicals, translated numerous German, Russian, and Japanese books, and became identified with the great *New Youth* magazine. It was in 1917 that the *New Youth* began the *pai-hua* (vernacular) movement which ultimately was to march triumphantly across China. The publication was then edited by Chen Tu-hsiu, who later became a Communist and is now serving a long sentence in Nanking for his political heresy. At that time Chen was an ardent reformist, and his most radical step was to publish the essay which made Hu Shih famous—the manifesto advocating the adoption of *pai-hua* as the national language. Until the *New Youth* appeared, published entirely in *pai-hua*, almost all Chinese writing had been in the classical *wen-li*.

None of China's 'revolutions' caused greater agitation than the language revolution, and no war was more bitterly fought than the 'brush war' begun by the *New Youth*. Gradually it enlarged its offensive to include the whole social and political ideology of the conservatives carried over from the Manchu Dynasty, and attacked the rulers of the time. It was the beginning of critical thinking in living China. The more advanced Chinese demanded sweeping changes in politics, and in the system of government. They openly denounced the sickeningly corrupt Peking *régime*, and helped to organize opposition to it on a national scale.

Foremost among these was Lu Hsün. A colleague of Chen Tu-hsiu, he was an early contributor to the *New Youth*. In it was published, among other short stories, his *Medicine*, which is included in this volume. He first became noted, however, chiefly for originating a new form of short essay in *pai-hua*, called *tsa-kan*, or 'random thought.' In the intellectual combat then going on it proved a facile weapon, and it is to-day still in wide use. Examples of it are found in Lu Hsün's *Hot Wind*, *Wild Grass*, and one or two other books.

But it was the mordant *Real Story of Ah Q*, published in 1921, that made him nationally known. His subject as well as his technique in shaping it into fiction were then considered strikingly unusual for Chinese literature. *Ah Q* at once became widely discussed and debated. As a topic of conversation it rivalled the latest exploit of what conservatives called the "cracked-brain theorist," Sun Yat-sen, who had just been elected "President of China" by his followers at Canton. The long story was denounced by the *literati*, who regarded it as the ignoble epitome of all that was vile in the modernists. By the latter it was warmly praised as a work of art definitely proving the literary possibilities of *pai-hua*, in which it was written. Around Lu Hsün for a while the whole 'brush war' was fought, and out of it he emerged as a recognized leader of the new *pai-hua* literature.

When it was shortly afterwards published in his *The War Cry* the first edition was immediately sold out. New printings of the book have been issued once or twice a year ever since. It is one of the few works by living Chinese that has been widely translated, having appeared in French, German, Russian, Japanese, and other languages.[1] Romain Rolland, a great admirer of Lu Hsün's work, said that he was so moved by it that he wept.

But the authorities did not appreciate what critics call his 'fat' humour. The appearance of *The War Cry* made things more difficult. Charged with organizing students' unions and inciting revolt, he was forced to resign from the Ministry of Education. Suddenly, during the *régime* of the dictator Tuan Chih-jui, a warrant was issued for his arrest. Friends warned him, and he escaped from Peking and probable death.

He lived for a time in Amoy, where he wrote and taught. When Sun Yat-sen admitted the Communists to the Kuomintang he went to Canton, where some of his friends were Left Wing leaders. In 1927 Chiang Kai-shek's anti-Communist 'purgation' of the Kuomintang, which resulted in the killing of thousands of students, workers, and peasants, caused him to change his address again. Thoroughly disillusioned by these events, he went into hiding in Shanghai, to escape arrest.

[1] This story, which for reasons of length has had to be omitted from this collection, is obtainable under the title of *The Tragedy of Ah Qui*. See Bibliography, p. 356.

It was the 'purgation,' with the attendant horror of blood-drenched streets that he saw in Canton, and realization of the depth of the reaction, which finally caused Lu Hsün to swing decisively to the Left revolutionaries. This is not the place to interpret the various historical meanings of the word 'Leftist' in China. Here it must be sufficient to say that with the destruction of the Left Wing in the Kuomintang the term came to include, for a while, all remaining reformist activity. In the 'revolutionary literature' movement which grew out of the Kuomintang reaction there were, for example, disgruntled *bourgeoisie*, *salon* socialists, liberals, Communists, Menshevists, Trotskyites, and what-nots.

Quarrels in this Leftist intellectual movement ensued. Divided mainly into Creationists, Sun Society members, pink radicals of Hu Shih's Crescent Moon group, and Marxists, they began to attack one another. From among them Lu Hsün rose to become an outstanding champion of the proletarian cause. "Mere *bourgeois* revolution without a thoroughgoing socialist change," he now believed, "is utterly lacking in meaning for the masses." The Kuomintang promptly banned all publications in which his writings appeared, and he was forced to adopt a number of *noms de guerre*.

It was in 1930 that I first heard of him, and then he was being sought as a leader and organizer of the League of Left Writers, which the Government was determined to stamp out. By 1931, and especially after the Japanese invasion of Manchuria, the Kuomintang militarists began a more rigorous 'intellectual purgation.' It became dangerous to write realistically about peasant or working-class life, and to have such books in one's possession was a crime punishable according to the whim of the generals. Since then great numbers of young men and women have been imprisoned, tortured, and killed as suspected Reds, but none of these incidents was more tragic than the execution of half a dozen talented Left writers at Shanghai, on February 7, 1932.

These youths, all under thirty, and including one woman, were arrested by British police in the Shanghai International Settlement and, like many others, were turned over to the Kuomintang military authorities. They were Li Wei-hsen,

Hu Yeh-ping, Jou Shih, Tsung Hui, Yin Fu, and the girl Feng Kung. After being given the usual torture, they dug their graves and were then executed. The incident aroused indignation among liberals throughout the world, and in the United States such writers as Sinclair Lewis, Theodore Dreiser, John Dewey, Upton Sinclair, and about a hundred others protested to the Chinese Minister at Washington. A year later Ting Ling, most popular of woman authors, was kidnapped by Government agents, and is believed to have been put to death. About the same time Dr Yang Chien, a brilliant young scientist of the Academia Sinica and a Left sympathizer, was murdered by hired assassins. All of these and other victims of the harsh intellectual repression were friends of Lu Hsün, and he lived in constant fear of arrest or assassination. With Mao Tun, Ting Ling, and Kuo Mo-jo, who together represent a great part of modern China's literary genius, he is branded as a source of especially 'dangerous thought,' and eleven of his books are now banned by the Kuomintang.

As a matter of fact Lu Hsün is no more a true proletarian writer than Upton Sinclair, who is also on the black list in China, together with that arch-radical John Dewey and many other foreigners whose books have been translated into *pai-hua*. He does not rank himself as one, and thinks that China as yet has produced none of distinction. He retains the logical detachment of an intellectual reformer in most of his 'brush attacks' against such specific evils in Chinese society as squeeze, bribery, usury, child slavery, selfishness, superstitious 'Confucianism,' militaristic exploitation of workers and peasants, muzzling of the Press, destruction of the people's organizations, non-resistance to Japan, and other phenomena observable in modern China.

An eloquent and powerful speaker, with a contagious passion for social justice, Lu Hsün will draw a large audience anywhere. Such appearances involve risk, but the veneration in which he is held somewhat safeguards him. He has too much sense of humour to be a slogan-shouter and is impatient with the type. His message to Chinese youth rings with an appeal to logic.

"Think, and study the economic problems of society," he advises, "travel through the hundreds of dead villages, visit the generals and then visit their victims, see the realities of your time with opened eyes and a clear mind, and work for an enlightened society, but always think and study." Only the resurgent, educated youths, he believes, are capable of diagnosing China's fundamental diseases. "Reared in a class which is fast decaying, they alone can understand it, destroy it, and create an intelligent social order."

But, like Gorki, Lu Hsün has always been more at home in the social and cultural phases of the revolution than in its politics. In life and work he remains essentially an individualist. His belief in the socialist state is based on deep personal realizations of the economic and spiritual needs of the masses, rather than on any academic concern with dialectical materialism. He scoffs at art for art's sake, and believes writing is of value only for its propagandist message; but, whether he wills it or not, much of his work is art, and as near great art as anything produced in modern China.

While Lu Hsün has been deeply influenced by Russian writers like Turgenev, Artsybashev, and especially Gorki, whose works, along with those of the most important European writers, have been translated into Chinese only since the *pai-hua* movement began, he remains distinctly a product of his environment and everything he writes is informed and shaped by his subjective impressions in transitional China. This comment by a Chinese critic is just :

> Although much influenced by Western literature, Lu Hsun writes with lucid and elegant grace, in a natural and forceful style that is completely Chinese. It is there that he differs from the many imitators of Western technique. He has now, in fact, numerous imitators of his own. His stories of rural life and his many volumes of collected essays . . . lead the thought of the younger generation.

I have read and helped to translate a number of Lu Hsün's best stories and essays. Most of his stories seem rather loose in form, and from a Western point of view are extremely sketchy in plot; many are only character drawings. The great charm of his writing lies in his style, and that the translator struggles in vain to interpret. But for me the one value that stands out in nearly all his writing is the genius of his laughter, his Attic humour poised between pathos and mirth—which is the unique quality of China no foreign writer has ever quite grasped. What

that is like is succinctly described in this excerpt from a recent
issue of Lin Yu-tang's magazine, *The Analects* : [1]

> Like Chekhov's intellectuals of old Russia, like Dickens' classtypes
> of nineteenth-century England, Lu Hsün's characters will continue
> to live in the future because of their basic soundness and reality. . . .
> The depth of his portrayals is such that he not only makes us feel the
> truth and realism of his stories, and provokes mirth with every line,
> but he brings to us a new realization of our social conditions. . . .
> Our amusement when reading him is not merely superficial, but
> rather complex. In the midst of laughter we suddenly comprehend
> the inevitability of the obliteration of our feudal society in which his
> characters live. He is a subtle artist. . . .

The "miasmatic political atmosphere of China" prevents him
from solid work on the great revolutionary novel which his
friends urge him to complete, but meanwhile he writes barbed
essays, under pseudonyms, and translates more foreign literature.
He is a rapid reader, and has been through dozens of German
and Russian books, but most of his translations are from the
Japanese. He knows little English. China is indebted to him
for introducing much of the world's best literature, now available
in the new language, and he has led a whole movement to
invigorate Chinese thought by bringing it into contact with the
modern intellects of the West. In that, of course, much opposition is still encountered.

He is now forced to live in seclusion. Much of his time is
spent in collecting and preserving old forms of proletarian handi-
craft art now fast dying. He himself draws and paints and is a
skilful calligrapher. He has done much to stimulate the development of woodcut art in China and of the most interesting new
school of painting. He has made one of the finest collections
of rubbed prints of inscriptions and stone engravings in existence.
Recently he edited a set of books of the Ch'ing and Ming
Dynasty letter papers, printed from ancient woodblocks—an art
now nearly extinguished.

And because, like other intellectuals of the transitional period,
he has after all a classical background, he is inclined to think of
himself as belonging to the day of woodblocks. "I am too old,"
he says, "really to lead in the new ways. All I can give to the

[1] *Lun Yu*, August 1, 1934.

younger leaders of the inevitable new destiny are *no han*"—which literally means "cries of encouragement." But he still keeps the "vigour of his brush," and is to-day, as he has been for the past decade, the one figure in contemporary Chinese literature whose genius is universally unquestioned.

EDGAR SNOW, *in "Asia," January* 1935

MEDICINE

[MANY critics rank *Medicine* as one of the best pieces of short fiction produced during the Chinese 'literary renaissance' period. It was originally published in the *New Youth*, leader of the language reform. Its power of expression and its originality of subject-matter made a deep impression on the then nascent *pai-hua* movement, and in form it is now widely imitated.

While the story does not adequately reflect the interesting conflict between old and new which one finds in Lu Hsün's later writing, it still has value as an interpretation of rural China. Foreigners who know only Chinese treaty ports, where much progress in modern medicine is apparent, will be inclined, perhaps, to think that it exaggerates. Unfortunately it does not. Therapeutics, for many millions, still consist largely of a strange combination of exorcism, acupuncture, and quack medicines made of such remarkable substances as deer horns and powdered tiger bones. In England, by way of contrast, there is a competent doctor for every 1000 people, in China not one for 80 times that many.

Dried blood is believed by many ignorant people in China to have miraculous remedial effects. Pig's blood and sheep's blood are common ingredients of medicines. The superstition on which this story is based is widely credited, particularly in Southern China. The right to sell the warm blood of decapitated persons was regarded as the executioner's prerogative.

Medicine is a veiled attack on the Government for not more actively combating such practices. As in much of Lu Hsün's work, the story deals with the pathos of the philosophy of defeat and frustration which ignorance engenders among the Chinese masses. It is more gruesome than most of Lu Hsün's stories; nevertheless, even here "if one feels the death in his humour, one also feels the humour in his death," as somebody has said.

In even the best translation of Chinese much of its original savour and power are lost, and this is especially true of Lu Hsün, whose genius is largely stylistic. Every Chinese character has, of course, an atmosphere wholly its own (with elusive implications acquired during its millenniums of use) which it is often impossible to suggest by any single

English word, or group of words. The essence of good Chinese writing lies in its structural restraint, in what is left to the reader's imagination. "When I have presented one corner of a subject to anyone," said Confucius, "if he cannot from it learn the other three I do not repeat my lesson."

Lu Hsün's *doubles entendres* are recondite, and his numerous puns and allusions, his delicately shaded irony and censure, are frequently said to defy translation. Fortunately, *Medicine*, though simply conceived, is more elaborately constructed than most of his fiction. Hence it can be appreciated for its inherent story-value even though the richer qualities of style possessed by the original are denied us. One can see in *Medicine* at least the materials of his art, if not the finished portrait.]

IT is autumn, and late at night, so that the moon has already gone. The sky is a sheet of darkling blue. Everything still sleeps, except those who wander in the night, and Hua Lao-shuan. He sits up suddenly in his bed. Leaning over, he rubs a match and touches it to a lamp which is covered with grease. A pale greenish light flickers, and reveals the two rooms of a teahouse.

"Father of Hsiao-shuan, are you leaving?" queries the voice of a woman. There is a series of tearing coughs in the small room in the rear.

"M-m."

Lao-shuan, listening for a moment, fastens his garments and then stretches forth a hand towards the woman.

"Give me it," he says.

Hua Ta-ma fumbles beneath her pillow and drags forth a small packet of silver dollars, which she hands to him. Nervously he thrusts it into his pocket, then pats it twice to reassure himself. He lights a paper lantern, and blows out the oil-lamp. Carrying the lantern, he goes into the small rear room. There is a rustle, and then more coughing. When it is quiet again Lao-shuan calls out, in an undertone, "Hsiao-shuan . . . don't bother about getting up. . . . The shop—your mother will see to that."

His son does not answer him, and Lao-shuan, thinking he will sleep undisturbed, goes through the low door into the street. In the blackness nothing is at first visible save a grey ribbon of path. The lantern illumines only his two feet, which move rhythmically. Dogs appear here and there, then sidle off again. None even barks. Outside the air is cold, and it refreshes Lao-shuan, so that it seems to him that he is all at once a youth, and possesses the miraculous power of touching men into life. He takes longer strides. Gradually the sky brightens, till the road is more clearly marked.

Absorbed in his walking, Lao-shuan is startled when, almost in front of him, he sees a crossroads. He stops, and then withdraws a few steps to stand under the eaves of a shop, in front of its closed door. After a long wait his bones are chilled.

"Uh, an old fellow?"

"High-spirited, up so early."

Opening his eyes, Lao-shuan sees several people passing near him. One of them turns back and looks at him intently. He cannot distinguish the features clearly, but the man's eyes are bright with a cold, lusting gleam, eyes of famish suddenly coming upon something edible. Looking at his lantern, Lao-shuan sees that it has gone out. He feels quickly at his pocket; the hard substance is still there. Then he peers out, and on either side of him are numerous strange people, loitering, and looking oddly like ghosts in the dim light. Then he gazes fixedly at them, and gradually they do not seem unusual at all.

He discerns several soldiers among the crowd. On their coats they wear, both in front and behind, the large white circle of cloth of the Government troops, which can be seen for some distance. As one draws nearer the wine-coloured border of their uniforms is also evident. There is a trampling of many feet, and a large number of people gather, little groups here and there merging swiftly into one crush that advances like the ocean's tide. Reaching the crossroads, they halt and form a semicircle, with their backs towards Lao-shuan.

Necks stretch forth from collars and incline towards the same point, as though, like so many ducks, they are held by some invisible hand. For a moment all is still. Lao-shuan seems to hear a sound from somewhere beyond the necks. A stir sweeps through the onlookers. With a sudden movement, they abruptly disperse. People jostle one another hurriedly, and some, pushing past Lao-shuan, almost tumble him to the ground in their haste.

"*Hai!* One hand gives the money, another hand gives the goods!" screams a man clad entirely in black, who halts before Lao-shuan. In his eyes is a metallic glitter; they resemble the bright lustre of a pair of swords; they stab into Lao-shuan's soul, and his body seems to shrivel to half its normal size. The dark man thrusts one huge, empty paw at him, while in the other he offers a steamed roll, stained with a fresh and still warm red substance, drops of which trickle down to the earth.

Hurriedly Lao-shuan fumbles for his dollars. He attempts to hand them over to the black-garbed man, from whose hand slowly depend the drops of red, but somehow he cannot embolden himself to receive the saturated roll.

"What's afraid of? Why not take it?" the fellow demands, brusque and impatient. Lao-shuan continues to hesitate until the other roughly snatches his lantern, tears off its paper shade, and uses it to wrap up the roll. Then he thrusts this package into Lao-shuan's hand, and at the same time seizes the silver and gives it a cursory feel. As he turns away he murmurs, "That old fool. . . ."

"And to cure what person?" Lao-shuan seems to hear some one ask him. He does not reply. His attention is centred upon the package, and he embraces it as if it were the only child descended from a house of ten generations. Nothing else in the world matters, now that he is about to transplant into his own home the robust life which he holds in his hands. He hopes thereby to reap much happiness.

The sun lifts over the horizon. Before him the long
street leads straight into his teahouse. Behind him the light
of day caresses a worn tablet at the crossroads, on which
are four characters limned in faint gold: "Ancient ——
Pavilion ——"

II

Lao-shuan, reaching home, finds the teahouse swept
clean, with the rows of tables smooth and glistening, but
as yet serving no customers. Only Hsiao-shuan sits alone
at a table by the wall and eats his food. Large drops of
sweat drip down his forehead, and his little lined coat
sticks against his sunken spine. His shoulder-blades project
sharply from under his coat, so that there appears on his
back, as though embossed, the character *bah*. Seeing it
causes Lao-shuan to pinch his brow together. His wife
emerges hastily from the kitchen, her mouth open, her lips
quivering.

"*Te-liao-mah?*" she asks.

"Yes, I have it."

The pair disappear into the kitchen for a time, where they
consult. Then Hua Ta-ma comes hurriedly forth, goes out,
and in a moment returns with a dried lotus-leaf, which she
spreads on the table. Lao-shuan unwraps the crimson-
stained roll, and neatly repacks it in the sheet of lotus.
Meanwhile Hsiao-shuan has finished his meal, and his
mother warns him, "Sit still, Little Door-latch. Don't come
here yet."

When the fire burns briskly in the mud stove the father
thrusts his little green and red parcel into the oven. There
is a red and black flame. A strange odour permeates the
rooms.

"*Hao!* It smells good, but is it? What are you eating?"
demands Camel-back Fifth, who arrives at this moment,
and sniffs the air questioningly. He is one of those who
pass their days in teahouses, the first to come in the morning,

C

the last to leave at night. Now, tumbling to a table by the lane, he sits down to make idle inquiry.

"Could it be baked rice congee?"

Nobody replies. Lao-shuan silently serves him boiled tea.

"Come in, Hsiao-shuan," Hua Ta-ma calls from the inner room, in the centre of which she has placed a stool. The "Little Door-latch" sits, and his mother, saying in a low voice, "Eat it, and your sickness will vanish," hands him a plate on which is a round object, black in colour.

Hsiao-shuan picks it up. For a moment he gazes at it curiously, as though he might somehow hold his own life in his hand. His heart is unspeakably moved with wonder. Very carefully he splits the object. A jet of white vapour gushes forth, and immediately dissolves in the air. Now Hsiao-shuan sees that it is a white flour roll, broken in half. Soon it has entered his stomach, so that even the taste of it cannot be clearly remembered. In front of him there is the empty dish; on one side stands his father, and on the opposite side his mother. Their eyes are potent with a strange look, as though they desire to pour something into him, yet at the same time draw something forth. It is exciting. It is too much for Hsiao-shuan's little heart, which throbs furiously. He presses his hands against his chest, and begins to cough.

"Sleep a little; you'll be well."

So Hsiao-shuan coughs himself to sleep, obeying the advice of his mother. Having waited patiently till he is quiet, she now drapes over him a lined quilt, which consists mostly of patches.

III

In the teahouse are many customers, and Lao-shuan is kept engaged in his enterprise. He darts from one table to another, pouring hot water and tea, and seemingly intent on his tasks. But under his eyes are dark hollows.

"Lao-shuan," inquires a man with whiskers streaked with white, "are you not a little unwell?"

"No."

"No? . . . But I already see that it's unlikely. Your smile now . . . " the bearded one contradicts himself.

"Lao-shuan is always busy. Of course if his son were——" begins Camel-back Fifth. His remark is interrupted by the arrival of a man whose face is massive, with distorted muscles. He wears a black cotton shirt, unbuttoned and pulled together carelessly around the waist with a broad black cloth girdle.[1] As he enters he shouts to Lao-shuan:

"Eaten, eh? Is he well already? Lao-shuan, luck is with you! Indeed lucky! If it were not that I get news quickly . . . "

With the kettle in one hand, and the other hanging straight beside him in an attitude of respect, Lao-shuan listens and smiles. All the guests listen with deference, and Hua Ta-ma, her eyes dark and sleepless, also comes forth and smiles, serving the new arrival some tea-leaves, with the added flourish of a green olive. Lao-shuan himself fills the cup with boiling water.

"It is a guaranteed cure! Different from all others! Think of it, brought back while still warm, eaten while warm!" shouts the gentleman with the coarse face.

"Truly, were it not for Big Uncle Kan's services how could it be!" Hua Ta-ma thanks him, in deep gratitude.

"Guaranteed cure! Guaranteed cure! Eaten up like that while still warm. A roll with human blood is an absolute cure for any kind of consumption."

Mention of the word 'consumption' seems to disconcert Hua Ta-ma, for her face suddenly turns pallid, though the smile quickly creeps back. She manages to withdraw so inconspicuously that Big Uncle Kan still shouts with the full vigour of his lungs, and does not notice that she is gone

[1] The apparel of an executioner.—TRANSLATOR.

till from the inner room, where Hsiao-shuan sleeps, there comes the sound of dry, raucous coughing.

"So, it is true Hsiao-shuan has come upon friendly luck. That sickness will unquestionably be cured utterly. There's no surprise in Lao-shuan's constant smiling." Thus speaks the whiskered old man, who walks towards Big Uncle Kan. "I hear," he says to the latter in a suppressed voice, "that the criminal executed to-day is a son of the Hsia family. Now, whose son is he? And, in fact, executed for what?"

"Whose?" demands Big Uncle. "Can he be other than the son of the fourth daughter-in-law of the Hsias? That little *tung-hsi*[1]!" Observing that he has an alert audience, Big Uncle expands, his facial muscles become unusually active, and he raises his voice to heroic heights, shouting, "The little thing did not want to live! He simply did not want life, that's all.

"And I got what from the execution this time? Not the merest profit! Even the clothes stripped from him were seized by Red-eye Ah Yi, the jailer. Our Uncle Lao-shuan was the luckiest. Second comes the Third Father of the Hsia family. He actually pocketed the reward—twenty-five ounces of silver!—all alone. He gave not so much as a single cash to anyone!"

Hsiao-shuan walks slowly from the little room, his hands pressed to his chest, and coughing without respite. He enters the kitchen, fills a bowl with cold rice, and sits down at once to eat. Hua Ta-ma goes to him and inquires softly, "Hsiao-shuan, are you better? Still as hungry as ever?"

"Guaranteed cure, guaranteed!" Big Uncle Kan casts a glance at the lad, but quickly turns back to the crowd and declares, "Third Father of Hsia is clever. Had he not been the first to report the matter to the official his whole house would have been beheaded, and all their property confiscated. But instead? Silver!

[1] Literally, 'thing.'—TRANSLATOR.

"That little *tung-hsi* was an altogether bad egg. He even attempted to induce the head jailer to join the rebellion!"

"*Ai-ya!* If it were actually done, think of it!" indignantly comments a youth in his twenties, sitting at a back table.

"You should know that Red-eye Ah Yi was anxious to gather some details, so he entered into conversation. 'The realm of *Ta Ching* Dynasty really belongs to us all,' he told Red-eye. Now, what do you make of that? Is it possible that such talk is actually human?

"Red-eye knew that there was only a mother in his home, but he could not believe that he was so poor that 'not a drop of oil and water' could be squeezed from him. His rage already had burst his abdomen, yet the boy attempted to 'scratch the tiger's head!' Ah Yi gave him several smacks on the face."

"Ah Yi knows his boxing. His blows must have done the wretch good!" exults Camel-back Fifth from a corner table.

"No! Would you believe it? His worthless bones were unafraid. The fellow actually said, what is more, that it was a pity!"

Black-and-White Whiskers snorted, "What is it? How could pity be shown in beating a thing like that?"

"You've not listened well," sneers Big Uncle contemptuously. "The little *tung-hsi* meant to say that Ah Yi himself was to be pitied!"

The listeners' eyes suddenly dull, and there is a pause in the conversation. Hsiao-shuan, perspiring copiously, has finished his rice. His head seems to be steaming.

"So he said Red-eye should be pitied! Now, that is pure insanity!" Black-and-White Whiskers feels proudly that he has logically solved the whole matter. "Obviously, he had gone mad!"

"Gone mad," approvingly echoes the youth who spoke earlier. He too feels like a discoverer.

Equanimity is restored to the other teahouse visitors.

They renew their laughing and talking. Hsiao-shuan, under cover of the confusion of sounds, seizes the opportunity to cough hoarsely, with all his emaciated strength.

Big Uncle Kan moves over to pat the child's shoulder, repeating, "Guaranteed cure, Hsiao-shuan! You mustn't cough like that. Guaranteed cure!"

"Gone mad," says Camel-back Fifth, nodding his head.

IV

Originally the land adjacent to the city wall beyond the West Gate was public property. The narrow path that curvets through it now was first made by feet seeking a short cut, which in time came to be a natural boundary line. On the left of it, as one goes out from the gate, are buried those who have been executed, or have starved to death in prison. On the right are grouped the graves of the paupers. All of these graves are so numerous and closely arranged that they remind one of the sweet buns laid out in a rich man's home for a birthday celebration.

The Clear and Bright Day, when graves are visited, has dawned unusually cold, and willows have just issued new buds about the size of a half-grain of rice. Hua Ta-ma has laid out four fishes and a bowl of *mi-fan* in front of a new grave on the right side, has left tears over it, and has burned imitation money. Now she sits dazedly on the ground, as though waiting for something, but nothing which she herself could explain. A light breeze sweeps by, and her short hair flutters. It is much more grey than last year.

Down the narrow path comes another woman, grey also, and in torn rags. She carries a worn round basket, lacquered red, with a string of paper ingots hanging from it. Now and then she halts her slow walk. Finally she notices Hua Ta-ma gazing at her, and she hesitates, embarrassed. A look of confused shame crosses her pale, melancholy face. Then emboldening herself, she walks to a grave on the left of the path, and lays down her lacquered basket.

It so happens that the grave is directly opposite Hsiao-shuan's, with only the narrow path between them. Hua Ta-ma watches mechanically as she lays out four fishes and a bowl of rice, burns paper money, and weeps. It occurs to her that in that grave also there is a mother's son. She watches curiously as the woman moves about absently, and stares vacantly into space. Suddenly she sees her begin to tremble and stagger backward, as though in a stupor.

Hua Ta-ma is touched. "She may be mad with sorrow," she fears. She rises, and, stepping across the path, speaks to her quietly. "Old Mother, don't grieve any more. Let us both go home." The woman nods stupidly, her eyes still staring. Suddenly she utters an exclamation, "Look! What is that?"

Looking along the woman's pointing finger, Hua Ta-ma's eyes take in the grave before them, which is unkempt and has ugly patches of yellow earth on it. Looking more closely she is startled to see, at the top of the little mound, a circlet of scarlet and white flowers.

For many years neither of them has seen clearly, and yet now both see these fresh blossoms. They are not many, but they are neatly arranged; they are not very splendid, but they are comely in an orderly way. Hua Ta-ma looks quickly at her son's grave, and at the others, but only here and there are a few scattered blossoms of blue and white that have braved the cold; there are no others of scarlet. She experiences a nameless emptiness of heart, as if in need, but of what she does not wish to know. The other walks nearer, and examines the flowers closely. "What could be the explanation?" she muses. Tears stream from her face, and she cries out:

"Yu, my son! You have been wronged, but you do not forget. Is it that your heart is still full of pain, and you choose this day and this method of telling me?" She gazes around, but seeing only a black crow brooding in a leafless tree, she continues: "Yu, Yu, my son! It was a trap; you were 'buried alive.' Yet Heaven knows! Rest your eyes in peace, but give me a sign. If you are in the grave, if you are listening to me, cause the crow to fly here and alight on your grave. Let me know!"

There is no more breeze, and everywhere the dry grass stands erect, like bristles of copper. A faint sound hangs in the air, and vibrates, growing less and less audible, till finally it ceases entirely. Then everything becomes as quiet as death. The two old women stand motionless in the midst of the dry grass, intently watching the crow. Among the straight limbs of the tree, its head drawn in, the crow sits immobile, and as though cast in iron.

Much time passes. Those who come to visit graves begin to increase in numbers. To Hua Ta-ma it seems that gradually a heavy burden lifts from her, and to the other she says, "Come, let us go."

The old woman sighs dejectedly, and gathers up her offertory dishes. She lingers for still another moment, then at length walks away slowly, murmuring, "What could it have been?"

When they have walked only some thirty paces they suddenly hear a sharp cry from above.

"Yah-h-h!"

Turning round with a shudder, they see the crow brace itself on a limb, and then push forth, spreading its broad wings and flying like an arrow towards the far horizon.

A LITTLE INCIDENT

Six years have gone by, as so many winks, since I came to the capital from the village. During all that time there have occurred many of those events known as 'affairs of State,' a great number of which I have seen or heard about. My heart does not seem to have been in the least affected by any of them, and recollection now only tends to increase my ill-temper, and cause me to like people less and less as the day wears on. But one little incident alone is deep with meaning to me, and I am unable to forget it even now.

It was a winter day in the Sixth Year of the Republic, and a strong northerly wind blew furiously. To make a living I had to be up early, and on the way to my duties I encountered scarcely anyone. After much difficulty I finally succeeded in hiring a rickshaw. I told the puller to take me to the South Gate.

After a while the wind moderated its fury, and in its wake the streets were left clean of the loose dust. The puller ran quickly. Just as we approached the South Gate somebody ran in front of us, got entangled in the rickshaw, and tumbled to the ground.

It was a woman, with streaks of white in her hair, and she wore ragged clothes. She had darted suddenly from the side of the street, and crossed directly in front of us. My puller had tried to swerve aside, but her tattered jacket, unbuttoned and fluttering in the wind, caught in the shafts. Fortunately, the puller had slowed his pace, otherwise she would have been thrown head over heels, and probably seriously injured. After we halted the woman still knelt on all fours. I did not think she was hurt. No one else had seen

the collision, and it irritated me that the puller had stopped
and was apparently prepared to get himself involved in
some foolish complication. It might delay and trouble my
journey.

"This is nothing," I told him. "Move ahead!"

But either he did not hear me or did not care, for he
put down the shafts and gently helped the old woman to
her feet. He held her arms, supporting her, and asked:

"Are you all right?"

"I am hurt."

I thought, "I saw you fall, and it was not at all rough.
How can you be hurt? You are pretending. The whole
business is distasteful, and the rickshaw man is merely
making difficulties for himself. Now let him find his own
way out of the mess."

But the puller did not hesitate for a moment after the old
woman said she was injured. Still holding her arm, he
walked carefully ahead with her. Then I was surprised as,
looking ahead, I suddenly noticed a police-station, and saw
that he was taking her there. No one stood outside, so he
guided her in through the gate.

As they passed in I experienced a curious sensation. I do
not know why, but at that moment it suddenly seemed to
me that his dust-covered figure loomed enormous, and as
he walked farther he continued to grow, until finally I had
to lift my head to follow him. At the same time I felt a
bodily pressure all over me, which came from his direction.
It seemed almost to push out from me all the littleness that
hid under my fur-lined gown. I grew weak, as though my
vitality had been spent, as though the blood had frozen in
me. I sat motionless, stunned and thoughtless, until I saw
an officer emerge from the station. Then I got down from
the rickshaw as he approached me.

"Get another rickshaw," he advised. "This man can't
pull you any more."

Without thinking, I thrust my hand into my pocket and

pulled forth a big fistful of coppers. "Give the fellow these," I said.

The wind had ceased entirely, but the street was still quiet. I mused as I walked, but I was almost afraid to think about myself. Leaving aside what had happened before, I sought an explanation for the fistful of coppers. Why had I given them? As a reward? And did I think myself, after my conduct, fit to pass judgment upon a rickshaw-puller? I could not answer my own conscience.

Till now that experience burns in my memory. I think of it, and introspect with pain and effort. The political and military drama of these years is to me like the classics I read in childhood: I cannot recite half a line of it. But always before my eyes, purging me with shame, impelling me to better myself, invigorating my hope and courage, this little incident is re-enacted. I see it in every detail as distinctly as on the day it happened.

K'UNG I-CHI

THE wineshops in Lo Ching differ from those of other districts in China. There is, for example, invariably a right-angled counter within which hot water is prepared for warming wine at any time. When released at noon or sunset workers go to these shops for a bowl of wine—the price twenty years ago was but four cash, though now each bowl costs ten—and, standing beside the counter, drink the stuff hot, and relax themselves. One cash will buy a dish of salted bamboo-shoots or spiced beans, for 'wine-escorts,' and a little more than ten cash buys a meat dish of some kind; but most of the customers are of the short-coat class, and seldom have more than a few cash. Only the few long-gown[1] men, who stride past the counter and into the small room adjacent, indulge in both wine and meat, and sit down to feast at leisure.

When I was twelve years old I became a waiter in one of the Lo Ching wineshops, a place called the "Luck for All," which stood at the mouth of the town. The shopkeeper considered my appearance too silly to be displayed before the long-gown guests, so I was given work behind the counter. Short-coat customers were easier to handle, but they were a chattering lot and caused endless nuisance. They even leaned over to watch with their own eyes when the wine was being spooned from the keg, craning their necks to see whether there was water in the bottom of the tankard before it was filled with wine, and then closely inspecting the immersion of the tankard in hot water to make sure that no adulteration took place. Under such

[1] Long gowns were usually worn only by the gentry.

44

scrutiny it was extremely difficult to water the wine, and after a few days the shopkeeper decided that I was too stupid to fill the job. Fortunately for me my recommender had great 'face' in the establishment, and it was finally agreed that I should stay on, charged with the tiresome task of heating wine.

I stood all day behind the counter, assiduously attending my duties. I performed satisfactorily, but I could not help growing weary at times with the monotony of the days. The shopkeeper was a stern-faced individual, the customers were dull and had harsh, unpleasant voices, and ordinarily it was impossible to be gay. Only when K'ung I-chi came to drink could I join in hearty laughter, and perhaps because of that I still remember him.

K'ung I-chi was the only long-gown man who stood at the counter to drink his wine. He was tall in stature, altogether a large man, with a curious pale face, tinted a faint blue, and among its wrinkles were often cuts and wounds. From his chin straggled a grey beard. The garment he wore was indeed a long gown, but it was ragged, dirty, and appeared not to have been mended or washed for ten years. He always spoke with a mouthful of empty words like *chih*, *hu*, *chêh*, and *yeh*, which, being exclusively used as flourishes in classical writing, were altogether unintelligible to the common man. Whenever he came came into the shop every one would look at him and chuckle. Some one would call out, "K'ung I-chi, there are new scars on your face!"

He pretended not to notice. Turning to the counter, he would demand, "Heat two bowls of wine and give me a dish of spiced beans!" Then he would count out his nine cash in a row.

"You must have been stealing again!" one of the on-lookers once cried out, in an unnecessarily loud voice.

"How could you so groundlessly question one's integrity?" he asked, opening his eyes very wide.

"What integrity? Didn't I see you with my own eyes getting a beating the other day for stealing the books of the Ho family?"

K'ung I-chi, his face contorted and the blue veins standing out on his forehead, argued: "Stealing a book cannot be reckoned theft! Stealing a book—the affair of a scholar—is that what you call theft?" And he went on, with irrelevant quotations, such as, "The perfect man is content with poverty," and ending with strange words strung together like *chih*, *hu*, *chêh*, and *yeh* till the crowd roared with laughter and everybody somehow seemed happier.

Behind K'ung I-chi's back people gossiped that he had once studied the classics, but had been unable to enter the academy. He had no means of earning a living, and it had become more and more difficult for him till finally he reached the verge of begging. He happened, however, to be an exquisite calligrapher, so that he was able to find enough copying work to earn his rice. But he was too fond of wine, lazy at work, and after a few days of copying he would suddenly disappear, taking with him books, papers, brushes, and inkstones. Repeated occurrences of this sort had made it impossible for him to get work, and, finding no other employment, K'ung I-chi occasionally indulged in some petty thieving.

In our wineshop his behaviour was always exemplary. He never failed to pay his debts, though sometimes, when he was without a cash, we kept his name on the white board where credit customers' accounts were posted. At the end of the month it was erased, for he invariably settled up.

On the occasion mentioned, having sipped half a bowl of wine, his face gradually returned to its normal pallor, and some one asked him, "Do you really know the characters?" He looked indifferently at the inquirer, who continued, "If you do, how is it that you could not even get half-way towards a *hsiu-ts'ai* degree?" Instantly K'ung I-chi was dismayed, over his wrinkled face came a greyish veil, and he ground some incoherent words from his mouth, but nothing that was in the least intelligible. Again the crowd became hilarious and the atmosphere was charged with merriment.

At such times the shopkeeper did not reproach me if I joined in with the rest. He liked to keep his customers amused, and sometimes he even asked K'ung I-chi to make people laugh. But K'ung I-chi renounced the folly of conversing with the customers, and turned instead to the little children scampering about.

One day he asked me if I had ever read any books. I nodded my head.

"*Hao*," he said, "since you have, I'll give you a test. How do you write the character *wei* in 'spiced beans'?"

I thought to myself, "Is this beggarly sort of man fit to examine me?" and, turning my head, completely ignored him. He waited a while, and then said with great earnestness:

"So you can't write it, after all? Come, let me teach you. Remember! Such words as 'spiced beans' ought to be memorized. When you some day become a shopkeeper you will need to know them in writing your accounts."

I said to myself that I was still very far from becoming a shopkeeper, and besides I had never noticed my employer marking down spiced beans in the account-book. But amused and yet annoyed, I answered without enthusiasm:

"Who wants you to teach? Anyway, isn't it written with the *wei* radical under the radical for 'grass'?"

K'ung I-chi was cheered, and exuberantly rapped his two long finger-nails on the counter.

"*Tui*, right!" he exclaimed. "But the character *wei* can be written four different ways. Now, do you know those?"

I was offended. I twisted my mouth and walked off. K'ung I-chi had dipped his long nail into the wine, and intended to trace the correct character on the counter, but, seeing that I was not interested, he uttered a sigh and into his eyes came a hurt look of regret.

Sometimes when he came, and laughter with him, the children of the neighbourhood ran up and surrounded him. He gave each of them a spiced bean, and after those had been eaten they would stand in front of him still, waiting for more, their eyes glued to the dish. Roused to excitement, K'ung I-chi would stretch his fingers over the beans, bend down from the waist, and whisper to them, "There are only a few left, and I've not had many." Then, straightening up, he would say to himself, "Not many, not many! Many *hu tsai*! Not many *yeh*!" thus dragging in his absurd flourishes again. The children always scattered amid a crackling of laughter.

One day, shortly before the Mid-autumn Festival, my employer was closing his accounts. Taking down the white board from the wall, he remarked, "K'ung I-chi hasn't come for a long time. He owes me nineteen cash!"

Not till then did I realize how many days had passed since he visited.

"How could he come? He has been beaten! This time both legs broken!"

One of the customers offered this news.

"Ah!"

"Yes, at his stealing again. Utterly mad, that fellow! He actually stole from the home of Magistrate Ting! Who could expect success at that?"

"How was it afterwards?"

"How was it! First he had to write a confession; then he was beaten, and during the beating, which lasted half a night, both his legs were broken."

"Afterwards?"

"Afterwards—*his legs are broken!*"

"How was he after that?"

"Who knows? Probably dead."

The shopkeeper said nothing more, but proceeded methodically to total up his accounts.

The Mid-autumn Festival had passed, and each day the

wind grew colder. Early winter was approaching. Though I stood near the stove all day I had to wear a padded coat to keep warm. One afternoon, when not a single customer was in the shop, I sat with my eyes closed.

"Warm a bowl of wine."

Startled, I opened my eyes. The voice was very feeble but rather familiar. I looked round, but saw no one in the shop. Standing up, I leaned over the counter. K'ung I-chi was sitting on the ground, facing the threshold. His face was dark, lean, and wretched. He wore a ragged lined coat and sat on his limp legs, which were crossed and enclosed in a rush basket trussed up to his shoulder with a straw rope. Seeing me, he said again in a low voice, "Warm a bowl of wine."

"The shopkeeper also poked his head over the counter and remarked impassively, "K'ung I-chi, you still owe nineteen cash."

He lifted up his head lifelessly and muttered, "That—let it be cleared next time. This is ready money, and the wine must be good."

As usual, the owner smiled and remarked, "K'ung I-chi, you have been stealing again."

He did not argue or offer any denials, but replied briefly, "Keep your joke."

"Joke? If not theft, what was it? Why were your legs beaten and broken?"

"Broken?" he said in a faint voice. "Broken of falling, falling——" A look in his eye seemed to implore that the discussion be pursued no farther.

By this time several people had gathered, and they all laughed with my employer. I warmed the wine, carried it out, and placed it before K'ung I-chi. He fumbled in his pocket for four cash, and gave them to me. I saw then that his long, straight hands were muddied, and understood that he had come by dragging himself along the road. He stayed only long enough to swallow the wine. Then, while the

D

shop still buzzed with gossip and the laughter of onlookers, he sat up and pulled himself off on his hands.

For a long time after that he was seen no more. At the end of the year the shopkeeper took down the white board and said, "K'ung I-chi still owes that nineteen cash." At the Dragon Boat Festival the next year he said the same thing again. In the autumn he did not mention it. Since then I have not seen K'ung I-chi. Perhaps he is really dead.

BENEDICTION

THE end of the year according to the lunar calendar is, after all, the right time for a year to end. A strange almost-new-year sort of atmosphere seems to overlay everything; pale grey clouds at evening, against which flash the hot little fires of crackers giving a thunderous boost to the kitchen god's[1] ascent into heaven. And as one draws into it the scene grows noisier, and scattered on the air is the sting of gunpowder.

On such a night I return to Lo Ching—my 'home town' as I call it, but in reality I have no home there at all. I stay with Lo Shih Lao-yeh, a relative one generation older than myself, a fellow who ought to be called "Fourth Uncle," according to the Chinese family way of reckoning. He is a *chien-sheng*,[2] and talks all the time about the old virtues and the old ethics.

I find him not much changed; a little aged of course, but still without a whisker. We exchange salutations. After the "How are you?" he tells me I've grown fat. With that done, he at once commences a tirade against the 'new party.' But I know that the phrase to him still means poor Kang Yu-wei,[3] and not the Renaissance, of which he probably has not even heard. We have at any rate

[1] The kitchen god is supposed to report at this time to the Heavenly Emperor about the conduct of the family during the past year. He returns to earth after seven days.

[2] A *chien-sheng* is an honorary degree equivalent to the *hsiu-ts'ai*, but is purchased, whereas the latter is given only to scholars.

[3] A scholar who led in the attempted reform movement under the Emperor Kuang Hsu, towards the end of the Manchu dynasty. The movement was suppressed by the Empress Dowager.

nothing in common, and before long I am left alone in the study.

Next day I get up very late, and after lunching go out to call on some relatives and friends. The day after is the same, and the day after that. None of them has changed much, each is a little older, and everywhere they are busily preparing for New Year prayers-of-blessing. It is a great thing in Lo Ching: every one exerts himself to show reverence, exhausts himself in performing rites, and falls down before the god of benediction to ask favours for the year ahead. There is much chicken-killing, geese-slaughtering, and pork-buying; women go round with their arms raw and red from soaking in hot water preparing such fowl. When they are thoroughly cooked they are placed on the altar, with chopsticks punched into them at all angles, and offered up as sacrifices at the sixth watch. Incense sticks and red candles are lighted, and the men (no women allowed) make obeisance and piously invite the blessing-spirits to eat away. And after this, of course, the crackers.

Every year it is that way, and the same in every home—except those of the miserable poor who cannot buy either sacrifices or candles or crackers—and this year is like any other. The sky is dark and gloomy, and in the afternoon snow falls—flakes like plum blossoms darting and dancing across a screen of smoke and bustle, and making everything more confused. By the time I return home the roof-tiles are already washed white, and inside my room seems brighter. The reflection from the snow also touches up the large crimson character, LONGEVITY, which hangs on a board against the wall. It is said to be the work of the legendary Chen Tuan Lao-tso. One of the scrolls has fallen down and is rolled up loosely and lying on the long table, but the other still admonishes me: "Understand deeply the reason of things, be moderate, and be gentle in heart and manner." On the desk under the window are incomplete volumes of the K'ang Hsi Dictionary, a set of Recent Thoughts, with collected commentaries, and the *Four Books*. How depressing!

I decide to return to-morrow, at the very latest, to the city.

.　　　.　　　.　　　.　　　.

The incident with Hsiang-lin Sao also has very much disturbed me. This afternoon I went to the eastern end of the town to visit a friend, and while returning I encountered her at the edge of the canal. The look in her staring eyes showed clearly enough that she was coming after me, so I waited. Although other folk I used to know in Lo Ching have apparently changed little, Hsiang-lin Sao was no longer the same. Her hair was all white, her face was alarmingly lean, hollow, and burnt a dark yellow. She looked completely exhausted, not at all like a woman not yet forty, but like a wooden thing with an expression of tragic sadness carved into it. Only the movement of her lustreless eyes showed that she still lived. In one hand she carried a bamboo basket: inside it was an empty broken bowl; and she held herself up by leaning on a bamboo pole. She had apparently become a beggar.

I stood waiting to be asked for money.

"So—you've come back?"

"Yes."

"That's good—and very timely. Tell me, you are a scholar, a man who has seen the world, a man of knowledge and experience"—her faded eyes very faintly glowed —"tell me, I just want to ask you one thing."

I could not, in ten thousand tries, have guessed what she would ask. I waited, shocked and puzzled, saying nothing.

She moved nearer, lowered her voice, and spoke with great secrecy and earnestness.

"It is this: after a person dies is there indeed such a thing as the *soul*?"

Involuntarily I shuddered. Her eyes stuck into me like thorns. Here was a fine thing! I felt more embarrassed than a schoolboy given a surprise examination, with the teacher standing right beside him. Whether there was such a thing as the 'soul' had never bothered me, and I had speculated little about it. How could I reply? In that brief moment I remembered that many people in Lo Ching believed in some kind of spirits, and probably she did too. Perhaps I should just say it was rather doubtful—but no, it was better to let her go on hoping. Why should I burden a person obviously on the 'last road' with even more pain? Better for her sake say yes.

"Perhaps," I stammered. "Yes, I suppose there is."

"Then there is also a *hell*?"

"Ah—hell?" She had trapped me, and I could only continue placatingly, "Hell? Well, to be logical, I dare say there ought to be. But, then, again—there may not be. What does it matter?"

"Then in this hell do all the deceased members of a family come together again, face to face?"

"H'mm? Seeing face to face, eh?" I felt like a fool. Whatever knowledge I possessed, whatever mental dexterity, was utterly useless; here I had been confounded by three simple questions. I made up my mind to extricate myself from the mess, and wanted to repudiate everything I had said. But somehow I could not do so in the gaze of her intensely earnest and tragic eyes.

"That is to say . . . in fact, I cannot definitely say. Whether there is a soul or not in the end I am in no position to deny or affirm."

With that she did not persist, and, taking advantage of her silence, I strode away with long steps and hastened back to Fourth Uncle's home, feeling very depressed. I could not help thinking that perhaps my replies would have an evil effect on her. No doubt her loneliness and distress had become all the more unbearable at this time, when every one else seemed to be praying for benediction—but perhaps there was something else on her mind. Perhaps something that had recently happened to her. If so, then my answers might be responsible . . . for what? I soon laughed about the whole thing, and at my absurd habit of exaggerating the importance of casual happenings. Educators unquestionably would pronounce me mentally unbalanced. Hadn't I, after all, made it clear that all I could say was, "Cannot definitely say"? Even should all my replies be refuted, even if something happened to the woman, it could in no way concern me.

.   .   .   .   .   .

"Cannot definitely say" is a very convenient phrase. Bold and reckless youths often venture so far as to offer a positive opinion on critical questions for others, but responsible people, like officials and doctors,[1] have to choose their words carefully, for if events belie their opinion then it becomes a serious affair. It is much more advisable to say, "Cannot definitely say"; obviously it solves everything. This encounter with the woman mendicant impresses upon me the importance of that practice, for even in such cases the deepest wisdom lies in ambiguity.

Nevertheless, I continue to feel troubled, and when the night is gone I wake up with the incident still on my mind. It is like an unlucky presentiment of a movement of fate. Outside the day is still gloomy, with flurrying snow, and in the dull study my uneasiness gradually increases. Certainly I must go back to the city to-morrow. . . . To be sure, there is still unsampled the celebrated pure-cooked fish-fins at Fu Shing Lou—excellent eating and very cheap at only a dollar a big salver. Has the price by now increased? Although many of my boyhood friends have melted away like clouds in the sky, there must remain, at least, the incomparable fish-fins of Lo Ching, and these I must eat, even though I eat alone. . . . All the same, I am returning to-morrow. . . .

[1] The author was formerly a doctor, having studied medicine in Japan.

Because I have so often seen things happen exactly as I predicted—but hoped against, and tried to believe improbable—so I am not unprepared for this occasion to provide no exception. Towards evening some of the family gather in an inner room, and from fragments of their talk I gather they are discussing some event with no little annoyance. Presently all the voices cease except one, that of Fourth Uncle, who thunders out above the thud of his own pacing feet:

"Not a day earlier nor a day later, but just at this season she decides upon it. From this alone we can see that she belongs to a species utterly devoid of human sense!"

My curiosity is soon followed by a vague discomfort, as if these words have some special meaning for me. I go out and look into the room, but every one has vanished. Suppressing my increasing impatience, I wait till the servant comes to fill my teapot with hot water. Not until then am I able to confirm my suspicions.

"Who was it Fourth Uncle was blowing up about a while ago?"

"Could it after all have been any other than Hsiang-lin Sao?" he replies in the brief and positive manner of our language.

"What has happened to her?" I demand in an anxious voice.

"Aged."[1]

"Dead?" My heart twinges and seems to jump back; my face burns. But he doesn't notice my emotion at all, doesn't even lift his head, so that I control myself to the end of further questioning.

"When did she die then?"

"When? Last night—or possibly to-day. I cannot definitely say."

"What did she die of?"

[1] The word 'die' and its synonyms are forbidden at this season, and 'aged' is commonly used to describe death. Ordinarily Chinese refer to the dead as 'not here,' or 'outside.'

"What did she die of? Could it indeed be anything else than that she has been strangled to death by poverty?" His words are absolutely colourless, and without even looking at me he goes out.

My terror at first is great, but I reason that this is a thing which was bound to happen very soon, and it is merely an accident that I even know about it. I further reassure my conscience by recalling my non-committal "Cannot definitely say," and the servant's report that it was simply a case of "strangled to death by poverty." Still, now and then I feel a prick of guilt, I don't know exactly why, and when I sit down beside the dignified old Fourth Uncle I am continually thinking of opening a discussion about Hsianglin Sao. But how to do it? He still lives in a world of religious interdicts, and at this time of year these are like an impenetrable forest. You cannot, of course, mention anything connected with death, illness, crime, and so on, unless it is absolutely imperative. Even then such references must be disguised in a queer riddle-language in order not to offend the hovering ancestral spirits. I torture my brain to remember the necessary formula, but, alas, I cannot recall the right phrases, and at length have to give it up.

Fourth Uncle throughout the meal wears an austere look on his face. At last I suspect that he regards me also as "belonging to a species utterly devoid of human sense," since "neither a day earlier, nor a day later, but just at this season" I have put in an appearance. To loosen his heart and save him further anxiety I tell him that I have determined to return to-morrow. He doesn't urge me to stay very enthusiastically, and I conclude that my surmise was correct. And thus in a cheerless mood I finish my meal.

The short day is ended, the curtain of snow dropping over it earlier than usual even in this month, and the black night falls like a shroud over the whole town. People still busy themselves under the lamplight, but just beyond my window there is the quiet of death. Snow lies like a down mattress over the earth, and the still falling flakes make a faint *suh-suh* sound that adds to the intense loneliness and the unbearable melancholy. Sitting alone under the yellow rays of the rape-oil lamp, my mind goes back again to that blown-out flicker, Hsiang-lin Sao.

This woman who once stood among us in this house, thrown now, like an old toy, discarded by a child, on to the dust-heap. For those who find the world amusing, for the kind for whom she is created, no doubt if they think about her at all it is simply to wonder why the devil she should so long have had the effrontery to continue to exist. Well, she has obliged them by disappearing at last, swept away thoroughly by Wu Chang,[1] and a very tidy job. I don't know whether there is such a thing as the 'soul' that lives on after death, but it would be a great improvement if people like Hsiang-lin Sao were never born, would it not? Then nobody would be troubled, neither the despised nor those who despise them.

Listening to the *suh-suh* of the leafy autumnal snow I go on musing, and gradually find some comfort in my reflections. It is like putting together an intricate puzzle, but in the end the incidents of her life fit together into a single whole.

II

Hsiang-lin Sao was not a native of Lo Ching. She arrived in early winter one year with Old Woman Wei, who bargained in the labour of others. Fourth Uncle had decided to change the servant, and Hsiang-lin Sao was Old Woman Wei's candidate for the job.

She wore a white scarf wrapped round her head, a blue jacket, a pale green vest, and a black skirt. She was perhaps twenty-six or twenty-seven, still quite young and rather pretty, with ruddy cheeks and a bronzed face. Old Woman Wei said that she was a neighbour of her mother's. Her

[1] A sheriff-spirit who 'sweeps up' the soul at the last breath of life.

husband had died, she explained, and so she had to seek work outside.

Fourth Uncle wrinkled up his brow, and his wife, looking at him, knew what he meant. He didn't like hiring a widow. But Fourth Aunt scrutinized her carefully, noting that her hands and feet looked strong and capable, and that she had honest, direct eyes. She impressed her as a woman who would be content with her lot, and not likely to complain about hard work; and so in spite of her husband's wrinkled brow Fourth Aunt agreed to give her a trial. For three days she worked as if leisure of any kind bored her; she proved very energetic and as strong as a man. Fourth Aunt then definitely hired her, the wage being five hundred cash[1] per month.

Everybody called her simply Hsiang-lin Sao, without asking for her surname. The Old Woman Wei was, however, a native of Wei Chia Shan (Wei Family Mountain), and since she claimed that Hsiang-lin Sao came from that village no doubt her surname also was Wei.[2] Like most mountaineers, she talked little, and only answered others' questions in monosyllables, and so it took more than ten days to pry out of her the bare facts that there was still a severe mother-in-law in her home; that her young brother-in-law cut wood for a living; that she had lost her husband, ten years her junior, in the previous spring; and that he also had lived by cutting firewood. This was about all people could get out of her.

Day followed day, and Hsiang-lin Sao's work was just as regular. She never slackened up, she never complained about the food, she never seemed to tire. People agreed that Old Lord Lo Shih had found a worthy worker, quick

---

[1] This is about 50 cents. Wages for similar work to-day would be from $2 to $6 (2s. 6d. to 7s. 6d.) per month.

[2] 'Sao' means 'sister-in-law.' The Chinese call a woman married to an eldest son by that son's given name, suffixed by 'Sao.' Thus, her husband's name was probably Wei Hsiang-lin.

and diligent, more so in fact than a man. Even at New Year she did all the sweeping, dusting, washing, and other household duties, besides preparing geese and chickens and all the sacrifices, without any other help. She seemed to thrive on it. Her skin became whiter, and she fattened a little.

New Year had just passed when one day she came hurrying up from the canal, where she had been washing rice. She was much agitated. She said she had seen, on the opposite bank, a man who looked very much like her late husband's first cousin, and she was afraid he had come to take her away. Fourth Aunt was alarmed and suspicious. Why should he be coming for her? Asked for details, Hsiang-lin Sao could give none. Fourth Uncle, when he heard the story, wrinkled his brow and announced:

"This is very bad. It looks as though she has run away, instead of being ordered."

And, as it turned out, he was correct. She was a runaway widow.

Some ten days later, when everybody was gradually forgetting the incident, Old Woman Wei suddenly appeared, accompanied by a woman who, she claimed, was Hsiang-lin Sao's mother-in-law. The latter seemed not at all like a tongue-bound mountaineer, but knew how to talk, and after a few courtesy words got to the subject of her business at once. She said she had come to take her daughter-in-law back home. It was spring, there was much to be done at home, and in the house at present were none but the very old and the very young. Hsiang-lin Sao was needed.

"Since it is her own mother-in-law who requests it, how can we deny the justice of it?" said Fourth Uncle.

Hsiang-lin Sao's wage, therefore, was figured out. It was discovered that altogether one thousand seven hundred and fifty cash were due. She had let the sum accumulate with her master, not taking out even a single cash for use. Without any more words, this amount was handed over to the mother-in-law, although Hsiang-lin Sao was not present. The woman also took Hsiang-lin Sao's clothes, thanked Fourth Uncle, and left. It was then past noon. . . .

"*Ai-ya!* The rice? Didn't Hsiang-lin Sao go out to scour the rice?"

Fourth Aunt, some time later, cried out this question in a startled way. She had forgotten all about Hsiang-lin Sao until her hunger reminded her of rice, and the rice reminded her of the former servant.

Everybody scattered and began searching for the rice basket. Fourth Aunt herself went first to the kitchen, next to the front hall, and then into the bedroom, but she didn't see a shadow of the object of her search. Fourth Uncle wandered outside, but he saw nothing of it either till he came near the canal. There, upright on the bank, with a cabbage near by, lay the missing basket.

Apparently not until then had anyone thought to inquire in what manner Hsiang-lin Sao had departed with her mother-in-law. Now eyewitnesses appeared who reported that early in the morning a boat, carrying a white canopy, anchored in the canal, and lay there idly for some time. The awning hid the occupants, and no one knew who was in it. Presently Hsiang-lin Sao came to the bank, and just as she was about to kneel down for water two men quickly jumped out, grabbed her, and forcibly put her inside the boat. They seemed to be mountain people, but they certainly took her against her will; she cried and shouted for help several times. Afterwards she was hushed up, evidently with some kind of gag. Nothing more happened until the arrival of two women, one of whom was Old Woman Wei. Nobody saw very clearly what had happened to Hsiang-lin Sao, but those who peered in declared that she seemed to have been bound and thrown on the deck of the cabin.

"Outrageous!" exclaimed Fourth Uncle. On reflection, however, he simply ended impotently, "But after all . . ."

Fourth Aunt herself had to prepare the food that day, and her son Ah Niu made the fire.

In the afternoon Old Woman Wei reappeared.

"Outrageous!" Fourth Uncle greeted her.

"What is this? How wonderful! You have honoured us once more with your presence!" Fourth Aunt, washing dishes, angrily shouted at the old bargain-maker. "You yourself recommend her to us, then you come with companions to abduct her from the household. This affair is a veritable volcanic eruption. How do you suppose it will look to outsiders? Are you playing a joke at our expense, or what is it?"

"*Ai-ya! Ai-ya!* I have surely been fooled and tricked. I came here to explain to you. Now how was I to know she was a rebel? She came to me, begged me to get her work, and I took her for genuine. Who would have known that she was doing it behind her mother-in-law's back, without in fact even asking for permission? I'm unable to look in your face, my lord and my lady. It's all my fault, the fault of a careless old fool. I can't look you in the face. . . . Fortunately, your home is generous and forgiving, and will not punish insignificant people like myself too strictly, eh? And next time the person I recommend must be doubly good to make up for this sin——"

"But——" interjected Fourth Uncle, who, however, could get no farther.

And so the affair of Hsiang-lin Sao came to an end, and indeed she herself would have been entirely forgotten were it not that Fourth Aunt had such difficulty with subsequent servants. They were too lazy, or they were gluttonous, or in extreme cases they were both lazy and gluttonous, and in truth were totally undesirable, "from the extreme left to the extreme right." In her distress, Fourth Aunt always mentioned the exemplary Hsiang-lin Sao. "I wonder how she is living?" she would say, inwardly wishing that some misfortune would oblige her to return to work. By the

time the next New Year rolled round, however, she had
given up hope of ever seeing her again.

Towards the end of the holidays Old Woman Wei called
one day to k'ou-t'ou [1] and offer felicitations. She had already
drunk herself into semi-intoxication, and was in a garrulous
mood. She explained that because of a visit to her mother's
home in Wei Village, where she had stayed for several
days, she was late this year in paying her courtesy calls.
During the course of the conversation their talk naturally
touched upon Hsiang-lin Sao.

"She?" the old woman cried shrilly and with alcoholic
enthusiasm. "There's a lucky woman! You know, when
her mother-in-law came after her here she had at that time
already been promised to a certain Hu Lao-liu, of Hu
Village. After staying in her home only a few days she
was loaded again into the Flowery Sedan Chair and borne
away!"

"Ai-ya, what a mother!" Fourth Aunt exclaimed.

"Ai-ya, my lady! You speak from behind a lofty door.[2]
We mountaineers, of the small-doored families, for us what
does it matter? You see, she had a young brother-in-law,
and he had to be married. If Hsiang-lin Sao was not
married off first, where would the family get money enough
for the brother-in-law's presents to his betrothed? So you
understand the mother-in-law is by no means a stupid
woman, but keen and calculating. Moreover, she married
the daughter-in-law to an inner mountain dweller. Why?
Don't you see? Marrying her to a local man, she would
have got only a small betrothal gift, but, since few women
want to marry deep into the mountains, the price is higher.
Hence the husband actually paid eighty thousand cash for
Hsiang-lin Sao! Now the son of the family has also been

[1] The prostration made at this time in wishing greetings.
[2] That is, an upper-class family. It is not against the mother-in-law's
tyranny that Fourth Aunt protests, but her lack of virtue in remarrying
her widowed daughter-in-law.

married, and he gave his bride presents costing but five thousand cash. After deducting the cost of the wedding there still remained over ten thousand cash profit. Is she clever or not? Good figuring, eh?"

"And Hsiang-lin Sao—she obeyed all right?"

"Well, it wasn't a question of obedience with her. Anybody in such a situation has to make a protest, of course. They simply tie her up, lift her into the Flowery Sedan Chair, bear her away to the groom's home, forcibly put the Flowery Hat on her head, forcibly make her *k'ou-t'ou* in the ancestral hall, forcibly 'lock her up' with the man—and the thing is done."

"*Ai-ya!*"

"But Hsiang-lin Sao was unusually rebellious. I heard people say that she made a terrific struggle. In fact, it was said that she was different from most woman, probably because she had worked in your home—the home of a scholar. My lady, I have seen much in these years. Among widows who remarry I have seen the kind who cry and shout. I have seen those who threaten suicide. There is in addition the kind who, after being taken to the groom's home, refuse to make the *k'ou-t'ou* to Heaven and Earth, and even go so far as to smash the Flowery Candles used to light the bridal chamber! But Hsiang-lin Sao was like none of those demonstrators.

"From the beginning she fought like a tigress. She screamed and she cursed, and by the time she reached Hu Village her throat was so raw that she had almost lost her voice. She had to be dragged out of the sedan chair. It took two men to get her into the ancestral hall, and still she would not *k'ou-t'ou*. Only for one moment they carelessly loosened their grip on her, and, *ai-ya!* by Buddha's name! she knocked her head a sound whack on the incense altar, and cut a deep gash from which blood spurted out thickly! They used two handfuls of incense ash on the wound, and bound it up with two thicknesses of red cloth,

and still it bled. Actually, she struggled till the very last,
when they locked her with her husband in the bridal room,
and even then she cursed! This was indeed a *protest*. *Ai-ya*,
it really was!"

She shook her gnarled head, bent her gaze on the floor,
and was silent.

"How was it afterwards?"

"They say she did not get up the first day, nor the
second."

"Afterwards?"

"After that? Oh, she finally got up. At the end of the
year she bore him a child, a boy. While I was at my
mother's home I saw some people who had returned from
Hu Village, and they said they had seen her. Mother and
son were both fat. Above their heads was fortunately no
mother-in-law. Her husband, it seems, is strong and a
good worker. He owns his own house. *Ai-ya*, she is a
lucky one indeed."

From that time on Fourth Aunt gave up any thought of
Hsiang-lin Sao's excellent work, or at any rate she ceased
to mention her name.

III

In the autumn, two years after Old Woman Wei had
brought news of Hsiang-lin Sao's extraordinary good luck,
our old servant stood once more in person before the hall
of Fourth Uncle's home. On the table she laid a round
chestnut-shaped basket and a small bedding-roll. She still
wore a white scarf on her head, a black skirt, a blue jacket,
and 'moon-white' vest. Her complexion was about the
same, except that her cheeks had lost all their colour.
Traces of tears lay at the corners of her eyes, from which all
the old brightness and lustre seemed washed away. Moreover, with her once more appeared Old Woman Wei,
wearing on her face an expression of commiseration. She
babbled to Fourth Aunt:

E

"So it is truly said, 'Heaven holds many an unpredictable wind and cloud.' Her husband was a strong and healthy man. Who would have guessed that at a green age he would be cut down by fever? He had actually recovered from the illness, but ate a bowl of cold rice, and it attacked him again. Fortunately she had the son. By cutting wood, plucking tea-leaves, raising silkworms—and she is skilled at each of these jobs—she could make a living. Could anyone have predicted that the child itself would be carried off by a wolf? A fact! By a wolf!

"It was already late spring, long after the time when anyone fears a wolf. Who could have anticipated this one's boldness? *Ai-ya!* And now she is left only her one bare body. Her late husband's elder brother-in-law took possession of the house, and everything in it, and he drove her out without a cash. She is, in fact, in the 'no-road no-destination' predicament, and can but return to beg you to take her in once more. She no longer has any connexions (such as a mother-in-law) whatever. Knowing you want to change servants, I brought her along. Since she already knows your ways, it's certain she'll be more satisfactory than a raw hand."

"I was truly stupid, truly," said Hsiang-lin Sao in a piteous voice, and lifting up her faded eyes for a moment. "I only knew that when the snow lies on the mountains the wild animals will sometimes venture into the valleys and will even come into the villages in search of food. I did not know that they could be so fierce long after the coming of spring. I got up early one morning, took a small basket of beans, and told little Ah Mao to sit in the doorway and string the beans. He was very bright, and he was obedient. He always listened to every word, and this morning he did so, and I left him in the door. I myself went behind the house to chop kindling and to scour rice. I had just put the rice in the boiler and was ready to cook the beans, so I called to Ah Mao. He didn't answer. I went round to the door, but there was no Ah Mao; only beans scattered on the ground. He never wandered to play, but I hurried to each door to ask for him. Nobody had seen him. I was terror-stricken! I begged people to help me hunt for him. All the morning and into the afternoon we moved back and forth, looking into every corner. Finally we found one of his little shoes hanging on a thorn bush. From that moment every one said that he had been seized by a wolf, but I would not believe it. After a little while, going farther into the mountains, we . . . found . . . him. Lying in a grassy lair was his body, with the five organs missing.[1] But the bean basket was still tightly clutched in his little hand." Here she broke down, and could only make incoherent sounds, without stringing a sentence together.

Fourth Aunt had at first hesitated, but after hearing this story her eyes reddened, and she instantly told the widow to take her things to the servants' quarters. Old Woman Wei sighed with relief, as if she had just put down a heavy bundle. Hsiang-lin Sao quieted somewhat, and without waiting for a second invitation she took her bedding-roll into the familiar room.

Thus she once more became a worker in Lo Ching, and everybody still called her Hsiang-lin Sao, after her first husband.

But she was no longer the same woman. After a few days her mistress and master noticed that she was heavy of hand and foot, that she was listless at her work, that her memory was bad, and over her corpse-like face all day there never crossed the shadow of a smile. One could tell by Fourth Aunt's tone of voice that she was already dissatisfied, and with Fourth Uncle it was the same. He had, as usual, wrinkled his brow in disapproval when she had first arrived, but since they had been having endless difficulties with servants he had raised no serious objection to the re-employment of Hsiang-lin Sao. Now, however, he

[1] Completely eviscerated.

informed Fourth Aunt that, though the woman's case seemed indeed very lamentable, and it was permissible because of that to give her work, still she was obviously out of tune with Heaven and Earth. She must not, therefore, be allowed to pollute precious vessels with her soiled hands, and especially on ceremonial occasions Fourth Aunt herself must prepare all food. Otherwise the ancestral spirits would be offended and, likely as not, refuse to touch a crumb.

These ancestral sacrifices were, in fact, the most important affairs in Fourth Uncle's home, for he still rigidly adhered to the old beliefs. Formerly they had been busy times for Hsiang-lin Sao also, and so the next time the altar was placed in the centre of the hall and covered with a fine cloth she began to arrange the wine cups and bowls and chopsticks on it exactly as before.

"Hsiang-lin Sao," Fourth Aunt cried, rushing in, "never mind that. I'll fix the things."

Puzzled, she withdrew and proceeded to take out the candlesticks.

"Never mind that, either. I'll get the sticks," Fourth Aunt said again.

Hsiang-lin Sao walked about several times in a rather dazed manner, and ended up by finding nothing to do, for Fourth Aunt was always ahead of her. She went away suspiciously. She found the only use they had for her that day was to sit in the kitchen and keep the fire burning.

People in Lo Ching continued to call her Hsiang-lin Sao, but there was a different tone in their voices. They still talked with her, but smiled in a cool way, and with faint contempt. She did not seem to notice, or perhaps did not care. She only stared beyond them, and talked always about the thing that day and night clung to her mind.

"I was truly stupid, truly," she would repeat. "I only knew that when the snow lies on the mountains the wild animals will sometimes venture into the valleys and will even come into the villages in search of food. I did not know that they could be so fierce long after the coming of spring. . . ."

Retelling her story in the same words, she would end up sobbing and striking her breast.

Every one who heard it was moved, and even the sneering men, listening, would loosen their smiles and go off in depressed spirits. The women not only forgot all their contempt for her, but at the moment forgave her entirely for her black sins—remarrying and causing the death not only of a second husband but also of his child— and in many cases ended by joining with her in weeping at the end of the tragic narrative. She talked of nothing else, only this incident that had become the central fact of her life, and she told it again and again.

Before long, however, the entire population of Lo Ching had heard her story not once but several times, and the most generous old women, even the Buddha-chanters, could not muster up a tear when she spoke of it. Nearly everybody in the town could recite the story word for word, and it bored them excessively to hear it repeated.

"I was truly stupid, truly," she would begin.

"Yes, you only knew that when the snow lies on the mountains the wild animals will sometimes venture into the valleys and will even come into the villages in search of food. . . ." Her audience would recite the next lines, cruelly cutting her short, and walk away.

With her mouth hanging open, Hsiang-lin Sao would stand stupefied for a while, stare as if seeing some one for the first time, and then drag away slowly as if weary of her continued existence. But her obsession gave her no rest, and she ingenuously tried to interest others in it by indirect approaches. Seeing a bean, a small basket, or other people's children, she would innocently lead up to the tragedy of Ah Mao. Looking at a child three or four years old, for instance, she would say :

"If Ah Mao were still here, he would be just about that size."

Frightened by the wild light in Hsiang-lin Sao's eyes, the children signalled for a retreat by pulling on their mother's skirts. She would therefore soon find herself alone again, and falter off until the next time. Pretty soon every one understood these tactics too, and made fun of her. When they saw her staring morosely at an infant they would look at her mockingly.

"Hsiang-lin Sao, if our Ah Mao were still here, wouldn't he be just about that big?"

Probably she had not suspected that her misery had long since ceased to afford any vicarious enjoyment for anyone, and that the whole episode had now become loathsome to her former sympathizers, but the meaning of this kind of mockery pierced her armour of preoccupation at last, and she understood. She glanced at the jester, but did not utter a word of response.

IV

Lo Ching never loses its enthusiasm for the celebration of New Year. Promptly after the twentieth of the Twelfth Moon the festivities begin.

Next year at this time Fourth Uncle hired an extra male worker, and in addition a certain Liu Ma, to prepare the chickens and geese. This Liu Ma was a 'good woman,' a Buddhist vegetarian who really kept her vow not to kill living creatures. Hsiang-lin Sao, whose hands were polluted, could only feed the fire and sit watching Liu Ma working over the sacred vessels. Outside a fine snow was matting the earth.

"*Ai-ya*, I was truly stupid," sighed Hsiang-lin Sao, staring despondently at the sky.

"Hsiang-lin Sao, you are back on the same trail!" Liu Ma interrupted, with some exasperation. "Listen to me, is it true you got the scar by knocking your forehead against the altar in protest?"

"Um-huh."

"I ask you this: If you hated it that much, how was it that later on you actually submitted?"

"I?"

"Ah, you! It seems to me you must have been half-willing, otherwise——"

"Ha, ha! You don't understand how great were his muscles."

"No, I don't. I don't believe that strength such as your own was not enough to resist him. It is clear to me that you must have been ready for it yourself."

"Ah—*you*! I'd like to see you try it yourself, and see how long you could struggle."

Liu Ma's old face crinkled into a laugh, so that it looked like a polished walnut. Her dry eyes rested on Hsiang-lin Sao's scar for a moment, and then sought out her eyes. She spoke again.

"You are really not very clever. One more effort that time really to kill yourself would have been better for you. As it is, you lived with your second man less than two years, and that is all you got for your great crime. Just think about it: when you go into the next world you will be held in dispute between the spirits of your two husbands. How can the matter be settled? Only one way: Yen Lu-t'a, the Emperor of Hell, can do nothing else but saw you in half and divide you equally between the two men. That, I think, is a fact."

An expression of mingled fear and astonishment crept over Hsiang-lin Sao's face. This was something she had not considered before, had never even heard in her mountain village.

"My advice is that you'd better make amends before it is too late. Go to the Tu-ti Temple and contribute money for a threshold. This threshold, stepped on by a thousand, stepped over by ten thousand,[1] can suffer for you and perhaps atone for the crime. Thus you may avoid suffering after death."

Hsiang-lin Sao did not say a word, but felt intolerably crushed with pain. Next day dark shadows encircled her eyes. Right after breakfast she went off to the Tu-ti Temple to beg the priest to let her buy a new threshold. He stubbornly refused at first, and only when she released a flood of tears would he consider it. Then, unwillingly, he admitted that it might be arranged for twelve thousand cash.

She had long since stopped talking with the villagers, who shunned her and the tiresome narrative of Ah Mao's death, but news soon spread that there was a development in her case. Many people came now and inquisitively referred to the scar on her forehead.

"Hsiang-lin Sao, I ask you this: Why was it that you submitted to the man?"

"Regrettable, regrettable," sighed another, "that the knock was not deep enough."

She understood well enough the mockery and irony of their words, and she did not reply. She simply continued to perform her duties in silence. Near the end of next year's service she drew the money due to her from Fourth Aunt, exchanged it for twelve silver dollars, and asked permission to visit in the west end of the town. Before the next meal she returned, much altered. Her face no longer seemed troubled, her eyes held some life in them for the first time in months, and she was in a cheerful mood. She told Fourth Aunt that she had bought a threshold for the temple.

During the Coming-of-Winter Festival she worked tirelessly, and on the day of making sacrifices she was simply bursting with energy. Fourth Aunt brought out the holy

[1] It is believed that the stone threshold acts as a kind of proxy body for the sinner, and every step on it is a blow subtracted from the total punishment awaiting him in Hell.

utensils, and Ah Niu carried the altar to the centre of the
room. Hsiang-lin Sao promptly went over to bring out
the wine cups and chopsticks.

"Never mind," Fourth Aunt cried out. "Don't touch
them."

She withdrew her hand as if it had been burned, her face
turned ashen, and she did not move, but stood as if trans-
fixed. She remained standing there, in fact, until Fourth
Uncle came in to light the offertory incense, and ordered
her away.

From that day she declined rapidly. It was not merely a
physical impoverishment that ensued, but the spark of life
in her was dimmed almost to extinction. She became
extremely nervous, and developed a morbid fear of darkness or the sight of anyone, even her master or mistress.
She became altogether as timid and frightened as a little
mouse that has wandered from its hole to blink for a
moment in the glaring light of day. In half a year her hair
lost all its colour. Her memory became so clouded that
she sometimes forgot even to scour the rice.

"What has got into her? How has she become like
that? It's better not to have her around," Fourth Aunt
began saying in her presence.

But "become like that" she had, and there did not seem
to be any possibility of improving her. They talked of
sending her away, or of returning her to the management of
Old Woman Wei. Nothing came of it while I was still
in Lo Ching, but the plan was soon afterwards carried out.
Whether Old Woman Wei actually took charge of her
for a while after she left Fourth Uncle's home or whether
she at once became a beggar I never learned.

        .   .   .   .

I am awakened by giant crackers, and see yellow tongues
of flame, and then immediately afterwards hear the sharp
pipipapao of exploding gunpowder. It is near the Fifth

Hour, and time for the prayers and blessings. Still only drowsily aware of the world, I hear far away the steady explosive notes, one after another, and then more rapidly and thickly, until the whole sky is echoing, and the whirling snowflakes, eddying out of little white balls themselves like something shot from above, hover everywhere. Within the compass of the medley of sound and gentle storm I feel somehow a nostalgic contentment, and all the brooding of the dead day and the early night is forgotten in the stir around me, lost in the air of expectancy that pervades these homes about to receive benediction. What a satisfaction it is to understand that the Holy Spirits of Heaven and Earth, having bountifully inhaled their fill of the offertory meat and wine and incense, now limp about drunkenly in the wide air. In such a mood they are certain to dispense boundless prosperity on the good people of Lo Ching!

KITES

I<small>T</small> is something of surprise and melancholy to me that in the spring at Peking, while there is still snow on the ground and the black leafless branches fret the clear sky, there are already several kites drifting in the air.

In my native town the season for kite-flying is about the second month of spring. If you hear the sound of wind-wheels you can always see, by lifting up your head, a grey crab-kite or a blue centipede-kite. There are also silent tile-shaped kites, without wind-wheels, flying low and looking lonesome and distressed. But at this time willows have already pushed up new shoots and early peach flowers have also blossomed in harmony with the children's sky decorations, all of them together sending forth the warm message of spring. But where I am now? All around me is the severity of winter, yet the gone-by spring of my youth and my old home town breathe in this sky.

I was not fond of kites; indeed, they disgusted me. In my opinion they were playthings for good-for-nothing children. But, quite the contrary, my younger brother, who was then about ten years old, and was continuously sick and ever so thin, liked kites so much that, unable to buy one for himself, and not allowed to play with me, he stood for half a day at a time looking attentively at the sky, with his mouth hanging open. He would cry out at the sudden fall of a crab-kite in the distance, or dance with joy at the release of a couple of tile-shaped kites. I considered him an imbecile.

One day I suddenly realized that I had not seen much of him for some time, and then I remembered that I had last found him in the back garden, picking up decayed bamboos.

I comprehended that something was happening, and I rushed towards the deserted store-room. Pushing open the door, I beheld him in the midst of a pile of dust-covered furniture, seated on a small stool set in front of a big one. At the sight of me he was astonished, and he stood up, pale and trembling. Before him was the skeleton of a butterfly kite, not yet pasted together, and leaning against the big stool. On it was a pair of wind-wheels, intended for the eyes of the kite, decorated with red paper, and nearly finished. Highly gratified at my discovery of the little wretch, at the same time I resented his working so secretly behind my back. And all this painstaking work over a mere worthless toy of children! Snatching up the kite, I broke one of its wings, and threw the wind-wheels on the ground and crushed them with my foot. I was his superior in age and strength, and therefore the victory was mine. I walked off proudly, leaving him standing there heart-broken. What became of him after that I did not know, nor did I care.

However, the day for my punishment at last arrived. After we had parted from each other for a long time and I was already middle-aged I unfortunately happened to read a foreign book about children, and I began to understand that play is quite the proper kind of behaviour for them, and that toys are their angels. And then this scene of spiritual triumph and slaughter in my childhood, of which I had not thought for twenty years, suddenly stretched out before my eyes. My heart seemed to have become a slug of lead, and heavily sank downward. It did not become so heavy as actually to sink away entirely, but just dropped down, down, down.

Of course I knew how to mend my fault. I might send him a kite, help and encourage him to play. Moreover, I might play with him myself, as he had so often wished. We would shout and run and laugh. Well, but he had, like me, meanwhile already grown a beard! Too late!

Suppose, then, that I just begged his pardon, until he said, "Oh, never mind that." I believed that my mind would then certainly be put at rest. It was really the solution.

When I next saw him our faces were carved with life, and my heart sank again. Gradually our talk turned nostalgically to the days of our childhood. At last I took courage, mentioned the kite episode, and confessed that it was due to my youthful ignorance. "Oh, never mind that," I expected him to say, and grant me a pardon at once, so that henceforth my heart would be lightened.

"Did such a thing really happen?" he smiled in surprise. He listened as if to a story concerning some one else. He could not remember a thing about it.

Complete forgetfulness, no hatred, and no forgiveness! How could I beg his pardon? The whole thing existed only in my imagination.

What more could I desire? I had only to carry the burden in my heavy heart.

And so once more spring flies again across the sky of this strange land, borne from my native town. It reminds me of my long-forgotten childhood, and it brings to me a kind of intangible melancholy. Ah, well, I had better return to earth and the severe winter.

"MOTHER'S"

Every one who has lived in China must have often heard the phrase, 'his mother's,'[1] or one of its many popular variants. The frequency of the oath among us is, I estimate, about as great as our footprints are numerous; it is as common as the polite salutation, "How are you?" If it is true, as some people claim, that the peony is China's national flower, then 'mother's' is beyond doubt our national oath.

I was born and reared in eastern Chekiang, where this invective still retains its original simplicity. In that part of the country the curse is clearly confined to your mother, without bothering other members of the family. It was only when I left there and travelled to different regions in China that I understood its amazing ramifications and came to marvel at its profound thrust and depth of meaning. I found it being applied far back, against people's ancestors, stretching sidelong to sisters, passing ahead into posterity, and in fact embracing every relative of the family whose name was execrated! Its timelessness is truly magnificent, and it is "as infinite as the Yellow and the Han rivers."

Moreover, it is not only invoked against men, but comes in very usefully against animals. The year before last, for

[1] The full expression, in its commonest form, is *ts'ao ta ma-ti pi*, here shortened to *t'a ma-ti*, 'his mother's.' It is, however, used in first, second, or third person; and, as the writer says, it ranges over all nature in its application. As usually employed it means that the person (thing, object) is the offspring of an adulterous mother; often that the speaker is the accursed one's father. The oath 'hangs on the lips' of many of Lu Hsün's famous characters, as well as those of other writers, and has come to have a revolutionary connotation. It is for this reason that Lu Hsün's essay on the oath is included in this book.

instance, I saw a coal-cart with one wheel trapped in a deep rut. The driver was jumping about in a rage and beating the unhappy ass hitched to the cart with all his strength.

"Your sister's!" he screamed. "Your sister's!"

I do not know what the practice is in other countries, or whether any one of them can rival 'mother's.'

I remember reading a great deal of crude swearing in the Norwegian novel *Hunger*, by Knut Hamsun, but none of it could be compared with our favourite oath. Gorki has plenty of rogues in his novels too, but in those I have read I do not find any similar curse. Artzibashev, it is true, has his passive Aladejev say "Your mother's" on one occasion, but it was when Aladejev had determined to make a sacrifice for love, and Chinese readers are not inclined to laugh at what looks to us like his self-contradiction. This phrase could very easily be translated into Chinese, incidentally, but in other languages it has been rather difficult. I notice that the German translation renders it, "I have used your mother." The Japanese translation is, "Your mother is my bitch." Both of these seem much too involved to me—too complicated.

At any rate it is evident that there actually was some such term of abuse in Russia, but not so exquisite, perhaps, not so all-inclusive, as ours. The glory remains with us. At bottom it may not, it is true, be a very great distinction, and it is possible that the Russians will not even contest our claims. Certainly when contrasted with the awe-inspiring qualities of the word 'bolshevization' the power of 'mother's' is insignificant; the 'swell'[1] men, the notables, the elect, cannot be frightened to death by it.

Yet even in China only the so-called lower-class flavours its speech with the rich pungency of this oath; it is reserved for the use of cart-pullers and their kind. Men of position, high-class individuals like the historic 'courtier-officials,'

[1] This expression is the same in Chinese as in English.

permitted no such oath to escape from their lips, and, needless to say, they did not brush it down in their books.

I cannot myself go back to the Chou Dynasty and become a *Ta-fu* courtier, or a *Shih* courtier, and, living in this day, I could, if I wished, unsheath my brush and proceed to dally as candidly as I chose. Somehow, probably because I have never pulled a cart and am therefore not entirely cleansed of the 'aristocratic taint,' I find that modesty forbids such frankness of display, and in using the expression in my writing I abbreviate it. I omit the verb and the object used with it in speech, and prefer to make the reference to the third person instead of the second.

Incidentally, since the use of 'mother's' is confined to one class of Chinese, it may appear to some critics an exaggeration to call it a 'national' oath. I am forced to disagree. Ask yourself, does the 'lower class' regard the peony, cherished and delicately tended by great men as the "flower of wealth and nobility," to be the 'national' symbol?

II

I do not know the historic origin of 'his mother's,' nor when it first came into wide popular use. We do not find it among the abusive expressions which here and there crop into the canons and the annals—such words as 'slave,' 'coolie,' 'dead man,' and, in still stronger language, 'old dog,' and 'badger's son.' The most emphatic insults to one's ancestors we see are at worst only something like, "Your mother is a slave girl," or, "The disgraceful remnant [offspring] of a eunuch." Thus far I have not anywhere found the equivalent of 'mother's' this or that. Perhaps it was censored from the records.

In a dialogue in the *Kwang Hung Ming Tsi*, however, which concerns Ying Tsu-tsai, a scholar in the Northern Wei Dynasty, there is something very interesting.

He was of the opinion that the chastity of women cannot be guaranteed. He asked his friend, Wang Yuan-ching: "How can you be sure that Wang is your true surname?" Wang flushed.

But Ying Tsu-tsai continued:

"I myself am not sure that my correct surname is actually Ying. Can *anyone* prove it for even five generations back?"

This may be a clue in our search, for it certainly seems to suggest that something like 'mother's' was then already in current use.

During the Chin Dynasty a great deal of emphasis was placed upon the social standing of the family—too much emphasis. Descendants of nobles and illustrious folk found it easy to become officials, and even if they were mere wine-bags and rice-sacks they never lost their rank among the exalted. When North China was lost to the T'o-pa Tartars the scholars did not for a moment relax their religious devotion to the symbols of 'House.' They closely guarded and still preserved the family distinctions, and refused to invigorate officialdom by drawing upon the talent and ability of the common people. The lower-class men could not rise to such a lofty plane.

Hence, already decadent, the privileged had to fall back upon inherited, ancestral glory to hold power over the masses. The rulers were proud, arrogant, overbearing, and cordially disliked. Since they used their ancestors as 'protecting talismen,' or guardian angels, it was quite natural for the oppressed classes to come to regard those ancestors as their common enemies. Though it is not clear whether Ying Tsu-tsai's remarks quoted above were uttered against the prevailing order of things, it is obvious at any rate that they were a sarcastic thrust at people who kept their position by shielding themselves behind the protection of 'House.' Their pomp, their vanity, and their power were all based on their one and only 'protecting talisman,' the ancestor. And once the prestige of their

F

ancestors collapsed the whole edifice which supported them fell into ruin also, and such is inevitably the end of men who depend upon inherited glory.

That which contains the same meaning as Ying Tsu-tsai's words, but lacks a little of their literary polish, comes from the lips of the common man—"His mother's!" This kind of indirect war against the stanch old fortress, the 'lofty-doored' big family, this roundabout attack at the blood-relations, must be considered an unusually clever tactic from the standpoint of military strategy. The man who invented 'his mother's' really was a genius, though, alas, a genius who was not, I fear, a gentleman.

III

After the T'ang Dynasty it was no longer fashionable to boast of one's illustrious family, and during the Gold and the Mongol dynasties, when 'barbarians' were our emperors, it made very little difference to anybody whether a Minister or an official was the son of a butcher or a wine merchant. For a long time afterwards it became difficult to assert clear demarcations between any of the classes of Chinese. They were all conquered subjects.

Still this ideal of climbing to the 'upper class' stayed with many people, and it continued to be associated with the Ancestor. In one of his plays Liu Shih-chung makes these observations:

> Laughable are the people of the street,
> Audacious and roguish,
> 'Men of the rivers and lakes,' to be sure,
> Yet calling one another by titles of virtue and pomp!
> In their shouting there is an exchange of polite nomenclature,
> And their names are words of utmost refinement.
> Listen to some of them, one by one:
> The rice-dealer is called "Son of Liang"; [1]

---

[1] Liang was a famous Minister of the Han Dynasty.

The butcher is named "The Honourable Chung";
The restaurant keeper "Jewel of the Sovereign";
And the miller "Man of Virtue"!
Truly, can such things be?

That was your *bourgeoisie* of the time!

Before reaching such lofty heights, however, the common man usually had various 'his mother's' expressions hanging on his lips. Given a chance to steal into a position, and to learn a few characters, he became all at once a gentleman. He adopted a poetic name, something implying inherited rank, and proceeded to edit his genealogical records. He suddenly discovered a celebrated scholar as his early ancestor, or a famous Minister of history.

Gradually such people were transformed into high-class gentlemen, they became refined and cultured in speech, and gravely imitated their aristocratic 'ancestor.' But among the masses there were always some clever men who knew what had gone on behind the ridiculous shadow play. Many years ago they coined a proverb to apply to such cases: "In their mouths are 'rites, wisdom, benevolence, righteousness';[1] in their hearts the males are robbers and the females are prostitutes!" Thus the lower class was not altogether naive.

In protest against hypocrites they revolted and cried out, "His mother's!"

IV

But the fact that men arbitrarily adopt other people's ancestors for their own, and are unable to shake off with contempt, to smash asunder, the idea of inherited glory, either for themselves or for others, is itself very strange and not the sort of thing one would expect of gentlemen.

[1] This was written several years ago, and hence had no reference to Generalissimo Chiang Kai-shek's "New Life Movement," which, curiously enough, invokes these same Confucian virtues, *li*, *yi*, *lien*, and *ch'ih*, in an effort to win mass support for the Nanking Government.

Sometimes the masses did actually attack such 'mother's lives' with violence, but in most cases it has happened quite by accident and acquired no historical significance. Hence these cases of action are likewise considered 'ungentlemanly' even to-day, and we still have classes dividing the Chinese people. The house still depends for its prestige on the ancestor as its 'protecting talisman.'

Until notions of this kind are dispelled we will also have with us our famous national oath, whether you always hear it or not. In time of peace 'his mother's' will everywhere continue to express the people's disgust, and in time of turmoil in the future it will be voiced in action.

There are, however, exceptions to this general significance of the expression. It may, for instance, denote surprise; it may even become an exclamation of praise. Thus, I once saw in my native village a young peasant lunching with his father. He pointed to one of the dishes and said:

"This isn't bad. Mother's. Help yourself to it."

"I don't feel like eating it," the old man replied. "Eat it yourself. Mother's."

In this case, you see, the oath has acquired all the delicacy of that now fashionable importation, "My dear!"

DIVORCE

"Ah, Uncle Mu! Happy New Year and good luck!"
"How are you, Pa San? Happy New Year!"
"*Ai, ai*, Happy New Year. So Ai-ku is here too. . . ."
"Greetings, Grandfather Mu, greetings. . . ."

Several voices harmonized in this shouting from within the cabin of the small boat when Chuang Mu-san (Uncle Mu) and his daughter Ai-ku stepped aboard from the Mu Lien Bridge Wharf. Some of the passengers clasped their hands together and swung their arms up and down while bowing, and four people got up to make room for them. Chuang Mu-san replied to their salutations and sat down, leaning his long pipe against the side of the boat. Ai-ku sat on his left, and just opposite Pa San.

"Going up to the city, Grandfather Mu?" asked one fellow, who had a face like the shell of a crab.

"No, not to the city," he replied. His voice sounded a little depressed, but there was no noticeable change in his heavily wrinkled features, ruddied by exposure. "Merely paying a visit to P'ang Village."

For a while every one was silent and simply stared at the old man and his daughter.

"Is it Ai-ku's business again?" Pa San finally asked.

"It's Ai-ku. Really, it is worrying me to death. It has already dragged on now for three years—how many times, fighting and talking peace! In the end it is still unsettled. . . ."

"Back to Wei's house then, eh?"

"Back to Wei's. He has tried to settle the affair between Ai-ku and her husband several times, but I have rejected

85

his terms. Never mind, this time they are celebrating New Year, and even old Squire Seventh will be there."

"Squire Seventh!" Pa San opened his eyes very wide. "Even the old Squire is putting in his word?"

"Well, as a matter of fact," said Uncle Mu, lowering his eyes, "we smashed their kitchen stove last year, and blew a breath of bad air in their place. Besides, actually, there would be no point in Ai-ku's returning to her husband now; it's too late."

"Moreover, I don't want to return," said Ai-ku, lifting her head indignantly. "I won't easily forget. Think of it! The young beast found himself a widow, and then wanted to get rid of me! But is it such a simple thing to throw out a wife? The *old* beast took his son's part, and he decided to *dismiss* me too. Entirely too simple! What about Squire Seventh? Can he be unjust merely because he has sworn brotherhood with the magistrate? He cannot be so unreasonable as Mr Wei, and only repeat, 'Separate, better separate, better separate.' I will tell him what troubles I've endured these years, and we'll see who he decides is right!"

Pa San was silenced by Ai-ku's eloquence.

Nobody spoke, and there was only the soft slap of the water against the bow of the boat. Chuang Mu-san reached for his pipe and filled it. A fat man sitting next to Pa San brought out a flint from his girdle and struck a light, which he held for Uncle Mu.

"Too much, too much," Uncle Mu said, thanking him.

"This is our first meeting," replied the fat man, "but I heard your name long ago. 'In the eighteen villages bordering the sea' is there anyone who does not know of you? We all have known for some time also about that young fellow Shih's becoming stuck on the little widow. When you went last year with your six sons and destroyed their kitchen, was there anyone who denied that they had got exactly what they deserved? You move in and out of lofty doors, the big gates open for you, you have plenty of face, what can *they* do to you?"

"Here is a discerning man," remarked Ai-ku enthusiastically, "though I do not know who he is."

"I am called Wang Teh-kuei," he promptly answered.

"They cannot discard me in this way," Ai-ku insisted. "I don't care whether they call in Squire Seventh or Eighth! I will pursue this and demand my rights until their house collapses and their men are all dead! Hasn't Wei tried to get me to make an agreement four different times? Even my father has been made dizzy-headed by the sight of the settlement-money he offered."

"*You*—rape your mother!" Chuang Mu-san muttered under his breath.

"But, Uncle Mu, isn't it true that the Shih family sent a feast to Master Wei last year?" commented the crabshell-faced Pa San.

"Never mind that," said Wang Teh-kuei. "Can a mere feast make people so addle-pated that they lose their sense of justice? If so, we might try giving a *foreign* banquet to them! Those who know the classics and are reasonable men always pronounce justice. For example, if a man is ill-treated by others they are the first to step forth and defend him—whether there is wine to be got for it or not! Just last year Yung Ta-yeh, from our wretched village, came back from Peking. He is a fellow who has seen the face of the world—unlike the rest of us. Now, he said there is a certain Madame Kuang up there——"

"Wang's Jetty!" shouted the boatman just then. "Passengers ashore for Wang's Jetty!"

"Here, me!" cried fatty, hastily snatching up his pipe and rushing from the cabin of the moving boat. He leaped to the shore as the boat drew near. Then he turned and politely nodded farewell to those left in the little craft, which was soon moving forward again, amid stillness broken only by the splash of the oars.

Pa San fell asleep, gazing at the feet of Ai-ku opposite him. Two old women in the rear cabin began chanting Buddha's name over their beads, looking at Ai-ku also, and nodding knowingly.

Ai-ku stared thoughtfully at the awning above her. She was thinking of ways and means of punishing her husband's family "until their house collapsed and their men were all dead," so that both the young beast and the old beast would find no way out. She had seen Wei several times, and she was not afraid of him. He was merely a fat dwarf with a round head, and there were many such people in her own village, only they were slightly darker than he.

Chuang Mu-san smoked his pipe to the end, and it wheezed a *ch'i-ch'i finale*, but still he kept on puffing. He knew that, having passed Wang's Jetty, they would soon reach P'ang. Already, in fact, the shrine of Kuei-hsin, God of Literary Examinations, was visible at the mouth of the village. Well, what was to be feared? He had been to P'ang Village more than once; it was not worth any serious consideration, nor was Wei himself.

Old Mu still remembered very well the day his daughter had returned, in tears, and how he had loathed them—the young beast and the old beast—and vowed revenge. The whole history of the affair renewed itself in his mind. Ordinarily when he recalled the scene in which his son-in-law's parents had been punished he smiled with contempt and satisfaction, but this time he did not. For some reason Squire Seventh obscured the view. There he was, in the midst of the whole picture, and he confused it and changed the total effect.

The boat moved on and nobody spoke, but there was the murmur of the old women, chanting holy words. The others seemed to be meditating with Ai-ku and Chuang Mu-san over that affair that stretched before them.

"Well, Uncle Mu, here you are. P'ang Village. Put your venerable bones ashore."

Startled from his musing, Chuang Mu-san looked up to see the shrine of Kuei-hsin immediately in front of him. Ai-ku followed him ashore. They passed the shrine and moved on in the direction of Master Wei's home, where the negotiations between the two families were to take place.

They passed about thirty doors, moving in a southerly direction, turned a corner, and they were there. Four dark-sailed boats stood at anchor in front of the big gate.

Stepping across the black-lacquered door-sill, they were greeted by the gateman and invited into his room. Behind him, already seated at two tables, were some boatmen and a number of tenant farmers. Ai-ku gave a quick glance at them merely to make certain that neither the young nor the old beast was in the group.

These working people brought out portions of New Year cake and tea and offered it to them, and Ai-ku, without knowing quite why, felt suddenly uncomfortable and embarrassed. She began to speculate about Squire Seventh. Was it possible that because he had become the magistrate's blood brother he could no longer render an impartial decision? "Those who know the classics and are men of justice must always defend the oppressed," she thought. "I'll just tell Squire Seventh all the details, beginning from the time I married, at the age of fifteen. . . ."

Finishing their refreshments, father and daughter were ushered into the great hall, round a corner, and into the guest chamber. It was a luxurious place. There were so many articles of furniture that she had no time to observe them all, and there were so many guests—dressed in purple and blue satin coats—that the room shimmered with radiance. In the midst of this splendour sat a gentleman who, she concluded, must certainly be Squire Seventh. Although fat and round of head he was taller and altogether bulkier than Master Wei, and two narrow eyes looked out over his shining black whiskers. The top of his head was utterly bald, but his face had a ruddy glow to it, and was soft and smooth. That wonderful texture, indeed, for a moment puzzled Ai-ku, but she concluded that it must have been attained by applying pig's fat to the skin. . . .

"This is an anus-stop," Squire Seventh was proudly announcing, holding up an ancient piece of jade, "and was buried with our ancestors, as was the practice then." He caressed his nose with it as he spoke. "It's too bad it came from a fairly recent tomb, probably not much earlier than Han.[1] Nevertheless, it is worth owning. See here, look at this spot. This is a mercury stain, the result of the mercury that was put in corpses in olden times to keep them from decaying too rapidly."

Several heads at once concentrated around the anus-stop to see exactly what the Squire meant. One of them of course was Master Wei. The rest were those of rich young men whom Ai-ku had hitherto failed to notice, due to the fact that Squire Seventh had altogether obliterated them by his imposing bulk.

Ai-ku did not comprehend the meaning of the latter part of the comments reported above. She did not, more-over, dare to begin, just as this point, any inquiry or research into the exact nature of a 'mercury stain.' Instead, she stole a glance around the room and saw, behind herself, the old beast as well as the young one. They stood quite close to the wall and beside the door. This one glimpse gave Ai-ku the impression that both of them looked older and wearier than even half a year ago.

Suddenly everybody dispersed, and the marvellous jade, with its 'mercury stain,' was left in Master Wei's possession. He held it affectionately, moving it warmly in his fingers, as he turned to Chuang Mu-san.

"Only you two?" he asked.

"Yes."

"Your sons haven't come?"

"They were too busy."

[1] The Han Dynasty, 206 B.C. to A.D. 220.

"As a matter of fact, why should you yourself be bothering in the New Year—and in the First Moon? But it is still the same affair, you see. . . . You have had enough of disputes, I dare say. Isn't it already more than two years? As for myself, I believe that we should attempt to untie old knots rather than make new ones. Since Ai-ku has not lived in harmony with her husband, nor been liked by her parents-in-law—well, as I said before, better separate, better separate. I haven't enough face to have my words accepted, but here is Squire Seventh, who is, as you know, the very image of justice, and he thinks as I do. However, he suggests that both parties confess to a little bad luck, and compromise. The Shih family will add ten dollars to the offer previously made, bringing the total settlement money to ninety dollars."

". . . . . ."

"Ninety dollars! Even if you took the case before Uncle Emperor you would not get such a bargain! Only Squire Seventh could suggest such generous terms!"

The Squire opened his narrow eyes very wide and, looking at Chuang Mu-san, nodded his head in agreement.

Ai-ku felt that events were rapidly impinging towards a crisis. She was annoyed at the meekness of her father, a man who was used to putting other people, those who lived along the sea-coast, in awe. Now he did not seem to have a word to say, and she did not understand his timidity. What was there to be afraid of? She had heard Squire Seventh's opinions on the jade relic, and, although she did not clearly comprehend the full profundity of his remarks, she could find nothing very terrifying in them. On the contrary she concluded that he was a kindly and benevolent person, not as intimidating as she had imagined, and so she spoke up boldly.

"Squire Seventh is a man of wisdom and learning, very different from us villagers, with a knowledge of what is right. I have been wronged, and I wish to appeal, therefore, for justice.

"After I became daughter-in-law in the Shih family I tried my best to fulfil the duties of a faithful wife. I kept my head low, and I did not omit a single rite. But they mistreated me from the beginning, and posed before me like the god who chases evil spirits. One year a weasel killed a cock that belonged to them, and they blamed me for it, saying that I had forgotten to shut the chicken-coop. Actually it was because of their mangy dog—cut off its head!—who knocked open the door of the chicken-coop to steal some rice-chaff. But, without investigating at all, without distinguishing between green, red, black, and white, the little beast smacked my face."

Squire Seventh glanced at her.

"I thought then that there was some other reason for it —and here is a fact which will not escape Squire Seventh's notice, for those who know the classics and wisdom know everything. Well, he acted that way because he had already become infatuated with that lewd harlot and wanted to get rid of me! But I, who was betrothed with the three teas and the six gifts, I who was formally borne to his home in the Flowery Sedan Chair, is it so easy to toss me aside? I must demand justice, and show them my colours, even if it means going to court. If the magistrate does not give me satisfaction, I can still appeal to the prefect——"

"Seventh Squire knows all about these things," Master Wei interrupted her. "Ai-ku, unless you change your attitude you will accomplish nothing. You are still the same, I see. Look at your father, how reasonable he is. But you and your brothers . . .! Well, suppose you do take the matter to the prefect? Won't the prefect also consult Seventh Squire? By then it will also have become a public scandal, there will be no face for anybody——"

"I am ready to stake my life on the outcome, even so, and although it may ruin both families!"

"This is not an affair on which to stake your life," spoke Squire Seventh at last. "You are still in the green of life, and while young one should seek harmony with others. 'Harmony brings forth wealth,' is it not true? I have suggested that your husband increase the sum by ten dollars, and this is already a kind of justice higher than heaven. Actually, if your father-in-law and mother-in-law tell you to 'Go!' then go you must. This is true not only locally but also in Shanghai, Peking, and even in foreign countries. If you distrust me, here is a young man who has just returned from Peking. You may ask him yourself."

He turned to a sharp-chinned young master near by and demanded, "Is that not so?"

"Precisely," replied the sharp-chinned one, making his body stiff and his voice suave and respectful.

Ai-ku began to realize that she stood alone. Her father had said nothing, her brothers had not dared to come. Master Wei had always taken the side of the Shih family. Squire Seventh had evidently been influenced in the same direction, and even this young sharp-chin (with his air of humility and his voice like a wounded bug) was beating his gong with the prevailing wind. Her mind in confusion, she made a last struggle.

"Can it be true that even you, Squire Seventh——?" Her eyes hesitated between surprise, perplexity, and despair. "Yes—we crude people know very little. Even father does not know the ways of man and the world, and age blurs his powers of judgment. He should not let them, the old beast and the young beast, make the arrangements! They know well enough how to crawl into the dog's hole and find out about things; they know well enough how to win favour by flattery and bribery——"

Young beast, who had remained mute, standing behind her, now broke in, saying, "Look at her, Squire Seventh! You see how she acts even in the presence of a great man? In our home she was such a pest that even the domestic animals could get no peace. She calls my father 'old beast' and me 'young beast,' or 'bastard'——"

Ai-ku turned upon him and shouted: "Who—you that were born of a lewd mother with ten times ten thousand lovers—*who* has called *you* a 'bastard'?"

Having silenced him she turned to Squire Seventh once more.

"I have something to say to all of you. Did he ever speak to me kindly or decently? When he opened his mouth it was to call me 'child of a debased womb,' and when he closed it it was by cursing my mother. After he made a mistress of that harlot he even reviled my ancestors. Squire Seventh, just consider this——"

She suddenly stopped, frightened by what she had seen. Squire Seventh had quickly rolled his eyes and turned his head up. A high wavering voice issued from behind his long thin whiskers.

"*Come!*" he yelled.

Ai-ku's heart seemed to stop beating, and when it began again it pounded and jerked furiously. She had lost her case now, she felt sure. She had taken a fatal misstep and fallen into the water.

A man wearing a blue gown with a black vest over it came in and stood in front of Squire Seventh like a wooden rod, waiting for instructions. There was not a cheep in the entire room. The Squire moved his lips. No one could make out what he had said except the man before him, who snapped his body even more rigidly to attention, as if the command had entered his very bones and brought new resilience to them.

"Yes, sir," he answered, and backed away a few steps before leaving the august presence.

Ai-ku knew that something unexpected was about to happen, and she felt helpless to prevent it. She understood now the austere power and greatness of the Squire, and she understood also how reckless she had been when a

moment ago she had spoken so freely. She had under-
estimated him. She regretted her rashness, and, wishing to
mollify him somehow, she said, in spite of herself:

"Nevertheless, for all that, I shall still accept whatever
decision Squire Seventh may reach."

There was still not a cheep in the entire room. Although
she had spoken very softly, spinning her words out as thin
as a strand of silk, Master Wei had heard her, and, jumping
up as if a clap of thunder had just been detonated, he
shouted out:

"Good! Squire Seventh is really just, and Ai-ku is after
all a sensible woman."

Having extolled her, he next turned to Chuang Mu-san.

"Honourable Mu, since your daughter has already given
her consent, you have nothing more to say. Have you
brought along the red and green marriage cards, as I asked
you to do? Now, then, let both families bring them
out."

Ai-ku saw that her father had already reached into his
girdle and was fumbling for something. Then her attention
turned to that rod-like man who had received the Squire's
command. He had reappeared, carrying a small, flat, jet-
black object shaped like a tiny tortoise, which he handed to
his master. Fearing that the affair might yet take a turn
for the worse, she glanced quickly at her father, and was
relieved to see him already unfolding a blue cloth pack.

Squire Seventh now removed the head of the tortoise,
and from the inside poured something out of the neck into
the palm of his hand. The rod-like man took the object
and left the room. The Squire pressed one of his fingers
into the substance in his hand, and then rubbed it into his
nostrils, staining his upper lip a faint brown. He wrinkled
up his nose to sneeze.

Chuang Mu-san was counting the silver pieces. Master
Wei removed some dollars from an uncounted pile and
handed them back to the old beast. The two copies of the

red and green cards, bearing the birth-characters of bride and groom, were returned to both families, and Wei remarked:

"You have kept them in good condition. Count the money carefully, Lao Mu; this is no joking matter—counting money is a serious business."

"*Ah-choooo!*" Ai-ku knew that it was Squire Seventh sneezing, but she could not help turning to look at him. She saw his mouth hanging open and his nose wrinkled up comically. Between his fingers he again held in his hand that same jade instrument—"buried with our ancestors, as was the practice then"—and was rubbing it against the side of his nose.

Chuang Mu-san finished counting the money with some difficulty, and both sides put away their marriage cards. Every one seemed to relax, tense expressions gave away to relieved looks, and an air of harmony pervaded the guest chamber.

"Good! The matter is at last settled up in round perfection," announced Wei. Noticing that every one was preparing to leave, he sighed and said, "Then there is nothing else. Congratulations to both families! The knot is finally broken, and we can drink a cup of New Year wine before you go. This is a rare occasion."

"We won't drink," Ai-ku thanked him. "Let it wait until next year."

"Thank you, Wei Lao-yeh. We won't drink just now. We have things to do," old beast and young beast responded in chorus.

"Ah-h-h. Not just a drop or two before you go?" Wei asked, looking at Ai-ku, the last to leave.

"No, not now, thank you, Master Wei."

PART II
STORIES BY OTHER CHINESE WRITERS

JOU SHIH
(1901–31)

JOU SHIH was born in a country town in Chekiang province, and was educated in the provincial schools there. After leaving a training college he began to teach. For a short time he was educational commissioner of the Ninghai district of Chekiang. He became interested in writing, and was strongly influenced by radical thought, which he expressed in most of his work.

Jou Shih was one of the most active of the League of Left Writers, organized in Shanghai after the counter-revolution in 1927. This society was made illegal by the Kuomintang, and membership in it was threatened with punishment by death. Jou Shih, together with five others, paid this penalty in 1931. He was arrested in January of that year by British police in the Shanghai International Settlement. Extradited at the request of the Chinese authorities he was killed on February 7 at the Lunghua Garrison, on orders from Nanking. Feng Kung, a girl novelist 24 years old, Tsung Hui, 21, Yin Fu, 22, Li Weisen, 28, and Hu Yeh-ping, 26, were the other writers killed at the same time.

Published works by Jou Shih included *February, The Great Impression,* and *Death of the Old Order. Slave Mother* is considered his best short story, and had a permanent influence on the 'revolutionary realism' movement in Chinese literature.

SLAVE MOTHER

By JOU SHIH

HER husband dealt in skins—that is to say, he collected cow-hides and the skins of wild animals from hunters all over the countryside, and took them to the larger towns to sell. Sometimes he supplemented this occupation with a little farm labour. During the busy planting season he used to assist the farmers in transplanting the young sprouts. He knew just how to set out each row perfectly straight, and for that reason if there were five working together in a paddy-field he was always put in the head position to act as a marker. Circumstances were against him, nevertheless, and his debts mounted year after year. Probably it was the hard times that made him take to smoking, drinking, and gambling. Soon he had become a surly, hot-tempered fellow, continuing to grow poorer and poorer until people were afraid to make him even the smallest loans.

Illness followed in the wake of poverty, and his body turned a withered yellow colour. His face grew as yellow as a small brass drum. Even the whites of his eyes changed colour. People said that he had the jaundice, and children began calling him "Yellow-belly." One day he said to his wife:

"There's nothing more I can do. If we go on like this we'll soon have to part with the kettle. I think it would be better to let you save us with your body. If you stay and go hungry with me what can I do for you?"

"With my body?"

His wife sat behind the mud oven, holding her three-year-old son on her lap, nursing him at her breast. She spoke in a subdued tone, haltingly.

"Yes, yours!" replied her husband, his voice weak from illness. "I've already leased you——"

"What's that?" she asked, seeming almost to faint.

The room was silent for a moment, and then he spoke, breathing hard.

"Three days ago Wolf Wang sat here for hours demanding his money. When he left I went out too. When I got to Nine-Acre Pool I felt I didn't want to live any longer. I sat down under a tree. All I needed to do was to climb it and let myself drop off into the pool. I kept thinking about it, but I hadn't the courage to jump. All the time there was an owl screeching in my ear. It turned my heart cold and I came away. But on the road I met the Sun woman. She asked me what I was doing out so late, and I told her. I asked her to try and raise me a loan, or to borrow some girl's clothes or jewellery that I could pawn, so that I wouldn't have to see Wang's wolfish green eyes glittering in my house every day. But the Sun woman laughed at me, and said:

"'Why do you keep on, then, supporting that wife of yours at home, and you as yellow as you are?'

"I hung my head and said nothing.

"'Of course you can't spare the son,' she said, 'having only one. But the wife . . .'

"I said to myself, 'Surely she isn't telling me to sell my wife!'

"'But the wife,' she went on, 'even though she is your proper wife—you're poor, you can't help it—what's the use in keeping her at home?'

"Then she came straight to the point and said:

"'There's a *hsiu-ts'ai*[1] who has no son, although he's already fifty. He has had it in mind to buy himself a

[1] *Hsiu-ts'ai* is a Chinese literary degree roughly corresponding to the B.A.

secondary wife, but his first wife won't let him. She'll
allow him only to lease one for three years or five years,
and he has asked me to look out for a woman who might
suit him; one somewhere around thirty, who has had two
or three sons already, who is quiet and honest and willing
to work, and who will be submissive to his major wife.
Recently the *hsiu-ts'ai's* wife spoke to me about it herself,
and said that if the conditions were satisfied they would be
willing to pay eighty or a hundred dollars purchase price.
I've been searching for a suitable woman a good many days,
but haven't located one.'

"Then she said that as soon as she met me she thought of
you, and that you were just the right one. So she asked me
straight away what I thought, and after I had cried a little
I let myself be persuaded."

At this point his head dropped, while his voice trailed off
until it stopped completely. His wife said not a word.
She seemed wholly stupefied. After a moment's silence he
went on :

"Yesterday the Sun woman went to the *hsiu-ts'ai's* house,
and she says he is quite keen, and that his wife is pleased too.
The price is a hundred dollars, and the lease is for three years
if there is a son in that time. If not, for five years. The Sun
woman has set the date too. It's the eighteenth—five days
yet. To-day she's sending the lease agreement."

The wife was quivering in every limb. "Why didn't you
—tell me earlier?" she stammered out.

"I walked a circle in front of you three different times
yesterday, but I couldn't get it out. Really and truly, apart
from using you as a means, there is absolutely nothing we
can do."

"You've decided on it?" she asked, with trembling lips.

"Just waiting for the agreement to be written out."

"Oh, what a shameful thing! Isn't there any other way
at all, my own Spring Treasure's father?" That was the
name of the boy in her arms.

"Shameful? Yes, I've thought about it. But we're poor, and we don't want to die. What else can we do? I'm afraid I'm not going to be able to do any transplanting this year."

"Have you thought about Spring Treasure? He's only three. What will he do without a mother?"

"I can look after him, can't I? He's ready to be weaned, anyway."

Little by little he seemed to have grown angry. He now strode out through the door. He began to sob, brokenly.

Out of her memories of the past emerged the thing which had happened just a year ago. She had borne a daughter then, and she lay on the bed like one who had died. No, the dead die whole, but her body was shattered into fragments. On a heap of dry grass on the floor the new-born baby was crying loudly, "Caa, caa!" and perking its arms and legs. The navel string was twisted about it. She made a supreme effort to rise and wash the child, but only her head would lift; her body remained inert on the bed. It was then she had seen that brutal husband of hers, with flaming red face, take a pail of boiling water beside the infant. She had put forth a final effort to shout at him, "Wait! Wait!" But the brute had not allowed a moment's discussion, nor had he returned any answer. Like a butcher holding the lamb he was about to slaughter, he had taken in his hard rough hands the new-born life, the little daughter with the cries of "Caa, caa!" and, *plop!* dropped her into the water. She had heard nothing but a splash and the hiss of steaming water. The little girl made no sound. She wondered now why it had not uttered one loud cry. Had it been content to go silently to this undeserved death? Ah, yes! She remembered why she had heard nothing! She had fainted away then, fainted as she would have done if her heart had been cut out.

When she thought of this it seemed as though all tears were drained away. "Ah!" she sighed softly, "fate is bitter!"

Spring Treasure dropped the nipple and looked up at her. "Mamma! Mamma!"

.   .   .   .   .   .

On the evening before her departure she chose the darkest corner of the house to sit in. An oil-lamp was burning in front of the stove, giving out a firefly-like illumination. She held Spring Treasure in her arms, and let her head rest on his hair. Her thoughts seemed to have floated very far away, to what far place she could not tell. Slowly they travelled back, back to the immediate present, back to the child. She called to him in a low voice:

"Spring Treasure, my precious!"

"Mamma!" he answered, pulling on her breast.

"Mamma is going away to-morrow. . . ."

"H'mm," he replied, only half comprehending, but instinctively rubbing his head against her.

"Mamma's not coming back. She can't come back, not for three years!"

She wiped her eyes.

"Where mamma going?" asked the child, freeing his mouth. "To temple?"

"No, she's going ten miles away, to a family named Li."

"I'm going too!"

"Precious can't go alone."

"Ng!" he grunted rebelliously, returning to the little trickle of milk.

"You stay at home with daddy. Daddy will look after my Precious. He'll sleep with Precious, and take Precious out to play. You do what daddy tells you, that's all. And after three years——"

"Daddy will beat me!" the child interrupted in a tearful voice.

"Daddy won't beat you any more," she said, at the same time stroking his right cheek, where a scar was left by the blow from a hoe-handle that his father had given him on the third day after murdering his little sister.

She seemed to have had something more to say to the child, but just then her husband came stalking in through the door. He walked over to her and, reaching in his pocket with one hand, said:

"I've got seventy dollars of the money already. The other thirty will be paid ten days after you arrive there."

There was a pause.

"And they've agreed to send a sedan chair for you."

Another pause.

"And they've agreed that the chair-bearers will come directly after breakfast."

With that he left her, and went out through the door again.

That evening neither her husband nor herself ate any supper.

. . . . . .

The next day there was a drizzle of spring rain.

The sedan chair arrived early. She had not slept the whole night. First she had mended all of Spring Treasure's ragged store of clothing. Spring was almost over, and summer would soon be here, yet she brought out even the torn quilted coat that he used in the winter, and turned all his things over to the father, who lay asleep in bed. Then she sat down at his side and tried to talk with him. But the long night dragged slowly through without her having said a word. Once or twice she worked up the courage to call out to him, but she said nothing intelligible, nor was it loud enough for him to hear. Finally she had lain down in silence.

Just as her mind was drifting off into unconsciousness Spring Treasure awoke. He tugged at his mother and wanted to get up. As she put on his clothes she said to him:

"Precious must be a good boy at home here, and not cry,

so that daddy won't beat you. And mamma will buy Precious lots of candy to eat. Precious mustn't cry."

The child, without a trace of sadness, opened his mouth and began to sing.

"Don't sing," she said, kissing him beside his lips. "You'll wake daddy!"

On a bench near the door sat the chair-bearers, smoking long pipes and telling each other stories. Shortly after the Sun woman arrived from the neighbouring village. She was an old woman, a matchmaker, with a wealth of worldly experience. On entering she brushed the raindrops from her cloak and said to them:

"It's raining! It's raining! That's a sign that there will be growth after this in your home."

She took a turn or two about the room in a businesslike manner, and made a few remarks to the child's father, the general import of which was that she would appreciate a commission. It was due to her efforts, after all, that the lease agreement had been arranged so smoothly and profitably.

"To speak quite frankly, Spring Treasure's father, for another fifty dollars the old fellow could have bought himself a concubine," she said.

Then she set about hurrying the woman along, but the latter sat motionless with Spring Treasure in her arms. The old woman shouted at her in a high-pitched voice:

"The chair-bearers want to get back to their own place for dinner. You had better get ready to leave."

The woman looked at her as though saying:

"Really, I don't want to go! Let me stay here and starve!"

The matchmaker understood what was on her lips. She went over to her and gave her an engaging smile.

"You are a simple wench, right enough. What more has Yellow-belly got to give you? Over there is a family that has enough to eat and to spare, two hundred acres of fields, enough money, their own house, hired men and cattle. The wife is very good-natured and extremely polite to others. Every time she meets people she makes them presents of food. As to the old fellow—he isn't really old— he has a white face and no beard at all. From so much studying he has grown round-shouldered in an elegant way. But there's no need for me to tell you. As soon as you step down from the sedan chair you will realize that I never tell lies in my matchmaking."

The woman brushed away the tears.

"Spring Treasure," she said softly, "how can I give him up this way?"

"Don't worry about him," said the old woman, placing a hand on her shoulder, and putting her face close to the two of them. "He's three. The ancients said, 'Three or four years and he leaves his mother.' He's ready to leave you. If you'll just put forth an effort with your belly and bear a child or two while you are there everything will be fine."

The chair-bearers at the door were urging departure. "She isn't a young bride," they grumbled, "to be doing so much crying!"

The old woman took Spring Treasure out of her arms.

"I'll take him with me," she said.

The child cried and struggled, but was finally bundled out through the side-door. Just as his mother was getting into the chair she called out to them:

"Bring him back into the house. It's raining out there."

Her husband sat resting his head on his hand, and neither moved nor spoke.

. . . . . .

It was ten miles from one village to the other, but the second time the chair was set down they were there. The fine spring rain had blown in through the cloth curtain of the sedan chair and soaked her coat. She was welcomed by a plump-faced lady of fifty-four or -five, with crafty eyes. "That must be the wife," she said to herself, and looked at her in silence, full of embarrassment. The other conducted her in a friendly way to the steps, while a tall, thin man with a delicate round face came out from the house. After carefully scrutinizing the new arrival he smiled broadly and said:

"You arrived very early, didn't you? Are your clothes wet?"

The older woman paid no attention to his presence.

"Do you have any things in the chair?" she asked.

"No, I have nothing."

A number of women from the neighbourhood had gathered outside the door and were peeping in as they passed into the house.

She did not understand why it was that she should keep thinking of her old home, and why she could not forget Spring Treasure. Certainly it was obvious that she ought to be congratulating herself on the three years of life that were commencing. Both this house and the husband to whom she had been leased were better than the ones she had left. The *hsiu-ts'ai* was unquestionably a kind and good man, with a quiet way of speaking, while even the wife was unexpectedly pleasant, with her attentiveness and her unceasing flow of chatter. She related the whole history of her life with her husband, from the time of her beautiful and happy marriage down to the present—a period of thirty years. She had borne one child, she said, fifteen or sixteen years previously. It was a son, and, according to her, a very beautiful and clever child; but it had died of smallpox before it was ten months old. She had never had a second child. Apparently she had wanted her husband to marry a concubine, but, whether he had refused because he loved her or because he didn't love her, he had not done so up to the present. As she listened to her the simple-natured young woman felt alternately cheered and pained, elated and depressed. Finally the old lady referred to their expectations. This brought a blush to her face, but the old lady said:

"You have raised several children already. Of course you know all about it. I am sure you know more than I do." And with this she left her.

That evening the *hsiu-ts'ai* also talked in great detail about family affairs, partly in a boastful way, to be sure, and partly to be attractive to her. She was sitting beside a chest of drawers, a red wooden one, such as she had never possessed in her own home. She was looking at it wide-eyed when he came and sat down in front of it.

"What is your name?" he asked her.

She did not return an answer or a smile, but, rising, went towards the bed. He followed, and laughingly asked her:

"Are you shy? Ha! You're thinking about your husband, eh? Well, I'm your husband now." But his voice was gentle. He put out a hand and pulled at her sleeve. "Don't be sad. I suppose you're thinking about your child too. But——"

He did not finish what he was going to say. With another laugh he began to remove his outer gown.

She could hear the wife's voice outside roundly cursing some one. She could not make out who it was. It might be the cook, or it might be herself. Somehow she appeared to be the cause of it.

"Come to sleep," called the *hsiu-ts'ai* from the bed. "She is always carrying on like that. She used to be very fond of the hired man, and so she always scolds Mrs Wang, the cook, because the hired man liked her."

.   .   .   .

The days passed, one after the other. Gradually the thoughts of her old home grew distant, while her immediate surroundings became closer and more familiar to her.

Sometimes she would hear Spring Treasure crying, and on several occasions she had dreamed about him. But the dreams grew more vague, while the duties with which she was surrounded increased daily. She discovered that the old lady was extremely suspicious. On the surface she appeared generous, but actually her jealousy turned her into a sleuth, for ever spying on every action of her husband in regard to the new woman. If the *hsiu-ts'ai* came in from outside and spoke with the other first she was immediately suspicious that he had brought something special for her, and it became imperative for her to call him into her room that very night and impose on him an angry lecture. "Are you bewitched by a fox?" "Do you know how much your old bones weigh?" Such expressions were commonly heard. From then on, if the young woman happened to be alone when the *hsiu-ts'ai* came in, she hastened to avoid him. Even if the old lady were near by it was wise to retire some distance, although she attempted to be as natural and unobtrusive about it as possible. Otherwise the lady would flare up and accuse her of trying to make her appear harsh in the eyes of bystanders. As time went on all the responsibilities of the house were heaped on to her shoulders, as though she had been a servant. She acted wisely, and often washed the old lady's clothes, although she was told:

"There is no reason for you to wash my clothes. Even your own clothes can be given to Mrs Wang to wash."

Directly afterwards, however, the old lady would generally say, "Sister, go down to the pigsty, will you, please, and have a look around. I don't know why those two pigs should be making such a fuss. Probably they haven't enough food. Mrs Wang always refuses to feed them."

After eight months, in the winter, her appetite underwent a change. She did not care to eat rice; only fresh noodles or sweet potatoes. After a few meals she was tired of these too. If she ate too much it would not stay down. She had

a desire for squash and plums, but these grew in the sixth
month. Where could one get them now? The *hsiu-ts'ai*
appreciated the message that these signs conveyed, and
smiled the whole day long. Whatever it was possible to
buy he procured for her. He went personally into the
street to get her oranges, and ordered little golden oranges
to be bought for her. He would walk up and down the
veranda, muttering things to himself that no one heard.
Once he saw her helping Mrs Wang grind flour for the
New Year cakes, and called to her before she had finished
as much as three pints, "Take a rest. The hired man can
do the grinding. They all share in the cakes, anyhow."

Sometimes in the evenings, while the others were chatting, he would bring a lamp and sit by himself, reading from
the *Book of Odes* in the lamplight. Then the hired man
would say to him:

"Why do you still study those things, sir? You are not
sitting for an examination now."

Then he would stroke his smooth cheeks and answer
merrily:

"Aha! Do you know about the joys of life too?

" Flower-candles for the wedding night.
    A list of gold for the candidates' names.

"Do you understand those two phrases? Those are the
two happiest events in a man's life. Both of them belong
to my past, and yet I have a joy now greater than either
of them."

When he said this every one except his two wives would
burst into laughter.

These things were very annoying to the old lady. At
first she had been pleased over the woman's pregnancy, but
when she noted how the *hsiu-ts'ai* humoured her she was
angry that her own belly had not been able to pay the debt.
On one occasion—it was in the third month of the following
year—the young woman remained in bed for three days

because of a slight illness and a headache. The *hsiu-ts'ai* was quite willing for her to rest. Not only so, but he was continuously asking her whether she needed anything. This sent the old lady into a violent temper. She said the woman was putting on airs, and muttered about it for three days, heaping malicious ridicule on her. As soon as the woman had arrived, she said, she had taken on a high opinion of herself, what with her pains in the side and her pains in the head—strutting about like a first-class concubine. She was quite sure that she had never been so pampered while she had been in her own home. There she had probably been obliged to do as the bitch on the street does —go hunting her own food with a bellyful of puppies inside her. Now, just because that old rascal—this was what she called her husband—was comforting her, she was pretending to be delicate.

"A son!" she once said to Mrs Wang. "We have all had children. I carried one myself for ten months. I'll never believe it is as bad as all this. In any case, this son of hers is still on the roll-book of the underworld. Who can guarantee that it won't be an ugly toad when it is born. After the little beast has crawled out it will be time enough for her to strut haughtily in front of me, but it is a little early for her to be puffing out now, while it is still a lump of flesh."

The young woman had not eaten that night. She listened in bed to all these abusive sneers, and cried quietly to herself. The *hsiu-ts'ai*, sitting half undressed on the bed, broke into a cold sweat and trembling as he heard it. He had the impulse to rise, dress himself, and administer a beating to her, pull out her hair, give her a sound thrashing, to give vent to his wrath. But he seemed not to have the strength. His fingers were trembling, and his arms felt weak. "Alas!" he sighed. "I have been too kind to her. During thirty years of married life I have never slapped her; never even flicked her with my finger-nail. And now she is as irritable as a crusty dowager."

He moved closer to the young woman and spoke in her ear:

"Don't cry! Don't cry! Let her bark! She's only a castrated hen who can't stand seeing others hatching out eggs. If you really bear a son this time I have two jewels for you. I have a green jade ring and a white jade——"

The continued jeering of his wife outside interrupted him. He threw off his clothes and pulled the blankets over his head. Laying his face on her breast, he whispered:

"I have a white jade . . ."

Day by day the abdomen grew more distended, until it was the size of a bushel measure, and the old lady finally made arrangements for a midwife. She even went to the length, while other people were looking, of getting out brightly coloured cloth and sewing clothes for the baby.

The cruel hot summer had come to an end, and the whole family had passed the sixth moon in an attitude of expectancy. At the start of autumn cooler breezes began to caress the village. Then one day the hopes of the household rose to high-water mark. The atmosphere in the home was one of thrills, and the *hsiu-ts'ai* especially was in a tense state. He walked back and forth continuously in the courtyard, carrying an astrological almanac, out of which he appeared to be memorizing something. "The Tiger influence is dominant," he muttered over and over to himself. Sometimes his anxious eyes turned towards the closed window of a room in which could be heard the low voice of the midwife. Sometimes he stared up at the cloud-covered sun.

"How is it now?" he asked of Mrs Wang, who stood inside the door of the room.

Mrs Wang nodded silently at him several times, adding after a moment:

"It will be here soon! It will be here soon!"

Then he took his almanac and began walking up and down the courtyard again.

H

This went on until the twilight haze had commenced to rise from the ground, and the lamps blossomed out here and there like flowers in spring. Then the child—a boy—was born. One could hear his voice as he was crying lustily from the room, and the *hsiu-ts'ai* sat in a corner ready to cry with happiness. No one in the house had any desire to eat, but they gathered about the plain supper table. There the wife said to the servants:

"Keep the matter hidden for a while, so that the little baby may escape noxious influences. If anyone asks, say that it is a girl that has been born."

Then they all nodded and smiled knowingly.

After a month the baby's soft white face appeared in the autumn sunshine. He was being nursed by the young woman, surrounded by curious women from the neighbourhood. Some of these praised the child's nose, some his mouth, and some his two ears. Others remarked that the mother was looking well, better than before; she had grown fairer and put on flesh. But the old lady was about, giving commands and dispensing care in the manner of an old grandmother, and she now said:

"That's enough! Don't start the child crying!"

Regarding a name for the baby the scholar indulged in long and painful meditation, but was not successful in finding appropriate characters. The old lady's notion was to select a name from the phrase "Long Life, Riches, and Honour," or from "Happiness, Prosperity, Joy, and Old Age." Best of all, she thought, would be the "Longevity" character or one of its synonyms, such as "Ripe Old Age." The *hsiu-ts'ai*, however, did not agree, considering these names too common and trite. But, though he pored over the *Book of Changes* and the *Book of History*, hunting for something out of these volumes, a half month, a whole month, passed without his having discovered a name that struck him as suitable. He wished the name, on the one hand, to pronounce a blessing on the child, and, on the other hand, to express by implication the fact that he had secured the son at an advanced age. It was not easy to do this. One day he was sitting with the three-months-old baby on his knee, holding his book under the lamplight and peering through a pair of spectacles still in search of a name out of it. The mother was sitting idle at one side of the room, with her thoughts far away. Suddenly she spoke up:

"I think it would be nice to call him 'Autumn Treasure.'" All who were in the room turned their eyes towards her and listened. "He was born in the autumn, wasn't he? A precious gift from the autumn! Call him 'Autumn Treasure.'"

"Excellent!" The *hsiu-ts'ai* took her up immediately. "What a lot of effort I wasted! Yes, I have reached the autumn of life. I'm over fifty. Then the child was born in autumn, and autumn is the ripening season for all nature. 'Autumn Treasure' is a perfect name! Besides, it can be found in the *Book of History*. 'Still there will be autumn harvest,' it says, and, indeed, I am having my harvest!"

Then he praised the child's mother, saying that mere study was worthless after all, and that intelligence was a gift from Heaven. These remarks made the woman feel very uncomfortable. She dropped her eyes, and mused bitterly and tearfully, "It was only that I was thinking of Spring Treasure!"

Autumn Treasure grew daily sweeter and more attached to his mother. He had amazingly large eyes, with which he stared long and inquisitively at strangers, although he recognized his own mother at a glance, even from a distance. All day he clung to her, but in spite of the *hsiu-ts'ai's* great affection for him the child did not care for his father. The wife of the scholar was superficially fond of him and gave the impression that she loved him as much as a child of her own, but in the baby's large eyes she remained a stranger and was favoured with the persistent stare of curiosity.

The tighter the hold that he took on his mother, the nearer approached the day of her departure. Spring came biting on the tail of winter, while summer's feet followed close behind. So the fact of the nearing end of the mother's three years began to figure prominently in the minds of all.

The *hsiu-ts'ai*, because of his love for the son, took up the matter first with his wife. He wished, he said, to pay another hundred dollars and purchase the woman in perpetuity.

"If you want to buy her just give me poison first!" was his wife's answer.

The *hsiu-ts'ai* said nothing for a long time, merely snorting with rage. Then he forced a smile and asked:

"Don't you think a child without its mother——?"

"So you don't consider me a suitable mother for him?" replied the old woman sarcastically.

In the mind of the child's mother a struggle was going on between two conflicting feelings. In the first place, she had long had echoing in her brain the words 'three years.' Three years, she had thought, would pass quickly, and so she had accepted the life of a slave in the *hsiu-ts'ai's* household. She found the Spring Treasure of memory as lively and appealing in her thought as the Autumn Treasure of reality. If she could not bear to give up the latter, how much less could she relinquish the former! She had an earnest desire, on the other hand, to spend the rest of her life in this new home. She felt that Spring Treasure's father had not long to live, that his sickness would very likely carry him off within three or four years to the unknowable realm. She planned to ask her second husband to adopt Spring Treasure so that he could be with her also.

Daydreams came most easily in the early summer sunshine on the veranda outside the house. Sometimes as she sat there nursing Autumn Treasure in her bosom she seemed to see Spring Treasure too standing beside her. She would put out a hand to draw him closer, and begin to talk to the two brothers—but the other was not there.

In the doorway not far off stood the old woman with the kindly face and cruel eyes, watching her attentively. Then she would come to a startled realization. "Better to get away as soon as possible! She watches me just like a spy!" When, however, the child in her arms gave a cry she knew that nothing else mattered but this, and this controlled her.

Later on the scholar-father modified his plan somewhat. He decided to send for the Sun woman and have her go to Autumn Treasure's mother's first husband to ask whether he would be willing for thirty dollars—at the very most fifty—to renew the lease on his wife for another three years. "When Autumn Treasure is five," he said to his wife, "then he can leave his mother."

The old lady was saying her prayers, with a Buddhist rosary in her hand. She continued to mutter "*Mamu Amitabba*" as she replied:

"She has a child of her own at home. You ought to give her the opportunity of associating with her lawful husband again."

He hung his head and said hesitatingly:

"But think of Autumn Treasure being deprived of his mother at the age of two!"

"I can raise him," said the old woman, putting down her rosary. "I can look after him. Are you afraid I'm going to assassinate him?"

At her last words he rose and strode away. She continued to call after him:

"It was to help me that we had this son. Autumn Treasure is mine. And though it is your family, not mine, which would be in danger of extinction, nevertheless I have to eat the food of your family. You have gone daft, childish with age. You have lost all your senses. How many more years do you have to live that you hang on to this woman

with might and main? I don't intend my memorial table
to sit beside a rival!"

But he had moved too far away to hear the rest of the
vicious and cutting things that the old lady had to say.

During the summer a boil came out on the baby's head,
and sometimes he suffered from a slight fever. The old
lady, therefore, busied herself consulting the gods and
procuring Buddhist remedies to rub on the boil or pour
into the baby's stomach. The mother did not consider
the matter serious, and she objected to having the child
kept in a perspiration from crying so much. She often
threw out the medicine secretly after it had been barely
tasted.

"You see!" complained the old lady to her husband,
sighing loudly. "She isn't at all concerned over the baby's
illness, and won't admit that he is getting thinner. Love
in the heart is deep, but love on the surface is merely
false."

The young woman wept secretly, and the *hsiu-ts'ai* said
nothing.

On the occasion of Autumn Treasure's first birthday there
was a busy celebration all day long, to which thirty or
forty guests came. Some brought gifts of clothing, some
brought noodles, some brought silver lions to be hung
about the baby's neck; others brought gilded images of the
God of Long Life to be sewn on the baby's cap. Presents
of every kind emerged from the sleeves of the guests. They
wished the child an illustrious career and immortal life,
while the host's face glowed as though his cheeks reflected
the glories of a sunset.

Towards evening of that day, just as the feast was beginning, there came a guest into the courtyard, walking
through the twilight mist. The people, staring at him,
saw a frightfully haggard country yokel, with clothes all
patched and with very long hair, carrying a paper package
under his arm. The host went over in surprise to receive

him, and asked him where he came from. The tongue-tied response conveyed nothing to the host until of a sudden he understood: this must be that trader in skins!

"Why have you brought a present?" he asked in an undertone. "You really didn't need to do that!"

The guest looked timidly about him before answering.

"I want—I wanted to—I came to wish the lady long life and a thousand——"

He broke off to pull out the paper package, and with trembling fingers removed two or three layers of paper. Then he produced four characters each about an inch square, made of brass and coated with silver. The characters read: "Longevity Rivalling Southern Mountain."

The *hsiu-ts'ai's* wife approached and inspected the visitor, appearing not too pleased. The *hsiu-ts'ai*, however, conducted him to the festal board, where the guests were already whispering to one another.

Two hours of meal and wine put the company into a state of maudlin boisterousness. They played at 'guessing fingers' in loud voices, filled up large bowls with wine and challenged each other to drink, and made so much confusion generally that the house tottered. The skin-trader alone, although he drank two cups of wine, remained still and silent, nor did any of the guests pay the least attention to him. When the influence of the wine was wearing off each guest hastily gulped down a bowl of rice, uttered congratulations, and the company departed by twos and threes, carrying lanterns.

The skin-trader ate till the last, and only when the servants came to clear away the dishes did he finally leave the table. He sought out a dark corner of the veranda, and there met his leased wife.

"Why did you have to come?" she asked in a melancholy tone.

"You don't think I wanted to come. I couldn't help it!"

"Then why did you come so late?"

"How do you think I got the money to buy a gift? I tramped about the whole morning, begged and pleaded the whole morning. Then I had to go to the city for the birthday present. The walking made me tired and hungry —and it made me late."

"And Spring Treasure?" asked the woman quickly.

The man heaved a sigh.

"It's about Spring Treasure that I came."

"About Spring Treasure?" she echoed in alarm.

"All through the summer," he said slowly, "Spring Treasure grew terribly thin, and with the autumn he has fallen sick. I hadn't the money, of course, to get a doctor or medicines for him, so now he is worse. If we don't do something for him it looks as if he will die." He paused a moment. "And so—I came to borrow some money from you. . . ."

It seemed to the woman as though there were cats clawing and biting her breast and gnawing at her vitals. She wanted to weep, but on a day like this, when all had been voicing happy wishes for Autumn Treasure, how could she follow with sobs? Restraining her tears, she said:

"I have no money, either. Here they allow me only two mao[1] a month for spending money. As a matter of fact I have no use for it, so that it all goes for the baby. What can we do?"

They were both silent for a while.

"Who is looking after Spring Treasure now?" the woman asked.

"I left him in charge of a neighbour. I expected to be back again by this evening. I had better start now."

He wiped the tears from his eyes.

"Wait a moment," said the woman, a lump rising in her throat. "I'll see if I can borrow from him."

And she went.

.   .   .   .   .   .

[1] A mao is equivalent to sixpence.

Some days later the *hsiu-ts'ai* suddenly asked her one evening:

"Where is the green jade ring that I gave you?"

"I let him have it that night. He took it to pawn."

"Didn't I lend you five dollars?" he asked angrily.

"Five dollars wasn't enough."

"Ah, yes!" sighed the gentleman. "It's always the first husband and the first son of whom you think, no matter how I treat you. Well, I had been thinking of keeping you another two years, but you had better leave next spring."

The woman was too amazed to cry.

A few days later he referred to the matter again. "That ring was a treasure. I gave it to you so that you could hand it on to Autumn Treasure. I never dreamed that you would pawn it at the first opportunity. It's lucky that *she* doesn't know about it. Otherwise there would be a good three months of wrangling."

The woman grew paler and thinner day by day, and a dull look crept into her eyes, while her ears rang with the mockery and abuse that was thrown at her. She thought constantly of Spring Treasure and his sickness, and kept on the watch for friends from her village, or travellers who might be going to it. She waited anxiously for the news that the boy had recovered completely, but no news came. She also sought to borrow a dollar or two and to buy delicacies to send him, but there was no one to take the things. Much of the time she sat holding Autumn Treasure at the side of the highway that ran past the door, watching those who came and went. This situation was very annoying to the old lady, and she constantly said to the old man:

"Don't you see she doesn't like being here at all? She wants nothing better than to fly home as soon as possible."

On several nights, dreaming with Autumn Treasure in her arms, she cried out suddenly, waking the baby and making him cry. The scholar persecuted her with questions.

"What's the matter? What's the matter?"

There was no reply from the woman, who was patting and crooning to Autumn Treasure.

"Did you dream that your other son was dead? How you yelled! You have wakened me!"

"No, no!" she said hastily. "I thought I saw a tomb in front of me."

He asked nothing further, and the mournful vision continued to unfold before the woman. She would have liked to walk into that tomb.

Winter drew to an end, and the little birds that were sending her away had begun to sing uninterruptedly beneath her window. First the child was weaned, Taoist priests being called in to assist the baby over this crisis in his life. Then the separation—the separation for ever of the child from its natural mother—was decided on.

On that day Mrs Wang asked the *hsiu-ts'ai's* wife quietly, "Shall I call a sedan chair for her?"

"Let her walk," said the old lady, still counting over the beads of her rosary. "The fare would have to be paid at that end, and what money does she have? I understand her husband hasn't even food to eat, so she needn't be asking for luxuries. It isn't so far, anyway. I have walked ten to fifteen miles myself in my time, and her legs are longer than mine. She can do it in half a day."

As she dressed Autumn Treasure that morning the mother's tears flowed in a torrent. The child kept saying, "Auntie, Auntie!" This was the name that the scholar's wife had ordered should be used, as she wished the baby to call her 'Mamma.' The mother answered the baby with sobs. She would have liked to say something to him, something like, "We are leaving each other, my darling baby. 'Mamma' will be good to you. Be kind to her in return and never think of me again." The words would not come out. In any case, a baby only a year and a half old would understand nothing.

The *hsiu-ts'ai* came sadly up to her and slipped his arm through hers. In his hand were ten twenty-cent coins.

"Take them," he said gently, "these two dollars."

She finished fastening the buttons on the child's clothes, and dropped the coins into her own inner pocket.

The old lady came in, and watched the retreating back of the *hsiu-ts'ai*. Then she said:

"Let me have Autumn Treasure, so that he won't cry when you leave."

The woman said nothing, but the baby refused, and slapped the old lady repeatedly on the face, making her very angry.

"Well, take him and have breakfast with him, but turn him over to me afterwards."

Mrs Wang urged her to eat heartily.

"You have been acting like this for two weeks and you are much thinner than you were. Have you looked in the mirror? Take a whole bowl of rice to-day. You have ten miles to walk yet."

The woman answered lifelessly, "You have been good to me."

The sun had risen very high and the weather was splendid. Autumn Treasure still would not leave his mother, until the old lady dragged him violently from her arms. He kicked her in the stomach with his little feet and pulled her hair with his tiny hands, yelling loudly. The mother, standing behind them, said:

"Let me stay till after the noon meal."

The old lady turned on her savagely. "You make up your bundle in a hurry and get out. You have to leave some time."

The baby's crying sounded more distant to her.

As she was tying up her belongings she heard him crying again. Mrs Wang stood beside her, trying to cheer her up and at the same time noting what she was taking away. Finally the woman set out, the old bundle under her arm.

As she went through the front door she heard Autumn Treasure again, and even after a mile of slow, weary walking the cries seemed still there. The road stretched away before her under the burning sun, endless as the sky. When she reached a creek she thought of ending this wearisome tramp, and leaping down into the clear, mirror-like water. But after sitting awhile beside the stream she again moved her shadow forward in the same direction.

It was past noon. An old peasant in one of the hamlets told her that five miles of the journey remained.

"Uncle," she said to him, "would you be kind enough to get me a sedan chair from the neighbourhood. I can't walk home."

"Are you sick?"

"Yes."

She was sitting in the pavilion at the entrance to the village.

"Where did you come from?"

She hesitated before replying.

"I'm just going in that direction. I thought this morning that I could walk it."

The old man said a few words to her and found her two bearers and a chair—one without a canopy, because it was the planting season.[1]

About four o'clock in the afternoon a chair with no canopy was borne down the dirty narrow street of the village. In it lay a middle-aged woman with a face withered and faded as a dry leaf of yellow cabbage. Her eyes were closed and her breath came feebly. The people in the street stared at her in surprise and pity, while a group of children ran noisily after the bearers as though some wonder had descended on the village.

Spring Treasure was among the children who followed

---

[1] *I.e.*, not warm enough for a canopy.

the chair. He hooted behind it as though driving a herd of pigs, but when it turned a corner down the street which led to his home he stretched out his arms in amazement. He watched it stop at his own door, and stood stupefied, leaning against a post, while the other children gathered timidly around it. The woman got out, but she was too dazed to see that Spring Treasure was there, dressed in rags, with hair unkempt, and hardly larger or taller than he had been three years before. Suddenly she called out with a sob:

"Spring Treasure!"

The other children were startled. As for Spring Treasure, he fled in terror to his father in the house.

In the dirty, gloomy room the woman sat a long time, but not a word passed between her and her husband. When twilight fell on them he lifted his bowed head and said to her:

"You had better get supper ready."

She forced herself to rise, and went to a corner of the room. After a moment she said weakly:

"The rice-bin is empty."

The man gave her a sardonic smile.

"You have been living in the house of the great. Rice? It's in that cigarette-box."

That night the man said to his son, "Spring Treasure, you sleep with your mother."

The boy, who was standing near the stove, began to cry. His mother went near him, murmuring, "Spring Treasure, my precious!" but as she reached out to fondle him he darted away.

"Acting strange already? A beating is what you'll get!"

She lay with wide-open eyes on the dirty narrow cot, Spring Treasure beside her, strange and unfamiliar. Into her dull brain came the impression that it was Autumn Treasure, fat and lovable, at her side. She put out her arms to take him without recognizing who he was. In his sleep he had turned over, and as she clasped him tight the boy, snoring gently, buried his face between those breasts that his hands instinctively clutched.

Quiet and cold as death the long interminable night dragged on . . . dragged on. . . .

MAO TUN

(1902–)

SHÊN YEN-PING is best known by the above *nom de plume*, but has written widely also under the names Pu Lao and Ping Sheng, as well as other pseudonyms.

He began his literary career humbly, as a proof-reader for the Commercial Press of Shanghai, which is said to be the world's largest private (non-Government) publishing house. He became nationally known as editor of the famous *Short Story Magazine*, which introduced to Chinese readers many of the best tales of the West, as well as first publishing most of China's leading contemporary writers.

He joined the Nationalists during the revolution, working in the political department dominated by the Left-wing Kuomintang. With the capture of Hankow, in 1927, he was made editor-in-chief of the *Min-Kuo Daily Post* in that city. Counter-revolution and the subsequent triumph of the Kuomintang Right Wing of Chiang Kai-shek forced his retirement. He returned to Shanghai and resumed his writing. He has since taken no active part in politics, but his essays and criticisms have been strongly in sympathy with the radical opposition. He is forced to live in seclusion. Nine of his books have been banned by the Kuomintang.

Mao Tun is perhaps the outstanding novelist of China to-day. His *Midnight*, now available in English and French, his long story *Spring Silkworms*, and his trilogy, *Pursuit*, *Turmoil*, and *Disillusion*, are distinguished examples of the new realism or 'revolutionary naturalism' invigorating Chinese literature.

Of his several volumes of short stories *Wild Roses* is generally considered his finest achievement. This has gone through many printings, and ranks with Lu Hsün's *No Han* in popularity. He is, incidentally, very close to Lu Hsün in personal friendship, as well as in social, political, and literary tendencies. Like Lu Hsün also, he believes that art divorced from the living social realities is devoid of significance.

SUICIDE

By Mao Tun

Huan Hsiao-chieh stood idly before the window gazing absently towards the lake through the foggy dusk. She heard the sound of voices faintly coming up from the shore, and she saw the black peak leaning out in front of her like a brooding giant. The little lanterns strung along the beach were in reality the lights in lake villas, and people who lived in them were beautiful and thought this scene beautiful too.

Huan Hsiao-chieh did not think so. She had no part in it. She felt broken, no longer intact, no longer young. The beauty of the world outraged her. She wished only to remain shut up in her small room, where over and over again she sought to heal a *malaise* of the soul.

Her embarrassment in the presence of other people had forced her into voluntary isolation. Whenever people were laughing and talking and suddenly ceased she was certain that she had become the focus of all eyes. The upturned mouths seemed to say, "We know, we know." Among even her former intimate friends she detected a different attitude towards herself, and while they talked she noticed some hidden significance in their smiles, and she believed they were making insinuations against her.

If they gossiped of a commonplace romance between this person and that, or concerning a total stranger, she perceived that this was only a method of satirizing her. They were simply "mocking the mulberry tree on behalf of the locust." So she preferred to live like a cowardly rabbit, hiding alone in her den. But when she read stories to amuse herself it appeared that every author knew of her secret, and in every story she was the central tragic figure. For only one thing she was genuinely thankful, and that was that neither her aunt, her cousin, nor her cousin's wife, with whom she lived, knew anything about her adventure, otherwise . . .

She turned her shoulders nervously and tears curtained her eyes. The world *was* really lovely; why should her own fate be so absurd? Whenever such a thought occurred to her, whenever she understood that human happiness could no longer be hers, she felt more than ever the value of life. The decision which had brought upon her this endless remorse had been made, and was no more to be cancelled than the brief rapture which had followed it. What would never be over, however, was the human cruelty she felt in every face and mouth turned towards her. She fell back upon the bed, sobbing, and held the pillow fast in her arms. Her heart beat furiously and seemed to murmur, "Suicide! Commit Suicide! Suicide!" And yet suicide was not enough. She longed to bring the whole beautiful world tumbling down with her, to fire the torch herself, ending all things, people, grievances, and the memory of the human race.

Jumping up in anger she glanced venomously around the room. Her rage coloured her face and a fierce kind of beauty radiated from her. She hurried to the desk, pulled open a drawer, took out a key and with it opened another drawer. There were some old letters in it, several pictures, and a square leather folder, which she tore open. Fumbling inside, she slid out a picture and promptly tore it into pieces. Then she sank into a chair and continued to weep. At last she raised a perplexed face, and told herself, "He is not to blame—but me."

She bent over and picked up the torn bits of photograph and carefully pieced them together, spreading them out on her lap like a mother soothing a hurt son after having

I

wrongfully punished him. She really did love him, she assured herself; she loved him eternally. Passionately she kissed his photograph, his eyes, his lips. Why had she imagined that she hated him? He was the most important thing in her life, even if the event at Fei Lai Peak was now causing her nothing but pain. Once more she thought of her sensuous abandon with him, and now it seemed to her that she should wear the memory of it like a decoration, always. Her face was suddenly on fire and her body grew weak as that strange ecstasy poured through her from deep in her heart. She said to herself slowly:

"I cannot blame him. Did I not also desire him? The man as he was and the place as it was, could anyone loving him have done otherwise? Buddha, who sat there in the stone wall, let him bear witness. There was nothing indecent about it, there was nothing carnal. I seemed to be dreaming, and his kisses, his caresses, were to me part of that radiant dream. It was a mistake, of course, to see him in his hotel next day, and yet it was inevitable; some force beyond me took me there, as Heaven knows."

She tried to recall her thoughts on that day. How had she persuaded herself to go? Actually, it had amounted to this: since he had possessed everything else of her entrancing body, was there any longer a reason for denying him the last conquest? It was with this thought that she had yielded to him, finally, completely, and with that great happiness that comes from largeness of soul. The third time she called upon him at the hotel he had already gone. He had left a letter for her, and his picture. That was all. That was the end. That was the beginning.

Huang Hsiao-chieh sighed and put the picture back in the leather folder. She moved to the window and stood once more gazing foolishly at the sky, at the wreath of clouds behind which rose a full moon, and at the crowded stars that were like dancing children. Her thoughts turned in confusion back to the same problem, which, however many times she pondered it, always made new patterns in the fabric of her mind.

Had she, after all, been too bold, too reckless? Should she ever have entered the cave? Perhaps her lover was a charlatan, a fellow who made a practice of collecting virgins? Perhaps he was inwardly a monster who wove a web of deceit around his victims, simply to have the satisfaction of capturing them and forcing them to think of him? Had he not planned the whole thing carefully in advance? And the letter, couldn't that too be part of the base trick? Who knew whether he had not practised the same treachery on scores of girls? And were his written words the only lies? Why was she so shallow that she could not distinguish a fake from other young men? Was it because he was so handsome? So intelligent? So gentle? Was it true that she must sacrifice her life because she had lived through this dream? Was it possible that he had sexually contaminated her?

"No! No!" she insisted. "It cannot be. Other girls have been far more careless than I, and nothing of the sort happened to them. He is not that wicked. His departure was unavoidable. I believe him. It is precisely because he forces himself to sacrifice his own happiness for others that he has left. He is great and his responsibilities are tremendous. He compels himself to avoid talking of love and marriage . . . in his kind of life he cannot think of it.

"But didn't he also say that he was passionate and sensuous? That he could not resist feminine charm?"

Huan Hsiao-chieh recollected now that she had contrived to 'charm' him, that she had willed that he hold her in his arms. She became all at once ashamed, and covered her face with her hands. She regretted very much that she had not immediately followed him when she learned he had left, that she had not gone with him, through fire and water, to the corners of the earth. A new hope shook her heart. Suppose he did come back? If you had a lover who had risked his life for something magnificent, a great cause of humanity, you could be proud of it!

"But, according to his letter, there is no chance of a return unless the revolution triumphs. He said he must fight for it as long as he lives, and that he cannot neglect his tasks until death relieves him of them. He said that he preferred to go there alone, that he could not take me with him to be needlessly sacrificed."

She let the darkness shelter her heart, and its comfort entered her and brought her a kind of peace. As she mused, more calmly, she understood that he had not been unworthy, and that the quality of their love was really pure. The weight on her heart lifted. She smiled. Why had she been unable to realize this before? Why had she thought of their love all day as sinful? She had nothing to hide from the world. She had loved a man and she had consummated that love, and the significance of that love was all the more deeply revealed because he had sacrificed it in an unselfish devotion to a great human purpose. How enchanting a thing it was!

In the gentle arms of the night she dreamed. Many people gathered and listened attentively as she disclosed the heroic story of her love. Everybody acclaimed her. Everybody admired the courage and self-sacrifice of her lover, the revolutionary. Again she dreamed. He had returned, and on his strong chest were hung many scarlet decorations, stars of his courage and bravery.

But the night moved on and day flooded her room with bright reality. She awoke to the sound of voices outside, and was reminded of a dreamless world. Her last night's recovery vanished. Her distrust of every countenance returned. She clung to the sanctity of her room just as wretchedly as the day before.

Well, she could distract herself by reading the newspaper. But under the headlines there was nothing except the meaningless stories of bloodless people, and it seemed to her that every square Chinese character looked back at her gravely and with condemnation. She picked up an old novel. "A foolish sentimental girl and a man with a cold heart" was the kind of expression she read. She turned to another, a modern novel, and this was even more stupid.

Tossing down the book she lay again on the bed, determined to think of nothing. She looked morosely at the clouds in the sky and noticed their varied shapes. She fancied that one surely had the features of her aunt. There was another that resembled a galloping horse, coming nearer and nearer. But now didn't it seem like a long, sinuous train? "Yes," she said to herself, "it does." There were actually windows in it; besides, there was a man's head. Like a drop of water on a sheet of paper the contour of the head grew and grew and seemed to be coming directly towards Huan Hsiao-chieh. It was he! But no sooner had she recognized her lover than the whole image faded into total emptiness.

Her eyes gradually closed, and she found herself thinking again. Perhaps he really was on the train, perhaps he would arrive here some time to-day. She might meet him if she went outside, unexpectedly. Or maybe he was now waiting at the very place where they had formerly made their appointments. Or—— She turned and went out. Nobody saw her leave, and she rushed down to the beach and into the little park, sheltered by trees and flowers. The lake was only a placid mirror, and in front of it, on the stone balustrade, sat a young man. She leaned forward, pressed his shoulders, and exclaimed in an excited voice:

"So you've come back!"

"I have come."

"As a matter of course, then, we shall at once get married. I'll announce it to my friends. Every one must know that you are not faithless, that you are not a false lover——"

"Not false, and yet not your husband either."

"But we——"

"We have been lovers? True, but you had better forget it. I cannot be your husband. You're still young, beautiful, capable of making any man happy—very happy. It will be a much grander happiness than I can give you, richer than anything we've known together."

She could not utter a word. She only held his head softly in her arms and wept.

"You are meant for a tranquil, joyous life. Though we have been lovers, your real happiness belongs to some one else. Suppose I am killed?"

"Ah, but you haven't been killed yet!"

"Then I'll die right now!"

Turning round, he jumped far into the lake. Astonished, Huan Hsiao-chieh jumped after him, pursued, and at last caught up with him. . . .

She awoke clutching the pillow tightly. Her satin gown was wet with perspiration. She shivered in the faint breeze.

Horrified, she turned her head to see whether anyone had been listening. There was nobody, and yet some one was crying out, "I know! I know!" She had a moment of sinking despair, and then more quietly she reasoned, "This was not the voice of my cousin's wife, it was not from the lips of the sharp-tongued Miss Chin, it was not—— There it was again! 'Huan Hsiao-chieh further confessed——' Good heavens! It was nothing but a cicada whose nasal scolding drifted in with the ragged breeze."

She sat quietly before the window, reflecting on that dream. She feared that it was an unfavourable omen. Yet she had said really nothing that was not in his own letter. There was no mystery about it. Nevertheless she considered his argument banal.

"Is it such a simple thing as that? I am not what I was. I have suffered a serious change. I have become a piece of broken white jade. Are these facts easy to deny? Are they easy to forget? Let's see. . . . I am now still as I was, I remain quite intact, I am in no way blemished. To him who shall win my love I offer a virgin body in return, and all bliss, limitless happiness!

"But, as a matter of fact, why not? Why should anyone else know about it, even if I cannot forget? He has promised to carry the secret with him to his grave. If that is true, then I can also imprison it in my heart. No one else need know of it, not a single soul."

Life coloured again before Huan Hsiao-chieh's eyes, and her imagination built many-storied buildings of hope. She would, to be sure, bury this experience. She would again open her arms to the world. She would—but how regrettable it was that one could never be sure about *them*, about the third persons.

"Can I ever be absolutely certain?" she asked herself. She had to admit that she could not.

They were so many—malicious folk, unkind folk, people who made a business of prying into the private affairs of others.

They swam before her eyes, one after another.

She closed her teeth, hung her head in her hands, and said over and over that it was not a bad world and that the privilege of living in it was still hers. No one had any right to restrict her, no one was cunning enough to ruin her happiness.

How hateful *they* were! How she longed for a pestilence to destroy *them*.

At dinner her cousin's wife suddenly suggested that Huan Hsiao-chieh go with her to the cinema. A new film was showing, called *The Tragedy of Ma Chen-hua*. Would she consent to go? The young wife described the story in vivid synopsis, and every word of it seemed a dagger pricking her heart. She glanced up secretly to see whether she was being ridiculed, but the young woman's face was quite innocent, so she felt comforted. Her cousin's comment, however, landed upon her quivering nerves like heavy lead. He said:

"My opinion of such a story is that it is totally worthless as dramatic material. Tragedies of Ma Chen-hua's kind happen every day; there is nothing unusual about it. Since nobody knows, it amounts to nothing. The only difference is that in real life the girl never commits suicide."

Huan Hsiao-chieh's eyes darkened as she listened, and she sat paralysed in her chair. Showers of suffocating cotton seemed to be smothering her, falling down and down. Fortunately her cousin did not even glance at her as he slid his eyes around the table; had he done so she would certainly have collapsed on the spot.

"Since you want to go, I'll accompany you," she said to her cousin's wife, forcing the polite phrase from her mouth with a supreme effort.

At the table every one grew silent. They were all pleased that Huan Hsiao-chieh seemed to be coming to life again after her moodiness, and her cousin gave her a grateful smile. His wife smiled softly too. Huan Hsiao-chieh felt gratified at the success of her deception. At any rate she knew that no one in the house suspected her.

They met several acquaintances at the cinema, and she carefully scrutinized their faces. They all seemed to be perfectly guileless. None of them looked unkindly at her, and she could detect no hidden implications in their remarks. "I really believe they do not know about it," she informed herself. When she saw the pair of lovers on the screen she felt more than ever encouraged. She believed profoundly in her lover's word. She doubted more than ever that two brief meetings with him could have been noticed by anyone else.

Her own conduct, however, had differed somewhat from that of Ma Chen-hua. She had been too nervous these last two weeks; she had been too obvious; she had invited wondering and doubt. She ought to make some effort to explain herself. She could tell people that she suffered from the heat. She could say that at the beginning of summer she always had a slight attack of sunstroke. She began to feel that *they* were not so much to be despised as she had imagined. She had overrated them. Her way of living still offered some hope, and there was perhaps even some happiness on horizons which she could not yet glimpse.

But the fact is that she did at last suffer from 'sunstroke.' She began to grow tired very easily, she wanted to sleep all day long, she felt an inner discomfort. Her appetite was active enough, but as soon as she raised a stickful of food to her mouth she lost interest in it. A week later she made another discovery. At that droll time of the month nothing whatever occurred. "Do such things really happen? Can it be true?" But it was. The many-storied buildings immediately crashed, and the little hopes she had framed so neatly fell into ruins.

Neither day nor night henceforth seemed to have any meaning to her. They fled past as if driven on by a relentless hunter. She felt that she stepped nearer and nearer her tomb. She stepped alone, without any understanding, without help, without sympathy. She longed for her dead mother, for any mother, however severe and exacting. But she could not even remember her mother's voice. It seemed to her that she had no friend in the world. Her aunt was a good woman and a kind guardian, but after all a guardian. Her cousin was a cousin. It was true that before he married they were much closer to each other, but they had spoken few words of intimacy since his wife had come.

At night she sat before the window looking dully at the myriad of stars, and her mind rambled over the hills between them. In the blurred bars of light she saw his face again, she heard him speak. "Incredible, incredible, that this could happen after so brief a meeting! I asked you to forget me, but now that is impossible. Let him be a memorial, I beg of you, to our love." This was the echo of her soul, sent back by the heavens and by all the nodding stars.

She took courage. This was the way out. She would keep her secret no longer. She would inform the whole world of her unshakable faith. She would stand alone before them with her child.

"Fancy! It's madness. And do you think you will be accepted by this cruel fellowship? Do you really believe *they* would forgive you? Now, if there were some one to defend your honour that might be different. Society demands that you produce a father, even if in name only. You will get some one to stand beside you if you are wise."

She pondered wearily. Which was better? Her mind swayed dizzily between the moon and the stars, between one road and the other. It was very tiresome. It was no longer tragic. She had forgotten tears just as she had forgotten how to smile. There seemed to be no capacity for feeling left in her.

She grew thinner every day. It became more difficult for her to hide her distress. Worried by her illness, her old aunt propelled herself to Huan Hsiao-chieh's bedroom and sat there for half an hour. She spoke repetitively.

"Huan, you are getting alarmingly thin. If you don't feel well, just tell me what's wrong. What is the matter? What are you thinking about? Don't you want something to eat? You are so thin! If it's something I can get for you just tell me and I'll have it prepared. Has some one hurt you? Maybe it was your cousin's wife? Did she say something unpleasant? Or is it the maidservant? Is she serving you badly? Can't you confide in me? You are my only one in my sister's family. If something were to happen to you how should I be able to face them in the next life?"

The old woman's eyes filled with tears. Huan Hsiao-chieh with difficulty suppressed her own tears, forced a smile, and shook her head. How she would have liked to cry out, "You love me, Aunt, because you are faithful to your duty, but would you love me if you knew about my misconduct?

Would you?" But she only opened her eyes widely and looked into her aunt's long face and replied, "I have no complaints whatever, honestly. . . . It's the hot weather, I think. Really, it's not any kind of mental pressure."

She knew that her aunt loved her from a sense of responsibility to her mother, that her cousin loved her because of his aunt, and that her cousin's wife tolerated her because of her cousin. Each had a different reason for 'loving' her; none of them loved her for herself alone. There was one man who understood the soul of her, and yet he had abandoned her. Had destiny assigned to her a violent death? If that was so then she wished that she might die with him. Suppose that there were another man who really loved her, would it matter? She would still have to die. She would have to tell him the terrible truth, and die under his angry blows.

Her cousin's wife came in also and wanted to know what had made her so melancholy. She too commented on her loss of weight, and expressed concern about it. Had she said or done anything to hurt her? If so she was sincerely sorry. She hoped that Huan Hsiao-chieh would speak frankly to her, and without any ceremony, if she had in any way offended her.

All this terrified her. She was in inward panic. She realized that her behaviour was exciting every one's curiosity. Her lack of composure had aroused suspicion in the whole family. An ambuscade of predatory eyes surrounded her. She no longer could enjoy the solitude of her bedroom. She began to hear noises outside her door continually.

"What weird sounds! Are they the footsteps of Death? But you can't die in that way. You're young, your life is before you; you need not die simply because of one cup of wine!"

And yet, wasn't that the only refuge left for her?

"Suppose," she thought, "that I just boldly make a

declaration, and reply to every sneer with a smile of contempt? Why not?"

But as she tasted this she realized that she had not the courage for it. The act of self-immolation demanded only one moment of triumphant courage; the act of self-denunciation demanded a sustained strength of heart that she did not possess. If she sought another man to share her burden their relationship could never have a lasting foundation. Besides, rushing headlong into a marriage was a certain guarantee of its failure. What was worse, she might be linked with an intolerable person for the rest of her life.

She thought of other girls she knew who had had several lovers. How had they met such difficulties? Had they carefully chosen men of whom they could demand marriage, or men who had proposed it? How innocent and ingenuous she had been! "Too honest, too generous, too foolish . . . to live."

A small white star sparkled coldly beyond Shu Pao Pagoda, and another night covered and hushed the earth. Huan Hsiao-chieh's mind became extraordinarily active, and her thoughts flew past as if sped by electric power. She recollected everything of any importance that had happened during her twenty-three years of life. She remembered vividly how in her seventeenth year the tide of new freedom had broken across China, and how it had excited her, how it had intoxicated her with its splendid promise.

She remembered the white radiance that had seemed to fill her soul. How glad she had been that she was not betrothed, how she had intimated to her aunt and to her cousin her own wish to choose her comrade for life.

The world pressed close to her, seemed to be shattering all around her, noiselessly shattering.

She took a long silk sash in her trembling fingers, and an oath tore through her body. Frauds! Cheats! Liars! Everything was a deception—liberty, freedom, enlightenment! Better by far to have submitted to a marriage arranged by her elders! Then, at least, this kind of grief would never have been hers, nor this kind of fate! She could have been at any rate as contented as her cousin's wife with her contented man!

She stood upon the edge of the bed and her body shook with agony. Her eyes seemed filled with blood. Her mind did not turn at all, except to demand an immediate end to it, to demand an action that would save it from explosion and would reveal to every one the shallowness of "Liberty, freedom, and enlightenment!" Without further hesitation she drew a noose rapidly in the sash, which she had tied to a pillar. Then she pushed herself forward and hung suspended.

Precisely at that moment a vague thought fought for light somewhere in the darkness of her benumbed brain. "There is still a way out," it seemed to say, "if you bravely join the world struggle to change society . . . if you move forward . . . if you keep pace with the urgent advance of social devel——"

But the sash had gripped into her throat and the idea was choked into silence.

MUD

By Mao Tun

[THIS story is based on events during the Northern Expedition of the Kuomintang Nationalist Revolution in the winter of 1926–27.

The Kuomintang and the Communist Party of China for a time co-operated as allies against the northern war-lords, many Communists being also members of the Kuomintang (People's Party). But after April 1927 the Right Wing of the Kuomintang, under the leadership of General Chiang Kai-shek, staged a counter-revolution, began the suppression and execution of Communists, formed a new *régime* at Nanking in opposition to the Nationalist Government at Hankow, and declared war on Reds as well as Left-wing Kuomintang adherents

It is in this critical turning period that the story *Mud* is laid. The army of 'child soldiers' is a Nationalist Army, the political department of which is apparently composed chiefly of Communists. They do not, however, remain in the village long enough to carry out any of the changes they have promised to the peasants. The last army to enter the village, the army whose chief orders the execution of Huang Lao-tieh, belongs to the war-lord General Feng Yu-hsiang. General Feng evidently has already joined the counter-revolution headed by General Chiang Kai-shek, and hence the execution of all villagers suspected of having been exposed to the Red influence.]

MACHINE-GUNS barked wolfishly throughout the broken night.

A little before dawn three armoured cars rolled up to the Temple of Earth, army headquarters (nobody knew whose army!) in the village, and down from them jumped several uniformed soldiers. They hastily went into the temple, looking tired and discouraged. When they came out, accompanied by others, they were carrying two heavy, bulky boxes between them. These were put into the cars, they climbed aboard themselves, and there was a grinding sound from the engines as the cars lumbered off. A moment later a mass of defeated troops swept through the village in retreat, moving like a great tide.

Intermittent firing on the outskirts did not cease till about seven o'clock. In the light of morning three dead men could be seen lying in the street. A provision store was on fire. By its door there was the corpse of a naked woman, whose face was the colour of pig's liver. One of her feet had been cut off.

Half an hour elapsed and then, through the three mouths of the village, some of the victorious soldiers, looking even dirtier and wearier than those who had retreated, rushed down the roads like a grey wind. They posted sentries here and there, but the bulk of them moved on. A few horsemen coming up to the Temple of Earth tore off the Government posters there, and replaced them with sheets of white paper spread with red characters. Four armed men were stationed at the temple gate.

After that came a startling innovation. Several unarmed but uniformed men began distributing leaflets to the various huts, and placarded the village with slogans. They knocked at doors and ordered every one out. One young fellow, clad in a grey uniform, with a pale face sticking out of it, and round eyes, shouted in the street through a megaphone made of galvanized iron.

Gradually, from behind shuttered windows, some sun-blackened yellow men with short queues and wide-open eyes poked out their heads to look at the stranger who knocked. It somewhat reassured them that, although he indeed wore a 'tiger skin,'[1] he was apparently quite unarmed and in appearance not altogether savage. One by one, step by step, the villagers emerged from their shabby houses and stood—some distance away—listening to the youth who was talking furiously through the megaphone. It was like going to a show.

[1] A soldier's uniform.

From the megaphone, however, came words that seeme
very strange—strange, at least, from a soldier. The meanin
of his harangue escaped them. All they understood clearl
was his last sentence, "Don't be afraid of us." Handbil
and coloured paper slogans were passed on to them, an
when the speaker had finished they carried these back t
their homes. The whole procedure baffled them.

Huang Lao-tieh and his two sons squatted beside the mu
oven and talked in low voices. "Nonsense! The Republi
of China!" muttered old Huang.

"It is not one bit better than the Empire of China! Thi
is the sixteenth year of it, and every year has been celebrate
with a new war. It gets steadily worse, and this is th
banner year for disaster: in the spring came the troops o
Marshal Wu Pei-fu, later on the army of Fengtien, an
now——" but he suddenly closed his mouth. He pulle
in his neck and cautiously looked around him, as if fearfu
that some one had overheard his complaints.

Huang noticed two sheets of coloured paper that ha
been pasted on the mud wall, and, inspecting them closely
he tried to read. He had been a scholar, having passed th
local literary examinations forty years ago, and he had als
been a teacher. Therefore he knew characters, and ye
here were new combinations that seemed to him to mak
no sense at all.

His son Lao San imitated his father and held his head u
to examine the paper too. He was able to recognize only
two characters, 'farmer' and 'united,' the latter because i
was used in the name of the village provision store whic
had that morning been gutted by fire. "United Prosperity,"
it was called.

Lao Chi, Huang's younger son, was also interested in th
poster. He who had lived as a cowherd and from early
childhood had been kept busy cutting grass, with no tim
for memorizing characters, was entranced by the picture o
the modern girl (wearing a *short-sleeved gown!*) shown on

one of the posters. She had a slender waist and a pretty face, and she stood with outstretched arms.

"Mother's!"[1] scolded old Huang, half to himself. "This means the coming of those communal wives!" Looking closer he saw, moreover, the white-armed girl standing in the midst of four or five men. She was smiling in a friendly way, and she clasped hands with one man on her right and another on her left. The same discovery astonished Lao San, but it did not displease him as it did his father. He congratulated himself that his wife had died last spring, for he felt that he was now in a position where nothing prevented him from enjoying himself with these modern women.

"Speak softly, Father, or they will hear you. H'mm . . . after all, this idea of common wives isn't so bad. What do we lose? There's no woman in our family now, eh?"

The old man stared at him, horrified, and then at Lao Chi. He attempted to silence his son by quoting, somewhat falteringly, the righteous maxims of the great sage Confucius, and for him that closed the subject. Nothing more was said about it, and they sat meditating glumly.

Bang! Bang! They jumped up, frightened. Should they dive into their cellar? Before they could move there came another loud hammer against the door. Lao Chi crept up and let down the latch. It was a student soldier, accompanied by Li the Pock-face, a native of the village.

They came inside, the soldier smiling.

"This is Huang Lao-tieh, the only one among us who can read and write," Li said, introducing old Huang.

"Very good. We want you to come along with us."

Huang Lao-tieh's lips were shaking, and he could not find a word.

---

[1] *T'a ma-ti* is the expression here; literally, "His mother's." It is a curse of vast range of implication, but in its simplest form may be held to mean, "Rape your mother." Other variations are explained in Lu Hsün's *Mother's*, included in this volume.

K

Pock-face said that the officer wanted to organize the villagers in order to take care of village business. They needed a literate man to help them, he added. He pointed to a bundle of papers under his arm, and said that the printed proclamations would be explained to all of them.

"I am old, old, and my eyes can't see clearly enough to read. I'm not suited for this kind of work," begged Huang. He wanted to stay out of it, and was determined to become in no way involved, but in the end he was pulled off to do as they said. Lao San stayed behind, squatting on the floor and looking depressed. Lao Chi, anxious to witness any excitement, went after them of his own will.

In a short time a Farmers' Union had been organized, and Huang Lao-tieh was kept busy copying down names in the *Hua Ming Ts'e*, a registration list. Beside him sat a youth about seventeen who wore a uniform, and whom Huang regarded as his 'superior officer.' It was with him that new-fangled ideas originated. He sent young men everywhere looking for landlords (who had fled) and to pull forth the villagers (who had hidden in their huts), and had all of them brought in and made members of the new association.

Lao Chi found this quite interesting, but it did not in the least make up for the absence of 'communal wives.' He concluded that perhaps it was simply a phrase used to deceive people.

"Mother's!" he thought. "Rape their mothers!"

The sounds of machine-gun fire and cannonading had pulled far away and the detachment of soldiers at the entrances to the village had been withdrawn. Only four sentries remained at the gate of the Temple of Earth; within it were another ten men. Order had been restored, and women and girls ventured forth upon the streets again.

"Join the Union!" shouted groups of men gathered in the village.

One day five or six 'child soldiers' arrived. They wore grey uniforms, like the rest, but they had high voices like youths who had not yet attained puberty. They made straight for the huts and hunted out the women and girls, talking earnestly to them. Consternation spread throughout the village—till it was revealed that the 'child soldiers' were in fact women themselves! They had come to unite the females into a union of their own, and for that purpose only.

Huang Lao-tieh returned home and began to scold his sons. "That turtle Li the Pock-face is the cause of it all —and you two also probably instigated him to get me mixed up in it. Organizing the men, that might be all right, but now they're actually unionizing women too! Is it or isn't it the first step to socializing wives? Sooner or later the whole thing must lead to communism. By Heaven, the skies will thunder if this comes about. To think that an honest fellow like me should be dragged into the mud in this way! Heaven may forgive me, but the villagers?—never!"

Lao San opened his mouth, but he did not utter even half a word. Lao Chi looked slantingly at the picture on the wall, and at the white-armed girl. How, he wondered, will the communization be brought about? Various methods occurred to him that night in his dreams.

The village grew tense with excitement. Young men ran here and there, making news or bringing it. Lao Chi trailed the women soldiers all day long and eagerly awaited some wonderful development.

In Pock-faced Li's house seven or eight of the village riff-raff gathered. They denounced him vigorously for assisting the southern troops. "Turtle! You guaranteed that these people are not Communists, but see what's happening! Organizing women! The first step! What do you get out of it? You have a wife; well, we'll communize her first." As a matter of fact, Li Ma-tzu had a wife, with no pock-marks, but she had hidden herself in the pigs' shelter, where she lay trembling in fear.

It was not till that afternoon that Huang Lao-tieh's 'superior officer' learned of these apprehensions concerning the communization of women, and called a meeting of the villagers. He shot forth his young neck and for half an hour shouted at the top of his lungs. He hoped there would be no more misunderstanding: this idea of 'communal wives' was a *bourgeois* falsehood put out against them. A woman soldier also lectured.

The villagers listened, but made no comments. It was apparent that they were not entirely convinced, for when they reached home they shut their doors and barred them, and their women hid themselves once more. . . .

Ten or more of the toughest villagers met one day in the woods that skirted near by. The sun beat down heavily, and the wind had rolled up great layers of fine dust and sand that lay piled everywhere like the ruffled coats of dogs. One of the group, a narrow-faced fellow, nicknamed "Living Ghost," took his seat on the root of a large tree. He gazed upward and angrily burst out:

"These promises, I tell you, are simply meant to deceive us! I haven't seen anybody giving me even so much as a morsel of land. How about the fields we were supposed to get? When does it happen? Dog out of a turtle! They are simply the same as the rest, only with their unions, their associations! Rape their ancestors! Under the same hot sun we still stand here, their fathers, sweating and toiling! Huh! This is the extent of their benefit to us!"

"They are not exactly dog-tortoise sort of men," said some one else. "They are having their own fun in the temple and plenty of it. Lao Chi claims to have seen them in person. How can we believe in them when they act so falsely?"

A younger man, narrowing the corners of his eyes, sagely observed: "They may yet give a gay festival, and then we can all participate in their pleasures."

Said another: "If there are no common wives, what are

the five or six women soldiers doing with them? Are these soldiers the only ones permitted to communize? Suppose we communize *them*! Whoever refuses to accept the offer isn't a human being, eh? Mother's!"

"Never mind! That long slender woman with the graceful stride—not bad, eh?"

Everybody broke into laughter, and could not help swallowing hungrily and in envious desire.

"Let's start something! We've lived without women too long! Our time has come! Let's go! The man who doesn't follow is a dog out of a turtle!"

Living Ghost jumped up and danced with joy. These were bold words that appealed to him. Unfortunately a sudden burst of wind interfered with the speech he intended to make. It swept up in a great billowy canopy, driving the yellow sand around them and wrapping them in its folds. . . .

No doubt news of the rascals' intention leaked out through Lao Chi, and the women soldiers very soon left the village. Huang Lao-tieh meanwhile lost sight of his 'superior officer.' Generally, every one felt more at ease. The Southerners evidently were losing.

With these changes Living Ghost and his group of toughs became more active, though they did not make attacks in the open. No one knew at first who had beaten Li the Pock-face; several people thought the local toughs had punished him because he had acted carelessly. Others maintained that his troubles were all traceable to his unblemished wife. Then the Changs' house was robbed of several piculs of wheat that had been hidden under the floor. Who had done it? Everybody began to suspect that the marauders were actually men in their own village, but old man Chang would not say a word.

Huang Lao-tieh also had his new worries. When he went out in the street now he noticed that many of his neighbours avoided talking to him, but from a distance smirked contemptuously, using only one side of the face.

One day the four soldiers posted at the Temple of Earth disappeared, and this was a grave thing indeed. All sorts of rumours floated through the village, and on top of these rumours there was general rioting, with some desperate combats—about what nobody seemed to know. Living Ghost was among those injured, and he disappeared. Several counter-casualties were inflicted against the toughs by the newly unionized villagers. Fire broke out during the night. Stealing out to investigate the conflagration, one man identified the spot as the Temple of Earth, and he crept back into his hut well pleased.

Next morning a detachment of northern troops arrived at one end of the village. The officer at once dispatched a messenger to bring the village headman of the landlords to him for an interview, but not an elder was to be found. They had scampered away hastily, along with most of the gentry, before the arrival of the leaflet-distributing troops. Even old Huang was in bed, ill, and could not go to answer questions, so finally Chang, who had been robbed, was summoned to headquarters.

Everybody waited uneasily for his return.

A number of the newly arrived soldiers proceeded to make camp in the open air. They were mostly tall men, and they spoke northern dialects, and also carried leaflets, but did not distribute them.

Presently a squad of soldiers arrived at Huang Lao-tieh's bedside and commanded him to get up. Ill as he was, the old man had to obey, and his son Lao San was dragged along too. Huang Lao-tieh shook with fright. What 'mother's' sort of mess was this? He felt somewhat better when he saw a familiar flag stuck in the mud.

"Who are you?" demanded an officer. He was wearing a parted beard,[1] which also reassured the old man.

Huang Lao-tieh answered him truthfully.

[1] *I.e.*, a moustache, not then worn by the 'beardless youth' of the revolutionary troops.

"Is this your son?" he asked, pointing to Lao San.

Huang Lao-tieh nodded.

"Isn't there a younger one?"

"Yes, but Lao Chi didn't come home last night," the old man said.

The officer smiled knowingly, nodded to his aides, and gave a glance at the revolver that lay beside him. Huang Lao-tieh and his son Lao San were marched out of the camp between two soldiers. They were executed promptly and efficiently.

That afternoon soldiers were sent out from the camp to raid the villagers' stores of provisions. They got a pig from Pock-faced Li's house, more wheat from the underground storeroom of Chang's, and articles of various kinds from other huts, all of which things they carried away. The villagers understood this kind of conduct. These soldiers acted like soldiers, and everything appeared normal again.

Lao Chi, his clothes spattered with blood, lay in the woods beyond the village, holding his dizzy head. He felt that his body was arching, now upward, now downward. Sometimes in fancy there danced before his eyes very faintly that lovely girl holding forth her two wide-open arms—the very girl he had been seeking among the Reds when he had evidently met some disaster.

In his spangled vision now that girl seemed to appear. But he fell back dizzily, saying:

"It is simply a fraud! Mother's!"

TING LING

(1905-)

TING LING is perhaps the best known of all living Chinese women authors, and is popular especially with the youth of China. She is also widely read in Japan. Some of her stories have been translated into Russian, Japanese, and French.

A native of Changteh, Hunan, she was the daughter of a poor family, and had a difficult struggle for her education. During middle-school days she became involved in revolutionary activities, and wrote stories of revolutionary youth. Her author husband, the noted Hu Yeh-p'ing, was a revolutionary leader. For a while Ting Ling, Hu Yeh-p'ing, and Shên Ts'ung-wên lived together in Shanghai. Their unique friendship attracted much comment and became historic; it was broken up with the assassination of Hu Yeh-p'ing during one of the Kuomintang 'purgations' against the Communists. Shên Ts'ung-wên later lived with her, and attempted to deflect her from radicalism, without success. She was kidnapped by Government "Blue Jackets" in 1933, and was at first thought to have been executed. At present she is a prisoner in Nanking. Seven of her books have been banned by the Kuomintang.

Most famous of Ting Ling's books are *Wei Hu, A Man's Birthday, Diary of a Suicide*, and, best known of all, *The Diary of Sophie*. Her work is distinguished by its psychological treatment of modern youth, and also for its freshness and vitality.

A highly interesting account of the Hu-Ting-Shên triangle is given in Shên Ts'ung-wên's *Biography of Ting Ling*.

THE FLOOD

By TING LING

THE relatives who had arrived from a neighbouring village sat with most of the family, intently listening. The room darkened gradually, and across the open doorway, under the thatched roof, the moon cast a bar of pale blue light. Five-year-old Lao-yao rested his recently shaved head in his mother's lap, and perked his tiny ears upward, like everybody else. He didn't know why he was listening, he didn't know what he expected to hear, but it was obvious that at this particular moment the thing to do was to listen.

A dog barked somewhere not far off. The wind rustled uncertainly. Perhaps that swishing noise was in fact only the wind filtering through the trees. . . .

"Listen! Don't you hear something? Hush!"

Sure enough there was a sound as of some one very faintly crying.

"There's somebody shouting out there."

"Nonsense! I didn't hear a thing."

"But wait, that is certainly a voice!"

Nobody said anything for a while. Then there was a restive moment. Old Grandma, half-deaf and completely bald, suddenly began muttering through her toothless gums:

"Heavenly grandfather, what to do! The fortune-teller predicted this would be my dangerous year. . . . Hope it doesn't get here, that flood. Something always saves me, though. Think of the calamities I've lived through! Of course nobody can tell for certain . . . but, mind you, I'm not afraid to die. For these old bones it's time; but leaving the sons and the grandsons—that makes it hard."

"Son or grandson, fate doesn't show any preferences! It takes them all alike, and that's the worst of it."

"Why, you fatherless son! Keep still! Suppose she hears you!"

"She ought to be in bed. *Hai*, Sister, put grandmother in bed. She must be very tired after her long walk."

"Bed! Time for bed, Grandma!" Sister shouted in her ear.

"Nonsense! No bed for me. I'm going to wait for them. What time will they get back?"

"Who knows? We don't even know where they are. We can't hear a sound, either, at the moment. Do you think anything may happen to-night?"

"How can I tell? The Great Buddha Himself won't tell you that!"

"Buddha? Down with him! What's he got against us? Flood, flood, flood, and behind it every year this same Buddha. The devil with him! What we ought to do is to unite to overthrow Buddha. Why should we repair the dikes? Why these long vigils at night? Rush in, waters of blood, rush in! Drown this Buddha! Down with this enemy of ours, I say!"

"Quiet, Ta-fu. Why get so excited about an image that can't even see you?"

"Yes, but what he says is true enough. Flood, flood, flood, repeated every year!"

"This one is going to be worse than the others. Just wait!"

Nobody listened any more. Ordinarily not very talkative, tense nervousness and excitement now made the strong peasant women garrulous, and they all began chattering at once. The older boys, prevented from accompanying their fathers to work beside the dikes, joined in heartily, and in the midst of it all the old grandmother steadily kept up a monologue:

"I can't remember how many years now ago—I was about the size of little Lung-erh—when we had to eat clay and the

bark of trees! Actually! I went from one person to another
in the family—we kept getting fewer and fewer, our big
number getting smaller every day—famine, disease, and all
kinds of hardship—corpses all over the place! Good meals
for the crows and dogs! How many died? I don't know:
there was first of all my little brother—he died sucking
my mother's dry breast. Then my sister went, and my
aunt, and then Uncle Mien. . . . I was seven years old.
Somehow I've managed to live till now, still alive. Would
you believe it? A beggar, and I didn't starve to death!
A slave girl, and I stood up under the beatings! And now
I am over sixty—sixty-five, in fact—yet I remember all that
very clearly. About the size of Lung-erh, I tell you, and I
wore a queue like a sparrow's tail. . . . That was my first
flood. Since then . . ."

Lung-erh didn't like it at all, hearing himself compared
to the bald old woman. Her arid droning voice blew on
endlessly and somehow frightened him, and he moved
stealthily across the room towards his brother. Lao-yao,
his eyes half-closed, nevertheless kept his little ears wide
open. As grandmother droned on his gaze moved from
one to the other of the dim figures. Then he looked again
at the old woman; her sunken cheeks inflated and deflated
with every mouthful of words. She looked very funny,
and Lao-yao wanted to laugh, but some unspoken command prevented him. No, not a command, but some
warning in the air. Anyway, he couldn't laugh.

Bing-bang! It was a noise startling as a shot, but it was
evidently only somebody striking against an object—or it
may have been a teacup knocked down. Everybody suddenly stopped talking, chilled to the heart, and ominous
silence hung over the room. Now they were able to hear
the wind again, shrilling noisily. And they were able to
hear grandma, who continued talking to herself :

"Whose fault is it? Who can say? My husband, a good
man, reliable and dependable—and the boy just like him.

Never a day of laziness in either of them! And yet they are both dead. Why? What kind of justice? Where is the God in Heaven? Myself, I don't matter any more—the hours aren't many ahead of me. But you younger ones, won't it be the same with all of you? Yet you go on hoping, I guess—like me when my own life was young— hoping for the world to turn over, with everything that was up suddenly come down, and everything down, *up*! Absurd dreams! Honesty is stupid, I tell you. . . . And after I die, what? The world goes on, the same thing—only bitterer, much bitterer."

"Rot! Bitterer, bitterer, bitterer—but when it gets *bitterest* the turning-point *must* come! Why——"

A dog barked outside and the sharp note quivered into the hut and lost itself in the mud walls. Out of the foggy grey night a shadowy figure rose, close to the cinnamon-tree beside the pond. Now, through the door, could be seen distinctly a man. He flung a word of recognition to the dog, and in a moment entered the room.

"Oh, it's San-yeh? How are things? How are the dikes? How is Erh-ke?"

"Isn't there a lamp in the whole house?" he asked. "No light at all?"

"What's the matter? Do you think the heavens are going to fall down, eh?"

"Not a drop of oil left! We've only got two candles, and they must be kept for the gods."

"Well, how is everything? We can't hear a whisper of a noise. Has the flood gone down or not?"

"Down? No, not this flood! On the contrary, we're down. What, you didn't even hear the gong? Things are bad at Tang Village. The dikes are weak and it's too late to strengthen them now. It's like building a latrine after you've got dysentery, eh! Tang Village will be a lake in a little while—watch and see!"

"How about here?"

"Yes, how about it? We forgot our pigs when we left. Can we go back for them to-morrow or not?"

"It's hard to say. If the flood goes over Tang Village we ought to be safe here. But we haven't as much ground here as they have, and if we're flooded we'll have to move over to Tang Village. They won't dare prevent us coming—at the point of death, eh? But come along, Ta-fu, Erh-fu! We want more men. Come along, and watch out! With the smallest break in the dikes we're done for." He moved to the doorway and stood marked against the dull sky, a powerful figure with a great chest and knotted muscles. He hesitated for a moment. "Don't get excited," he said. "Why worry your heads off? H'mm. Well, let's go! Hey, Ta-mao, you might as well come, and you too, Erh-mao. The younger they are the sharper their eyes! Lao-yao needn't come if he isn't feeling well."

They were all anxious to go, glad to have the chance to get away from the chattering women, glad to be there on the spot to see the flood come if it must come. They dived nimbly here and there searching for their jackets. Though summer, the night was cool, and one didn't want to go into it with bare shoulders.

"What is it like? I can't rest till I've actually seen it."

"And you won't rest when you *have* seen it! Nothing but a limitless mass of water, roaring this way and that. If you heard it late at night and weren't frightened to death I'd be a turtle!"

San-yeh the fearless, the powerful, San-yeh who had defied the gods of heaven and earth! To hear even San-yeh speak of fear deepened anxiety in the hearts of the timid women.

"What time is it? I'm going with you. I can't stay behind to-night; the house is full of ghosts! Really I'm scared. I want to go along."

"Nonsense! What can you do? Stay home and look after Lung-erh and Chu-chu. If it's ghostly here it's all the more so outside."

San-mu didn't say anything more, but turned slowly back to her seat. Little Chu-chu stirred beside her.

Ta-fu and the others ran outside, where a cool wind greeted them. They looked up at the high veiled moon, and the tattered cape of sky, torn by innumerable stars. In a moment they had disappeared, taking the two dogs with them. Beyond the cinnamon-tree nothing could be seen but the dull blanket of night. Those inside felt abandoned, cut off from the world.

Lung-erh rubbed the warm spot on the bench where Ta-fu had been sitting. He thought of crying for his father; then it occurred to him that it would be better to run after his brother. He couldn't make up his mind to do either. He had seen them vanish in the direction of the dikes, and he knew very well that the dikes were fun. He had been there during the day and he had seen the lovely swirl of yellow waters, and best of all the things borne along—chairs, boxes, tables, beds, pretty lacquer, and live chickens and dogs, and even people squatting absurdly on pieces of timber or floating motionless in the hollow of a wave! It had been so fascinating a spectacle that little Lung-erh in fact forgot altogether about his rice and had just sat watching the river mightily drifting. But somehow at night it didn't seem so alluring. Especially just now there didn't seem to be anything friendly about the fast dark stream, and he couldn't help wondering uneasily about those *things* drifting, drifting all alone. Old grandmother started up again:

"I know, I tell you I know. The rich are not afraid of the flood. We poor people are afraid, because it's only us it gets—and our pigs and dogs. I remember a flood that came when I was slave girl in the Chang house. How many beggars there were! I lost count—not real beggars, understand, but people ruined by the flood. What about the Changs? The young masters went up to the Pavilion of Stars and had drinks there—to enjoy the sight of the flood, they said. As a matter of fact Old Master Chang made a fortune that year by cornering all the grain and raising prices six or seven times. Can you believe it? The heart of the rich is neither flesh nor blood. And even the Buddha takes sides, I'm beginning to think. All these years I've begged mercy, and not once any help comes my way, but always the rich get richer. Of course they have enough money to keep Him right there in the family—it makes a difference. . . ."

A mouse scampered across the room, brushing against something and making a little noise.

"The flood hasn't come, but they begin to move already. Wonderful, the instinct of these little animals. . . . It *does* look bad. Believe me or not, things are going to happen. There was a time——"

Ta-niang, the family story-teller, hit upon a theme, and without any urging began a tale which she partly remembered from somewhere but mostly made up as she went along. Only the young girls listened to her; the women were too distracted to take any interest, although ordinarily they would have clung to her words with delight. She soon gave up, and once more the room was silent.

A gust of wind blew in suddenly and the house filled with the smell of fresh water and damp earth, and very faintly came the sound of voices. Looking out, they saw a string of torches circling in the distance above the shoulders of the flood-fighters, and the glimpse heartened them. Those were their men down there, strong and well-loved, bravely meeting the threat of the swollen river. Hope ran along from those torches into the eyes of the women and lighted them for an instant. The little flames crept gradually round a corner of the dikes again and were lost to view, so that only a hail or a cry came drifting back, and then that too was no longer audible. The moon lay pale upon the equally pale faces of the women. For a time nothing could be heard but the wind, and little could be seen but the darkness, which seemed to have mysterious life in it. Presently the barking of dogs broke out near the cinnamon, and a figure appeared; then another, a third, and a fourth. As they came nearer it could be made out that they were two women with two small children.

"Have pity on us! We are refugees from New Mao-tan."

"New Mao-tan? It was flooded only the day before yesterday, wasn't it?"

"Yes, flooded indeed. It's about fifty to sixty li from here."

"Lower than here, of course!"

"Come in! Draw nearer! Tell us what happened!"

The two women from New Mao-tan entered the room, and their exhausted children dropped on the doorstep.

"Night before last, very dark and raining heavily, it came. Our whole house simply melted away. We hadn't time to seize a thing. Our small mud house, what's that in the way of just a ripple of the flood? But it was worse with our neighbours—not only their houses but *them* too! A little too late in leaving—trying to save some of their things, probably. . . . We haven't eaten since half a bowl of congee yesterday morning."

"Poor creatures! I'll see what we have—perhaps a little rice."

"What about your men? Where are you going? Is New Mao-tan still under water?"

"Our men stayed behind."

"What's the good of that? No place to live, nothing to eat, nothing to wear, no work——"

"Well, they don't want to leave. There's nothing there, you see, and the water has destroyed the crops, but underneath the earth is still sound, and that's what they won't leave."

"Where are you going?"

"We intended to go to her place at Wu Ya Shan. We're sisters-in-law. But this morning we heard that things are

L

even worse at Wu Ya Shan. The roads are blocked. Heaven knows where we'll go. Our men still think we are going to Wu Ya Shan." The woman was young and inexperienced, and the perplexity of her situation terrified her. She began to weep aloud.

"We . . . must turn back, I suppose."

"To New Mao-tan?"

"What else to do? And as long as it's safe here——"

"Not so safe! Our men are all at the dikes at this moment. Nobody knows what the world will be like to-morrow!"

"Good God! Suppose we are cut off here, and the men still thinking we are in Wu Ya Shan. . . ."

She groaned and started sobbing and hoarsely crying. Old Grandmother, unable to hear, looked up and asked anxiously, "Why all the fuss? Has it really turned bad?"

No one answered her; no one in fact noticed her. Every heart was wrapped tight, as if held by string, and every eye was turned into the night. . . . And at that very moment the great gongs began to ring out.

The *dong, dong* rolled across the fields from the direction of the dikes, a confused clamorous note shaking people out of their houses, rousing all the animals and fowls, startling even the roosting birds. The whole village burst into life. The universe itself seemed to have been strung on a line, ready to break at this touch of sound. One of the women dashed from the house, and then every one emptied from it, streaming towards the cinnamon—every one except grandma. There was a weaving crowd of excited people, with children wailing and dogs yelping, and above it all the incessant hammering of the gongs. Men barked through the filtered darkness:

"To the dikes! The dikes must be saved! No male shall stay at home now! No one shall run away! Everybody come! The dikes!"

"Bring hoes! Bring torches!"

The dogs yelped maddeningly, cocks crowed, and the

wind rushing through the crowd twisted the mingled sounds with the voices it carried of the excited men at the dikes and the rising waters they fought. Torches lined the river-bank —down there hundreds of people were working frantically.

"Father in Heaven, protect us! *A-Mi-To-Fu!* Watch over us, oh, Buddha! King of the Dragons! God of Rain and Water! Stop it, stop the flood!" Some one had knelt down and was praying.

The villagers grouped themselves like ants, and the more numerous they became the more their fear increased. Children wailed, dogs howled out their lungs, women screamed into the tumult, and still louder and ever faster beat the gongs, and brighter flared the torches.

"To the dikes, to the dikes, comrades!"

"Save the dikes! Save our people! Save our families!"

"Hurry up, comrades! There's no time . . ."

"Hold up the torches! Hold them higher!"

A stream of men, a winding row of flame-points, moved towards the weakening mud defences against the river. Quickly another group followed, and in its wake more yells of encouragement and appeal, more torches cutting red lines down the night.

The wind died now to a breeze that fluttered daintily across this wild open stir, this angry ferment of men. The moon moved over a little and looked down on trees and the rich crops and silvered the lush green life which reached everywhere.

"San-mu, don't! Where are you going?"

"Never mind. I can't stay here any longer. I'm going down there to join the workers."

"I'm coming too!"

They stumbled down the slope, their long hair streaming. Soon afterwards another group rolled along darkly, and left behind it more tremulous voices of mothers and frightened-eyed children. Flickering shadows, the women's figures, danced in silhouette against the village walls illumined by moving torches. But soon those shadows diminished. One by one women carrying hoes and wheeling barrows joined their men at the dikes . . . and still the waters rose.

Overhead the sky looked on serenely and the new moon shone benignly now over the thatched roofs. Stars sparkled, and up there the Milky Way itself seemed to be in flood. The breeze blew itself down to a pleasant zephyr. It whispered gaily along the fields and down the long aisles between rows of bourgeoning grain.

"The fortune-teller said this was my year of danger," Grandma muttered to herself.

NEWS

By Ting Ling

"OFF to the kitchen, old woman!" said her son Ah Fu, who climbed through the small door from the ladder. Behind him followed that same young man once more, his short grey gown folded under his arm.

She sat beside a narrow window covered by a piece of board about two feet square. When this board was pushed away it let a banner of light into the room, so that she could see to repair the trousers of her grandson.

They came in, and Ah Fu took off his blue gown without even looking at his mother. He sat down on the bed and asked his companion to sit beside him.

The old woman realized that it was the same business again. Since it had begun her son seemed to her to have ascended into a world which she did not understand, a world which she could not enter. From the threshold of it Ah Fu somehow looked down on her, his mother, and she could not help feeling resentful because of his indifference. But, anyway, she now rolled up her bundle of rags, stooped, and went out, furtively eyeing the guest.

Yet she did not go down to the kitchen after all. Instead she crawled from the ladder through a small door and into an adjoining attic room, which was just big enough for one person to lie down in at full length. It was quite dark in there even when the sun was out. But it was separated from the other room by only a thin wooden partition, and every word spoken by her son could be clearly heard.

Several of Ah Fu's fellow-workers soon arrived from the

factory. Before her eyes they all crept up the shaking ladder and into the single-windowed cell.

When they had begun talking in earnest the old woman held her breath and scarcely breathed, so that she could listen with utmost care, not missing a single syllable.

It was evening, and people in the cramped lane were numerous. Some men were massaging themselves or each other, and many sat half-naked on little stools in the lane, driving away mosquitoes with broken rush fans. They talked a great deal, they laughed and joked, or they sang folk-songs known only to workers. Sometimes this noise interfered with the old woman's hearing, but she kept her ear fastened to the wall, and listened with the greatest attention to everything that was said.

It grew dark, and each family began cooking dinner. Smoke from wood fires and cheap cooking-oil curled out of every hut, filled the lane, and gradually drifted away. But in the crevice where the old woman lay it simply lodged and did not seem to move at all, so that the air was heavy with it. She could not help coughing.

"Kah, kah, kah, kah, kah, kah, kah—ah-ke!"

"Is your mother sick? What a rotten cough!" some one said in the other room when she choked painfully in the smoke-filled air.

Then Ah Fu knew that she was there, and he called to her, "Get out of that hole, Mother! It's too hot. Why do you creep in there, anyway?"

She stuffed a piece of cloth into her mouth, and refused to budge. She knew they did not want her, but despite her running eyes and nose she was determined to hear all they had to say. She did not even reply when her daughter-in-law and her grandson, eating their meal below, called out to her to join them. Battalions of mosquitoes assailed her. She brushed them away, but they left large bumps on her thin bloodless hands before retreating.

At length the guests got up and left. Ah Fu entered the

kitchen and scratched about for some cold food. Not until then did she crawl out of her little cave and join the others.

"What is it, are you sick?" asked her daughter-in-law, who was sitting at the back door, with Little Dog at her breast, and Ah Fu beside her filling his bowl.

"Nonsense, I'm quite all right."

Pleasure and satisfaction were written in the wrinkles of her face and flowed out with the words from her heart. Neither her son nor her daughter-in-law observed it.

II

Son and daughter-in-law had gone to work in the factory. Little Dog played with other children in the lane.

The old woman sat knotted over a garment ragged beyond identification, which belonged to Yeh Ta-fu, who lived upstairs. Yeh's wife, a factory worker too, spent all her leisure hours cooking and washing. How could she find time for mending?

The old woman stirred uneasily as she sewed. Something troubled her mind. She wanted to talk to some one. She felt the need of action. Yet to whom could she talk, to whom could she appeal? Even her own son regarded her as insignificant, and besides it was not entirely clear to her what it was that she wished to say or do. She sat alone, feeling rather miserable, for a long time. Still she did not give up thinking about the business, and presently, without knowing exactly why, she found herself calling on old Mrs Wang, who lived near by.

Wang Po-po was hanging over a wooden tub, scrubbing clothes. The mother stood beside her, and for a while said nothing of any importance, until finally she burst out, without thinking:

"Remember Permanent Abundance Place? Do you remember, eh, when we went there to eat that time?"

"Could I forget it? Everybody cooked and everybody

ate. Everybody shared what he had. I said then it would be a wonderful thing if we could live that way for ever."

Mrs Wang paused in her task and wiped her dripping hands against her thighs. Old Mrs Li, who lived next door, had wandered up, and she now interrupted excitedly:

"*Hei*, we didn't believe it at first! Everybody said Ah San was a liar when he told us about it. It was hard to believe, even when we found it was actually a fact, and we didn't risk a bite till those people invited us. Too bad it lasted such a little while. But of course the defile-your-mother police had to come and the Japanese spies, and they destroyed every stick, stove, and kettle."

"Is it against the law to eat? Actually? Those living corpses——"

"Who paid for it, do you know that?" the mother of Ah Fu asked in an earnest tone.

"Certainly it was that rich man named Liu, and afterwards he was driven out of town by the police."

"Named Liu, eh? And where could he get the money? Would a rich man do such a thing? No, indeed, he would hire us to work for him. Now the truth is this money actually came from . . ." She lowered her voice and turned out each word very carefully.

"*Ai-ya!*" Mrs Wang and Mrs Li exclaimed together.

"Not a man at all," explained the mother of Ah Fu. "Not one man, but many, many. One hundred ten-thousands of people got together a huge sum of money and sent it to Shanghai during the war. And some of it, you see, came to us, because we were on strike against the Japanese factory, and the Japanese bandits were attacking Shanghai! Because we had nothing to eat, don't you see, and so they were giving us this big meal together."

"So! This is as it should be. The poor help the poor. I should have known this man Liu wasn't such a fool after all. But where did you learn it?"

The mother of Ah Fu had forgotten her resentment over

being neglected. It seemed to her that she had become an authority on a number of things, and she spoke out with pride.

"Formerly I was as ignorant as a person asleep in a drum. But I heard about this, and I heard that they had won a victory, and I hear that we are making plans to send some gifts——"

"*Tui-la!* And that's good too. Since they helped us we ought to help them," broke in old lady Li, as if she had been coming to such correct decisions all her life.

"But who knows when they will get to Shanghai?" Mrs Wang wanted to be assured.

"They will come, don't worry, some day they will come. How soon depends on us. If we tell them we are in a great hurry, if we send them something, if we send them a telegram, they will come that much sooner. If we let them know that we are suffering then they will certainly come here first," the old woman explained to Mrs Wang, as if she knew all about it, though this was nothing that she had heard, but only what she imagined to be true, and therefore felt certain was true.

Mrs Li said, "I think we should try to send them something. Never mind how rough it is; as long as we mean well they won't laugh at us. Or is this right?"

The old woman felt extremely happy, and Mrs Wang agreed with her too that it was the thing to do. What to buy? They could scrape together only a shallow fistful of coppers, and what would they buy? They worried about it, until Mrs Li at last suggested that it would be easier if they asked some other women to join them. Having decided on this they set off as gaily as children, and, showing their few teeth in wrinkled smiles, they separated to enlist recruits.

III

There was new work for all of them to do.

Three old women went to buy cloth, and two were

commissioned to buy thread. But thread was out of reach at three coppers a twist. The thread-buyers decided to beg some from their daughters-in-law, and if that wasn't enough to ask contributions from others. They took back their coppers still wrapped up and fully intact.

The cloth-buyers could not decide what kind of material to choose, and they walked from shop to shop. At last they found something which seemed about right, and they counted out their coppers with some hesitation. It wasn't an easy task, and they felt their responsibility. Suppose the material proved unsatisfactory after all, think of their humiliation!

"This will have to do. Let's not be too particular. It costs us thirty-six coppers for a foot."

The shopkeeper wanted to know how they intended to use it, but the old women said nothing, while inwardly they smiled.

"All right, let's take it. Is two feet enough?"

"Yes, we'll ask him for a little extra."

"Banditry! A foot of red cloth, thirty-six coppers!"

They carried away their purchase as if entrusted with the Emperor's jewel-case.

A dozen or more old women sat together around the materials and debated about the work. Some thought that there should be a flower in one corner,[1] because they had seen other women use flowers, and since it was a gift it should be entirely correct. They got together a few more coppers, and one of their number went off to buy a piece of black cloth.

At last it was finished. The flower was slightly out of place, and the needlework was none too good, but the heart of every one of them was gladdened. They stared at the gift a long time before they folded it up, and then they sat and talked of their hopes. Just consider it: Shanghai another world; seven hours' work a day, increased wages,

[1] The Chinese call the hammer and sickle a *hua*, or flower.

no work on Sunday, and actually free tickets for box-seats in the theatre. . . .

The mother of Ah Fu was delegated to make the presentation, and she pledged that it would be safely delivered. But among the others some of them thought, "After all, will they really accept such a thing from old women like us?"

IV

Ah Fu came home again with that man. When she heard their feet on the ladder her heart pounded fearfully, and the hand that held her needle shook outrageously. She dared not even look up at them, but sat there without moving.

"Mother, out with you—to the kitchen!"

She tried to utter a friendly reply, but somehow nothing came out of her. She folded up her rags, and her hands touched the precious parcel. She raised her head to look at that man, and found his eyes very kind, and this encouraged her. She hesitated before them as she limped towards the ladder.

"Well, Mother, what is it?" Ah Fu demanded, noticing her strange behaviour.

She turned and walked to his companion. Taking the gift from her breast, she thrust it at him in a determined manner, and said:

"This is for them. Please deliver it for us!"

"'Them'? Who is 'Them'?"

"You know. *They!* Those you so often talk about. We old women know——"

"Oh!"

"Fourteen of us got together to help out with some small thing, and here it is."

He opened the package, and a delighted smile spread over his face. Ah Fu shouted out excitedly:

"Do you mean you old women made this?"

She trembled with mixed joy and pride, and she

could not suppress her smile of triumph as she nodded her head.

"We hope they will come quickly——"

"Mother! How did you know about this?"

"I heard you talking, and I understood." She smiled, a hundred per cent. satisfied with herself.

"Ha, ha, ha, ha!" They laughed happily, but as the old woman watched them her uneasiness returned. At last she gathered courage to ask a question.

"Is it true or not? Does your society admit old women?"

"Not wicked old women like you!" laughed Ah Fu. Then he nodded his head, and told her that it admitted all humanity that wanted to work.

"That's what I want to know. Then you only tell me what they want, and we old women will carry it out. Twenty or thirty of us will get together whenever we are called."

"*Hao, hao*—very good, good indeed!"

The others by this time had climbed into the little room and they all wanted to hear the story. The old woman blushed under her copper-coloured skin, and bundled herself towards the ladder with her rags.

"Wonderful! wonderful!" she heard the young men shouting at each other. "The old women are actually organizing themselves!"

She looked at them with bright eyes and took a last glance at the flag. The red field burned satisfyingly around the black flower.

Later on she could not even remember having descended the ladder.

PA CHIN
(1896–)

PA CHIN (pronounced Bah Gin) ranks with Lu Hsün, Mao Tun, Ting Ling, Shên Ts'ung-wên, and Yü Ta-fu as one of half a dozen important writers who have given form and vigour to modern Chinese literature, especially since the 'literary revolution' of 1917. His novels and short stories are widely read by Chinese youth. All his books have been translated into Japanese, for he is more popular and more widely appreciated in Japan than in China. Several of his works have also been translated into Russian, German, and French.

This is the first English translation made of any of Pa Chin's writings. *Dog* is considered by many Chinese to be the best short story written in China during the past decade. Unfortunately much of its savour and power, its freshness in form and technique, are lost in the English translation, which can at best convey only the shape of the meaning, but not the emotional values, the allusions, the bitter satire, and ironic humour inherent in the arrangement of the original Chinese characters.

Pa Chin's most famous books are *The Dead*, *The Tempests*, and *The Withered Sun*.

Like a number of other contemporary Chinese writers, his political views have brought Kuomintang censure on his head, and he now lives in exile in Japan. He calls himself an anarchist. Some of his writings have been banned.

DOG

By PA CHIN

I DO not know my own name (if, indeed, I was ever given any) or my true age, for evidently I arrived in the world a thing of chance, picked up from nowhere and dropped down again without thought—like a stone carelessly tossed from one place to another by some passer-by, to no particular purpose. I do not know who my father was or my mother. I was simply a thing abandoned, left behind, forgotten, marked by the same brown skin, dark hair and eyes, the same flat nose and short build you see in hundreds of millions of others, among whom Fate placed me, for a while, to live.

I went through a period of childhood, as every one does, but mine was in many respects unique. No one gave me any affection, no one warmed or comforted me; my earliest memories are of hunger and cold and bitterness. . . . Yet I remember (not exactly, for I had little idea of time, but nevertheless there was such a day) a lean, tall, wrinkled old man who stopped before me and, nodding his head, remarked, "At your age you certainly should be in school, studying. Education—that's what is important to a man." He spoke in a low voice which seemed full of tenderness, and his face was very serious. His advice impressed me, and, forgetting my anguish and the raw cold, I earnestly set forth to seek an education.

Buildings stood here and there, some splendid as a palace, and others not quite so magnificent. It was the latter, people told me, that were called 'schools,' where one might get an education. I kept thinking all the time of what the old man had told me, and finally, without waiting for an invitation, I stepped boldly into one of the schools. . . .

"Get out! This isn't the place for you." . . . Everywhere it was the same. Later I tried all the buildings, from the richest structures to the humblest, but no matter where I went, whether I was greeted by cruel faces or kind, that same sentence was repeated over and over again:

"Get out!"

The words struck me like a lash, and, frightened, full of fear and pain, I lowered my head, cringing, trying hard to think, while the echo of children's laughter and merriment in the schools rang in my ears.

Was I, after all, I began to wonder, really a human being? The more I thought about it the more my doubts increased. I tried to put the question aside, to avoid answering, but all the time there seemed to be some mocking voice in my ears for ever asking, "Is it really possible that you belong to the human race?"

Lonely, depressed, helpless, my very existence utterly ignored by the world, I at last sought refuge in the ruined temple where I sheltered at night, determined to seek an explanation from the God who dwelt there. "God is merciful, God knows all," I thought. "He will solve this question for me."

The curtain that once hung before Him had been torn aside; the image sat alone, bare, rotting, covered with dust, with one arm missing. I knelt before Him and prayed.

"Almighty God, help me to understand, to find a solution to the riddle: *Am I a human being?*"

Silence. His dusty mouth did not move, his eyes gave no answering gleam of response. . . .

Eventually I reasoned things out for myself. "How, indeed, is it possible for a thing like me to claim any relation to other men, who are obviously quite different?" I thought. "Warmth, comfort, human feeling, the privileges of man —all these are denied me—and I live on refuse, stuff that real people cannot eat and throw away. It would be an insult to humanity if I were considered a part of it! Certainly I don't belong to the world of men. . . ."

But if not a man, I thought, still I must have been put on earth for some end, and perhaps there was a use for my body. Everything could be bought and sold; why not me? Putting a straw price-tag on my back I went to the market, to offer myself for sale. I stood first at one place, then another, exhibited all angles of my head and body, inviting buyers to bargain for the object. If anyone should actually buy me, and feed me the left-overs, I was determined to be as faithful as a dog to his master.

I waited there in the market all day, shifting from one corner to another, but nobody made any proposals. Wherever I went people only looked at me with jeering eyes. Only some small boys took any real notice of me, and they were interested simply in making fun of the price-tag on my back. Hungry and tired, I crept back to the temple, stopping on the way to pick up from the road a crust of dry black bread, hard and covered with dust, which I swallowed without any hesitation. It occurred to me that if I could eat such things I must have the stomach of a dog.

The ruined House of God was very still. There was nobody there but me, and I lay down heavily, disgusted at my utter uselessness in the world. Whatever I was, it seemed clear that it was an article of no value to men. I wept bitterly, but even tears, though a precious gift, brought no relief to an unclassified monster like me. Nevertheless, I went on crying, for I had nothing else to do, and I had nothing to give myself, in fact, but these tears. I wept not only in the temple, but going forth and standing before the doors of the rich I continued to weep there.

Outside the gate of a great house I hid myself, starved, half-frozen, crying, bitterly swallowing my own tears, and then crying even louder to forget the pain in my stomach. A young fellow in foreign clothes passed close by and went into the house, but did not seem to notice me at all, and then a middle-aged man followed him in, but he too failed to see me. Along the street people moved to and fro, but none even glanced at me. Did I really exist?

Finally a towering fellow came out, and he saw me, beyond question, for drawing near he cursed and shouted, "Get out! This isn't the place for you to cry!" He began to kick me, as he would a dog.

My tears were at last exhausted, and pulling my limbs together I dragged them wearily back to the temple. There I knelt once more before the battered God, this image my only friend, and again I prayed:

"Almighty God! Though it is apparent that I am not a man, Fate has put me here, and I must live in the world. I'm a lost orphan. I don't know my father or my mother, and yet I need some one. Adopt me then, Just and Generous One, take me as Your son. . . . I don't belong to the human race at all, and I shall never know the love of man."

The God did not open His mouth. He did not reject me. At last I had a Father—the armless image, the Just and Generous.

II

I had to go out every day to beg something to eat, and when I had filled my stomach with what I could pick up I hurried back home with a new pleasure, for I felt somehow for the first time that I belonged in the world. I had a Father—the God of the temple. It is true He never opened His mouth, and He offered me no word of comfort, but He was always there, one Person who did not desert me. . . .

Time winged swiftly along and I grew up.

I remained convinced that I was not human, and repeatedly assured myself that this explained my curious existence, but nevertheless I felt now and then the sensations of a man

M

inwardly moving me. I could not help longing for fresh food, clean clothes, and a warm, comfortable bed inside a beautiful house. "But these are the appetites of a man!" I told myself. "How can you dream of enjoying such privileges?" Nevertheless, I continued to think about the enticing goods I saw displayed in the shop windows. And then, yes, even women allured me, with their flashing smiles, their soft white legs, smooth as jade, but warm to the touch, I imagined. Could you believe it! A thing like me—I wanted to touch them, to caress them. . . . Always I put down such wild desires, remembering, on going nearer, that I was but a thing of unknown origin.

But one day I saw, walking close to a pair of the softest, the shapeliest, the loveliest legs, a small white dog, and considering this I thought, "You see! Not all the privileges belong only to men. We dogs also have our rights!" Becoming suddenly brave, I rushed to embrace those legs. To my amazement somebody seized me, tripped me, and threw me to the earth.

"Are you mad?" exclaimed the man, who kicked me fiercely.

Returning to the temple I concluded sadly that I was even lower than a dog. "Father, God, my Father," I prayed, "make me into a real dog, a small white dog like that one, sharing the love and comfort of men!"

III

Brown skin, black hair, flat nose, short stature—these, like many genuine men, I possessed. But I observed that there are in this world people belonging to the human race and yet with white skin, yellow hair, a high nose, and very tall.

These men, I noticed, strode boldly down the street, singing, shouting, laughing, as if they alone existed, and indeed the others, walking at a distance, dared not pass near them. This was a discovery for me, that human beings were divided, and above those I saw most there were others, higher still. I began to notice these especially privileged ones more and more often. Among them were many who wore round white caps, white shirts bordered with blue, and white trousers,[1] and they were always laughing and playing, sometimes fighting, sometimes smashing bottles over the heads of the brown men, sometimes kissing women or riding with them in rickshaws, the women sitting in their laps and dangling soft bare legs.

People all seemed to respect these men very highly, everybody got out of their way, and evidently they were the noblest of mortals. I took care not to go near them, for my presence was certain to be offensive; but one evening, when I sat resting beside a wall, rubbing my bloody, mud-covered feet, hungry as usual, and tired, some people came suddenly before me. I looked up, and was terrified to see that it was some of this noblest class of humanity. Too late! I could not escape, but dully sat waiting for what fate had in store for me. They yelled at me to get out; they kicked me and called me a "dog."

Dog? And nothing worse? When I went back to the temple that night I thanked God, my Father, that these lofty beings considered me no lower than a dog. It gave me new hope. If I were recognized as no less than a dog, that should entitle me at least to the rights of a dog, and once more I thought of that small white animal running beside his mistress's shapely body.

The very next time I saw a pair of entrancing legs moving gracefully down the street I rejoiced, and, remembering that in the eyes of the white men I was now definitely a dog, I at once exercised my rights. I leapt at the legs, tightly embracing them, and forgetting everything else. Mingled shouts and screams came to my ears, heavy blows landed on me, hundreds of pairs of hands pulled me from every side,

[1] Foreign sailors.

but I neither felt nor heard anything: I clung on joyously to that pair of twinkling legs.

When I opened my eyes again I was lying in a cold dark cell, and no human sound was to be heard. My whole body ached and I could scarcely breathe. . . .

God, the Father, the Just and Generous One, still sits dustily in his temple, but never, never again shall I pray to that armless image!

SHÊN TS'UNG-WÊN
(1902–)

BEFORE the age of thirty Shên Ts'ung-wên was called the Dumas of China, for he had already produced more than forty books. Of these his stories of camp-life, of soldiers, and of aborigines in the frontier districts are best known and best liked.

Shên began to write when still a boy, and continued writing while leading the life of a soldier, a career at which he had already had some experience when only twelve years old. When he was fifteen he enlisted in the army of Hunan, his native province, and served as regimental scribe. In that capacity he lived for three years on the western frontier, in the midst of the Miao and Lolo tribesmen, who furnished material for many of his later stories.

When he was nineteen he resigned from the army and went to Peiping, where he worked as a reporter. In 1924 he joined the staff of the *Modern Critic*, a literary monthly, and made the friendship of Yü Ta-fu, the famous poet Hsü Chih-mo, the scholar Hu Shih, and other writers, who helped to make his works known. Going to Shanghai he began to write prolifically. There he met Hu Yeh-p'ing and his wife, Ting Ling. Together they formed a trio which provided literary gossips and the mosquito Press with scandal, and publishers with an abundance of copy.

Shên's most famous work is *Alice in China*, a long satire in a form entirely new to the country. *The Husband* is his short story that he likes best.

He was until recently literary editor of the *Ta Kung Pao*, China's leading 'liberal newspaper.' He now devotes himself exclusively to writing.

PAI TZU

By Shên Ts'ung-wên

THE anchor slid into the water at Chengchow and a junk settled to rest beside the quay.

A shore plank about fifteen feet long was lowered to the stone steps, and passengers began to file down it. They lined up, one after another, loading their baggage on their shoulders, and then moved across the space, rhythmically swinging from left to right like a pendulum. They all managed to balance themselves safely ashore.

Many other junks lay strung along the river, so many that their slightly swaying masts looked like waving trees, with the bundles of rope and sail clustering to them like the tangled confusion of strange foliage. On every junk blue-clad sailors worked or stood about smoking long pipes. Their large hirsute hands and feet, seen against the sky, seemed to hang in the wind, like those of the monsters out of a child's imagination. They reminded one very much of "Flying Hairy Feet," that fabulous hero of our youth, especially when some of them shot up the tall masts to disentangle the ropes. They enjoyed such hazardous tasks, and the more difficult the knot up there the better.

Up one would go, scaling the smooth, slippery mast so easily one couldn't help wondering if his hands and bare feet weren't equipped with hooks. How did they do it? And, once up in that dizzy height, how did they have the courage to sing and jest so carelessly, with only their feet tightly clutching the stem of the sail rigging, while their hands worked among the ropes?

Men on the masts of neighbouring junks sang out in

reply, or even set up a chorus, and this seemed to make them all the more reckless in exhibiting their skill high over the decks. Standing below other sailors looked up enviously, as if anxious to show that they were just as nimble and graceful as those above, and resented the *laodah's* order to them not to go aloft. They gazed wistfully as the acrobats on the yardarms joked with women on rival junks, and in annoyance shouted up at them.

"Fall down, my son, and crush yourself to death, ah!"

"Little grandson with a lark's voice, let's hear you sing when you've dropped and cracked your skull!"

"Bastard!"

Above, the sailor only became all the more musically inclined.

"Ho! Ho! little children," he cried down. "On the contrary I am *your* father!" They kept up this cursing back and forth till the job was done, everybody enjoying himself thoroughly. . . .

On windy and rainy nights the junks were canopied over with great sheets of yellow oiled cloth, and this was such a night. Beneath the covering sailors huddled and played cards, or chattered loudly, or simply sat quietly, listening to the tapping rain and the long wind riding down the River of Golden Sand. The junks were moored nearly abeam, fastened together with lines drawn almost taut, and now and then a wave swelled in, driving the vessels into collision. The jolt didn't disturb the sailors at all, and they hardly made a murmur about it. Nothing troubled them— not even the kind of pale moon, or the burnt sky, or the veil of morning dew that excite the mind soft with lyric impulse. What aroused the highest interest in them, how-ever, and were matters on which they had very definite opinions, were first of all whether they were fed meat or sour cabbage for dinner, and, secondly, whether the anchor was dropped in midstream or beside the shore. Meat was very much preferred to sour cabbage, and they didn't like to put down any distance from the river-bank.

Let it be told of one of these sailors how in the night blurred by rain he walked down the shore-plank and up the road, picking his way with difficulty through the mud. His heart beat rapidly. This was Pai Tzu. He never tired of climbing the masts, he sang all day, and at sunset was not in the least fatigued. His belt, as just now he groped along, was filled with coins that he had earned climbing up and down the masts. Lines of rain slanted against his head and curled down his bare legs and feet.

Pai Tzu finally reached the door of the house. He knocked, after the manner common to sailors everywhere, and whistled loudly. The door opened, and he thrust one of his muddy legs across the threshold. While the other was still outside, his body was girdled by a pair of long lean arms, and his newly shaved face, burned by sun and wind, was rubbed by the broad warm mouth of a woman. The perfumed smell of her, the curve of the embrace, and the powdered softness were all familiar to him. He moved his face and met her wet tongue, and for a long while they stood with their mouths sealed. At last he released her.

"You wretch!" she gasped. "I was afraid those Changteh women down the river had eaten you——"

"That long tongue of yours! I'll bite it right out of your mouth!"

"I'll bite off your——"

Pai Tzu laughed, picked up the woman in his hands, and carried her to the centre of the room. There he put her down under the lantern, and stood looking at her from his height, a head taller than she.

"To tell the truth, I'm tired of pulling the oars!"

". . . ?"

"Yes, I want to push the wheelbarrow!" he said, grinning.

"Immoral animal," she answered, and began all at once

searching his pockets. Each time she pulled something forth
and threw it on the bed she enumerated the 'contraband.'

"White-as-Snow Cream . . . fancy paper . . . new hand-
kerchief . . . a tin—— What's in it?"

"Make a guess!"

"I'm no good at guessing. Is it the powder you
promised?"

"Look at the brand; open the tin and see for yourself
what it is."

She moved closer to the lantern, opened the tin, and
sniffed. A look of mock disapproval came over her face,
and this seemed to make Pai Tzu exceedingly happy.
Without a word he seized the tin, and, taking her round the
waist, lifted her to the bed. You could not see them in the
room at all, but under the dim circle of light beneath the
red lantern were the prints of muddy feet.

Outside it now rained heavily, but their laughter muted
the noise of the storm. The walls of the room were so thin
that the sound of somebody smoking an opium pipe next
door was clearly audible. Pai Tzu and his woman were
totally oblivious to it.

"You're—strong. Strong as an ox."

"Um. . . . Believe me, I never went to a single woman
while I was down the river."

"Not once? Can you swear that you are as pure as the
sacrifice in the Temple of Heaven?"

"Really, I swear."

"Who can believe——"

But Pai Tzu indeed suddenly felt within him a great
strength and a power unutterable in words. His breath
came heavily and quickly, his muscles bulged, and then at
last he relaxed, became limp, and lay on the bed as lifeless
as a bundle of wet hemp.

After a while she brought forth a smoking set and put it
on the bed. It formed a Great Wall between them, and they
lay quietly smoking, one on each side of it. Presently she

began to sing snatches of song from the operas. Pai Tzu smoked on, now and then leisurely sipping tea. He felt like a king.

"But listen to me, woman, these females down the river —really they are rather beautiful!"

"Then why come to me?"

"Well—even if I love them, they don't love me."

"That's why you come here, eh?"

"You fox! When I'm not here how many others . . . what? You should protest!"

She made a wry face, and handed over another pipe to him. He smoked in silence for a few moments.

"Yesterday now—anybody here?"

"Why be such a wretch? I have been waiting for you for a long time. I counted the days, and calculated exactly that you, the wandering corpse, would certainly be here to-day."

"H'm. . . . Suppose I drown at the Blue Wave Rapids, you'll be happy, eh?"

"Yes, of course," said the woman. She was offended.

Pai Tzu enjoyed making her angry. It gave him a curious pleasure and a sensation of power. He pushed away the smoking set abruptly, and, reaching over, embraced her. He caressed her round full breasts and the curve of her thigh. He bit her. She lay looking up at him smilingly. From his back you could see wrapped around him only a pair of tiny feet bound in red silk. . . .

Pai Tzu plodded slowly back through the angular lines of rain towards the river. In his hand he held a piece of heavy rope, which was lighted and served him as torch. The rain was heavy, and the road was full of little wells of muddy water, but he did not feel uncomfortable. He was reflecting on the woman and the happiness she had given him. She filled his mind to the exclusion of everything else. He was thinking of the round softness of her body, of its warmth, and of its incredible curves, each of which he felt he could describe with perfect accuracy, even though separated a thousand miles from her.

What she had given him compensated for the hard labour of a month on the river, of bending at tasks in the heat of burning sun and driving wind and rain, and perhaps even made up, as a matter of fact, for his abominable luck at cards. And not only had she made this effort seem worth while; she had given him the strength to work, and climb up the masts, singing, during another month of toil. After that he would again lie beside her.

Pai Tzu stood staring at the painted empty hulk of the junk, and it seemed to him for a moment good to be back. New passengers and cargo had already moved into it, seeking temporary haven between its mothering flanks. Like most sailors he instinctively resented the strangers who intruded periodically into this curving shape of wood that for him breathed with life.

Suddenly, he did not know why, he thought of his woman, lying naked, and waiting, like this great dark-sailed ship. Dimly he perceived that there was something wrong with the world, and then he became conscious for the first time that his arms and legs were very tired. He went to his quarters and fell asleep.

SUN HSI-CHEN
(1906–)

SUN HSI-CHEN, author of illuminating stories of rural China, is one of the youngest and most talented writers of that country. He was born in Chekiang province in the town of Shaoshing, the native place also of Lu Hsün, and famous for the excellent wine it produces. In his infancy he became interested in literature through hearing the story-tellers repeat the ancient tales of his people. He began to write while still a child, and had published several books before he was out of his nonage. Since many of his earliest recollections are of civil war, which crossed and recrossed his home district, it is natural that conflict should be the theme for much of his work. He is in fact perhaps best known for his trilogy: *The Field of War, War*, and *After War*.

Sun has published six other novels, widely popular with Chinese youth. They are: *Beaten Gold, To Dairen, The Ring of Flowers, Miss Feng Hsien, Heart of Woman*, and *Woman of the Night*. Beside these, before the age of thirty this remarkable worker had to his credit a critical study of Upton Sinclair, another of Gorki, a *Life of Shelley*, a *Critique of English Literature*, and a volume of translated *East Indian Stories*. He has also written a text-book on Western literature and edited a book of anti-war literature.

Much of Sun's writing is marked with stinging irony, satire of poignant bitterness, and harsh cynicism, but at times he achieves an emotional impact rare in Chinese fiction. He is praised especially for his stories of rural life, which he knows perfectly. In his later work a deepening social consciousness becomes more manifest, there is a more highly developed sense of dramatic realism, and his writing begins to move, to drive, to have *power*—a quality strangely lacking in almost all Chinese literature.

Early in January 1935 Sun Hsi-chen was arrested by the Kuomintang authorities in Peiping on charges of radicalism.

At the time of his arrest Sun was lecturing on Chinese and Western Literature at several universities in Peiping, where he had lived for some time. He was one of over two hundred writers, artists, students, and professors arrested in Tientsin and Peiping during November, December, and January—a phase in the Fascist 'thought purgation' drive led by the so-called "Blue Jackets" of the Kuomintang.

AH AO

By Sun Hsi-chen

THROUGHOUT the day, from early dawn, Ah Ao had remained hidden under a bed in the small dark room, her head bent, her body still, scarcely daring to breathe. . . .

At the foot of the Purple-red Mountain, down which spilled a dense growth of fragrant pines and other trees, a small stream ran into the open cornfields, and beside it stood a row of seven houses, most of them old and dilapidated. This place was known as Tao Village. None of the inhabitants, however, was named Tao. In four of the seven houses lived the family Chen, the house on the western end was a family temple reserved for the spirits, while in the centre of the row stood a comparatively new and handsome residence (some eighteen years old) which was owned by Chin the Rich.

It was in the seventh house, poorest of all, consisting of five little rooms, where the Wang family dwelt, that Ah Ao lay hidden. Half of this house was in fact mortgaged to Chin the Rich, who, two years before, when old Wang died, had lent his widow forty thousand cash to pay for the funeral feast and obsequies. Consequently she now lived with her son, Small One Brother, and her daughter, Ah Ao, in only the nether part of the little hut, which did not belong to Chin the Rich. In the room next to the kitchen—or, rather, in one corner of the kitchen itself, for the bed was separated from it only by a few thin planks—Ah Ao, in secret dread, trembled and stifled her lungs all day. Some millstones and empty bamboo baskets leaned against the wall of the kitchen, which was just now very noisy. There were four square wooden tables, with long benches ranged on each side, and these, with their occupants, completely choked up the little room. Altogether one could count more than thirty men, including not only the male population of Tao Village, but also guests from the neighbouring villages of Yu and Red Wall. They sat drinking and feasting in exuberant mood. Most of them wore blue or white cotton shirts and trousers, and were in their bare feet. Chin the Rich, Wu the Merchant, who could read and write, and the Hairy-headed Village Elder, respected for his age, wore long gowns, however, made of linen. Only on rare occasions did these long-gown men visit such a lowly establishment, and it was plain that they were now quite aware of the extraordinary dignity their appearance lent to the feast.

The food seemed simple enough, with but four big bowls of meat, fish, turnips, and soup spread on each table, but they were refilled again and again, and each time emptied almost as soon as replenished. Later on, besides, the women of the village would have to be fed. Everybody gorged, helping himself to great hunks of meat and full bowls of wine, without any pretence at etiquette; their presence at the feast was not in the interest of goodwill, but a punitive measure against the mother of a shameless daughter. Never mind the financial burden to Widow Wang! It was the way of justice.

The fact was that only by mortgaging the other half of her house had the unhappy woman managed to get together the money to finance this strange banquet. A sentimental person might have observed that what the guests clipped between the blades of chopsticks was actually Widow Wang's flesh and blood, for the feast meant utter ruin to her. By this sacrifice, however, she was saving the life of her daughter, who was, no one could deny it, guilty of that crime. Now, although a crime of such a nature necessarily required two to commit it, the unwritten but powerful law of Chinese custom nevertheless made her alone responsible, and gave any villager the right to attack, insult, abuse, or kill her, as he saw fit. By what other means, then, could the child's life be saved than through this, an expensive banquet in honour of the offended villagers, and especially to win mercy from Chin the Rich, Wu the Merchant, and the Hairy-headed Village Elder? Even though it meant her own death in the end, still the widow would have gone through with it.

Two days before, in the afternoon, she had sent her son to Chin. He had bowed, begged mercy, and requested the loan of thirty thousand cash, pledging the rest of the Wang house as security. Then with this money the boy had, again at his mother's instruction, gone to the market, where he bought thirty pounds of meat, more than twenty pounds of fish, fully a bushel of turnips, and some other ingredients of the feast. Since early in the morning of the previous day she had busied herself with cleaning and preparing this food, making rice wine, and attending to other duties, so that she had not once had a moment to rest.

With the arrival of the guests she had become even busier. All alone, she worked ceaselessly, serving everybody, keeping all the bowls filled with food, pouring forth the warm wine that was like emptying the vessels of her own body, but all the same managing to smile and give the appearance of enjoying her duties immensely.

"Brother Lucky Root," shouted one coarse fellow, "don't hesitate! This isn't an occasion for ceremony, but a free feed. See, you don't have to give anything in return, so eat up! Fill yourself to the brim!"

"You are quite right," agreed Lucky Root. "Why be slow about it, eh? Let's eat, for such opportunities as this are rare indeed. . . . As a matter of fact, this girl, now, Ah Ao; shameless, but still rather good-looking. How many girls around compare with her? Actually——"

N

"The more girls like Ah Ao the more free feasts," yelled a third. "Personally I hope we'll have others——"

"*Ai-ya*, Old Fa! Always boasting. You, the hungry devil with women! But don't forget the facts in this case: the girl right under your nose chooses instead a fellow from a neighbouring village, not you!"

"Old Fa, ha, ha!"

"Ho! What an . . . Old Fa!"

The Widow Wang did not appear to understand these remarks, but bent her attention on the tasks of service, and on maintaining the smile on her face. She did not once frown. But Ah Ao heard, and trembled, and crawled still farther towards the wall. She did not know whether the feeling she experienced was humiliation, or terror, or indignation, or merely a heavy sadness, but something like a great stone seemed to be crushing her down, and her heart burned as though pierced by a shaft of red-hot iron. A few days ago she had boldly resigned herself to whatever fate might bring, but now she wanted only to crawl, crawl, crawl.

The Hairy-headed Elder at last came to the issue. "To be precise," he began slowly, "this is perhaps after all not so serious a matter. It is natural for a grown girl to want marriage, isn't it so? But to make love . . . to a young man . . . in secret, you know, and without anybody's knowledge . . . without the usual formalities . . . who can excuse it?"

"Exactly!" exclaimed Wu the Merchant. "Widow Wang, this is something that can only come to a mother as punishment for her own sins in the past. Such a daughter, just consider, is not only a disgrace to your own family name, but to the whole Tao Village as well. You very well know that according to age-old custom this crime merits nothing less than death. Recall, now, the case of the Chao girl—it happened three or four years ago in Stone Gate Village—who was beaten to death for the very same offence. Do you remember, she was buried without even a coffin?

Nobody could call it cruelty, but only justice, for she had violated the laws of right conduct. Moreover, the worst of it is that even after their death such girls continue to dishonour the good name of the community. Ending life does not end their sin. . . . No, indeed, and, as every one knows, death doesn't begin to make up for it!"

"What you have just said is undeniably true. Death doesn't cover up the crime at all. But, on the other hand, it's not altogether the girl's fault. . . . The mother is to blame also: a certain laxness, a waning of discipline. Again, in this case it may be that the mother was not herself very virtuous in some previous incarnation. . . . Widow Wang, let me advise you to take care. In this life you had better be more strict."

The Village Elder was the donor of this speech, which oddly did not seem to anger the Widow, but on the contrary encouraged her to speak. She moved forward timidly, her hands pulling nervously on the edge of her worn dress. She spoke, in a very low voice, and smiled painfully:

"Yes . . . Honoured Elder . . . that is correct. If she did wrong it was really my fault. I don't know what unpardonable sin I have behind me in some previous existence, but it must be as you say. And this terrible crime of my daughter, you're quite right, death would only be the punishment deserved. Still——" she broke suddenly into tears. "But I can't speak, I haven't 'face' to say—only I ask—*mercy*! Spare her life at least!"

This was a bold demand, an extraordinary request indeed, and were it not that the villagers were at that moment eating her food she would never have escaped ridicule by them. They believed in enforcing justice and morality to the letter, and ordinarily would stand no nonsense. Yet it seemed generally understood that because they had appeared, and had eaten, and had enjoyed themselves, and had some of them even come on their own invitation, they would not be altogether adamant. But their decision rested upon the opinions voiced by Chin the Rich, Wu the Merchant, and the Hairy-headed Elder. Everybody remained silent until Chin finally gave the verdict.

"Wu has, I agree, spoken very wisely, and very much to the point. 'Death doesn't begin to cover up the crime.' Precisely! Then, perhaps, or so it seems to me, little is to be gained by taking her life now. The guilt has been admitted, and the widow Wang, asking mercy, has begged us also to give 'face' to her late husband. She wants us to spare her daughter's life, and, everything considered, that is perhaps possible, but at the same time we cannot permit such an altogether immoral woman to continue to stain the village good name. She must leave at once!"

The Elder shared this view. "What is done is done. Though totally without honour, still it's no use, now, to kill her. . . . Better, as you say, expel her—move her out immediately!"

These two having rendered a judgment, the rest of the guests, who considered themselves a kind of jury, reined in their tongues. The decision was unanimously approved. The pale, weary face of Wang broke out suddenly into a genuine smile, she bowed low to the three wise men, and obsequiously thanked the members of the self-appointed jury. Back in the darkness the hidden Ah Ao heard, and yet curiously she did not feel happy at all at this reprieve. She understood well enough that life had been miraculously restored to her, but while the prospect of death had been terrifying she was after all too young to have a deep fear of it, whereas to be banished from the village, to leave and never again to see her mother, to bid farewell to her brother, to plunge into an unknown, uncertain future—that was something which she knew to be worse than death. Grief shook her body, seemed to break, to shatter it, so that it was no longer whole, but a heap of something that mysteriously still trembled with life.

II

It had happened two months before, in early April, on a day filled with an ineffable softness, an unbearable languor and gladness that made men dreamy-eyed, drowsy, and as if drunk with some wonderful wine.

Ah Ao, on her way home in the afternoon from the nearby Yu Village, thought that she had never known such a glorious day. There was a new warmth in her body, a strange vigour in her as if she had just begun to live. The fields bordering the road were touched from a withered yellow into a lush new green, the trees were coming to life, and in their budding limbs birds had appeared and were joyously chattering. The whole world, as far as she could see, was young, fresh, growing, awakened, expectant. She felt in harmony with all that she saw, and expectant too. Of what? She did not know, but somehow she found herself walking more slowly. Her face burned as from some inner fire, and she became all at once conscious of her body, vibrant and warm against the fabric of her garments.

"Ah Ao!" a voice called from somewhere.

Surprised and a little afraid, she stopped, looked round, peered over the fields, into the clustered pines and through the rocky pass, but saw no one. Above her head a pair of eagles circled. She blushed, rubbed her burning face, and walked on.

"Ah Ao!" some one cried again, this time much nearer. She stopped, more puzzled, but saw no one, and started to go on, when once more she heard the same voice, now quite close, speak out:

"Ah Ao, it's me."

Turning round quickly she saw, protruding from the bushes and greenery, a head. Then slowly a young man in a long linen gown gave her a full-length view of himself, including his handsome red-buttoned cap. He was perhaps twenty years old, not a bad-looking fellow, and he wore on his face a pleased look. Ah Ao recognized him. He was the son of Li, a shop-owner in the neighbouring village. His name, she knew, was Ah Hsian.

"*Ai-ya!* So it's you," said Ah Ao. "You frightened me almost to death. Where did you come from?"

Nevertheless, she seemed not altogether dissatisfied that he had appeared.

"I?" he demanded. "I? I just happened to be coming from town, saw you in the distance, and hid myself to have some fun with you."

"You impudent rascal!" she shouted gaily, raising her hand as if to slap him. "Frightening a person to death!"

"I apologize, Ah Ao, with all my heart. The truth is I have something very important to tell you."

"For example?"

But the youth suddenly became weak or timid. He kept murmuring "I—I—I——" Then he seized her hand.

"What is this?" Ah Ao started back quickly, but for some reason her legs refused to move. Her body quivered, as from some shock, and again she felt her flesh tingle under her cotton garments. All the strength seemed to run out of her. He put his arms around her, pulled her towards him, and then led her into the forest. She could not summon up any resistance, her mind did not seem to work as usual, she was hardly conscious that they moved at all; and she did not utter a sound. She only knew that within she felt intolerably buoyant and enlarged.

They sat down under the leafy arm of a tree, her head resting upon his shoulder. Her eyes closed and she breathed rapidly. She felt his hand close softly over her breast, over her beating heart. His lips touched hers, and suddenly she felt a bodily glow that she had never known before.

"Caw-w-w!"

A magpie, wheeling overhead, startled her, and for a moment recalled to her that the world existed. She trembled.

"Ah Hsian! No, no! Don't, please! Mother will beat me to death!"

"Don't! You must not worry. Trust me, believe in me. Everything will be wonderful, like this always. . . ."

His voice shook too, and some strange vibrancy of it, some summons she had never heard, and which would not be denied, completely overpowered her. He caressed her arms, her face, her throat. She ceased to resist.

III

"What is the matter with you, Ah Ao?" Widow Wang asked her daughter when, very much agitated, she returned home late that afternoon. "Fever?" She touched her forehead, which was covered with a short fringe of hair. "Have you caught a cold?"

"Nothing at all. I—I simply don't feel very well," Ah Ao murmured, half to herself. She went to the bed and lay down, and for a long time she did not stir. She knew very well the risks, the danger, the fate opening up ahead of her, but just as well she knew that she would meet Ah Hsian again, whenever he asked, yes, even to-morrow!

She expected something dreadful to happen; she prepared herself for it. In the future, after each interval with him, she waited dully for the exposure of their crime, and each time was rather surprised when no one came to denounce her. Nevertheless, she resigned herself to ultimate discovery, but found comfort in the thought that her lover would come to her defence, take punishment as pronounced. She imagined herself, in his moment of disgrace, going proudly to his side, sharing whatever fate imposed upon him. And what she constantly feared did happen at last, but its consequences were nothing like what she had romantically foreseen. It was just three days before the Widow Wang offered the villagers such a splendid banquet.

Behind Purple-red Mountain there was a small hill, the

name of which had long been forgotten. Half-way up its flank, nearly buried in the foliage, was a temple to the mountain god, but few visited it, and hardly anyone passed over the hill at all, with the exception of somebody now and then using a short cut to Stone Gate Village. The surrounding forests were owned by one of the great landlords; few ventured to trespass through the leafy lanes. The place was pervaded by a ghostly stillness, but it was gentle shelter for young lovers.

On this day Lao Teh, the Spotted Face, a woodcutter, had stealthily crept into the forest to steal wood. He had gathered a load and was prepared to leave just as the setting sun splashed ruddily against the wall behind the mountain temple. The sight invited him, and, lifting the burden from his shoulder, he sat down on the threshold of the enclosure, sighed, lighted his pipe, and leisurely gazed at the sky.

But was that not a sound? Thrusting the pipe into his girdle he seized his axe, and stood ready to combat with any wild animal that might rush forth. He waited for several minutes, tense and excited. He thought of running away, but reconsidered, remembering that an offensive is the best defensive. Picking up a stone as big as a goose egg, he threw it with all his strength into the thickest part of the forest.

To his astonishment it was not a wild beast but a man that burst from the trees. He did not stop or even look in Lao Teh's direction, but vanished like a devil. Lao Teh nevertheless saw enough of him to recognize Ah Hsian. Somewhat perplexed, he advanced towards the spot whence he had emerged.

Then in a moment he came upon Ah Ao, languidly spread out, with her dress loosened, her dark hair starred with bits of green leaves, and altogether wearing a look of abandon. The spectacle somehow aroused in Lao Teh, the Spotted Face, an intense fury, and he shook with his excess of indignation. He stared with wide-open eyes, and then he bent down and severely struck her.

"Ha! Ah Ao! The devil! You've done a fine thing!" She did not speak, but lifted up eyes that implored, and eloquently begged pity. "Scandalous and shameless one! To come here in secret and lie with him!" He viciously slapped her again.

Later on, this scene, and the subsequent abuse flung upon her by the infuriated Lao Teh, remained rather obscure in Ah Ao's mind. She could not remember how, under his guidance, she returned home in disgrace, nor how news of her love spread throughout the village in a few minutes. Only afterwards all the eyes she looked into were full of wrath: cold-gleaming eyes of hate. Even her mother gazed at her with anger and bitterness, yet deeper, deep down in those eyes, was a look of poignant sadness that troubled her heart. But the blows of bamboo sticks, the beatings that came in rapid succession, the curses hurled at her, not one of these caused her any pain, nor any shame, nor even the least regret.

She had expected all this, and now it had come. It was no accident, but had all along been in the certainty of fate, and she was prepared for everything that happened. The single unforeseen development that dismayed and depressed her was that her lover suffered none of the consequences, and did not appear to be in the least interested in her any longer.

IV

The three days had gone by as an incident in a dream, and now the verdict of the wise men had been pronounced. Not to die; it was true that she felt some relief at this decision; yet she was far from happy. Her body felt old, heavy, infinitely weary, and her spirit was completely crushed, crushed not by anything that had been said of her or done to her, not even by the bitter sadness of her mother's eyes, but by the singularly irresponsible and cowardly conduct of her lover.

Even before the men guests had finished sipping the last of their wine the women began to come for their share, and during all this time Ah Ao continued to press closely against the wall, hovering in her hiding-place, hungry and shivering, not because it was cold, not because she felt any longer the fear of death, but from some nameless malady that had seized her inmost being. The women ate no more lightly than their men folk. It was late at night when the last of them finished, and one by one began to return home. Like the men they dropped cynical, sardonic remarks meant to stab mother and daughter cruelly, as they ate, with enormous appetites, the food heaped before them.

The air seemed charged with heightened drama when Mrs Li, mother of Ah Hsian, unexpectedly appeared at the feast. She had come, it was soon apparent, not to apologize for the part her son had taken in the affair, but on the contrary to curse Wang the Widow for permitting her daughter to induce him to commit adultery. She began her vituperations even before she entered the house. The widow, seeing her fat body waddling along at a distance, went forth to meet her with a sinking heart. Mrs Li propelled herself across the stone bridge arched over the mountain stream, and rushed towards the Wangs' door. Then, seeing the unhappy mother, she drew back a few feet, pointed fixedly at her, and began to revile her in a loud voice:

"Miserable woman! Where there is such a daughter, there is such a mother also! And you have the 'face' to come out to meet me? Actually? My son is pure, chaste, good; he has made the genuflexions before the image of Confucius; he has understood well the teachings of the great sage. Yet you, shameless mother, and immoral daughter, attempt to seduce and ruin him! I am resolved to die with you this instant!"

And, saying this, she did indeed rush towards the Widow Wang and appeared to be determined to dash her brains out against her. Other women guests grouped round them, forming a little circle (not without experiencing an inner satisfaction at the scene), and comforted and soothed the wrath of the offended Mrs Li. In fact, the fat woman so far forgot her original intention that she permitted them to lead her into the house. She even partook heartily of the feast, and in the end contented herself with muttering now and then, "She abused my son, seduced him. . . . From now on he will be unable to raise his head above others."

When the last guest had gone the old widow stepped slowly into the little dark enclosure, carrying an oil-lamp in her hand. She called to Ah Ao to come out, and to eat, and she gradually dragged herself forth, but the whole day of hiding, lying cramped in such confinement, had so wearied her that now she had scarcely strength enough to stand erect. A moment ago she had thought herself famished, but now she could not swallow a morsel.

Midnight. Widow Wang was not yet in bed. She moved about in the little room, picking up articles from here and there, busily arranging them in the baggage which Ah Ao must take with her when she left at to-morrow's dawn. Finally she fastened the bag securely, and then at once opened it again, adding two more pairs of stockings. She stood silent for a moment, thinking; then from an old broken cupboard she pulled out a linen skirt, and that seemed to complete the traveller's wardrobe.

Spring nights are brief, and in a very short time the cocks began to crow. The widow awoke her son and daughter, lighted a lantern, gave them their morning food, and then accompanied Ah Ao to the barrow which stood beside the door.

"Understand, daughter, it's not I who wants to desert you—you have spoiled yourself——"

But the stooped figure shook with sudden tears. She

seemed to brace herself against the air, and continued, managing to smile very gently, "Just be careful, Ah Ao. From now on stand firmly on your own feet, and I shall have no more cause for worry. As for me, daughter, well, just think that I am dead, no longer in this world. If we can't meet here again, then perhaps after death . . . anyway, let's hope. . . ."

She sat beside Ah Ao on the barrow pushed by her son until they reached the great oak, at the main road, half a mile from her home. She alighted there, bid a last farewell to her daughter, and stood watching the receding lantern till, like the last flutter of life in a great void of death, its dim spark crept into utter darkness.

T'IEN CHÜN

(1908–)

Lu Hsün regards T'ien Chün (whose real name is Hsiao Chün) as one of the best writers thus far produced by the modern Chinese literary movement. He considers his wife, Hsiao Hung, as perhaps the most talented young woman writer, ranking her above Ting Ling.

T'ien Chün is very nearly a real 'proletarian writer,' a species very rare in China, if it may be said to exist at all. His book, *Village in August*, which describes the life and adventures of anti-Japanese volunteer bands who fight against the conquerors in Manchuria, was immensely popular when published in 1935, and was lavishly praised by critics. In response to a request from the editor, he has written the following biographical note of himself:

"I was born in Manchuria in 1908, in a not-too-small village separated by some seventy *li* of mountain paths from the nearest city. The population consisted of peasants, craftsmen, hunters, soldiers, and mounted highwaymen—*i.e.*, bandits.

"My grandfather was a peasant and my uncles and my father were at first farmers, then carpenters, and later on merchants, army officers, and 'mounted bandits.' At times my family had property, at times we owned nothing at all. After the Mukden Incident [September 18, 1931, when Japan invaded Manchuria] my father and three of his brothers—the youngest still clung to his carpentry—enlisted in the Volunteer Army against the Japanese. My third uncle is now imprisoned in 'Manchukuo.' The little property we had, including some houses and lands, has been confiscated by the 'Manchukuo' authorities.

"I received no systematic education, was invariably expelled by the authorities of every school I attended, and in all studied in school only six or seven years.

"In 1925 I joined the army, and remained a soldier for about six years. I was in the cavalry, infantry, gendarmery, artillery, and the cadet corps, and later became a junior officer. I joined the Volunteers in 1931 also, but after a while I began my literary career in a Manchurian city. I came to Shanghai in 1934.

"Besides my career in the army I have been a vagabond-tramp, a secretary, an apprentice to a professional boxer—one of those stunt-doers in open-air markets—a waiter, a millstone pusher in a bean-curd shop, and what-not. My ambition was to become a regular in the 'mounted-bandit' corps, and though I did not succeed, and am now writing novels, I still cherish that hope, and perhaps some day it will be realized.

"My interest in literature began in childhood, and about ten years ago I began to write. I was then in the army. At first I diligently studied Chinese classical poetry, the *shih* and the *tz'ŭ*, and later I read the works of Lu Hsün and Kuo Mo-jo— the former's stories, the latter's poetry. Among the earliest works of new literature I read was Lu Hsün's *Wild Grass*, which I have always loved most. Among foreign authors I have liked Goethe and Chekhov best. As I read more I discovered the Soviet writers, among whose works I especially liked Gorki's *Mother* and A. Serafimovitch's *Sheleznyi Potok*, both of which greatly moved me, especially the latter, which had a profound influence on me. I have read little of the works of contemporary Chinese writers other than Lu Hsün and Kuo Mo-jo, hence I have not felt their influence.

"I am stirred by the characters of my own creation; for me they are real beings. I become completely absorbed in the environment and atmosphere built up by my own pen, and I confess that I find it interesting to be 'deceived' by my own art.

"The only 'purpose' of my literary work is to help liberate all oppressed people from their unhappy lot.

" SHANGHAI
   May 21, 1936 "

ABOARD THE S.S. DAIREN MARU[1]

By T'IEN CHÜN

OUR friend W. accompanied us to the *Dairen Maru*, but left without permitting us to say good-bye.

Before we had even become accustomed to the odour of the air in the cabin we found ourselves surrounded.

My wife and I were preparing to spread out our bedding.

"Where are you going?" a fat, short fellow asked me. Behind him stood four men, two in police uniform with pistols, two in plain clothes.

"To Tsingtao."

My heart jumped a beat, even though we had expected this. I only hoped that the search would not be too severe. Once finished, I would soon stand on our beloved native soil on the other side of the sea, where everything would come to my rescue.

With their hands and eyes they examined my body, and went over my baggage like dogs.

My wife was pale. She had just recovered from illness, and her unusually hollow eyes now showed anxiety. We were gambling for life in the mouth of a monster.

"Where do you come from?"

"From ——"

I did all I could to control my pulsing blood.

"What was your profession there?"

"An office worker at the headquarters of ——"

I knew one of my friends worked there. I took his

---

[1] This story is a factually correct description of the close scrutiny now maintained over Chinese travelling between China and Japan's "Manchukuo."

profession for mine. I had long been—well, let us say an unemployed beggar.

"Tell me the name of your Commander, his headquarters, his family name, official name, private name, and his age."

My blood raced faster and faster, as if determined to burst its vessels.

"His family name is ——; official name ——; private name ——. Now . . . he is . . . about fifty years of age."

"What? *About* fifty?"

His narrow eyes widened and the relaxed muscles of his face tightened. The men behind him stared, open-eyed. I saw that the two armed men had rested their hands on their pistols. The batons of the other two swung back and forth.

My wife's eyes were wide with anxiety.

"My Commander was fifty years old last year. This year he would be fifty-one," I explained.

"Well, you even forget the age of your superior! Why do you now go to Tsingtao? Who is this woman?" he asked.

"She is my wife. We are going home," I explained.

"Why, then you are a Shantung man? You speak . . ." he began.

"I am a Manchukuo man." I became calm again.

"Then why is your home in Shantung?" he asked.

"My father is there."

"What does your father do there?"

"He is a business man."

"What kind of business?"

"Money exchanger."

"Name of his shop?"

"——"

"On what road?"

"—— road."

"Why are you going home?" Another series of questions seemed to begin.

"We married recently and wish to go home to see our parents."

"Married recently?" His eyes travelled back and forth from my face to my wife's, then back again. I did not really know if we looked like a newly married couple on a honeymoon trip.

"Did you resign your position or ask for leave of absence?"

"I resigned."

"Give me your name card and your certificate of resignation." He held out his hand. It was a fat, thick hand, on which one could read cruelty.

"I do not have . . ."

Silence, silence throughout the cabin. The sound of the sea lapping against the side of the steamer came to me. A sunbeam of late spring fell upon the mat on the floor before me, and with it a gentle breeze came through the porthole.

"I did not think these were necessary. I am not in official uniform, and do not require such certificates to identify myself," I answered.

"No—you do not look like a good man." The fat man's eyes covered my body from head to foot, then returned to stare into mine.

"Judging by your eyes alone, you are not a good man. . . . A good man would not have such eyes as yours. . . . Come along with me!" he ordered.

So it was my eyes that offended him!

In the other place the questioning went on for about an hour. Finally he said he would have to take me ashore for further examination. I remember now that a feeling of absolute despair came over me. If he took me to the maritime police-station I would be subjected to all kinds of torture—I would be whipped, have kerosene or pepper and water forced through my nostrils. Everything would be finished for me.

One is always calm when in despair. One may even be

o

more brave. So I now walked with determined steps before this man. Before we reached the door he halted me.

"No. . . . Come this way!" I turned in the direction his hand indicated. I thought he might want to take my wife also. So much the better, for then we could die or be imprisoned together.

I found my wife's examiners had left her. She stood, leaning against the porthole, gazing out at the sea. I saw how thin her back had become from illness. A pain darted through my heart.

"Bring your things here. I want to examine them," the man was ordering me.

I moved everything I had brought with me—a middle-sized canvas suitcase and a willow basket. Men with pistols and batons came back again.

The fat, stout man examined every shirt and every pair of socks. He was as thorough as a second-hand dealer or a pawnshop owner. The only thing lacking was the bargaining.

He also examined a pile of white letter-paper, holding it up to the light, one piece at a time. He was as faithful as a dog, I thought.

Everything was examined. When he found that I was eating an apple he remarked:

"You enjoy yourself very much!"

When leaving the cabin he repeatedly turned to look back at me as if to say, "It seems to me he is not a good man."

The sound from the turning capstan was heard. I knew the sailors were lifting the anchor.

The waves beat beautifully and free, but my heart and my body were cramped as if fettered. My wife and I gazed at each other in silence. We then turned to the sea—the unconquerable sea—thinking of that other shore.

When the night was deep and no one but we two were on deck my wife's low, vibrant voice asked, "When will the steamer enter the harbour?"

"Not until ten or twelve to-morrow morning," I replied.
Her hand lightly brushed over mine as I grasped the deck
railing.

"If . . ." We both turned to look, but still there was no
other person on deck but us.

"If . . . if they come to worry me again I would rather
leap into the sea. . . . I would rather feed the fish with my
body!"

My wife's face turned still more pale. "You . . . must
not say that!" I felt anxiety overtake her again.

The sound of the rough waves churning ceaselessly under
the steamer came to us. The wind was no longer gentle.
We returned to the cabin, and my wife fell asleep. I lay,
listening to the cry of the sea. An old, witchlike woman
was smoking opium on the next mat, unconcerned with
it all.

On the second morning the green mountains of Tsingtao
fringed the horizon. A little warmth crept into my frozen
heart.

"Oh, my own country!" we both cried, as if possessed.

THE THIRD GUN [1]

By T'IEN CHUN

THE fields were heavy with red-eared grain that burned tall and straight and unbending in the strong sunshine. Harvest-time was drawing near, and yet nobody seemed to care about it this year, and among the young farmers especially it was an event regarded with complete indifference.

Sickles were shelved and rusting under the eaves. Nothing was ready for the cutting of the grain. Young men were concentrating their enthusiasm on shouldering rifles and 'inspecting,' or guarding places to which they had been assigned. When occasionally they came together they discussed the latest news from headquarters, they talked about matters unknown to their ancestors, they told really *new* stories.

Nobody betrayed any fear. On the contrary each youth competed with the others to demonstrate his courage, and vowed his determination to destroy the Japanese troops— and especially the officers of the Japanese. They regarded these enemies with genuine contempt. They considered them utterly worthless *tung-hsi.*[2] Sometimes they even sneered at the Russians. The old people had told them that in the Russo–Japanese war many Russian soldiers had been

---

[1] In the mountainous regions of Manchuria there are still many thousands of Chinese who have never recognized Japanese authority. Organized as Reds, Red partisans, patriotic Volunteer Corps, and ordinary bandits, they frequently attack and decimate Japanese and Manchukuo troops.

[2] Literally, 'things.'

defeated by the Japanese. They said it was because the soldiers of Russia in those days were undisciplined drunkards.

"*Mother's*, in such a time as this there is no choice but to fight! In the end, unless they die we cannot live! Can we stand by and watch the Japanese becoming bolder and more arrogant each day and do nothing? Can we give up our wives and children without making any struggle? Can we watch them, together with our parents, knocked over by the invading turtles' eggs? . . . Our Commander—there is a real man now!"

"The Commander, eh? But if his whole family had not been killed by the Japanese he would never have fought so bravely! Men have to be grossly oppressed to make them fight like that. . . . By the way, the new recruits are seven people from Prosperous Town. Did you know? They all have guns." This came from young T'ang, who lay under a tree with his eyes half-closed and his gun lying ready beside him.

"I hear these seven began as nine. Two of them 'disappeared' on the way. I don't include Hsiao-ming, who is one of our own people."

"Hsiao-ming! There's a young fellow who will do! He was a student, but he hasn't forgotten to 'eat bitterness' like the rest of us. He hasn't spent his time reading for nothing."

Overhead the sun licked at them with fiery tongues. Everybody had moved into the shady comfort of the tree. The grain hung limply, and so did the grass. Even the insects, except for the grasshoppers with their incessant singing, were silent. At the end of the village the pigs and their young were burying themselves in the marsh. Dogs stood with long-hanging tongues in the shadow of the wall. Naked children, their bellies bulging, stole cucumbers from the gardens as their parents slept through the hot period.

It was like peace at midday centuries ago. The cry of the

cock rose slowly on the air and then descended just as slowly. How steady the noon!

But young T'ang could not sleep. First he pulled up a blade of grass and, sticking it between his lips, imitated the singing of the birds. People around him grumbled and cursed. He laughed, and, taking up his gun, strode away. Not far off, in a small cottage beside the road, lived a certain Mrs Li, and it was precisely in that direction that he ambled in his restless mood. . . .

Peering through an opening in the wall he saw her holding her baby close to a generous breast, with her hair shimmering down abundantly from her bending head. She was humming, and in her voice there was an invitation as irresistible to T'ang as the glimpse of her warm breast, opened darkly above the infant's head.

He picked up a small stone and tossed it against the shutter behind which stood Mrs Li.

"Who is it?" she cried in a hushed voice.

Pushing open the gate he showed at first only his face, and Mrs Li laughed shyly and sweetly.

"You—the impudent one! Why appear like a devil or a ghost? Afraid of the wolf, or afraid the Japanese will eat you?"

T'ang's eyes narrowed to a crack and his mouth lengthened towards his ears. He was a man of action and not words. He moved into the cottage and stood beside Mrs Li, resting his arms on the ledge of the window, which was made of thick cords of wood, as heavy and unfinished as arms. From here he could, if he chose, touch Mrs Li or anything about her, while the world slept under the midday sun.

"Why are you here again instead of at your duty?" she asked him, her eyelids heavy and her eyes very large and warming at his every movement. The deep blackness of his luxuriant hair, the golden line of his chest, and his round naked shoulders . . . they all disturbed her.

"Is the child sleeping?"

"Why do you ask? Does it concern you, you wind-blown thing? . . . What's on your mind again?"

He did not reply. He was busy caressing her blushing cheek, which only blushed all the more, accompanied by the beating of her heart, which raced all the more.

"Just you wait. . . . I'll put down the baby. . . . Unless I give you a full blow it's quite evident you will continue to under-estimate my strength!"

She pulled away and lay the child on the *k'ang*, but she did not strike him after all. Her cheeks were still crimson; she dared not raise her head. Instead she drew up and arranged her hair, and while she was shaping it into order the young peasant's beard somehow found her blood-filled lips, and in a moment his brown bare shoulders were throbbing against her own bountiful breast. For a moment they stood thus in peace. Then she began to resist. They cursed and struggled until anyone looking on might have thought each was determined to devour the other. . . .

He softly closed the door of the cottage, feeling weak as if faint. He did not return blowing a grass-blade in imitation of the birds, but carrying a gun on his shoulder that weighed at least five catties more than the one with which he had arrived.

Under the great tree the men sat holding their guns in their hands. Had anything happened? He grew suddenly alarmed.

"You donkey! Where have you been loafing? Such people as you will ruin us all! If it happens again we'll discuss it with headquarters——"

The Commanding Officer was enraged. His long body standing perfectly rigid, a revolver dangling from his wrist, he looked like a wingless eagle. He had been a farmer of Fengtien, then a soldier, then a bandit, and now he had joined the People's Revolutionary Army. He fought the Japanese, and every one who helped them in any way, or any one who opposed the Revolution. He wasted no sentiment over his victims. He was unbending in the discipline he imposed, and his men had nicknamed him "Iron Eagle" —an acknowledgment of his bravery as well as his severity.

"Take this man to headquarters, and bring him back," he ordered T'ang now, motioning to a newcomer.

T'ang could not find a word of explanation for his own conduct before such a Commanding Officer, and he docilely led away the new arrival, a man dressed like a farmer but really with the look of a worker about him. Judging only from his nostrils and the deep sockets of his eyes one would say that he had lived long in an iron foundry.

"From Straw Market, comrade?" T'ang asked him.

"Straw Market." He looked very tired, as if he had run too fast or too far. As they walked through the fields he inquired several times the distance to headquarters.

T'ang was curious about him and the kind of news he brought, or his errand, but he decided that it was not his business. Finally he asked, "Are you working in the railway shops?"

"Yes," he replied, and as he turned his head he saw the red badge, marked with a simple yellow star, that was bound on T'ang's sleeve. It was faded, but still you could see that it had once been red. The stranger smiled.

"*You* are all armed!" he exclaimed, "but the only weapon we have is the strike. And so we strike! Our factory is surrounded with barbed wire and trenches, and machine-guns are pointed at us day and night. Japanese troops are stationed around us. But they dare not——"

Suddenly he saw the red flag waving ahead, and he pulled off his cap. His eyes filled with happiness.

"Is that headquarters?"

T'ang confirmed it, and, noticing how deeply this comrade seemed to be moved by the sight, he felt queerly exalted himself. Everything else seemed insignificant beside the glowing splendour of their common purpose.

It was a strange kind of male happiness that poured through him then, something quite different from and greater than the glory of the adorable Mrs Li.

"What is your name, comrade?"

T'ang not only gave his name; he continued excitedly to tell this city-man all about himself and his regiment and their exploits.

A breeze rustled the grain and murmured its way through the throng of bean leaves. It brought to them the fragrance of wild raspberries and the chuckle of a running brook, and they thirsted.

"The Japs are the seed of urine! They are as stupid as bears, and yet imagine they can climb mountains! Up here all their fine equipment is useless—their heavy guns, their machine-guns, the droppings of their aeroplanes! We know the country, we know the highways and the byways, and where the caves are. Our numbers are increasing—nearly every day new ones come in to join us!"

"At headquarters you will see a girl. She will talk to you . . . she often lectures to us—and how she *can* speak! She shoots just as well! At the same time she teaches us characters and fully explains why we must fight the Japanese and drive them away."

His mouth felt very dry, and it was not easy for him to speak, but he was determined to tell all he knew.

"You cannot see that she is a foreigner. You would never know it, but she is really a Korean! Her father was a Korean revolutionary leader. Killed at Shanghai by the Japanese—or . . . She has studied in China. . . ."

They passed through the fortified gate of the mud-walled village. A guard questioned the new comrade and then led him away. T'ang went off to amuse himself with his friends.

. . . . . .

At dusk everything was ready for the attack.

No breeze was alive and the tall grain did not move at all.

Beside the silent rails that stretched tranquilly over their mattress of wooden sleepers lay thirty volunteers—with only twenty guns.

Iron Eagle, the revolver hanging from his wrist, walked back and forth, examining every man's position and turning his fierce eyes on their arms. If their rifles were levelled too high they would be seen. The oncoming enemy would stop, make preparations, and things would be difficult. Bullets would be spent for nothing.

"Comrades, wait for my order!"

He always spoke sharply, and took no back-talk. When he gave an order he seemed to become the living order itself. T'ang was not entirely satisfied with this; he thought some of the decisions should be discussed, but he never disobeyed. Just now he chewed to bits a piece of herb, spat it out, and then replaced it with another. He thought of Mrs Li's round dark breasts.

Wearing on their heads green wreaths made of leaves, instead of caps, they lay completely hidden from view. Behind them the ten men without guns searched about for sharp-cornered stones.

"Nobody in sight yet?" asked one.

"Can you hear anything on the rails?"

"Unlucky *tung-hsi*, having eaten fully, they now have to pay for it with their lives!"

"It is a hundred *li* from here to Straw Market. . . . Our turtles must have drunk well! Maybe they are also bringing us something on the train—wine, meat, tinned beef! True or not?"

"Hush!"

A prolonged whistle sounded not very far away, and in a little while the persistent and monotonous tune of turning wheels rumbled down the rails. High up on a tree a man signalled to them with a small red flag.

The mountains here rose up sharply on each side and the track lay imbedded between them as neatly as in a tunnel.

Iron Eagle now flung himself down at the head of the little detachment. The whistle still hung from his mouth, but the revolver no longer merely dangled from his wrist.

The chant on the rails deepened. In every face jawbones were hard and set, and eyes burned with excitement. They scarcely breathed. Though this was not their first encounter, still their hands trembled slightly on tightly held guns.

A sudden breeze danced capriciously across the fields, blowing cool and sweet. How deep the peace of evening!

There was a roar, and a cruel bellow. The whistle screamed in agony. The train hurtled from the track and lay on its side like a paralysed snake. Only its wheels continued to spin.

They soon restored order among the frightened passengers. At one side they collected the dazed Manchukuo guards—Chinese like themselves. Inside the train they found plenty of beer and food, *en route* to the Japanese troops at P'ing Ch'uan. There was ammunition, and there were rifles too.

"Thanks, brothers, our little ammunition-carriers. And thanks for bringing us so many rifles this time."

The Commanding Officer looked at his prisoners kindly, but warily. The revolver once more hung from his wrist. The train-guards were grey and weary, but their fear gradually faded. One of them, emboldened after a moment, called out the name of Iron Eagle.

"Commander," he said, "I know you. This is the second time you have disarmed me. Do you want the third gun or not? If you do, then you will free us! The third gun will be delivered promptly!"

"All right, it's a promise. I'm sorry we had to shake you up a bit, brothers—couldn't be helped. I'll release you immediately."

The two captains, however, were taken away to be shot.

Every man had two guns on his way back through the dark acres of grain. Only Iron Eagle, the Commander, still wore on his wrist that same revolver.

LIN YÜ-T'ANG

(1895–)

LIN YÜ-T'ANG has become internationally known through his deservedly popular book, *My Country and My People*, which depicts the present decay and collapse of quasi-feudal Chinese civilization in an attractive nostalgic manner.

Born in Changchow, Amoy, he went to St John's, a missionary school in Shanghai, graduating in 1916. From 1916 to 1919 he taught at Tsing Hua University. Subsequently he studied at Harvard University and at Leipzig, where he received doctorate degrees. He joined the staff of Peking National University in 1923 and taught there until 1926.

After 1927 he devoted himself exclusively to writing, at which he has been extremely successful, both in Chinese and English. His column, "The Little Critic," in the *China Critic*, a weekly published in English by the Chinese intellectual dilettanti of Shanghai, has long been the chief feature of that journal. Meanwhile Lin has edited two popular magazines of humour and satire, *The* [Confucian] *Analects* and *Jen Chien Shih*, which have contributed much towards the development of the art of humour in Chinese literature. He is also co-editor of the *T'ien Hsia* monthly, Shanghai, in English.

Besides *My Country and My People* Lin Yü-t'ang has written several books of essays, some English textbooks, plays, and serious works on philology.

THE DOG-MEAT GENERAL [1]
By Lin Yü-t'ang

So General Chang Tsung-chang, the "Dog-meat General," has been killed, according to this morning's report. I am sorry for him, and I am sorry for his mother, and I am sorry for the sixteen concubines he has left behind him and the four times sixteen that had left him before he died. As I intend to specialize in writing 'in memoriams' for the bewildering generals of this bewildering generation, I am going to begin with the Dog-meat General first.

So our Dog-meat General is dead! What an event! It is full of mystic significance for me and for China and us poor folk who do not wear boots and carry bayonets! Such a thing could not happen every day, and if it could there would be an end to all China's sorrows. In such an eventuality you could abolish all the five Yuan, tear up the will of Dr Sun Yat-sen, dismiss the hundred odd members of the Central Executive Committee of the Kuomintang, close up all the schools and universities of China, and you wouldn't have to bother your head about Communism, Fascism, and Democracy, and universal suffrage, and emancipation of women, and we poor folk would still be able to live in peace and prosperity.

So one more of the colourful, legendary figures of medieval China has passed into eternity. And yet Dog-meat General's death has a special significance for me, because he was the most colourful, legendary, medieval, and unashamed ruler of modern China. He was a born

[1] General Chang Tsung-chang, for many years a powerful North China war-lord, was assassinated in 1933.

ruler such as modern China wants. He was six feet tall, a
towering giant, with a pair of squint eyes and a pair of
abnormally massive hands. He was direct, forceful, terribly
efficient at times: obstinate and gifted with moderate intelligence. He was patriotic according to his lights, and he was
anti-communist, which made up for his being anti-
Kuomintang. All his critics must allow that he wasn't
anti-Kuomintang from convictions, but by accident. He
didn't want to fight the Kuomintang: it was the Kuomintang
that wanted to fight him and grab his territory, and, being
an honest man, he fought rather than turn tail. Given a
chance, and if the Kuomintang would return him his
Shantung,[1] he would join the Kuomintang, because he
said that the Sanmin[2] doctrine can't do any harm.

He could drink, and he was awfully fond of 'dog-meat,'
and he could swear all he wanted to and as much as he
wanted to, irrespective of his official superiors and inferiors.
He made no pretence to being a gentleman, and didn't affect
to send nice-sounding circular telegrams, like the rest of
them. He was ruthlessly honest, and this honesty made him
much loved by all his close associates. If he loved women
he said so, and he could see foreign consuls while he had a
Russian girl sitting on his knee. If he made orgies he didn't
try to conceal them from his friends and foes. If he coveted
his subordinate's wife he told him openly, and wrote no
psalm of repentance about it like King David. And he
always played square. If he took his subordinate's wife he
made her husband the chief of police of Tsinan. And he
took good care of other people's morals. He forbade girl
students from entering parks in Tsinan, and protected them
from the men-gorillas who stood at every corner and nook
to devour them. And he was pious, and he kept a harem.
He believed in polyandry as well as polygamy, and he
openly allowed his concubines to make love with other

[1] The province in which Chang Tsung-chang ruled as satrap.
[2] The "Three Principles" of Dr Sun Yat-sen.

men, provided he didn't want them at the time. He respected Confucius. And he was patriotic. He was reported to be overjoyed to find a bed-bug in a Japanese bed in Beppo, and he never tired of telling people of the consequent superiority of Chinese civilization. He was very fond of his executioner, and he was thoroughly devoted to his mother.

Many legends have been told about Dog-meat's ruthless honesty. He loved a Russian prostitute and his Russian prostitute loved a poodle, and he made a whole regiment pass in review before the poodle to show that he loved the prostitute that loved the poodle. Once he appointed a man magistrate in a certain district in Shantung, and another day he appointed another man to the same office and started a quarrel. Both claimed that they had been personally appointed by General Dog-meat. It was agreed, therefore, that they should go and see the General to clear up the difficulty. When they arrived it was evening, and General Chang was in bed in the midst of his orgies. "Come in," he said, with his usual candour.

The two magistrates then explained that they had both been appointed by him to the same district.

"You fools!" he said, "can't you settle such a little thing between yourselves, but must come to bother me about it?"

Like the heroes of the great Chinese novel *Shui Hu*, and like all Chinese robbers, he was an honest man. He never forgot a kindness, and he was obstinately loyal to those who had helped him. His trousers-pockets were always stuffed with money, and when people came to him for help he would pull out a bank-roll and give a handful to those that asked. He distributed hundred-dollar notes as Rockefeller distributed dimes.

Because of his honesty and his generosity he was beyond the hatred of his fellow-men.

This morning as I entered my office and informed my colleagues of the great news every one smiled, which shows that every one was friendly towards him. No one hated him, and no one could hate him.

China is still being ruled by men like him, who haven't got his honesty, generosity, and loyalty. He was a born ruler, such as modern China wants, and he was the best of them all.

P

HSIAO CH'IEN

No bibliographical note on this author could be obtained.

THE CONVERSION

By Hsiao Ch'ien

"THESE two unseeing holes! H'm . . . I used to embroider the Playful Dragon with them, and now they can't even recognize the nostril of a needle. I am a witless old-one indeed!"

She sits on the edge of the *k'ang* with a long brown gown in her hands, head leaning towards the dim light that filters through a window thickly pasted with Korean paper. She tries patiently to thrust a weak thread's end into a bit of stubborn steel. No matter how she encourages it, with wetting and twisting into a brave point, the thread-end is helpless. The needle resists. Several times it seems to penetrate, but when she drops the trembling hand that holds the needle the thread hangs out alone like a withered bough in winter.

"Ah, you sly devil-pin! You too try to fool this bitter-fated woman." Then she triumphantly raises her voice. "Let's put one deceiver against another."

She calls loudly, "Niu-niu, Niu-niu! Come help ma-ma [1] teach this silly thread."

But the reply is only the heavy ticking of that horse-hoof clock on the little eight-fairies table which her son had bought from the second-hand stall at the Heavenly Bridge.

"Niu-niu, deaf-girl, why don't you answer?"

A moment ago they had been sitting face to face with their sewing. The old woman rises to find her daughter. On the table in the next room she sees their supper unprepared: a

[1] The expression is exactly the same in Chinese as English.

228

slice of pig's-fat, a little cabbage, a piece of salty turnip, a sliver of raw ginger. A partly peeled onion thrown aslant on one corner of the table reveals how hasty the indolent cook had been at the moment of her departure. In the ceiling overhead several mice are scampering. Suddenly there is a crack. One of them must have fallen. Old dust drifts down like snow. She glares angrily at the ceiling, then at the table again.

"That lazy wench, where has she gone?"

She shuffles to the door and calls with all the energy her withered old body can summon. This is meant for that house south where Niu-niu frequently goes to visit with a girl named Lan-hsiang. Lan-hsiang goes to the Tsai's every other day, as Niu-niu does, to get socks to sew. They contend in speed, and compare their wage-money in copper *tiao*. If Niu-niu had been chatting with Lan-hsiang about the superior quality of her sewing or the sufficiency of work to do nowadays, she would have answered quickly, "Yes, ma-ma, I'm coming home now."

To-day the old woman has called twice and there is no answer except from the few ill-fed chickens lingering along the crumbling mud wall. They begin to chatter hopefully for food. Also the yellow dog lying beside the open privy-basin is wakened by the voice. He lifts his head, but when he understands that nothing has happened which requires action in his sphere of duty yawns and falls again into sleep.

In the grey sky of early winter there fly a few kites, dreamily giving themselves up to the whim of the winds. The old woman sees them, and curses into the air as though one of the kites were her errant daughter.

"You little wild goose, you are young and pretty. Is that the reason you leave this bitter-fated woman alone?" She spits on the ground and turns back into the house still muttering:

"Wait, little deceiving wench! When my son comes home I'll speak to him."

Seeing the half-naked onion lying indolently on the table, she becomes still more furious.

"I'll say to him like this: 'Niu-niu is not good. She runs out like a wild thing. Who knows what she does? If she is insulted again, don't you go out to fight for her like a cock.' Wretched girl, I'll show what this bitter-fated woman can do."

It grows darker. Thinking her son will be hungry as soon as he returns, she wraps up the unfinished gown and pettishly pushes Niu-niu's socks to the corner of their blankets, which are piled up like a hill on the *k'ang*. Then she sits by the door and begins to peel the onion, with streaming eyes, incessantly cursing her daughter in weary monotone.

The watchman is climbing on his ladder to light the street lanterns when Niu-niu returns. She walks in blithely, forgetting that when she left the house the sun was yet very far from the banner pole of the White Horse Temple. Under her arm is a pamphlet and in her mouth the humming of an unfamiliar tune.

The lamp, turned low to spare kerosene oil, whispers hoarsely to the flame in the little brick stove. The old woman is slicing the salty turnip with a dull knife. At sight of her daughter, young and cheerful, in the door she bursts out anew with complaint.

"You little sly fox, where have you been with your wicked man, leaving me, bitter-fated woman, at home alone?"

"Ma-ma, don't scold me!"

Niu-niu rushes to her mother's side like a bird and crouches down.

"Ma-ma, I have been seeing the most interesting, wonderful things——"

Then, sensing that she must reverse the order of her talk, the girl explains.

"Ma-ma, when I was peeling the onion this afternoon I heard a foreign drum playing before our gate, the same that we've been hearing all week from a distance. Did you hear it—*dum-dum, dum-dum*? Oh, I couldn't wait even to ask your permission. I ran out by myself. Oh, I saw——"

But the old woman bends her head deafly and slices her salty turnip without paying any heed. Niu-niu clutches at her mother's jacket.

"Ma-ma, listen to me! I saw people marching behind a huge banner. Near by the banner was a fat foreign drum which made the beautiful sound. Following this were many little drums with bells fastened on the edges."

The girl tries to illustrate how big the drum was and nearly causes the salty turnip to fall to the floor.

"Wild wench, even if it is that big, don't spoil my nice turnip."

"But, ma-ma, you must listen. There were many men in grey uniforms with red stripes on the shoulders. And they were clean and polite, not like the kind of soldier that our cousin is. And there were several girls too, also in grey with the same red stripes. All so clean and well-ordered and splendid. And they sang beautifully, ma-ma. As they sing they jingle the little drums in their hands."

Niu-niu begins to sway her head and waist as she imitates the various noises of the procession. This burst of joy inspires her mother to look even more offended.

"And so, wild goose, you chased them madly, leaving me alone. Didn't you?"

"No, ma-ma, I knew I couldn't go with them. How could I forget that I can't leave you: 'Now, Niu-niu, give me some boiled arrowroot.' 'Now, Niu-niu, the spitting-bowl is full.' 'Now, Niu-niu——'"

The girl succeeds in imitating her mother's plaintive orders so well that the old woman bursts into unwilling laughter.

"You mimic artful talker! When have I ever been all the time like that? See what I have done to-day, peeled this turnip, and that——"

She points to the steaming cauldron on the little brick stove, childishly exhibiting her merit.

"Well, anyway, I wouldn't have gone as I did—but they *invited* me, ma-ma. One of the girls in grey beckoned to me several times."

"Ah, did she?" The old woman can no longer conceal her interest. "Who was it?"

"Well, I couldn't recognize her since she had a grey lotus-leaf cap on. While I was staring at her she rushed out from the parade and pulled me by the sleeve——"

"No! Did she really?"

"And she said, 'Come along, Niu-niu.' I looked at her carefully——"

"Who was it after all?" the old woman bends to ask intently.

"It was Chu-tse, the girl who used to sew socks with me."

"You mean that girl who is fond of green string on her queue?"

"That one. But she no longer cares for green string. She has pretty clothes, and even her shoes are foreign-made leather now."

"And her father gambles." The old woman scratches her grey head sagely, trying to show off her memory. "Didn't he often beat his wife?"

"Listen, ma-ma," Niu-niu goes on breathlessly. "And so I joined their parade. That fat foreign drum was just three steps ahead of me. I was right in the front." Now both faces gleam with pride. The little brick stove puts out its red tongue saucily. "And I asked, 'Chu-tse, where are you taking me?' As she played her little drum with the bells on, she whispered to me solemnly, 'Don't call me Chu-tse any more. My name is Rebecca now. We are marching back to the HALL.' I worried about you, ma-ma. I wanted to come back home, truly. But she firmly dragged me on. And, oh, they really sing wonderfully. Ma-ma, listen: 'Jesus loves me . . . Lord in Heaven.' Look, this was what they gave me when I said good-bye."

The girl goes to the eight-fairies table and turns up the lamp. The flame gladly stretches its tongue. In the little room filled with steam, flame, and lamplight her face glows rosily. Mother and daughter look proudly at the pamphlet. On the cover is a coloured picture. Neither can read the context. The old woman peeps close, with her vacant eyes, rubbing her nose on the pamphlet. Dimly she discerns a man with a long beard, all naked, standing by two pieces of wood.

"Probably it's a 'barbarian.' . . . Such a sharp, hard forehead," she breathes.

"No, it isn't a real barbarian. It's Jesus."

Suddenly there appears in the mind of the old woman the scene of the Jesus-believers being killed by the Boxers. She has seen several round warm heads cut off and rolled along the dusty road. . . .

Niu-niu talks on excitedly. "They say we all have sin. Jesus died for us, and so we can live. Look, ma-ma, at the beautiful picture. Here He died on the Cross for us, for you and me. We must all believe in this religion, they say. . . ."

The girl tries to repeat all the fascinating new ideas she had heard in the daytime, unconscious of the horror that she has created in the heart of her mother.

"I just won't believe it. Sin, indeed! And why should I believe in those barbarians and have the Boxers kill me as they did before? And cause the barbarian soldiers to enter the city, too, destroying everything precious we have? Though the earth has already buried me half in length, I refuse to give up my old life so cheaply. From now on, Niu-niu, I forbid you to go near that place! Have you heard me clearly? If you go there no one would even dare to betroth you as a daughter-in-law." She stretches out her hand to grasp the pamphlet.

Niu-niu has been so proud of her vivid representation of

what she has heard and seen that the sudden unreasonable attitude of her mother greatly shocks her. She feels deeply hurt and offended. Recalling how gently and politely she had been treated by those grey-clothed people, she begins to hate her mother's insulting that new-found dignity. She grasps the pamphlet tightly, and stumbles from the room with quivering mouth.

Watching the disappearing figure of the girl, the old woman wags her head as if saying: "What experience have you had, little goose? I, this old woman, have eaten many more *catties* of salt than you. H'm."

Then she bends her back low, listening to the steaming of the cauldron, which hisses like reeds rustling in the evening breeze. After a time she sniffs along the lid of the cauldron, which is closed tightly with old newspaper to prevent the precious steam from escaping before the dumplings inside are fully cooked. She is trying to guess the condition of the cakes. She counts with her fingers. When the kettle began to steam the charcoal-vendor had just passed the door. Now there are many stars in the sky. Unquestionably the time has been sufficient. But, as a rule, both the mother and daughter are too prudent to trust their individual judgments alone in this important matter. Unless the other nods her head and says, "Open, don't worry about it being raw," the cover of the cauldron will not be lifted. As soon as this agreement is reached the seven or eight little naked white-skinned dumplings will be rolled out and the room filled with hot mist. In case the lifting of the lid happens too soon and the cakes are underdone, neither complains of the other. And when that young man working as a janitor in a school comes home and finds the dumplings sticky to his teeth and shows his temper they both bend down their heads, restrain their breathing, and patiently hear his unpleasant words. Thus it is that presently the old woman asks kindly:

"Niu-niu, come and smell the cakes. Let's see if they are ready."

The reply from the inner room is only a suppressed choking.

The evening bell in the Eastern City is tolling when a huge black shadow enters the house. The single bowl of vegetables is placed before the man, who has been working hard the whole day. Three blue bowls are filled with bean-soup by the old woman, one by one, all wreathed with hot steam. Usually Niu-niu places them cautiously on the little table. Then the man is expected to act as news carrier, relating what mass meeting in Tien An Men his school has recently participated in; how he helped the students prepare little banners written with various slogans; or how much money the proctor has squeezed when buying brooms for the school; or how the fat principal has made an overcoat out of the cloth bought for students' uniforms. Finishing with these items, he asks his old mother at random:

"I say, ma, what about Mr Li's long gown, the one I brought three days ago for you to sew? He asked me about it."

Ching Lung often gathers needlework for his mother to do to increase their meagre earnings.

"I haven't done much," she answers, putting down her bowl. "Niu-niu has been away the whole afternoon. When a needle cannot be penetrated my old eyes must have a holiday."

Ching Lung looks at his sister and notices her peculiar mood. Usually at supper she peeps brightly at him with her shining black eyes and begs to hear some 'revolution song,' picked up from the students. This evening she sits mutely, hanging her mouth on the edge of the bowl and indifferently allowing the sour bean-soup to flow into her throat. She is unable even to finish half her dumpling. No inquiry. No laughter. Behind the lock of hair on her forehead is a pair of red eyes swollen with weeping.

Ching Lung loves his sister. He never allows anyone to treat her with disrespect. Often he promises her: "Niu-niu, when I get promotion in life the first thing I'll do is to send you to school. Be patient for a few years, sew those socks, and some day I'll have you wearing silk hose yourself. Hold your backbone straight, the poor will some time have their day. The students often say, in those patriotic speeches they give on the street, 'The future belongs to us poor.'" Once his sister was insulted by a neighbour. Ching Lung was at the school erasing the blackboard when he learned of it. At once he ran back and had a fight with the man like two dogs in the street. This evening he is afraid some one has again insulted her.

"Niu-niu, what's troubling you?"

The girl bends down her head and says nothing. Two tears on her eyelashes are like little shy birds on a bough; one more teasing and they will certainly fly down.

"Tell me, Niu-niu." Intuitively he decides that the strength of a man is in need. He puts down his chopsticks and rolls up his sleeves fiercely.

"We are poor, but we won't bear any injustice. Tell me, I'll smash the bones of that——"

The old woman interrupts. She is angry with her son for his blind protection of the girl.

"Wait, you young brute. Listen clearly. I didn't treat her badly. A wild goose, she goes out when the sun was high in the sky, and returns in the dark, leaving me, old bone, at home alone. I only blamed her with a few words, and now she acts like this."

Ching Lung gathers that what has happened is within the family. He relaxes and picks up his chopsticks. With a stern look, he asks his sister reproachfully:

"Where have you been for the whole afternoon?"

This gravity is a comfort to the old woman and she perks up visibly.

"I went to—to the Save-the-World Army,"[1] Niu-niu answers hesitantly, her head still bent.

[1] The Salvation Army.

"What did you go there for? Those crazy barbarians, beating a big drum like mad on the streets and hiring poor Chinese for their monkey show. Those barbarian soldiers have killed our people by tens in Shanghai recently. Save-the-World indeed!" Now he recalls what he heard from the students' platform in Tien An Men the day he carried the huge flag for his school, marching in front of the parade. "They are Imperialists. Imperialists!" The word rolls out magnificently. "I'd rather have you sew your socks for ever than see you ruined by those exploiting savages. Listen to me: Never go there again! That is settled."

The old mother is delighted with her son's words. She takes the opportunity to bring out the historical knowledge stored away in that old stomach. She tells about the terrific flames of the French Cathedral in the West City when it was burned by the Boxers, of how the troops of the Eight-Allied-Nations robbed the nine cities of Peking to bareness.

"Then I was just eighteen. . . ."

When she goes on to repeat for the hundredth time the story of her wanderings with her family as a refugee in those days, her son, who has been moving desks and chairs for many hours, yawns with fatigue. Soon they extinguish the lamp. The three lie down together for the night, each on that place which belongs to him on the single k'ang.

Niu-niu, wrapped round in her thin blanket, is not convinced. Those historical tales have not pushed away the shiny dream of her splendid experience. In her fancy the coarse snoring of her brother sleeping by the wall becomes the rumbling of the fat foreign drum behind the gay flag. The spasmodic coughing of her mother is the rattle of those little drums with the bells on their edges. Niu-niu imagines herself walking before all eyes in the parade.

It seems to her that her mother and brother have been

unfair to the foreigners. That *chiao-shih*[1] not only had soft white hands but in her mouth flowed the native language so musically that you felt her one of your own people. . . . Niu-niu had been as timid and proud as a bride when she followed the parade into that big Hall. The Hall was certainly beautiful. Red and green stained-glass windows— all colours really, so dazzling that you felt you were entering a fairy world. Pretty little flags of all nations flapping all over the ceiling. And, oh, what a wonderful voice that foreign man in the brown uniform had! No wonder he leads the singing of the whole Hall!

Niu-niu turns over and over sleeplessly. The third watch has beaten. The resounding voice of the pork-dumpling vendor is reminding the night gamblers to have an interval of rest. She bites her lips in the darkness. If she does not go back to that *chiao-shih* to whom she is so much indebted . . . ? It was she who put that beautiful pamphlet in Niu-niu's pocket, patting her shoulder with those soft white fingers and saying, "Come to-morrow and I'll give you a much better one." That foreign woman had an alluring smile. As she said good-bye she had whispered in her ear with intense, startling seriousness:

"Remember, you belong to God."

God . . . Come to Jesus . . . Belong . . . The soft hands . . . The wonderful voice of the man in the brown uniform. . . .

.   .   .   .   .   .

Usually Niu-niu rose early to kindle the little brick stove and heat water for her brother to wash his face. Then she went out on the street to buy a piece of wheaten cake for his breakfast. All the morning she would sit with her mother, face to face, deftly sewing her socks. When the old woman had a bit of sewing too delicate for her eyes, those of Niu-niu came to the rescue. Often the girl sang

[1] The term for a woman teacher.

folk-songs in a low vibrant voice. Sometimes she wittingly teased the poor-sighted woman:

"Ma-ma, let's exchange our work, won't you? You sew my socks and I'll manage your button."

Then the old woman quickly hugged her work to her breast and said: "I don't care for your machine-made work. My old fashion is better."

When the blind fortune-teller passed by the gate sounding his brass gong Niu-niu always knew it was eleven o'clock. She would put away her socks, saying to her mother:

"Ma-ma, don't you touch my things. You are to pay for it if you spoil one thread-end." And she would go to the outer room to prepare their noon meal. . . .

But to-day Niu-niu does not follow this routine. She is too lazy to kindle the fire, and her brother has to devour the stiff dry cake without even a cup of hot water. When she picks up her socks and begins to work she is plunged into painful thoughts. She remembers what Chu-tse has told her.

"H'm, you earn only twenty-two coppers for a dozen socks. Even if you work your hands into pieces, can you get more than three dollars a month? Here, look, we get two uniforms like this each year, and receive six dollars every thirtieth day. And more than that, working in the Hall there is hope of promotion if you can bring new members to the Hall by your talking! And every day it is thrilling—no matter how much I might be paid for it, I'll never again sew the dirty socks. My hands are for God's work—to beat the drum and spread His Gospel."

Memory of these touching words causes Niu-niu's fingers, which used to work all day long energetically, to begin to feel weak and tired. Sitting on the k'ang, she peeps outside from time to time. The magnificent spectacle appears and reappears before her eyes. She begins to hate her brother —more directly, her mother, who sits before her.

In the afternoon comes the sound of the great drum again, beating in the distance like heavy raindrops under the eaves, beating right into Niu-niu's fidgety heart. Her face burns, her hands tremble uncontrollably. That fat foreign drum ... *dum-dum* ... the well-ordered parade ... *dum-dum* ... the beautiful hymns, the white soft fingers, the sweet kind words ... *dum-dum.* ... It comes nearer. Niu-niu seems to distinguish the word 'glorious.' The high-pitched girlish voice seems to be that of Chu-tse. A firesnake seems to be creeping in her heart, in and out.

There is a knot in the thread. Her brain is so disordered that she cannot untie it. She bites it off with her teeth. Lifting her head, her eyes meet with the watchful look of the old woman. It annoys her—as an iron bar maddens the beast in a zoo. And she is gladdened inexpressibly by the drum which comes ever nearer. Her needle jealously stings her finger. She sucks the blood with her mouth. *Dum-dum, dum-dum.* ... The drum is still nearer, louder and louder, as if boasting. So loud that the dog in the yard barks.

Niu-niu can no longer restrain herself. She pulls out that beautiful pamphlet from underneath the mat of the *k'ang* and whispers hysterically:

"I've got to go, ma-ma."

She tries to rush out. The old woman catches her gown.

"How dare you do this, Niu-niu. Your brother has told me to stop you from going there. Your forefathers committed no sin, why should you insist on disgracing us like this?" The old voice is tearful.

The sound of drum-beats and singing surrounds, besieges, the little house. The rustling of clothes tells that many people follow in the parade. Niu-niu's ears throb ... "Six dollars a month" ... and the mystic, strange, exciting whisper of the *chiao-shih*, "Remember, you belong to God."

Niu-niu throws off the sinewless hand from her shoulder. She runs insanely and exultantly into the street.

"Niu-niu, crazy girl, wild girl, cruel daughter!"

.   .   .   .   .

That evening when the huge black shadow draws near to the gate humming a popular revolutionary song he is surprised to find his old mother leaning over the gate.

"Ma-ma! What have you been doing here, so cold?" He looks in dismay at the trembling old body and tries to usher her into the house.

"Cold! No doubt it would please that girl if I am frozen to death." The old woman stubbornly refuses to move.

"Did you have a fuss with Niu-niu again? You must take care of yourself. Winter is always a hard time for old folk."

"Ah, the wings of that wild girl have certainly grown strong. She can fly away by herself and join the barbarians, leaving me alone here until this moment."

"What! She has gone there again. Ma-ma, go inside! I am going to find her."

The old woman gazes at the black shadow rapidly swallowed up by the night. Walking back into the house, she mutters, "Well, *he* is also gone. This bitter-fated woman is always left alone."

With hungrily hunting eyes, the janitor rushes rudely into the prettily decorated chapel. The evening prayer meeting has just ended. A servant is taking a bright-coloured picture from the wall, which has just been used for the sermon. It shows a man painfully encircled by a terrible snake. There are other pictures and slogans hung on the wall, as in the school. But Ching Lung has no heart to look at them. He merely stands outside the chapel, shouting loudly to the servant who is rolling the picture.

"Say, old man, where is my sister?"

Perhaps the way he addresses him is too intimate. The chapel servant does not even look at him squarely, but says in reply:

"Get out of here. There are people confessing in the next room."

"I'm sorry."

Q

The janitor now senses the need for politeness.

"I come to look for my sister."

"But your sister isn't here. This is a Sacred Hall. You get out. Some one is confessing and there must be absolute quiet."

"How do you know my sister isn't here? I must find out."

The janitor stalks noisily into the room. This greatly offends the chapel servant. The janitor ignores him. He sticks out his chest belligerently and walks directly to a little green door on one side of the platform. The servant's rage has turned to fear. The bold behaviour of this strange intruder is becoming a direct menace to "keeping his rice-bowl." The servant jumps before the green door like a hunting dog and stands with hands supporting his waist.

"Get out of here, you rascal! This is a sacred place. Inside the 'fruits' of to-day's holy work are confessing their sins."

"Sacred place, hey? My sister has been tempted by these creatures. Now she even refuses to stay at home."

Seeing that the chapel servant is bent on defending the door, Ching Lung immediately concludes that behind it his sister is imprisoned. He kicks at the door. A foreigner in brown uniform walks out, holding a thick book shining with gold on the edges. He stands firmly before the two quarrelling men, rearranging his gold-rimmed spectacles, and speaks to the chapel servant reproachfully but gently.

"What is wrong, Old Hsu?"

Old Hsu shrieks with fear. He points at Ching Lung.

"General James, he—a criminal-natured rascal from the street——"

Ching Lung is greatly enraged by these words. He grasps the collar of the servant menacingly.

"Curse you, who is the rascal you mean? Answer?"

"Don't, brother, don't!" A familiar voice checks the janitor's rough hand and he loosens his grasp.

The three men turn their surprised eyes into the room behind the green door. Ching Lung sees his sister piously kneeling before a platform beside several other 'fruits' of the day's gathering.

General James, realizing the relationship, softly puts a furry hand on the janitor's shoulder and speaks:

"Brother, since this nice girl is your sister, then you also are our friend. Welcome."

Feeling the palm on his shoulder, the janitor stops glaring at his sister and whirls upon the General.

"Who wants to be your friend? You—who tempt the poor Chinese, make them forget their mothers, neglect their honest self-supporting work to act in a mummers' show, and come here to be crazy!" He points his finger at the noble nose of the patient General.

He rushes into the room, dragging at his sister's weak, trembling arm.

"Come, shameless thing, our mother is waiting for you at the gate even."

"Wait, brother, she belongs to us now!"

General James walks up to the girl, placing his hands on her shoulders, and looking at the brother with head poised in solemn dignity. "When she has finished her confession she may go with you. Please wait at the door."

Ching-Lung stops short. This white-faced foreign-devil. . . . Intuitively he feels that this is no common situation. The words that he hears the students shouting daily at their meetings ring in his ears: "Down with the Imperialists! Away with the foreigners!" A fire sparkles in his eyes. Here is his chance of revenge. Those two meddling furry hands on his sister's shoulders seem to be a symbol of all the unwholesome power choking at the throat of his race. He pushes them away from her, stands back, and doubles his fist to strike the breast of that brown uniform.

General James falls helplessly beside the platform. Lifting his head with its dishevelled hair, he literally blinks his eyes in astonishment at the strange experience which he has never before had during six years of missionary work in this dark continent.

"How unlike a Chinese!" he quavers.

As her brother pulls her away fiercely Niu-niu looks back sympathetically at the splendid General who a moment before had had such a ringing dramatic voice for prayers.

YÜ TA-FU

(1896–)

LIKE Lu Hsün, Mao Tun, and several other popular modern authors, Yü Ta-fu is a native of Chekiang province. He was born in the town of Fuyang, and educated in the provincial schools until 1911, when he went to Japan. At eighteen he entered the Imperial University at Tokyo, where he graduated in economics. He lived in Japan till 1922, and Japan furnishes the *local* of many of his stories.

During the twenties Yü Ta-fu was perhaps the most widely read younger poet of China, and his short stories and novels greatly affected the thought of what is to-day the middle generation. He was one of the first Chinese writers to deal frankly with the forbidden theme of modern love, and his early work had a distinctly emancipating influence. In questioning the traditional Chinese conceptions of marriage, divorce, filial piety, and other phases of the institution of the family, and in boldly disregarding centuries-old taboos on sex relationships in general, he won the interest and admiration of youths then just beginning to taste a new social freedom.

He is considered a representative of Chinese impressionism. His characters are nearly always morbidly introspective, excessively sentimental, dissatisfied with life, but impotent to make any real attempt to change society. They are fundamentally ineffectual and pessimistic, and hence have little appeal for the more revolutionary youth of the present moment. Nevertheless, they are highly typical of contemporary life. Yü Ta-fu attempted in 1927 to make a transition to revolutionary literature, but was unsuccessful, and returned to what he himself terms "decadent romanticism."

His published works include a dozen novels and volumes of short stories and poems. He has translated a number of European novels, and was one of the editors of the great standard All-

Western Library of Translations being published by the Commercial Press.

As editor also of several eclectic magazines he has influenced modern literary trends, and has many followers of his own peculiar style and form.

He has now become a Government official in Fukien.

WISTARIA AND DODDER

By Yü Ta-fu

The wistaria and dodder
Cling to the pines and cypresses.
THE SHI CHING

UNHAPPY WOMAN:

It is afternoon, quiet, and I sit alone. Every one in the house has left but me, and in this tranquil atmosphere, unrippled by a sound, I should be calm too, yet there is nothing in my heart but loneliness, nothing in my head but the sentiment of sorrow.

It is just half-past three. Outside the road is dappled with sunshine and the air no doubt odours of spring. Why should this same air in my room feel stale and heavy? Young people in gay silks are probably wandering across the green meadows and under the peach trees in the groves at Lung Hwa, singing merrily to the open azure sky. Why should that same sky, seen through a corner of my window, seem like a cruel jest to the spirit? Why don't my vitality, my energy, my mind and body, lift and beat strong with new life? Why can't I respond to this season of summery cold and wintry warmth, and shoot out fresh tendrils like the emerald foliage of the earth?

Alas! Woman whom I must love and yet woman whom I cannot love! I despise the world because I despise myself for all my savagery to you!

Your train must have passed Sunkian by now. I imagine you sitting with an absent look on your face and gazing out at the fields, and those who thread over the paths. What are you thinking? It's not hard to discover that, either, for

247

there are tears in your eyes. You are recalling the vile treatment you've had at my hands while we lived together. Woman whom I must love, but cannot, listen to me! In spite of everything that has happened, understand that inside me there is a real sympathy for you, that all my petty insults, tyranny, and abuse are only an outlet for my passionate hatred of the society that breeds people like us. Really, if you could see into me it might even be possible for you to overlook all that I have done.

I suppose it helps not at all that to-day is Ching Ming Festival, with young people joyously rambling through the woods. Perhaps you can see many of them from the car window? Doesn't it make you all the more embittered against me? Go ahead, let your feelings flower darkly into the kind of relief you get from abhorring me! Hate me your hardest! Pray that I'll die soon! But, poor child, I know that you can't. You're utterly incapable of it, and even as you try you begin to find excuses, and reasons to forgive me. You are tender-hearted, there's no question about it, and the wonder is that I can feel any resentment towards you.

I don't know how many (or how few!) happy days we have ever had together, but the failure of our marriage was inevitable. You know when I went abroad I was only seventeen, yet even at that age I preferred living in a strange, inhospitable land rather than at home. I stayed away eight long years, and during all that time didn't return once even for the winter and summer holidays. Do you know why? Because I hated the thought of marriage! Not you so much, understand, but simply the feudal institution of 'arranged matches.' I was resolved to revolt against it, and as long as I stayed in Japan I couldn't be married.

Finally, four years ago, in the summer, I came home. Against my whole conscience, against my spirit, but unavoidably, I had to consent to the wedding. The rigid traditions of our country prohibit the breaking of a betrothal. Your mother and father kept insisting that the thing must not be delayed any longer, and my own mother, full of tears, charged me an unfilial son. All around these unfeeling people driving us into an unwanted union! My rebellion collapsed. And now it isn't us who are responsible for the tragedy of to-day, but our parents—not us, but China! Still, all this time I should not have denied you some explanation.

What an unsatisfactory ceremony it must have been for you! I wasn't worrying about that; I was determined at least to make as little fuss about it as possible, since it had to be endured. No reception, no interlocutor to justify the marriage, no guests at all—not even a pair of candles, not a single cracker fired! You simply came silently at dusk in a little sedan chair, carried from your home twenty-two *li* distant, and took supper alone with my mother. And then you groped your way up the stairs on your little bound feet and entered my room alone.

I had been told that you were suffering from malaria, and when at midnight I went to your bed I stood looking down at you without speaking. You were wearing only a thin gown of pongee. Your face was turned to the wall and you were asleep. I still remember your wistful expression when, as I started to get into bed, you awoke and under the candlelight gravely stared up at me. It was apparent that you had been weeping. Your lips quivered, and how tired and sickly and pitiful your little face seemed! Thinking of that even now brings tears of remorse to my eyes.

For the first time you were breathing the air of a large town. Reared all your life till then in a small, isolated village, kept in your house since childhood, and not once allowed to enter a public school, you were timid, shy, and frightened. Yet you had been perfectly educated in the tradition of Chinese womanhood. I remember you brought with you to my house a classical library—*Biographies of Distinguished Ladies*, the *Four Books for Women*, and other volumes you had read in your family study, and which had told you all about life. It's true you hadn't been taught the art of fascinating men, and you knew nothing about cutting out stylish dresses, but there wasn't a word in the Confucian code of 'submissive' behaviour that had escaped you!

After the 'wedding' we went to your home, to get away from the depressing city, and we really had a little happiness. If we could have stayed . . . But there was your insolent nephew, who so disturbed you, and who threw me into a towering rage, and you into uncontrollable weeping. On the very next day following that quarrel we rushed back to the city. I had been there only two or three days when I fell sick, and your malaria returned, and we were both miserable.

Then I made up my mind regardless of my illness to get out, to leave the oppressive atmosphere that seemed to hang always over us. The night before I left we did not exchange one word. You remember, I went out with some friends, got drunk, and, coming home, lay down on the bed, probably a very disgusting sight. I was dimly aware of you, sitting quietly under the pale-flowing lamplight. When I awoke next morning you were still there, and you had not once during the night ventured to come near the bed. Still, I could find nothing to say to you. Nor did you say anything, not even when I was ready to leave. It was mother who came to me, a little after dawn, to announce that the ship could already be seen at the foot of Deer Hill.

For two years I left you with the memory of that parting in your mind. Your letters spoke of my old grandmother, longing to see me, anxious that I should come home for a visit during some holiday. You reminded me, too, that mother wasn't growing any younger, and that I really should return to cheer her. But you didn't succeed; I was detained by worthless friends and the alien flowers of Japan. I had lost interest in China, and renounced all my responsibilities. What was the use of life in which there was no freedom to live? I began to drink heavily; in fact I managed to stay drunk most of the time. I don't remember how many strange women came and left. They were a soulless lot. Nothing mattered to me but that they should be amusing. Yet all this immersion in drink couldn't keep me from thinking of you sometimes, and then the breeze seemed to blow cold in the night, and the moon froze into the sky. Several times I cried bitterly, still hating myself for having given in and married.

I couldn't have shown my contempt better than I did by that visit the year before last, when I did come back to China for a short while. Instead of going to you I accepted an invitation from friends in Amoy, and stayed there for three months. Then I went to Shanghai and spent the New Year, and afterwards went back to Tokyo. But I couldn't stay in school for ever. Finally last spring I managed to produce a thesis, and had to prepare to face the world. I landed in Shanghai with a great many useless books, little else, and began to hunt for work.

But what work? What could I do? Thanks to an impotent Government and to my unenlightened country-men, I had qualified—a worthless but nevertheless harmless fellow—for subsidized study abroad. The Government allowance was hardly enough to feed me, but it was at least a regular income, and on various pretexts I managed to extort money from my mother and brother. It had enabled me to lead a riotous life in the splendid capital of the newly prosperous country for several years. But then the day fixed had arrived, and I had to give up my refuge in the heavily shaded library, cease my dreaming, and move on. Some Generals at home had in the meantime got hold of the funds giving income to us students, and last June my monthly allowance stopped altogether.

Well, I had been helped long enough. I was nearing thirty, and it was time for me to begin to find my way through the social struggle. And now that I was a graduate

of a foreign national university I hadn't the face to go on
accepting aid from my mother and my high-minded brother.
Do you know why I stayed in Shanghai last summer more
than a month before returning home? There's no necessity
for keeping that secret any longer. It's quite true that I
really did want to linger as long as my travelling expenses
lasted, but there was another reason. I was trying to decide
whether there was adequate excuse for my continued
existence. All the heart seemed crushed out of me. What
was there left of any earthly use?

One warm night I stood on the noisy bank of the Huangpu, staring into the shaking waters, and depressed to my
inmost being. The lines of a silly foreign poem kept
running through my mind:

> Come you home a hero,
> Or come not home at all,
> The lads you leave will mind you,
> Till Ludlow Tower shall fall.

Timid, thoughtful, too reflective, during all those months
abroad I had not done one thing to win any distinction for
myself! I had not even written an article, I had no exhorta-
tions to my credit—either on paper or in speech. I had not
once entered into the warm, excited debates of other students,
or urged action when modern youth took command of the
mass movement of our people. I had always felt dull. I
hadn't had the spirit for such activities. What was the
matter with me? What was the purpose of life under the
conditions that mastered me? I hadn't had any success at
job-hunting, and altogether I concluded the best thing I
could do in the world was to find a way to get out of it.
I meant to commit suicide.

Being in fact driven by such a thought I kept going back
with slow steps every night to stand beside the Huangpu.
But somehow I couldn't take leave without at first doing
something useful. My idea of something useful was to get

hold of a large piece of money somewhere, enter into a
hearty carouse, and end up by killing one or two people.
I had no particular person in mind and no feeling of class
preference in the matter; if it happened to be a rich man
I killed then so much the better for society, but if poor and
miserable then I would be doing him a service by ending
his vegetable career. Afterwards I would leap into the
Huangpu.

And do you know that all the time I was thinking these
insane thoughts it never once occurred to me to wonder
what would become of you after I was dead. I didn't
give a thought either to my grandmother or my mother.
You'll say I had little sense of responsibility. Exactly; and
in that I cruelly rejoice. In the first place it is the fault of
this barbaric competitive society in which we must live,
but which finds no use for us. Secondly, it is your parents,
who failed to teach you independence and self-reliance,
who are to blame. And then it is the responsibility of my
mother and my whole family—and of the generations that
weigh down upon and rule them with dead hands—who
were very well aware of my utter inability to support you
while I was in school, and yet obstinately forced me into
this marriage. But of course I didn't reason about these
things then; as I said, I didn't even think of you.

I don't know what would have happened if T. hadn't
come unexpectedly to my lodging one night with a letter
from my friend at Amoy. Ordinarily my meetings with T.
were one-way affairs, for he never repaid my calls, and so
when he entered that June evening I felt at once that he had
some extraordinary news. I was right. He had hardly sat
down beside my broken desk when he told me about the
letter.

"You've got a chance to teach at Amoy," he said. "What
about it?"

It isn't necessary to tell you once more how I loathe
teaching. It's the special purgatory of the literate but

penniless class of people. After half a year with me you can have no illusions about that. Worst of all, this college was full of intrigue, with several ambitious people in rivalry for the presidency, and anybody teaching there couldn't avoid being dragged into the mess. I don't suppose even now you understand how revolting the idea of taking a position under such circumstances was to me, though I was just then on the fringe of starvation. Ha! Do you remember the letters I sent home telling how busy I was?

Actually I was desperate, and I hadn't the courage to turn down this offer. At the moment T. handed me that letter nearly all my clothes, everything I owned, had been pawned. I was in exactly the same condition as that unfortunate German poet, Grabbe, who went to the city to seek fame. Before he left his old mother gave him a set of ancestral silver plate, that had been in his family many generations. Settled in the capital, he began to live by pawning this silverware, consuming it at the rate of a spoon or a silver piece per day. Before long he had eaten up the whole set. I had no such valuable antiques, and in fact the only article I had was a silver photograph frame that I bought for you in Tokyo. Many a time I had been tempted to pawn it, but somehow had managed to struggle through all the critical situations without doing so. I had determined that if at all possible I would cling to it and present this one little thing to you. Nevertheless (one more lash of irony!) after receiving that letter I had to turn over the gift to a moneylender in order to get passage money to return to see the Old Lady, and my mother, and you, the timid lamb!

It was an afternoon of heart-breaking beauty when last June I sailed from Hangchow over the wide-flowing Ch'ien T'ang river, past the rustic Bridge of Holiness and Li Hill, down through the thickly wooded valleys, and up to the wall of my native city. I rejoiced, and at the same time I trembled with apprehension. Looking at the mountains rolling back from the city gates I became aware that my heart was beating rapidly. I hummed, and yet, if two such contradictory emotions are possible, I was at the same time uttering an inward prayer. "Heavenly Father! Just let it be that none of my acquaintances shall see me disembark. I couldn't stand it, having them see me return in disgrace."

As soon as the ship dropped anchor I rolled ashore and with my two bags, one in each hand, hurried under the bright sun towards home. I lowered my head like a fugitive as I wound through the crowds of men and animals. I reached the house safely, entered the front door, and at once saw mother drinking tea alone in the alcove. Curious, do you know that I had intended to rush joyously to embrace her at first sight, to call out affectionately, "Mother! My mother!" but when I saw her sitting there all at once a rush of indignation came over me and I could not go near her. I couldn't help myself for hating the injustice of which I felt myself a victim. I said nothing, but flung my leather bags upon the bench and immediately ran upstairs into my rooms, wishing to avoid any emotional scenes.

To my surprise you were already there, kneeling before the bed, your body torn by sobs, and your face hot with tears! I stared down at you stupidly for some moments, feeling somehow resentful. "What's the matter?" I finally asked in a dry and downcast tone of voice. You only began to cry all the more bitterly! I repeated the question, and you didn't answer me, but went on sobbing. Good God, I am no one to stop another from crying, but, on the contrary, seeing people wretched brings out tears of my own, and in an instant I was embracing your head and releasing my own feelings in weeping with you. After a while mother broke in majestically from below:

"What a princess! At a few innocent words from me you leave the room, retiring in genuine anger! . . . And you, little beast, wandered in from Shanghai! After a month of idling in the city you return without a word of greeting for me and fling your bags at my feet. What sort of conduct is that? Even were you a prince such insults couldn't be tolerated! . . . I have long known: *You, man and wife, have been secretly corresponding, have no doubt even been planning to murder me!*"

My tears suddenly dried up and my blood cooled. Despite the oppressive heat my skin pebbled as if chilled by a blast of midnight wind in the depth of winter. I was deeply struck, and ready to cry out in retaliation. Had you not held me back I would certainly have done something dreadful, and ended by bidding eternal farewell to my mother. For this at least, for saving me from the crime of unfilial action, I thank you heartily.

Neither of you had expected me to return that day. Later on, after we had all been reconciled, I learned how mother had been abusing you and even blaming you for my long stay in Shanghai. It wasn't the first of such occasions, and no wonder you were inconsolable when you heard my plans to leave you again, to go to Amoy. But to oppose it actively would never have occurred to you! Resignation and submissiveness are the cause of your endless suffering, just as complete lack of resistance, helplessness to fight against the vile social order, are the root of mine! Oh, to revolt! *Revolt!* We know the word, but how, where to commence? That nobody tells weak and vacillating people like us!

After that miserable scene I began to notice that you were pale and even thinner than when you were sick with malaria. Your legs were thin and as fleshless as bamboo shoots. I decided to take you with me to Amoy, and to get travelling expenses I at once dispatched a letter to the college. While we were waiting for the two hundred dollars we didn't mention a word of the plan to mother. Yet when the money finally came you still hesitated.

"If you should lose your job there, if we should be without any money, what shall we do? Where shall we go?" Like a Greek prophetess, you sensed calamity in the future! But how could I know that we would end up as tragically as we have?

How stupid it is that a few days of living together should bring about such unwanted consequences! We had hardly settled down in Amoy when you began to lose what health you had. Your appetite waned, you vomited frequently, you were always lying wearily in bed. I didn't know the truth for a whole month, and several times spoke harshly to you. Even when, during the third and fourth month, there was no longer any question about your condition I acted indecently, releasing my wrath over many diverse stimuli.

I hated the routine of teaching, which I thought dry and tiresome. It oppressed me, and I went to and from classes feeling like a man unjustly arrested and undergoing torture. Always this weakness within me, but a greater pity for you and a leaning weakness that I continually fought against!

It happened that an essay of mine written long ago (before the renaissance) was published by a magazine, without my consent. It made me a target of attack from all sides, and especially from some jealous colleagues, and I felt thoroughly miserable. How angry I was, and how helpless to do anything concerning it! I had been used to independence of thought and action, yet I felt now that I could not resign my professorship. The prospect of repeating the experience of the previous June was not to be thought of, with you to support and a baby expected very soon. But how you suffered for it!

Looking upon myself as a helpless victim of society I excused my cowardice in the world of action, but in my home made up for it by tyranny to you. You, not I, were really the sacrifice made to society; you were the innocent lamb slaughtered on the altar of social tyranny, through the medium of me. What shallow pretexts I used to justify myself! Returning from some new indignity I criticized the food, or your household management, or equally as

R

often directly denounced you for causing all my troubles. When I worried about losing my job I used to shout at you excitedly. Such curses trail through my mind very vividly now.

"Why don't you die?" I would demand. "Why not? It is only when you are dead that it becomes possible for me to begin to live! What are you, actually? Why should I labour like an enslaved animal for you? Oh, for a little freedom—freedom from this endless drudgery, freedom to live! Ah, you living corpse! Why, in fact, do you continue to exist?"

When you had heard more than you could bear you always gave way to tears, although you wept silently, as if you didn't wish me to see. Remorse would come over me and I would apologize, and try to explain, and even caress you gently. Seeking to make you understand that it wasn't really you I despised but the world, I would unburden and make you the cistern of all my griefs and all my complaints against the world. And this only made you weep more bitterly, and very often we ended up sobbing in each other's arms! At first this occurred infrequently, but later on, especially about the time of the New Year holidays, it happened nearly every day and sometimes twice a day.

What is this tragic circumstance between us? Is marriage itself a crime, or is it the society which dominates it that makes the crime? If it's the first, then life is indeed pretty hopeless! But if it's society, if the trouble lies in the present order of conduct itself, then somehow we must struggle to change the rules. There ought to be some way to avoid deepening the tragedy by bringing along new successors to it, as we did. Before he was a month old the marks of our malady began to show in the child—this little bundle of protesting life, this vessel of future pain. For one thing notice how nervous he is, and how easily he cries out his unhappiness. Look how the blue veins stand out on his forehead when he isn't at once given his milk. How could

I, hating life and longing for the coming of death, bring this poor little unwanted creature into such a world? What a base self-contradiction! This is really criminal! I can't explain it or justify it in any way. Should some one ask you about it, just answer for me, please!

A month ago our affairs reached a climax. Perhaps you don't remember the event as clearly as I do—quite naturally you were dull with bewilderment—but every incident leading up to it is printed in my mind as if stamped by a seal of jade. It was at night and the moon shone only quarter full; it had indeed just risen in the east.

I had by then resigned my professorship. My brother had helped get me a position in a new bank, but its opening was delayed due to political developments. Meanwhile I was idle. I had come home that night full of wine, feeling more depressed than usual, so that the sight of you, and then the baby, suddenly roused me to an unreasonble fury. I poured out some oaths and burning sarcasm at you, I called you both the chains around my feet. I think I threatened to drown myself. Then I began urging you to go back to your native town, and to take the baby with you. Having thoroughly exhausted myself in this manner, I lay down and drowsed in a half-conscious feverish state. I remember looking at you vaguely through the netting draped over the bed. You were talking to Little Dragon, something like this:

"Don't . . . be naughty. Be good, little pet! . . . Sleep, sleep! Don't anger your father . . . after mother's gone."

You seemed, in the lamplight, to be weeping, and I remember that the familiar picture annoyed me. I turned impatiently and faced the other way. I was dimly aware of you there for some time, crying, and I knew too that you came over once, pulled up the net, and looked down at me. I was by then anxious to sleep and I didn't move.

When I awoke some one was knocking violently. I sprang up from the quilt and opened the door. It was some

rickshaw men from the street, and, utterly astounded, I saw
that they were carrying you in their arms. I stumbled to
wards you. Your hair was hanging loose, a tangled wet mass
Your gown was thoroughly soaked and the blue and black
colours had spilled over it in confusion. That quarter moon
hanging in the sky cast a grey light on your deathly pale
face, and gave it a ghastly radiance. Your eyes were closed
but your lips quivered feebly. Horrified, I threw my arm
around you, and called your name several times. At last
your lids lifted up for a moment, but almost immediately
closed. Beaded tears strung down from under the corner
of your lids! Alas! I knew very well then that you didn'
hate me. You really didn't, as I understood easily enough
from those tears, but why I don't to this moment compre
hend. I shouldn't have wept under the circumstances, but
in a moment, before every one, I felt my face wet and my
breath ripped out in gasps.

They carried you into the room and the sounds woke
Little Dragon. He too began to whimper. It was perhaps
because of his plaintive wail that you opened your eyes
again and looked at me. I began peeling your wet clothes
from you, and urged you to sleep, and not to worry about
the baby. By this time the *amah*, who had been asleep in
the next room, arrived to inquire what was wrong, and
knowing you wanted the child, I ordered her to bring him
Just at that moment, I remember, a steamer lying near by
suddenly gave off a deafening scream to announce it
departure for some river port.

Never has my mind been so clear and so pure as during
those next fifteen days when you lay ill in the hospital
My heart was really full of love and high resolves. I was
able for a while to forget myself entirely and convert all
my egotism into concern for you. I began to feel something
like human dignity. I sat beside you through hours of
delirium and fever that reached as high as forty-one de
grees.

"Little Dragon," you would ask, "how are you?"
"When are you going to the bank?"

When at last we left Amoy I intended to go with you
back to my native town, and there settle down. I was convinced that I was too stupid to get along in the modern
world and would always be having difficulties. Even if I
should get a job it could not be of much importance, and
was bound to be a droll task offering no opportunity. Our
old home, I decided, was the best place for me. The family
hasn't much, but it would be enough to feed us, and there
would always be a place to live. You are now twenty-
seven and I am twenty-eight. Suppose, I reasoned, that we
live to be fifty; that doesn't leave us many more years.
Besides, I had lost interest in fame and I had no desire for
great wealth. I know I haven't got that ruthlessness of touch
that is necessary to amass a fortune by climbing on the backs
of other luckless individuals—even if I had the chance.

Of all that I was convinced when we left Amoy. We
spent a great deal of time looking over building plans that
I brought out for you to inspect, and we elaborately drew
up a design of our own for the thatch-roofed cottage we
wanted to build just beyond the north wall of the town.
My mind hadn't altered about this when we were moving
along the waters of the Golden Sand river, and even after
we reached Shanghai. It was not until the second day that
my resolution began to wither. You remember well
enough, I suppose! We had had our photographs taken
and had finished dinner, when I went off to visit a friend
who had recently returned from Japan. I talked with him
and told him what I intended to do. He didn't approve or
disapprove of my viewpoint or my plans. He simply
pointed to several children playing about him and said:

"Just look here! These are my responsibilities, and I don't
intend to shirk them. My burden is heavier than yours,
but I'm not complaining about it."

Alas! I thought, how easily I had been defeated. At the

first real combat with the world I was turning away in panic. What sort of fellow is it who gives in as easily as that? Afterwards I kept thinking of my friend, and of my own decision, and all that night I could not sleep. You instinctively understood, and you kept silent, probably fearful that a word from you would bring some stabbing oath in return. For the first time since that night you entered the hospital the old emotional turmoil began working within me. For three long days I remained in this mood, until finally last night, feeling sorry for me, you said, as I lay motionless on the bed:

"I don't want to see you unhappy any longer. You stay here in Shanghai alone and I'll go back with the child. You need only escort me to the train. To-morrow I'll return to Chekiang without any more delay."

We had accepted an invitation for dinner to-night, but I suppose because you were afraid I might change my mind and decide not to let you and Little Dragon go after all, you insisted on leaving at once. I confess I felt grateful to you in a way, and yet at the same time I couldn't help feeling bitter towards you. That's why throughout your preparations, as you moved about picking up things here and there, I didn't say a word. We even reached the station, and you got into the train, without exchanging any conversation. At last I made that one inane remark about the weather:

"It doesn't look like a bad day."

You understood, and turned your face away. You looked for a long time, as if trying to observe the condition of the sky. Had you so much as glanced at me with your brimming eyes I should no doubt have been unable to control myself. Perhaps I might even have detained you, or accompanied you, or at least insisted upon going as far as Hangchow. But you did not look at me again, I said nothing more, and that is the way we parted. I stood for several moments on the station platform, gazing away from your panelled window, and not till the engine began moving did I turn to wave farewell. I saw a trail of tears on your left cheek.

For a long time, long after every one else had gone, I stared after the train. When I crawled away slowly with dragging legs I was thinking that I shall never, never see you again.

And yet my heart aches for you!

CHANG T'IEN-YI
(1907–)

THE author supplies the following autobiographical sketch:

"I was born in 1907. My family, having its home in Hunan, in the mid-Yangtse valley, used to belong to the land-owning class, but it began to decline after my grandfather's generation. My father had to take his family along while wandering adrift and away from home to struggle for existence; hence, since five years of age, I followed him and visited many places. It was not until I was eighteen that I finished my study in a middle school in Hangchow [Chekiang]. I went along to Peking in 1924, but did not enter any school there. It was then that I began to have definitely my new belief [indicating Marxism] and gradually to grasp that single truth of history. Later I lived the career of petty office-worker, assistant in the army, reporter and staff writer on a newspaper, school teacher, and what-not.

"As my parents and one of my sisters were all enthusiastic readers of literature, I was naturally influenced by them in this way. While in middle school I once wrote some puerile and ridiculous stories. In 1925 a Peking newspaper published a piece of mine which was in imitation of the so-called Symbolism. I had then a funny and absurd notion that literature and action are two separate things. Later I stopped writing.

"In 1928 I began to train myself to write in the realistic way, and wrote *A Dream of Three and a Half Days*, a short story. It was sent to the *Pên Liu (Rushing Torrent) Magazine*, edited by Lu Hsün, and was published. This encouraged me greatly to continue my writing. My writings include the novels *One Year*, *The Knights of Yangchinpeng*, and the collections of short stories, *Moving About*, *Counter-attack*, *Round Union*, *Ch'ing Ming Festival*, etc., and two stories for children.

"The characters in my stories are taken from my friends, relatives, and those with whom I have had frequent contact.

265

Formerly I had the weakness of making my characters ac merely for the sake of bringing out the themes of my storie thus neglecting their complex human natures. Recently I hav attempted to correct this mistake. I shall remember the necessit for 'creation of types' and learn to do it.

"The authors who have influenced me most are Charle Dickens, Guy de Maupassant, Emile Zola, H. Barbusse, Le Tolstoy, A. Chekhov, Maxim Gorki, and Lu Hsün. Nev works from Soviet Russia, especially A. Fadeyev's *Razgror* (translated into English as *The Nineteen*), have also greatl influenced me. As I read over the works of these writers I fee my humbleness. But, for the same reason, I am all the mor determined to learn and to write, as if I were under the guidanc of professors."

MUTATION

By CHANG T'IEN-YI

SANG HWA, her face glowing like a hill haw, looked through the open window for a moment, and then she gazed idly down at the table. A gentle breeze blew in and disturbed the silken tassels of a lamp which stood there; it brought from outside the voice of a minstrel singing an operatic theme of *Sad Vistas*. She frowned. She became aware of an unpleasant puckery taste in her mouth, like unripe plums. She moved over, selected a sweet, and put it daintily to her lips.

"Proceed, cousin," she invited, "with what you were saying."

The other woman, who was smoking and gazing in a detached way at a painting, turned her head. "H'mm? What was it?"

"I believe you were criticizing me."

"Oh—that." She collected herself and tapped the ashes from her cigarette. "Your life, my dear, seems to me . . ."

Sang Hwa looked at her intently as she began to speak, but presently her gaze slanted to a mirror. She changed her posture to achieve a more graceful line. She munched delicately and listened carefully, as she always did when anyone discussed her.

She enjoyed being discussed. Why not? Everybody praised and admired her. She was rich, and she could amuse herself lavishly, which she liked very much to do. Those ladies and gentlemen singing across the lake were all her guests, and this splendid garden was hers, this spacious suburban residence her summer home. Moreover, as

people often said, "It is apparent that she has been nobl
born."

Sang Hwa had once lived quite meagrely with he
mother, it is true; nevertheless, she had always behaved lik
a gentle lady. Many people envied her now, and with avi
sighs reckoned up her fortune and the profits of her husban
who was a broker in sugar and rubber. Yet, with all tha
most of her friends agreed that she had exquisite taste an
never made a vulgar display of her money.

"She certainly understands where to look for pleasur
and how to get it," they said. "No one could complai
about such life."

And this was in fact no exaggeration.

Whenever people talked about her Sang Hwa always di
her best to stand aloof and coolly and impartially consid
their comments. She convinced herself that she had locke
up her pride and was suspending judgment, or she affecte
the simplicity of a child awaiting condemnation. Som
times, however, try as she would, she could not prevent
smile creeping up, and then she slyly turned her head to th
mirrors. She studied her face to see whether it neede
powdering, or observed her posture to determine wheth
it produced the most charming effect of form.

Just now she decided that the attitude could not b
improved upon, and she gazed steadily at the moving lip
and the working mouth of her cousin, "What," sh
thought, "is the difference between a man and a woma
like her? She is an odd fish, really; neither male nor femal
She has a plain face untouched by cosmetics, her hair is cι
short, and above her hips there are simply straight stiff line
Her voice literally roars. When she talks you feel that sh
has a rope around you and is dragging you."

The cousin became excited and at last reached her poin
"Look around you, at the age we live in!" She blew dens
smoke from her mouth, not gentle whiffs but heavy puf
like those following an explosion. "Haven't you ever eve

thought of it? How long can you go on living in such magnificence, anyway? That is, if you call it living."

There was a pause.

"What I mean is, you simply have no conception of realities. You don't even read the daily paper, hidden away in this artificial world. Suppose, for instance, the rubber market breaks, where are you? You're afraid to think of such possibilities—it would spoil your fun, eh? As a matter of fact, a woman with your intelligence——"

She looked suddenly at Sang Hwa, who was thoughtfully examining her finger-nails, so pink and softly gleaming. She swallowed—and it was beautiful to watch her swallow! —the morsel in her mouth, and allowed a moment to elapse. Then, sighing wistfully, she said, "Oh, let us not talk about that. I merely enjoy to-day, each day, for itself."

"What if a great storm sweeps in—something far worse than the Shanghai war! Such things come suddenly, without warning. Maybe tens of years will roll by, maybe it will come to-morrow."

"To-morrow!" Sang Hwa lifted up her eyes. "I would rather die than think about it. If the collapse comes to-morrow—then to-morrow means my death."

Her cousin smiled and stood for a while facing the window. "Uncle and Aunt have given you a good education, I suppose," she said. "You are their only daughter. No doubt they determined to make you——"

"What?" Sang Hwa stole a glance at the glass, and was pleased with what she saw there and did not move.

"What? Well, a *bourgeois* wife."

Sang Hwa smiled. "But why?"

The other shrugged her shoulders. "To make you happy. Isn't it true they petted you in every way? They taught you to act like a *lady*, a real *lady*. And now they've succeeded in making you one. You've married a millionaire. You're happy, aren't you? And your whole family benefits too."

"Oh, no, it was not exactly like that! I was not so submissive. Do you remember how I refused the year my
father tried to betroth me to that fellow Chin? Did I not
repeatedly decline?"

"And now?"

Sang Hwa blushed. "This is a different matter. This
marriage was a thing of my own—my own——"

The cousin brushed her short hair back from her face
impatiently and sat down, crossing her legs, in defiance of
all etiquette.

"I dare say your philosophy is the result of your education, and yet—what has happened to you during these ten
years I don't know, but you . . ."

She scrutinized Sang Hwa as she talked along carelessly.
They had seen a great deal of each other in their adolescence,
but not once since they had become women. She remembered hearing that Sang Hwa had left college to take
a job of some kind. What was it? In this setting she
seemed to be merely living into a *rôle* carefully planned
and rehearsed during all those years—the *rôle* of a rich
wife.

"I suppose it's quite natural after all—living among
bourgeois women, with no ambition but useless married
pleasure. Such a background prepared your mind for this
sort of existence, and your own marriage simply fits into
what you were taught to believe——"

Suddenly Sang Hwa stood up, for a moment losing her
composure. She broke in passionately:

"No, no! That is all wrong!"

"Wrong? Then you——"

"Quite wrong. The reason I married him—indeed, it
grew out of conditions very different from those you
suggest. I—you see, in the beginning I accepted his company for—for the——"

Sang Hwa stood very gravely leaning on a table, but
instinctively assumed a graceful pose. She slightly bent her

willowy waist, and lifted one foot, poising the toe behind
her on the floor. She repeated again:

"I accepted his company—for——"

"For what?"

"For the Revolution," she finally uttered in a low voice.

"Revolution, you!" Her cousin shrank back, astonished.
"You mean you've been a Red?"

"Exactly."

Her cousin gaped at her stupidly, and then at the table
laden with sweets, an opium lamp, and a glass of half-
finished wine. She could not imagine Sang Hwa in an
atmosphere so remote from all the comforts and vices that
she saw surrounding her. Was it possible? Sang Hwa, who
sat in her boudoir four or five hours a day beautifying herself; Sang Hwa, who everywhere she went must have
friends to amuse her, foreign wine to drink, and dancing
and singing and mah-jongg; Sang Hwa, whose monthly
allowance was a thousand, two thousand, dollars, and who
bought a new car whenever she chose—this same Sang Hwa
a Revolutionist? And claiming she got her husband through
such an idea as that!

"But I don't like to talk about it. Let the past stay with
the past."

She lifted her arm and let it swim in the breeze as she
looked through a window. She felt her cousin's eyes on
her, and unwillingly she turned and met them, but immediately looked away.

"I don't understand what you mean. How could you
meet a man like your husband for Revolutionary purposes?
Or don't you want to explain?"

"It is not precisely that. But whenever I think about my
life at that time my heart is bound to . . ." She did not
finish. She moved up to the window and stood framed in
the opening, looking up at the sky. There was a moon
there in the middle of the night, a dull glowing circle that
looked like a slice of orange. . . .

II

It was under the very same moon that she had more than once walked down the dark streets, thick with filth, leaning on the firm arm of Lien Wen-kan.

He was a head taller than she. His hands were strong; they were cold, and they gripped hers with the hardness of steel. She pressed close to him, so close that a single shadow nailed them to the earth.

"Are you sure you can do it?" Lien Wen-kan asked her one night as they hurried along together.

"Certain of it," she smiled. "It is simply a matter of charm, the right kind of technique——"

"Oh, it's not that I mean. That's irrelevant. I simply refer to——"

In front of them a black shape loomed ominously. He stopped talking at once.

Sang Hwa shivered and felt terror rise in her. A special kind of noxious air seemed to sweep past with the threat of that dark figure, but nothing happened. It went by Lien Wen-kan's shoulder and did not stop. She turned and peered after the fellow, whoever he was, and then she sighed and looked anxiously into her comrade's face. His expression had not changed.

He went on: "Are you sure you can get the money from him? I mean that broker—what's his name?"

"Li."

"Yes, Li. Can you get such a sum from him?"

"Of course, I cannot guarantee it." She smiled. "It depends upon charm, unusual charm, and nothing else would succeed." She looked for an appreciative smile, and was prepared to expand upon this topic. She leaned closer to him, but he kept his lips shut and his eyes on the ground, as if in deep thought. He forgot all about her at times and walked so rapidly that she could not keep in step with him, and once or twice almost lost her balance.

"Is Little Hu at home?" She asked in a whisper.

"Eh? Yes, he's at home—been in bed all day."

Before her rose the picture of that pale inspired face, with its coffee-coloured freckles under the sombre eyes. She felt terrified again.

"We must cure him."

"But how? With what?" Lien Wen-kan made a wry face. "Plenty of other comrades have got the same thing. If we send them all away for rest and care, what'll we use for funds to do the work? Who'll direct the programme ahead?"

She suddenly trembled against his arm. "Then you take care of yourself. Oh, you must take care!"

He looked at her and smiled. "I haven't time for any special precautions. I'm ready for death, anyway. It's got to come some time, sooner or later; if not that way then at the hand of the enemy."

She sighed inwardly, and tried hard to keep from betraying her feeling of dread. She took her tongue between her teeth till it began to swell; her cheeks quivered. She wondered how much longer Little Hu could live. When they arrived at his house she was hardly able to control herself. She began to tremble all over.

The sick man had a high fever and his face was scarlet. When he coughed his features were pinched together and his body shook in spasms of pain. At length he spat up a mouthful of viscous stuff and that relieved his lungs. He fell back on the pillow and lay with his eyes shut, panting hard. After a while he began to talk to Lien Wen-kan in a slow, painful voice. The air in the room was bad, and everything seemed to have on it the marks of his sickness. Lien Wen-kan sat on the edge of his bed and spoke to him, interrupted now and then by harsh coughing. When Lien told the sick man that Sang Hwa had promised to get money enough for the present crisis he made a great effort and lifted up his face to smile gratefully at her. She was

S

sitting on a bench near the window, protecting her mouth and nose with a square of linen, but quickly withdrew it when Little Hu looked at her. She tried to smile back encouragingly.

"We can't keep up the struggle here unless we get some money. And yet we can't give up now. There," he gasped, "there are our martyred comrades—they also——"

He began coughing again with great ripping sounds that shook his body convulsively, as if he would end by turning up his whole viscera. His face went a deep crimson, and the swollen veins stood out piteously, like hempen cords. Little Hu's jerking body made the bed squeak, until he got relief by expelling more viscid mucus, and then he lay back, puffing through his wide-open mouth. His eyes half closed, but after a while Sang Hwa saw him looking at her shocked face. He smiled wanly, as if to say that he was not really sick enough to worry about.

"If our plans work out we can succeed in building a great movement here, greater than the Hong Kong rising." He paused to gasp dryly for breath. "If only we can hold together it's a real crisis. How much can you raise from that fellow Li? How is he related to you, by the way?"

"He is Li Ssu-yi, and no direct relation of mine. I simply met him in my aunt's home, when I stayed there. My aunt is trying to marry her daughter to him. He merely knows me as a relative, that is all. He is nevertheless very attentive."

She began to laugh. She explained that he was a droll and tiresome character, and she described him. "Never mind that," she said, "if I can only get what you want. The application of charm, with the right technique, ought to succeed."

The very next day she lunched with Li Ssu-yi, drank wine with him, and later on went to Chao Feng Park, where they sat listening to the music. She was heavily powdered and her cheeks were tinted a delicate apricot. She smiled constantly. Her face was as changelessly pleasant as a flower.

Li Ssu-yi made a great effort to be bright and entertaining. "What a beautiful moon there is to-night," he said in his Tai Shan accent. He made other romantic observations, following each with a prolonged sigh, as though half in jest. "Aren't you happy?" he asked her several times. He was very, very considerate. Wherever they went he offered her, in courtly gesture, the fat curve of his arm.

Li Ssu-yi was about forty years old. There was a little round bald spot on the top of his head, but elsewhere was a thick shining growth; he had a habit of threading the fingers of his right hand through it. Whenever sugar or the condition of the rubber market were discussed he lifted up his eyebrows with interest. He did not, however, discuss such subjects in the presence of ladies. He kept his eyes half closed, and he often wistfully remarked that people seldom understood him. He especially resented any references to his round little belly. He himself considered that he was not fat, but merely happened to have a bigger stomach than most. One explanation he offered for this phenomenon was that he drank beer.

Sang Hwa looked out of the corner of her eyes now at his oleaginous face and his protruding teeth. She thought to herself that some day her cousin, Pao Chen, would have to yield to those arms and feel those teeth against her face. The prospect highly amused her.

"Why do you laugh?" he asked tenderly.

"I was laughing at Pao Chen—thinking how jealous she would be if she found us here."

He frowned and absently scratched his head. "She doesn't suit me—temperamentally, you know. On the other hand, you—you're—— But what do you think of me, anyway? Do I weary you?"

She smiled and pressed his arm, employing one of the gestures in what she called her "technique." She said nothing.

A stiff wind blew against them and furled her silk gown

against her legs. The wine had affected her; she felt physically very light and as if walking along a bank of clouds. Some fragrance seemed to hang in the air and sweeten her tongue. Was it flowers, or the odour of green grass, or really a perfume somewhere? Looking into the faces of other strollers she saw that they were kindly and tranquil, as if there was no such thing as pain on earth. She drew in the air hungrily. "The world is after all rather beautiful."

She skipped rather than walked, and somewhere inside her a spirit bubbled into laughter over nothing at all. Her body seemed to hum behind every word she said. She found a new pleasure in the most insignificant gesture—a turn of the head, or a lift of the shoulder. She felt herself actually gliding round corners.

"I never knew before that Shanghai was real, that it was alive."

Before them little children rolled on the lawn, shouting and laughing. She felt like one of them. It seemed to her that she breathed more freely—as if a mask had suddenly been torn from her face. She felt liberated, and knew again the simple joy of just being alive, of knowing that everything in the world had been put there for her amusement, that even other people had been born only for that purpose. . . .

It grew dark, and the moon lay hidden behind a filmy garment of clouds. The wind blew colder and wrapped Sang Hwa's gown closer to her figure.

Li Ssu-yi suddenly put his pudgy hand on her shoulder, and she returned to the solid substance of herself.

"May I take you back to school?"

School! She had forgotten that he did not know her true address or her real life with Lien Wen-kan. He thought she was still at school.

"No, I shall not return to the dormitory," she said hurriedly. "Just take me to my aunt's home; I will stay there to-night."

They got into his car, and he put his face near hers. "It would be a good thing if I could go on being of service to you. Not a bad arrangement."

She thought otherwise, but she did not speak. "It would be a much better arrangement," she sighed to herself, "if Wen-kan were with me." But Wen-kan would spend no time looking at the moon: he would regard this evening as just so much money diverted from the Revolution, plus so much time. She had said nothing to Li about her real motive: let that be settled to-morrow. She made an appointment with him, and thought now about the most effective lie she could concoct. Tell him that she needed the money to buy a certain thing (very important!), or that she had debts? Well, let it wait. She shut her eyes.

"To-day, at least, I have been free and I have lived."

But even this freedom, she knew, was illusory; was but part of a drama being played to an end set by some greater destiny than her own. In this larger force she was but an atom of infinite smallness, and the joy she had felt to-day was, in fact, quite absurd. It could not last; it was not real. The miserable little house, to which she must soon return, the secret work in which she was united with others in a cause, these things had purpose and vitality, they were life and the meaning of life . . . *struggle*.

III

Again it was evening and again the orange moon, grown larger, burnt in the sky. Several people were in Little Hu's room, and Sang Hwa was one. She sat very far from his bed and dared not look at him. How the coughs tore into his poor flesh! She looked down steadily at her hands and could scarcely breathe.

"He's finished," some one whispered.

Lien Wen-kan began sprinkling the room with some disinfectant. Hsu lifted up the thin, withered body to a half-reclining position, and Ah Yeh Hsin sat beside the bed and held Little Hu's chin. He had not strength enough to support himself. He coughed now almost incessantly, and with each cough his lips were covered with blood. The sick man's nose and chin had turned ghastly, the colour of soiled old lacquer, and the rest of his face was a waxen yellow. He kept his eyes shut, and his facial muscles did not move. Whenever he coughed his body seemed to be crumpling up anew. Despite his suffering some powerful urge to speak presently took command of him, as though he had a thing of terrible significance to impart. His mouth began to move and he stammered unintelligibly.

"Don't talk! Lie still for a while."

Suddenly Sang Hwa shrieked, and then hysterically began to weep. Every one turned in surprise. "I can't bear it," she cried, "the life is being crushed out of him."

"Comrade Lien, take her home please," one of the group ordered.

She could hardly stand as Lien Wen-kan took her arm. He half dragged and half lifted her outside. She clutched the tightened muscles of her throat; as they stumbled along her fright was succeeded by a feeling of dull pessimism.

"Why," she said tonelessly, "why is it? Why is life like this to us, bitter, dangerous, full of pain, always with death very near?"

Lien held her even more firmly and told her to hush.

"But what is it for? What has he got out of it? Dying now, one great pain gathering up all the little pains and sufferings out of the past: is that what death is? Do you remember only a short time ago he was so full of life, so abundant with it? And now he is dead, or as good as dead, in the hand of that dark illness——"

"Shut up! Do you think we don't all feel the same way? Be quiet for a moment! Get control of yourself."

When they reached home the girl pulled away from him and threw herself on the bed. She felt her body quivering

like a taut rope. Her breasts stood out and seemed enlarged.
Lien stood gazing down at her in silence.

"Where can it lead us, Wen-kan?" she asked tearfully.
"Remember Old Pon too. Think of the bitterness of days
he lived through, and then in the end he died just like that!
Hasn't one got a right to want happiness?"

Lien sat down on the bed, but he did not look at her.
He could hear her beating heart and he felt her convulsive
sobs vibrating against him. She leaned over and let her
head fall on his shoulder.

"Happiness?" he said finally. "You mean roll yourself
up in a golden cocoon and to hell with the rest of the world
as long as you can feed on mulberry leaves? Isn't it precisely
because we can't live that way, because we're not vegetables,
nor insects, but human beings, that we believe in making
real happiness possible?"

She tried to control her resentment, and the effort gave
an unnatural tone to her voice. "I often think that after all
human beings can only live a few tens of years at best, and
why should we deliberately seek out pain?"

Lien started to protest.

"Listen," she broke in, "it's just because we are human
beings that we have a right to make a choice, and the
choice doesn't have to be a bitter one, does it? It seems to
me sometimes that I cannot live without light, the wide
open sky to breathe freely under, and happiness, just plain
happiness. And our life, always a secret existence, seems to
deny our right to clean joyous air and even the flowing
sunshine."

Lien Wen-kan looked at her sardonically, and there was
a note of weariness in his reply. "In order to make freedom
a reality we've got to struggle for a new society, out of the
old bondage—but, look here, you understand all this, you
have seen these things yourself."

Sang Hwa lifted her head and put her lips close to his
chin.

"Yes, I know—all that. But can we get that sort of freedom in our time?"

"If not our generation, then the next. Meanwhile we stand for something." He leaned over and embraced her simply. "You've had too much for one day. You'd better get some rest. To-morrow I'll have a thorough talk with you."

He helped her undress and she melted into the bed. He was going back to Little Hu's.

She took his hand. "Perhaps you are right, perhaps I am not quite sane. I feel like—but never mind. Tell me exactly what you think of me to-morrow."

She watched him snap out the light and shut the door, and listened to him go down the stairs. When she could no longer hear his footsteps fear crept into her again. After a while she imagined that she heard some one in the room, and she sprang up and switched on a light. She called out. No one answered, but then she felt sure that it must have been a 'black-gown'[1] outside her door. She fell back on her bed, exhausted.

"I can't stand it!" she said aloud. "Isn't it silly, when one thinks of it? Given a few years of life, one throws them away for an ideal one will never see, an ideal that may not come about in that way ever. . . ."

Early next day, before Lien Wen-kan had returned, she wrote a note and sent it over to him, asking the Party for a month's release. She packed her leather bags in a few minutes, and went to stay with her aunt.

IV

Although Li Ssu-yi was not the most lovable of people, he had his virtues. He responded promptly and generously, for instance, to the slightest expression of a wish of Sang Hwa, and he bothered himself a great deal thinking up ways

[1] Government spy.

in which to please her. She knew that his attentions to her were not altogether agreeable to her aunt, who seemed worried that she might lose a good prospective son-in-law, but Comrade Sang did not let that trouble her. She had a right to enjoy the few happy days stolen from her work.

Her happiness was genuine.

She covered her whole body with powder and spent hours making up her face. She abandoned herself to gaiety, every night going out with Li, and every night coming home late, smelling of wine and not a little drunk. During the day she amused herself driving here and there in his new car. She read nothing but romantic stories and the cinema advertisements.

Two weeks went by very rapidly, and one day she returned home in Li's car to find her little cousin waiting for her, important with news.

"A fellow named Liu came to see you," said the boy.

Liu! That was Lien Wen-kan's other name. "Did he leave a note?" she asked.

"No. He just says he come to see you. Nothin' particular, he says."

Sang Hwa frowned. She walked slowly to her room, suddenly ashamed, her eyes filled with the tall, straight figure of Lien Wen-kan and of his fine, grave face. Perhaps he had come to denounce her? Or to bring important news? Perhaps Lien was being chased? She shuddered. They might even be watching her. Looking round she saw only a warm clean room with furniture of rich wood shining under a flood of light, and she felt reassured. Here were no documents, no forbidden books. Everything was spotless and legal, everything was beautiful, and there were no germs of disease. Guiltily she remembered Little Hu, and thought of the others, working, toiling. Ought she have left without first getting approval from the Party?

Her aunt strolled into the room, smoking a silver-mounted water pipe. She began chattering at random, but gradually came round to the subject of her school friends. One had to choose one's company carefully these days, but Sang Hwa had a good fellow in that youth called "Liu."

"He's quite a friend of yours, isn't he?"

"Yes, we are comrades."

The old lady, her gold teeth flashing, began a long eulogy of his charms. He was certainly very handsome, he was brilliant, he had a winning manner, and all in all (judging from what she said) he was perhaps the most attractive young man she had ever met. She searched for more subtle and effective encomiums, and watched her niece keenly, to see what her expression revealed.

Sang Hwa smiled as if highly pleased, but inwardly she thought: "Don't imagine you are going to find out anything from me. I think I shall just hold on to this Li Ssu-yi and keep him out of your reach."

When her aunt had left she threw her stockings angrily on a chair and said again, "I shall hold on to him."

There were, however, but two weeks left, and after that she knew she must return to work, to the Revolution, and to a covert existence. Back there her individuality would cease to be a reality; she would again become but an atom in a movement that had its absolute in masses of men, and was concerned with the individual only as a conscious thought in an organism infinitely greater than any single ego. Back there with her comrades she would again have to be very careful, not only against sickness, but against the Terror—arrest, imprisonment, or, worse still, having her soft legs and body crushed in torture.

"Live in pain, die in pain!"

Why should she go back? She was not indispensable, and somehow now she no longer felt any interest in that work. But how they would despise her if she broke away! She could hear them saying of her, "Little Sang Hwa, who sold herself to the big-bellied sugar merchant! Ha!" She frowned angrily, and told herself that she ought not to think

about them at all, not for another two weeks, anyway.
And yet . . .

"Could they ever forgive me," she asked aloud, "if I gave
up? Could Lien Wen-kan?"

She thought that perhaps they had already expelled her.
If so, good. "Good!" she said with an air of finality, as if
to convince herself that it was already true. She sat motionless for a while, and the expression on her face was one of
extreme perplexity.

Presently she went into the tiled bath and stood before
the long mirror, looking first at her face, and then down
the gentle curves of her body that spun silkily up from the
floor to her gleaming hair. She moved her hips in a slow
arc, and she lifted her arms gracefully above her head. For
several minutes she stood thoughtlessly admiring the figure
before her, as she might have gazed in detachment at an
exquisite thing of art.

"What is it all for?" she suddenly asked herself.

Those soft rounded shoulders, the tragic beauty of those
high-arched breasts, and glistening down from them that
swift line to the firm ivory thighs! Was it fair to this
perfect body, to herself, to nature, to hide a work of such
splendour in darkness, risk it in perhaps altogether useless
ventures, expose it to barbaric tortures? Her eyes were
dazzled with the wonder of it; she had forgotten how
magnificent her body was. She put her hands over her face
and felt her temples throb. When she looked in the mirror
again she was impressed with that exquisite line that seemed
like a long note of music, clinging from breast to thigh.
She began to analyse this form of art in terms of æsthetics,
breaking it into parts.

"Parts?" If the Terror got hold of her, how many parts
would she be cut into? She shuddered.

Her face burned, and she moved over to bathe it, first
in hot water, then in cold. She drenched all the powder,
all the cream, all the mascara and lipstick, and they slid

away, leaving just a plain oval. This was the face she wore among the women labourers, when she did organizational work: no paint at all, and even her shaved eyebrows left completely bald. She looked at herself again, and again she thought of her comrades and of their tall dreams. She felt a blush of shame creep over her, and was indignant because of it.

She wanted to smash something, to protest with physical action. Why could she not break away from them? She pictured Lien Wen-kan before her, and angrily she cried aloud: "Be it good or bad, I have only one life, and only one choice for it! You can condemn me as you please, I am not going to risk this body, expose it to torture. I can't stand it!"

Every one had the free will to turn, this way or that. Why should not she have it?

She rushed from the bathroom into her boudoir and lay down heavily on the bed. Her heart pounded, and her temples seemed to leap out, they beat so hard. She put her chilled hands against her hot face. She could not think through to a conclusion; every statement posed another and brought its own denial. Finally she centred her wrath on Lien as an individual.

In the next room she heard her aunt's voice suddenly raised in conversation with her daughter, Pao Chen. She seemed to be complaining about Li Ssu-yi's attentions to Sang Hwa.

"So Pao Chen still wants to sell herself to him," she thought. "I think not. It is very bad for young women to sell themselves to fat old men. H'mm. I shall not let him go."

But how could she prevent it? Accept him herself, marry him? Before her she saw a multiple row of protruding bellies and jutting teeth. She saw Li Ssu-yi absently scratching his head, heard the dull heaviness of his voice, with every word interminably emphasized. The effect of thinking of him as a whole was like a dose of castor beans.

To yield to those short fat arms, to be pressed close to that round little belly . . . castor beans.

For the next five or six days she could not satisfy her conscience about Wen-kan and the others and she remained depressed. She seemed to hear them making fun of her, laughing with great amusement over her attachment to her rich and sentimental donkey. They did not understand her, she told herself, whenever the cynical smile of Wen-kan rose up before her. She even began to sympathize with Li Ssu-yi, who so often made the same complaint against the world; it was probably true that few people really understood him.

At last she decided to have a thorough talk with Lien Wen-kan.

When she reached the house she was very excited. She paused a moment to still her heart before mounting the ladder-like stairs to the room. Mentally she phrased her opening remarks. Out of that familiar door a strange face poked itself, looking at her suspiciously.

"Who d'ya want?"

"Mr Liu. . . . Isn't there a Mr Liu?"

"No. No Liu in this house."

She climbed down and left hurriedly, with an uncomfortable feeling that she was being watched, and perhaps followed.

But she did not give up the search. She went from one place to another, looking for former comrades. They had all left, and everywhere she encountered suspicious eyes. At last she did find Wang Chao-ti, formerly a close friend. He did not show any pleasure at meeting her, but simply listened coldly to what she had to say. He answered her questions briefly and non-committally. Exasperated, she grabbed his shoulder and shook him. She put her face close to his and demanded in a quaking voice:

"Chao-ti, am I poison? Where is Wen-kan living now? Why don't you tell me? You have nothing to fear from me. Tell me, where is he? I have something important to say to him and I must find him."

He smiled with the corner of his mouth, and looked at her impudently.

"I really don't know."

She had an almost uncontrollable desire to beat him, to knock the information from him. Then she thought of embracing him, or hanging on to him, weeping, begging him not to forsake her. But she only stood looking at him for a while in silent fury, and then she choked down her tears and left.

"It is not I who is to blame now," she kept repeating to herself. "It is they who have abandoned me."

Three days later she came once more to Chao-ti's place, and handed him a three-thousand character letter, asking him to deliver it to Lien Wen-kan. It was a thick, heavy package and very firmly sealed on the outside with the initials "S.H."

She had spent two nights composing this document.

It began with a careful analysis of her temperament, which she pointed out was in many ways unique; she was unlike other women. She proved beyond doubt that her spirit was not suited to revolutionary work, that the atmosphere of struggle did not fit in with her philosophy of life. She explained just what the latter was: it involved the right to live gladly in such freedom as she herself could find. She had discovered that human beings were given but one life, and somehow she was unable to find any justification in history for believing that men afterwards would worry about how she had used it. But even without this conflict with her philosophy which the work involved, had they not been the first to abandon her? She did not in a single line suggest that she had fled, or that they might have had cause to worry over possible betrayal at her hands. But now that it was all over she wanted them to understand her philosophy, that was all. It was not that she was afraid to die, but that she was eager to live. Finally she begged Lien Wen-kan to be careful, and she promised that she would remember him for ever. She was even willing to keep up their personal friendship, always, if it pleased him.

Sang Hwa was not happy. Even after she had written this letter she could not forget Wen-kan, and she kept thinking, "Never again to see him? Never?"

Her life problems were by no means solved. She could not go on living in her aunt's house much longer—Pao Chen's jealousy was becoming unbearable—and yet she was determined not to go back to her own poor home. The month which she had set for herself must see some kind of way out!

She felt carried resistlessly on the broad expanse of a great sea, with not a shore anywhere in sight. The break from the one thing that for a while had given meaning to her life left her now without any course or aim, without any chart, drifting purposelessly. . . .

In such a mood she saw Li Ssu-yi.

She looked once more at the little circle of baldness on his head, she considered the oily, well-fed face, and she gazed a long time at the unfortunate teeth. She tried to convince herself that these were but minor details, that love could in fact glorify them, and she repeated to herself over and over, "I do love him, I *love* him." Yet when she fell into his arms, when his big mouth sought and covered hers and he sighed into her, she could not escape the feeling that this was a bad-tasting medicine she was taking in atonement for some crime against herself.

"Whew!"

"Sang Hwa," he proposed, "let's get married right away —before I leave for Nanyang ! What do you say?"

She pulled a long breath. "I have no opinion in the matter."

He leaned forward hungrily, touched her lips to his, and kept them there for several minutes. When at last he drew away he was red-faced and panting. He gazed passionately at her, and his eyes came wide open with a light of happiness. Unconsciously he put his fat hand to his hair.

Suddenly Sang Hwa buried her face in the divan and began to sob.

"Why, what's the matter?" he asked, astonished. "What is it?"

After a long time she lifted her head, and her face was stained with tears. Nevertheless she forced it into a bewitching smile and put her cheek against his.

"Nothing," she said. "I am simply too happy."

v

The face of the lake before Mrs Li Ssu-yi's rambling summer home grew pale under the softening sky. A few boats sailed by in the moon-bathed night and the place was touched with a melancholy glamour.

Sang Hwa, standing beside the window, had not moved for a long time, nor had she answered any of her cousin's questions. The lake breeze blew strong now and the song of the minstrel crowded into the room. He was singing *Sad Vistas*. Why did he always come back to that song? It made her think of Wen-kan. What had become of him?

"Have you had a letter recently from him?" her cousin suddenly asked.

"Who?" Sang Hwa was startled.

"Your husband, of course."

"Oh!" She blushed. "Yes, of course."

She turned back abruptly and tossed her head, lifting her neck so full of poise and grace. Walking over to her cousin, she looked at her with that captivating smile for which she had become celebrated, and spoke to her in that soft voice of the very gentle lady.

"Let us go out for a sail under the moon, cousin. We will take along two bottles of wine—one for each of us, so? Come on, hurry! We shall get grandly drunk."

KUO MO-JO
(1892–)

POET, dramatist, literary critic, translator, short-story writer, and novelist, Kuo Mo-jo's versatility alone would seem sufficient to give him eminent rank among the leaders of the Chinese literary renaissance. The quality of his creative work makes this place assured.

Going to Japan while still of middle school age, Kuo Mo-jo (like his friend Lu Hsün) studied medicine in Tokyo. Before he returned to China he married a Japanese wife. That resulted in frequent trips to Japan, and long periods of residence and many friends there. His characters are often Japanese, and his stories frequently have Japanese settings. He is almost as well known among the Japanese as among his own countrymen. An order was issued for his arrest as a political 'reactionary' some years ago, and he is now forced to reside in Japan. Ten of his works, including some translations from foreign languages, have been banned by the Kuomintang.

Kuo Mo-jo is also an archæologist of distinction. His recently published volumes concerning the discoveries in the Honan diggings greatly interested scholars and scientists in both Japan and China. It is thought that his interpretations of the Yin bones may prove that Chinese civilization is a thousand years or more older than previously supposed.

DILEMMA[1]

By KUO MU-JO

" . . . When I was living in Shanghai I was a burden to you, I know, and when I finally departed I had to cause you even more trouble.

"The weather was not bad when we left, but that afternoon the sea was violent and we were all very uncomfortable. The three children were sick, Little Peace worst of all, but next day he recovered. It was snowing when we reached Nagasaki, and was still stormy when late in the afternoon we came into Fugun. We spent the night there in Shih Chuan's home. In the morning we went to Yuhu's.

"We had lived at Yuhu's for only two days, however, when we wanted to move. You know that second story of his is not safe. It is cold, and the timbers are unsound. Moreover, with children running in and out, and requiring to be watched, it is inconvenient to be living upstairs. I've therefore rented a house for twenty dollars a month, and it is attractive, with a little garden of orange-trees where the children can play.

"Perhaps you remember it? From where we lived before we could just see those trees. Don't you recall it? That's the place. At first I thought of consulting you by letter before taking it, as the rental is a little higher, but I finally took the decision by myself because for the children's sake I thought we should move in as soon as possible. I can afford the expense for the present.

"How are you living in Shanghai? I still feel desolate, with a lonely sorrow for ever whirling along in my mind.

[1] The Chinese title for this story is, literally, *The Cross*.

Outside it is still bitter, there is a heavy snowfall, and I am in a morbid mood. We have been parted only half a month, yet it seems to me already a year.

"The day before yesterday the sky cleared for a while, and I took the children with me to shop in the market. We passed by the cinema and they begged me to take them in. It was a task to sit through it. Returning, we stopped to have some noodles, and Sonny Fu then wanted to be carried; he had eaten so much! I took him on my back for nearly half the way. How heavy he is becoming! I ached with a sore back that night and could not sleep.

"There are so many things I want to write to you, and yet now that I have begun I can say nothing, and this all ends without any significance. I cannot help being depressed. I am no longer young, many of the things I once valued most in the world are gone, and those precious things I held in my hands have somehow slipped through them. I feel dreadfully uncertain about the future. How brief life is! Is there anything left of it for a woman after the age of thirty? What is your opinion, father of my children?

"But my head is a confusion of loneliness and fatigue! . . . I shall write to you later."

.   .   .   .   .   .

Mrs Ai-mao had been in Japan almost three weeks, and nothing had been heard of her. Her husband had written a letter asking for news, and when none had come he had been much annoyed. Then he had begun to worry. Here was a letter at last. He carefully read every character of it, his eyes taking it in eagerly, his nostrils turned out, his breath quickening.

It was written in pencil and was hardly legible. From the nervous scrawl he understood that she must be troubled by the children, moving, and adjusting herself. The end of it was so chaotic that he decided she must have written during a sleepless night. When she was not caring for the children evidently she was longing for him. Well, it couldn't be helped: they could not continue to live with him if he were to make a living. He reread her words, and at the end a few tears mingled with those that his wife had shed on the letter as she had written it.

"Yes, truly, men are mortal and their mortality is short! Yet living under such pressure as we do we are not even allowed to enjoy these few years! We are more to be pitied than cows and horses. Even the dog has liberty to go where he chooses and to sleep in peace, but we are denied this! We suffer deeply from suppressed griefs, and we struggle vainly in a sea of troubles.

"Why do we live? Why do we exert our brains at all? Isn't the whole process only conducted for the benefit of money-grabbers? Don't we do it only to impose upon our descendants exactly the same *rôle* as we ourselves are living in the present world? We are really insufferable creatures! We are vegetables, we are water, we are even baser! Art? Literature? Prestige and reputation? Finally, enterprise? Are they not all merely gold-plated trap-words, delusions?

"I don't want to sacrifice my character in order to be an artist. I want to create out of myself a man! In the end I may become a beggar, I may die abroad, but at least I want to be the sweetheart of my wife, I want to be the beloved father of my children, however many crosses I may bear! I am yours, now and to-morrow, permanently yours, my chosen wife! How I long for you! Should it prove impossible for us to live, we can at least destroy our children, and end everything by jumping together into the Poto![1]

"Sorrow no more! I shall return, I certainly shall return!

"Our magazine is publishing on a contract of only one year, and its first issue must appear within thirty or forty days. I am responsible for its publication. When these first thirty or forty days are over I shall return, certainly I shall return, whether the magazine appears or not! Whether we

[1] A river in Japan where unhappy lovers commit suicide.

are destined to live or to die, this I shall decide in that time, and nothing can stop me from following you! Where you go I shall follow you! Through fire, water, or suicide! Where you make your home there my home will be also."

He remonstrated to himself in this manner for some time, weeping bitterly. Then his senses gradually became more subject to discipline. He moved back and forth in his small room. It was early afternoon, scarcely two o'clock, and the sunlight billowed in from a side window. The warm rays seemed now encouraging, now cynical, disillusioning. The walls were bare except for his bookshelves and a portrait of Goethe on one side and on the wall adjacent to it a print of Beethoven.

"How insipid are your feelings! What a habitually complaining person you are! How self-pitying is your daily life! And how narrow and selfish are your thoughts! Such notions as you've had only prove the ease with which you profane the artist that's in you! You are a criminal-souled artist after all!"

Scolding himself in this way he felt that his spirit was repressed between two partitions, threatening to burst asunder both of them. But he ignored and mastered this conflict within himself and walked thoughtfully back and forth across the room. "My Beethoven! My Goethe! Don't stare at me! I no longer claim any kinship with you. I promise never to 'put on your sheep's head to sell my dog's meat'—no, never again! I shall bid farewell to you, farewell for ever." And actually he looked at the two images before him as if he were bidding them good-bye for all time as he muttered to himself.

Ai-mao had suffered deeply, and at last he decided to communicate to his wife the degree and nature of his sorrow after reading her letter. Just when he put brush to paper, however, he heard a knock at his door.

"Is it Ai-mao's house?"

"Yes."

"Is Mr Ai-mao in?"

"I am Ai-mao."

"Eh! Eh!"

The two guests bent deferentially to him, and yet they seemed not quite convinced. Ai-mao invited them into his rooms, and they relieved themselves of their names. That delivery was really perfunctory, as Ai-mao had already identified them from their features and their dialect.

They came from the city of C——, of the far western province of Szechuan.

Two weeks earlier Ai-mao had received a telegram from the Red Cross Society of C—— City, asking him to return there again and take up his post as a doctor. The message stated that the Red Cross was sending representatives to bring him money, and begged him to accept their offer. A few days later this long express letter had come from his eldest brother in C——:

> I have written to you several times, but thus far no letter has come in reply. I wonder if there is any special reason for it, and if so I wish you would tell me, fully, what it is.
>
> A letter has come to me from the Red Cross of C——. I enclose it, together with a copy of their telegram, and you will see what it is about. I want to tell you that it is very difficult finding a job now. It is especially hard to find a good permanent position. The Red Cross is organized on a big scale here, more so than in other places, and it is more dependable than any official connexion. I hope you will not reject this opportunity.
>
> You know your parents are getting older. They are expecting much of you. I will personally appreciate it very much if you can come back as soon as possible.
>
> With affectionate regards to you, and remembrances to Hsiao Fu (Mrs Ai-mao) and the children,
>
> Sincerely,
>
> W.

The letter enclosed read as follows:

Dear brother W,

We have come to a decision here to invite Ai-mao to join us. The salary offered is nominally 400 dollars a month, but actually, due to our financial condition at present, there will be a discount on this of 20 per cent., which means he will collect 320 dollars per month. When our finances are in better shape we will pay him accordingly.

We are hoping that you will write to him about this matter. I am afraid that Ai-mao will have taken another position in Shanghai by the time this reaches him, so that I have already telegraphed him our proposal. I shall be glad to send representatives of ours to meet him, and provide him with travelling funds.

I enclose a copy of my telegram to him.

With kindest regards,

K.

Ai-mao's eldest brother had already been in business in C—— City for a long time. He had found a good job for Ai-mao two years ago, and the Red Cross had promised to send him travelling expenses when he returned from Japan. The remittance had somehow gone astray, however, and he had lived in Shanghai for more than a year before his brother had learned his address and sent him a series of letters. Ai-mao had made no reply. His brother and parents loved him deeply and wanted him to return as soon as possible. They did not understand why he had no wish to go back.

Eleven years earlier he had been married at home, and immediately he had desired to be unmarried. Yet he was helpless. His parents were old, and he did not want them to suffer. He dared not divorce his wife because she was so dominated by old ideas that she would most certainly have committed suicide, and his parents themselves might die of anger and shame. So he had fled from his home instead.

Nine years ago, when his younger sister had been

betrothed, he had written some letters of objection, saying that wedding her off without her consent destined her, "if she married a chicken to live with the chicken, if she married a dog to live like the dog, for whomever she married she must obey and be dependent upon." His parents had bitterly resented his ironical comment, and they had been outraged by his unreasonableness. His own wife, due to his aloofness, had made several attempts to kill herself.

Then he had gone to live with Hsiao Fu, and for a while his parents had broken all relations with him. Later on they had slightly relented, because he was after all their son. Yet when they wrote to him they referred to his Japanese wife as his 'concubine' and to his children as 'concubine's sons.' This wounded him deeply, and often he longed to return home, to divorce himself, and win his freedom, but whenever he seriously considered doing it he was restrained by the thought of injuring his mother and father, and was moved by pity for his backward wife.

The first in the family to forgive him had been this eldest brother, who nevertheless did not really understand the mental torture through which he had gone. His ambition was to persuade him to return to C——, which was not far from his home town. But how could he go there? He often thought of his old father, whom he had not seen since he had left home, and his mother and his brothers and sisters, none of whom he had seen in all that time. Finally he thought fondly of his native town, and sometimes lay awake with a nostalgic yearning for a glimpse of familiar people and scenes of his youth. Yet it was impossible for him to return, impossible!

"My father and my mother! I think you will not see me again in this century. I weep when I think of your sorrow over my conduct, but I can do nothing to comfort you. I have only given you regrets to carry with you the rest of your life! My brothers and sisters! I am grateful for your kindness, but we cannot meet again either. Woman who has lived with my parents and who was queerly my wife! We were victimized by stupid customs of the past, and I have no complaint to make against you, and I hope you have none against me! I sympathize with you, and with your dull *rôle* as a mere guest in my parents' home for the rest of your life, yet I am powerless to free you from your yoke. . . ."

Whenever he thought of his home he could scarcely keep from weeping. But no one but himself knew the depth of his misery.

"We have come to see you, at the request of our president. Here is his letter, and here is a letter from your brother. I have a bank draft for you too. It's in here, in my blouse—there are many pickpockets about."

One of the visitors handed him the letters, loosened his coat, and from inside drew out a bank draft for a thousand silver taels. The letter contained little new information, but merely added a few words of introduction for the visitors. After he had read them Ai-mao declared that he could not accept. He explained why he must refuse, and he returned the bank-draft to them, and asked them to take it back with them to Szechuan.

"But we have been ordered by the Red Cross to turn the draft over to you. If you accept it then our duty has been performed; if you do not then we shall be criticized by our president. He expects you to come."

"Are there not two German doctors in the hospital?"

"Yes, yes, there are two, but there are also more than thirty Chinese doctors."

"Oh! But the staff must be well filled then. It is unnecessary for me to go."

"On the contrary, we are understaffed. The Second Army suffered a severe defeat, there were thousands of wounded, and we had to take care of all of them. At the same time the First Army had several thousands of wounded —and altogether our staff is inadequate."

"If that's the case, my coming or not cannot matter much. There is always fighting nowadays, and we cannot take care of all the wounded even if we make doctors out of the entire population of Szechuan!"

"Ah-ha! Ha, ha! . . ."

The guests refused to take back the bank-draft and at last Ai-mao accepted it. He made out a receipt for it and the two men left at once.

.   .   .   .   .   .

Sunlight sprayed in diffused banks of light into the little room, and dust drifted lazily in the air.

Ai-mao's intention to write a letter to his wife having been interrupted, he thought now about the thousand-tael draft before him. It was the biggest sum of money he had ever possessed at one time, and it was proving very tempting. He thought of cashing it, going at once to Japan, and bringing his wife and children back with him. They could then go on to C—— together. They would not have to worry about the materials of living, for with $320 per month he could recklessly squander even as much as $120 and still save a great deal. In three or five years they would be comfortably well fixed. He could look forward to salary increases from time to time; besides, there would be other commissions. Well, in case he went to C—— he would not return to his native town. His people would insist upon it, but if he did there was certain to be an explosion over his marriage. His parents would never become reconciled. . . . It was after all impossible for him to go back, reopen old wounds, and cause new despair, only because he wanted to make his fortune.

"Alas! My father and my mother, forgive your son! It is unfilial for me not to see you; it would be *more* unfilial for me to see you! If your unfilial son returns it will be only to ruin the lives of others, perhaps to endanger your

lives also. So how can you wish me to return? I will
not see you again in this life."

He thought with remorse of how often he had seen his
mother weep when his two older brothers were studying
in Japan. She had repeatedly said that she would never let
Ai-mao go abroad, because having her sons away from her
for so long had nearly broken her heart. When Ai-mao
had married he had insisted, however, upon being permitted at once to go to the provincial capital for higher
study. His mother had gone with him to the wharf. The
last thing she had said, as the boat was about to leave, was,
"Promise me not to go abroad without my knowledge,
son! Do you hear?"

It was over those words of parting that he felt profound
regret, for he had after all gone to Japan without asking
his mother's consent. How great and prolonged must have
been the sorrow, how numerous the tears of his mother
during his long absence! How many recollections she must
have borne with anguish! He thought now that she must
never see him again, and that she must die without seeing
him. Frequently he had told his sweetheart that he longed
to return only once, to visit his mother a last time to ask
her blessing, but he realized that the journey would never
be made. Ah, the cursed results of the arranged marriage!
How many parents had been separated from their sons,
how many had suffered under the same system, how final
and irremediable was the estrangement!

"Money! You will not ruin me, but I shall ruin you!"

He threw the bank-draft and letter on to the floor and
viciously stamped upon them. Strength to form his
decision, to refuse to return to C——, seemed to grow out
of this physical action. He sat down at once and wrote two
letters, one to his brother and the other enclosing the bank-
draft, to the president of the Red Cross Society of Szechuan.
Then he took up the letter from Hsiao Fu and read it again
and again. He made the following reply to her:

I have your letter, sweetheart. Before it came I was extremely depressed, and since I read it how depressed I have been again! You know that I thoroughly understand your distress, and I cannot greet you with trivial words. Just now I can only say that I shall be back with you again in three or four weeks. Perhaps this may cheer you a little.

I have repented my extravagant ambitions. I have come to recognize that I have no talent for literature. Now I do not feel the slightest hesitation concerning this decision. I shall stay here for several weeks only because our magazine, you know, will be prepared for a full year by that time. In any case, I must keep my word to my friends.

.   .   .   .   .   .

Several days ago I went to Wusih, and you remember that one of our friends told us of a beautiful house there? I saw it during my trip, and regretted a little that we did not move into it, so that it would not have been necessary for you to return to Japan. However, let's forget it now; it does not matter.

I am not worrying about my present living conditions here now. I have a last way to solve everything, but I shall not tell you about it until I return to Japan. One thing which makes me very happy is that I have just trampled upon a thousand-tael bank-draft—stepped on it indeed! Money! I won't bother my head about it again. After I return to Japan I think it may be possible for me to be an assistant in a physiology class—or I shall be glad to become a newsboy or milkman, for that matter. As a last resort there is this one way to solve everything, about which I'll tell you when I reach Japan.

Kiss the children for me.

When Ai-mao finished his letter it was past four o'clock in the morning. He seemed to have relieved himself of a great burden, and there was a peace in his body and brain. He drew some cold water into a basin and bathed his face. Then he put the letters into his pocket and went out by the back door.

SHIH MING

(1908–)

SHIH MING is the pseudonym of a Chinese woman writer who has thus far managed to shield her real name.

She was born in Hupeh, in a 'lofty-doored' family—that is, a large old-fashioned Chinese family of the upper class. Her father was an important landlord and high official of the Provincial Government.

Shih Ming's stories are not widely known, but she has had a strong personal influence on the development of several of China's youngest and most vigorous writers. Her courage and daring in utilizing social material heretofore tabooed in Chinese literature show an emancipation which will astound those who have persisted in believing that Chinese art is incapable of a sharp revolutionary break with the past. *Fragment from a Lost Diary* is a good example of the 'revolutionary realism' school in which she classes her work.

FRAGMENT FROM A LOST DIARY

By SHIH MING

May 24, Windy

THE heaviness of this long May day nearly suffocates me. Endless hunger, endless nausea, endless doubt and anxiety. I move from my side to my back and then to my side again. The wooden planks of the bed are harder than stone. Hard, hard. It is impossible to get any rest! It is impossible for one moment to relieve the constant throbbing pain in my body, however I turn and toss. I cannot read. Only writing—since there is no one to talk with—seems to take my mind out of itself, as small idle occupations do.

Ching's forehead has become noticeably more lined since he learned the reason of my illness. Often he stares at me with wide eyes, saying nothing. When I ask why it is he looks at me like that he answers vaguely, "Nothing, nothing. Rest and get well quickly, that's all."

Meaningless words! I know well enough how inconvenient a thing I am. What small regard the female womb has for the 'historic necessities'! It is its own history and its own necessity! It is the dialectic reduced to its simplest statement. What generosity of nature to make me this gift of the 'illness of the rich' at just such a time!

I can't even enjoy being heroic in bearing my personal discomfort. With the tyranny of helplessness I must drag the whole of our close-knit organization into this trouble. When conditions are critical, and the situation everywhere is hostile, the individual burden unavoidably becomes the group burden. It isn't that my own small *rôle* remains

302

unfulfilled. It's that my incapacity causes interruptions and irregularities for every one. Most of all for Ching. He has become the slave at a sick-bed. He is *amah*, nurse, cook, errand-boy—and beggar. His work is neglected, badly done, and he goes about his duties with an absent-minded-ness born of fatigue. This in turn means confusion in the organization, and all because of my demands. It is so terribly important that all our plans at this time should be unfailingly sure, so much more important than this strug-gling life inside of me. Ching never complains of this added worry and responsibility, but I know how greatly it weighs upon him.

Now that the 30th of May is approaching he drags himself out every morning at six and cannot return until late at night. Out of this precious day he must steal time for me —begging a few coppers from friend to friend to buy the small indispensable things for me, the invalid. I know this, and I know too how it troubles him to be away from me. Yet, under this unendurable sickness, I forget and quarrel with him again and again for his negligence!

Our house is like all the rest of the *kung-yu*[1] along Sha Tan. Our room is the middle one of three facing south. There is no window in it. The only opening is the door. When that is closed no air or sunshine can stir within. The room itself is very narrow, with space only for a bed and table and a small bench. I can reach over to the table from my bed. That at least is a convenience.

The boy hasn't cleaned our room for several days. Probably this is because we haven't paid the rent (four dollars a month!) since March. The wall-paper is cracked, and a corner of it hangs from the ceiling. Dust and cobwebs drop from it. Rats run back and forth in the bamboo rafters. Sometimes one of them, in a fight, tumbles down to the earthen floor. It has to lie there till Ching returns.

[1] A *kung-yu* is a lodging-house. Many are used as dormitories for men and women students in Peiping.

I myself cannot get up, however nauseating the sight and
smell of the creature may be.

Everything in the room is covered with dust, blown in
through the open door—open to anyone who wants to gape
in from the courtyard. Spiders work back and forth. I
look at them, entranced, as they crawl even up to my bed,
and spin their silvery threads in the sunlight. They are at
least *alive*. They are the only companions I have. They help
me to forget the oppressive loneliness and agony of this
dreary May day.

Our neighbour on the left is evidently a student at Pei
Ta.[1] He seems to be in some way related to the landlord,
and for that reason hasn't paid his rent for months. The
landlord has now begun to seize his mail, however, even
registered letters containing money. The student doesn't
complain about it. What is money to him? His fat red
face radiates peace and serenity. When he needs money he
tries to beg it from the landlord. If successful he goes out
with a handful of coppers, and soon returns with a bottle
of *pai-kan* and a piece of roast chicken. Locking himself up
inside, he proceeds to drink for the rest of the day, clucking
and imitating the opera stars in an impossible falsetto.
When the last drop is gone he gives a loud slap on his
thigh, rolls over, and is soon thunderously snoring in deep
contentment. Sometimes he cannot squeeze a single cash
out of his relative, but receives instead a large piece of harsh
criticism or advice. On these occasions he returns to his
room very depressed. "Ah! ... Sh! ... Ha! ..." Is he
actually planning to commit suicide? Nobody worries
about it, least of all the landlord.

On the other side there is a dramatist, also a student of
Pei Ta. He is often away for a whole day, for which I
offer thanks. When he stays at home he practises his chosen
profession, and this is very tiresome indeed. He sings like a
Great Painted Face of the theatre, in a froglike voice. Some-

[1] Peking National University.

times he attempts the lines of the Bearded Face, with his voice
ranging in all dimensions. But the most unbearable of all is
the sound resulting when he lifts his throat to a shrill
soprano and shrieks in imitation of the female lead. One
can picture him twisting his waist and swinging his hips in
rhythm with the singing. He frequently asks the landlord
in for a chat and 'refreshments.' At such times he joins the
villain in cursing the other lodgers.

"*Ai-ya*," he exclaims, "it's time even for me to pay the
rent. Only this morning I reminded myself to go to the
bank, but my wasteful memory has again failed me. Look,
here's the account book in my pocket. You see I really
intended to go there!"

This fellow looks after the house servant too. Bribing
him with a handful of peanuts he collects all the gossip he
can. How much money has the rickshaw-man's wife—she
in the corner on the western wing—squeezed behind her
husband's back? With whom has the actress been copulat-
ing? What dress did she wear? And so on. Between them
a most provoking conversation ensues, evidently to the
interest and high satisfaction of both. It never occurs to
him to give me any consideration. Yet when I am retching
with anguish he heaves audible sighs. "How unendurable!
How much better off dead!" Not content with exaggerated
groans to himself, he sometimes ventures to tap the thin
wall and whisper through the chinks in a soft, sympathetic
voice: "Madam, sister, would you bring peace to my heart
by permitting me to assist you? Ah, it is bitterly painful to
me, painful!"

However great my contempt of him I am helpless. I say
nothing. My very silence provokes him to actual savage
scolding and cursing. I am a pestilence to him! We paste
up the chinks in the wall, but he slits them open again with
a knife. Sweet are one's neighbours, unto whom one
should do as unto oneself.

The whole courtyard is crowded with quarrelsome

U

voices. Women curse and scold and beat. There is a droning voice somewhere for ever mechanically reading the old
Four Books and classical poetry. Eight different families,
living in a twelve-*chien* house, and each rivalling the other
to produce the loudest noise and create the greatest possible
friction! The whole day long this courtyard boils and
seethes, and only my damp, suffocating little room contributes nothing. Perfect Confucian harmony: *li, yi, lien,
ch'ih*.[1] I am seized alternately with chills and fever. All the
time I am half-famished. The hungrier I am the more I
want to vomit. But not a crumb to feed that twin torment,
either the hunger or the physical need for expelling food.
And all this suffering utterly without significance! That I
can have actually endured it for over two months! That I
should think, even now, of wanting to continue to exist
only as the vessel of a chemical experiment heartlessly, in-
exorably formulating itself within me! And against my will!

Am I insane to think of *that* way out? But it is obviously
the solution. Still, I won't consider it again to-day.

May 25

Ching returned last night looking like a mask of himself.
He fell on the bed almost as soon as he entered the door.
He was very gaunt, terribly thin, and his dark eyes opened
to show frightening depths, cavernous like wells and full of
foreboding.

He looked vacantly at me, while I asked him what he
had eaten. He admitted having had nothing since noon,
when he had bought six dry cakes from a street vendor.

At last he pulled himself from the bed and turned to
cook the little tubes of wheat-rolls he had brought home
with him. He lighted the tiny flame under the oil-lamp on

---

[1] Propriety, righteousness, honesty, humility, the "pillars of Confucian culture," which Generalissimo Chiang Kai-shek's "New Life"
Movement attempted to revive in 1934.

the table. When the water boiled over it he put the rolls into the pan. He did not speak until then. Going to the thin panels of the wall he pressed his ear close, listening on both sides to make certain our neighbours were asleep.

"I'm afraid we'll have to leave here soon," he whispered to me. "It's unthinkable while you're so ill; and yet . . ."

He looked questioningly at me, but I simply signalled that I wanted to hear the inner truth of it.

"It's the landlord. The rent. He kicked up another storm about it. Threatened to call in the police if we don't pay or get out."

I did not say anything. There was nothing to be said. I knew quite well that Ching had not told me the whole story. The rent problem can't have reached a crisis; it has already been at that stage for weeks. This alone wouldn't alarm him. He wouldn't at any rate speak so seriously about it were this not merely a screen hiding the real facts. I didn't question him further. No doubt he knows what is best for me to hear.

And yet to move! How? First of all money is needed, and after that my health has to be mentioned.

"Can't we stay a few days longer?" I finally asked him.

"Certainly—a few days. Only we *must* be out before May the 30th. Don't worry about it, anyway. I simply told you so that you won't be surprised when the time comes. It isn't a serious matter. I will have money very soon." He smiled a little wan smile with his mouth, but his eyes did not change at all. The effect was somehow terrifying. "It will do you good to get a change of atmosphere, eh?"

He blew out the flame and drew forth some of the boiled rolls. Sitting on the bed he helped me eat. Before we had finished half the food my stomach rebelled, and up it all came. Not only the miserable food! It seemed to me that a violent internal explosion was taking place, forcing up my very soul! My eyes felt like gates being hammered at by battering-rams inside. My whole head burned as if afire. I couldn't control myself at all. Even while my body was bathed in sweat it also felt cold, and I shook all over.

Ching wasn't suffering much less. He jumped about excitedly, in a rage because he was so helpless to ease my pain. He tried to hold me up. He rinsed my mouth and nose, and bathed my eyes. He soaked towels in the hot water and put them on my forehead. He got his four limbs mixed up trying to do everything at once.

I didn't sleep all night. I could not even keep my eyes closed. After this performance I kept thinking of that hope, and it seemed to me the only way to freedom. I must have been very delirious. I remember pinching and pressing and even sharply striking my womb. How I wanted the little creature to die! And yet at the same time my heart seemed to be protesting with all the vigour left in me, responding with a blow at *me* for every one I struck at *it*! With the conflicting instincts—the one selfish, for the preservation of my child, the other unselfish, for the preservation of my usefulness—I felt for a while that only through a double death could any solution be cleanly achieved. Traitorous thought!

And yet I love this little life! With all the pain of it, I long for the wonderful thing to happen, for a tiny human creature to spring from between my limbs bravely out into the world. I need it, just as a true poet *needs* to create a great undying work. No, more than that; for my little one shall be the instrument of Mother Nature to change nature. Of that I am certain, just as I am certain even now that it is already shaping into a—man! That little fellow, at first so helpless, so full of a need of me, curious with the curiosity of little eyes slowly opening, that little man will later on stand up and assert, with his great beauty and his great power, such fine true things about men and nature that all the authorities, all the rulers of heaven and earth, cannot but bow down to his will!

Ever since my lunar pause, ever since the first quivering in my womb, my heart has been unspeakably shaken with the wonder of this knowledge. My throat has ached to proclaim it to the whole world. Despite his purity and his splendour, it would actually be upon me whom this young man would bestow his first smile! It would be me whom he would call mother! Ah, yes, all that I've thought about, and of all that known the joy and the power and the longing!

Where is the woman strong enough alone not to dream such dreams? No, there is not one, and certainly not I. Not one—and yet perhaps many, thousands, millions of us together! Cannot the essential spirit of motherhood, strengthened in the unity of many women, reject its selfish little individual rights? Can't we become for once *conscious* in travail, dedicate that priceless fertility to the nourishment of a vast physiological act of Mother Nature herself, greatening her womb in our own time with a new *kind* of man?

I believe we can. Yet turning an abstract philosophy into a poisoned needle to thrust into my own womb, that is a different thing! I am full of the distress of mental and physical torment as these emotions battle ceaselessly. Still, I am determined. I am awake at last, after years of bovine slumber. I am more fully awake than when I first made up my mind to join the Revolution. Only when the beat of life is lifted to this pitch, this fury, and this danger, only when destiny (here in my case it is but a wayward sperm carrying its implacable microscopic chromosomes, but nevertheless it is a form of destiny!) poses the choice between irreconcilable desires at a given moment, only when a human being feels the necessity of ignoring personal feeling in the decision taken—only then can one talk of a revolutionary awakening!

Well, all that is to say that for the pauperized millions to bear children in society as at present disorganized is simply to increase the number of those living in hopeless misery. Every child thrust from the womb of a sick, underfed, unattended mother just so much further degrades the disinherited. For the child of poverty there lies ahead nothing but hunger, insults, ignorance, abuse, bitterness, and no hint of the spiritual exaltation that divides men from beasts of the jungle. For us the problem of new life is the problem of life as we know it now, ourselves, and this we cannot unconscionably impose upon the unborn.

And yet I still fondly amuse myself with maternal fancies! I still now and then dream of freeing my own life by projecting another one into the world!

Ching will meet a Korean friend to-day. With the help of this fellow I may bring my plan to a practical conclusion. I told Ching to seek out this man. It never occurred to me that he would be shocked, and his curious stare and his silence dismayed me. He just stood still for a while, with his hands thrust deep in his pockets. Then he turned his head, and ground out, in a decisive tone:

"Abortion! It isn't to be thought of! It's impossible."

"Abortion, on the contrary, is the only way. It is settled!"

He turned and looked at me with a strange look, as if he had been struck. He sat down on the bed and took my hands in his. His expressive eyes spoke half of compassion, half of remonstrance. I began to explain to him how I had reached the decision.

"We cannot," he broke in, and covered my mouth with his hands. Lowering his lips to my ear he whispered: "I understand, dear. I know everything you feel, but later on you will regret it. And it is dangerous, by such means——" He shook his head and for a while said nothing. I felt suddenly sick and lay back, silent too.

After a long while he whispered again: "However great the pain—two kinds of pain, I understand—it isn't so serious as this step. You do not know how dangerous it is

—dangerous first for Li, and then it is an attack on your very life. Besides we haven't time. We must move . . ." He choked and did not finish. We both sat staring at each other, profoundly miserable.

Just then we heard a scratching sound on one of the walls. Ching looked significantly at the slit cut open between the panelling, and then got up, gently stroking my arm.

May 26

Can Ching actually not have returned once during the entire night? Do I deserve to be forsaken? What have I done that I must lie here in torn anguish, helpless, uncomforted, hungry, with nothing to break the horrible monotony of these surroundings—that old broken washstand, the stained wrappings of food, stale spinach, and the ceiling webbed with the spider's spinnings, somehow making the room seem like a place where only discarded things should be?

Laid away like this, a dead one, is it possible for me to feel the same sense of value, to believe in my own significance as a social being, as I do when living with the working masses?

Ordinarily, even when busiest, Ching never fails to get back some time during the night. What can have happened?

I waited last night, as usual, for the sound of his footsteps. I kept my eyes on the door steadily after the landlord's clock struck eleven. I heard every sound it made after that: half-past eleven, twelve, half-past twelve, and then just as regularly one, half-past, two, half-past, three, and so on till after dawn. Every boom of the clock deepened my own anxiety; and, as sometimes happens to one, I became intensely aware of the irredeemable loss of each of those hours, aware of time actively destroying me.

It was quite unnecessary for me to torture my mind worrying about ordinary accidents, such as Ching being struck by a motor-car, or falling dead from exhaustion, or being bitten by a mad dog. And yet I did so. I even hoped that it was something like that. I invented several highly improbable situations to account for his absence. I refused to think about that most dreadful—and yet most likely —possibility.

Just now I would welcome even the arrival of some spies or *gendarmes*. I cannot stand the suspense any longer. Even to know that he is in police hands is better than this hovering dread, this awful uncertainty! It seems to me that I cannot breathe for another hour! What the devil is going to happen to me? It is perhaps preferable even to be in gaol than to be an abandoned lump lying lifelessly here. . . .

Later

Lao[1] Li has been here and has brought news of Ching! It is, of course, as I feared.

His thick brows were locked under his broad forehead, and I knew before he spoke what had happened. He came in, nodded his head in greeting, and simply said, "*En!*"

"What is it?"

"Ching has been arrested."

May 27

I won't die! I thought of it last night, the easiest way being simply to languish in the *kung-yu*, where nobody would lift a rice-bowl to save my life. But I won't die. Lao Li gave me some encouragement. He advised me to move to his house, where his wife, a doctor, can help me. This good news, now that Ching has already lost his freedom, is perhaps the only thing that made me want to live.

Li helped me to move. I am lying now in a bed placed in one of their two small rooms, which they rent from a

[1] Here "Lao" is not part of the name, but an honorific. Literally "Old," though Li is still young.

Korean landlord. He is a sympathetic fellow, and lives in the other part of the house himself.

Lao Li's Korean wife seems to me rather quaint in appearance, with a grey-tinted yellow face, greyish-brown eyes (very narrow), and thick lips. She is quite fat, a distinct contrast to the sharp, straight architecture of her husband's body. She has not been long in China, and has to dig for words to express herself, and often, failing to find them, she fills in the blanks with an embarrassed smile.

She was very moved when I told her what I wanted. At first she was speechless, and only shook her head violently. Then from her little eyes tears began to sprinkle her piteous face, and she jumped up impetuously and came to my bed. She held me close to her fat breasts while she shook with convulsive sobs. Almost hysterically she cried, "No, no, no! You shall not!" Her obviously deep emotion rather surprised me.

Lao Li pulled her up gently and spoke to her in Korean. I couldn't understand. She kept sobbing, as pathetically as if she were a small orphan girl. Gradually she grew quiet, under her husband's persuasion, and at last came to say that she would help me.

There is only one bed in the rooms, and last night Li and his wife had to sleep on stools set before me. During the evening Li *tai-tai* told me something of her life.

She is now thirty-nine years of age, but she has no children. She has, however, constantly longed for a son, but each time this desire seemed about to be fulfilled she was frustrated.

Li *tai-tai's* family were Christians and furious when she married her revolutionary husband. They disowned her. What annoyed them particularly was that, after they had spent so much money educating her and getting her medical degree, she had turned it to the service of such a worthless cause. They refused to extend to her even a copper of help.

Lao Li, extremely busy in revolutionary work, rarely had any money. Often he was compelled to go into hiding for weeks or even months, leaving his wife alone. Each time she was with child it happened that Lao Li was in danger, and she had to suffer the shock, worry, and nervous tension of this knowledge as well as being left with inadequate funds for either proper care or nourishment. Seven times she lost her unborn child!

Seven! Is it possible for a woman to go through this horror seven times? Women and revolution! What tragic, unsung epics of courage lie silent in the world's history!

At the time of his wife's eighth pregnancy Lao Li, in desperation, arranged to get leave for a while, borrowed some money, and took her to the seashore. He provided her with such material comforts as he could and bent every effort towards protecting her against disturbance. The result was that at last her son was born. It grew into a beautiful, healthy child, and by the time it was seven months old delighted its parents by the long and fascinating conversations carried on by the changing expressions of its face and by its adorable infant chucklings and babblings. Needless to say, the parents were enchanted with their precious possession.

At this time both Lao Li and his wife were suddenly arrested and thrown into prison, their baby with them. Ten days of that is sufficient to kill any child. Theirs died.

As the unfortunate woman talked on she wept freely. Her husband, sitting beside her, patted her gently and spoke to her in the most compassionate way. He was evidently glad that she had taken this chance to give expression to the repressed misery burning within her. Hardly less moved himself, he even reminded her of details she had forgotten, and helped provide her inadequate Chinese with words and phrases whenever she paused.

.   .   .   .   .

This morning I took an enormous capsule, administered by Dr Li. She promises that one of these is sufficient to abort a fœtus one month old, and three are enough to expel one gone three months. Three days after taking this medicine one can hope for the best.

Afternoon

The stormy May wind, carrying down tons of Gobi dust, seems to set fire to your eyes and nose and throat. It is enough in itself to make most people a little ill. Now, as it howls outside, and the fine yellow silt drifts in and covers everything, I take a savage delight in describing my own feelings! Perhaps it will be instructive to read later on. . . .

Well, then, I feel exactly as if there were dozens of repulsive hairy worms crawling back and forth in all my joints! It seems to me that if these worms managed to get out they would take with them the basic tincture of my life-blood! Ugh!

Later

I just saw Ching being tortured! An old man with red, blinking eyes bent over him, holding a huge kettle with a tiny spout, out of which he poured 'pepper water' into Ching's nose. "Among means for the regeneration of mankind," old red-eyes quoted Confucius, "those made with great demonstrations are of least importance."

Ching struggled to free himself, and let out blood-drying groans. He tried to turn his face, but that tore his lips on the rope binding him across the mouth to the floor. The water poured from his nose, his mouth, and his eyes. Several times he fainted. The torturers revived him by turning him over and emptying him of water.

More than forty kettles had been poured into him!

Now and then the torture would cease while Ching was cross-questioned. All the time I stood by, helplessly watching his agony. It seemed that already I had been shoved in front of him, and whipped on my bare back. They had demanded that I ask him to talk, to tell his address. It seemed also that my lips had already been burned by incense because I had refused to speak.

Apparently Ching did not recognize me. It may be that he could not see. His face was mottled with red, blue, purple, and greenish bruises. Blood clung to his hair. He looked dumbly at me without any comprehension in his eyes at all.

Since they already had me in custody, what was the object of torturing Ching for this information? Had he another address that they wanted? Having changed him into a different creature, why did they continue with this bestial abuse? Did they hope to break his spirit by making him confess to the fact that he was under arrest? I did not understand it. I wanted to scream. They came towards me, tore off my jacket, and prepared to whip my back and breasts in front of him. Then I did scream.

Opening my eyes I looked into the face of Li *tai-tai*, who had her arms around me. She held her narrow eyes close to mine, and they were as wide open as she could get them, full of fright and astonishment. "What is it?" she demanded. "What?"

The tortures of which I had dreamed were exactly like those used on Y—— and P——. But the significance of Ching's refusal to divulge his address? What was it? Obviously it betrayed my anxiety that Ching, thinking me still helpless in the *kung-yu*, was submitting to some ghastly inquisition rather than give the KMT his address.

May 28, windy

Windy indeed!

As the wind rises my fever rises, and as it dies I am shaken with chills. All the paper panes in the windows have been burst open by the storm. The wind screams like a woman, like a woman in torture and travail. It shows its torn face through the window—but am I still delirious?

Because of my fever Dr Li refused to give me another capsule to-day. I pleaded with her. I insisted. Now that this is begun I want it finished quickly. I am impatient to get into the world again, to carry on Ching's work and my own. Then, too, I cannot waste any more of the Lis' energy or money than is absolutely necessary—on this useless, pointless enterprise.

I swallowed two of those great cylindrical pills at once!

Midnight

Shao Feng just ran in breathlessly. His face lengthened when he saw me here. He had come to warn the Lis to move immediately. At the same time he wanted his wounds dressed by Dr Li.

The day before yesterday Shao Feng was carrying some things on a bicycle. As he was going along Pei Ho Yen another bicycle suddenly dashed against him. A spy jumped out, grabbed him, and yelled as loudly as possible for the police. Shao Feng succeeded in tripping the man over the rickshaw, and escaped by running down small lanes, jumping some walls, and crossing several low roofs. He tore his left arm, and it was swollen with neglect and covered with ugly dark blood. Dr Li dressed his wound, and he left immediately, giving an anxious glance at me.

"Move at once!" What mockery to me lying here, a helpless burden, endangering the lives of my friends! To-morrow is May the 30th,[1] day of awakening for China, day on which the masses everywhere rise up to show their growing strength and unity. To-morrow over the whole nation resolute young men and women will march forth,

[1] May 30, 1925, was the day on which foreign police in Shanghai killed many students and workers in a demonstration, an incident which inflamed the whole nation to anger.

defiantly, and some of them will be killed—and from their deaths new strength will arise. But I—weighed down by a stone! Women and revolution—strange pair!

To-day they will spare no search to get our people imprisoned before the demonstration. . . . The Lis are talking together in Korean. I want to tell them that they must go, that I don't want them here with me, that they must leave me! But on my lips there is only a silent scream which will tell them that suddenly my womb feels as though pierced with ten thousand hot needles. I want to keep on writing this, to hide that scream that will betray me. . . . My whole flesh itches and stings and burns. My entire body pulses as if with anchored lightning. Everything around me is poisonous, sickening. There is that hot stone ready to burst from within me at any moment—and another ready to burst from my head.

[*Here the diary ends.*]

SHA TING
(1904–)

THE author supplies the following autobiographical sketch:

"I was born in 1904 in a mountain town in the far north-western corner of Szechuan. My father, a scholar, died early. My mother was very able, having the character of a man. Wretched and in decline, the family depended on her alone for its maintenance.

"My maternal uncle was the *hsien* (district) leader of the Ko Lao Society (a Chinese secret society), and later became a brigadier-general in the army. That's how, when I was a lad, I came to know numerous swordsmen, gamblers, opium-traffickers, and even local bandits. When I began to take up study seriously it tortured my mind to remember how much of my best time had been taken up in such rough surroundings. But before long I realized the value of my early rough associations. Now I think of those years with gratitude.

"My literary life started in 1932. Up to the present I have written only about thirty short stories."

VOYAGE BEYOND LAW

By Sha Ting

[It is necessary to explain that this story describes a voyage on the Upper Yangtse river, between the city of Ichang and Hankow. For a number of years the banks of the river, and even the famous Yangtse Gorges, have for long distances been held by the Chinese Reds.

Foreign steamships, however, continue to operate under the protection of their river gunboats, or with guards of foreign marines or sailors on deck. Szechuan, a province of sixty million population, has long been ruled by brigand generals, who in cases have collected taxes from the peasants for as many as sixty years in advance, but these rulers and the officials they install are nevertheless confirmed in office by the Kuomintang Government. The river traffic with Szechuan, which lies in the far west, pays a rich reward to foreign shipowners, and adventurous foreign navigators and seamen can always be found ready to hazard the attempted blockade. A few journeys often suffice to enable them to retire with neat fortunes made in smuggling opium down from Szechuan, in collusion with Chinese officials.

Compared with that kind of graft, the petty racket of the ship's Chinese steward in this story—stowing away his young friends among the vegetables—seems to have been rather severely punished. But the dramatic significance of the situation presented here—and it is said to be historically accurate—is that the influence of foreign imperialism reaches into farthest China. The real "Voyage beyond Law" is not the venture into Red territory, but the embarkation on a foreign river steamer, which, though it operates on charter granted by the Nanking Government, is aloof from the legal processes of both revolutionaries and the Kuomintang—a law unto itself.]

THICK smoke shot out of the steamer's huge lung, her hot pulses of iron and steel throbbed and beat in the swirling waters, and she moved lustily ahead. Farther on, below Shihmen Shoal and Chu Dike, lay the coiling rapids, and narrowing overhead were the immense walls of rock, converging all the time, leaning nearer, becoming ever more majestic. They seemed like enormous living creatures, ready to crouch and pick up the snorting steamer and all on board. The passengers looked up, awed and terrified.

High on the flanks of the nearly perpendicular cliffs, so that they appeared to be suspended in space, were lines of men wearing red turbans and nothing else but tattered trousers. They shouted banteringly at the steamer, challenging the foreign marines. In such a scene nobody should have been surprised had they jumped down, like the heroes of ancient folklore, walked across the waters, boarded the ship, and struck off people's heads with great efficiency. But on closer inspection it could be seen that they were, after all, mere men with rather famished-looking bodies, and none of the marines guarding the steamer were in the least disturbed. . . .

Now the rapids bubbled at the stern, the gorges closed like shadowy gates behind, and the 'red spirits' no longer were visible. The river widened and the banks levelled out; above, the heavens expanded. An ashen pallor spread over the fields and the villages and even over the barking dogs, who seemed to glide back and forth like detached souls crying protest. It was the look of inland China everywhere: that half-living appearance, that deserted air, that inner sullenness, and that deep melancholy, which never disappears even in the golden wash of the sun!

Passengers on the ship gazed intently at the yellow shore. Some of their weary eyes took on such lustre that you could almost imagine lines stretching from them to some living heart pulsating out there in the midst of the matted grass, or in the moist clay, or hidden somewhere beneath the drab landscape. They held their breath and then let it out quickly, and stood listening carefully again. When would they see what they sought, in the next second or in the next quarter of an hour? The most illiterate refugees on board were as interested as the rest, and shouldered their

X

way to the rail, where they gaped shoreward with wide eyes.

"Look, isn't that——"

"No, stupid. Look over here! Watch carefully!"

They chattered and argued, some of them with such dignity and certainty that they seemed in anger. Others contented themselves with weak sighs or inward quakings, or sat open-mouthed, listening with absorption. They leaned over the railings, or against the bulkheads, or simply squatted on their bottoms. A lanky peasant from Hupeh, wrinkling his eyebrows and stretching out his neck, raised his voice high above the rest:

"Where did you hear that! It's a myth! They're in fact much stronger than the bandits in the lowlands! These Reds have their belief, and that's what makes the difference."

" . . . pirates! . . ."

"Robbing ships? Well, maybe; but why not? Take the case of the shipload of guns the Reds seized at Chenlanchi recently. Fighting for three days and nights over them! One of their comrades in Shanghai sent them advance information that the guns were coming up to the Szechuan militarist."

A fellow with a load on his back stood before the door leading from steerage into third class and gesticulated comically. He was talking excitedly with a student. Suddenly he turned and cried out in an obdurate tone:

"Listen to me! I say it won't work. The land has been divided, but still you admit there's nothing to eat under the Reds!"

"Not at all, not at all! I was talking of salt and a few luxuries. On the contrary rice is plentiful and it's much cheaper: the price is controlled and for only a few cents you can get a whole peck. But salt is more expensive than ginseng, that's true. And why? The Government prevents exportation of it into the Red districts. Still, despite the salt-guards, adventurous fellows smuggle it in and make a good profit."

"Do they really pay for it? If it's a fact I'll try it myself. . . . Hum; one man can't carry very much, though."

"Things won't be improved this way," abruptly remarked a grey old cynic, who stooped and knocked the bowl of his pipe on deck. "Nobody can improve things. How can the Reds change anything? There are too many of us. There haven't been enough people killed! Hummph!" He refilled his pipe and walked off angrily.

"Blind corpse!" cursed a waiter who almost collided with him. He was carrying a plateful of food; readjusting it, he triumphantly climbed upward. The old fellow stared after his white-clad back and frowned.

On the upper deck machine-guns, protected behind steel-plated wings, were mounted and uncovered for action. One of the foreign marines, smoking a big pipe, paced back and forth across the smooth floor, with a rifle slung over his shoulder. Behind him, in the first-class saloon, some people were drinking wine, and seemed gaily unaware of the toiling rhythm of the ship.

A Chinese soldier who had come aboard at Ichang crept to the door of the upper deck and lifted his head above the step.

"Be damned! The fellow's more splendidly dressed than our colonel."

He went to the stern and sat down before the door leading to a lavatory. Stretching out his legs and putting his hands on his knees, he glanced appraisingly at the crowd, spat with the wind, and commented, "In appearance not bad, not bad, but let's see him in action!"

Several people turned and stared at him. He stretched again, opened and closed his legs, and began to talk:

"I've been fighting for more than ten years, but never anything like these Reds! Do you know what? It's true their women pull off their trousers, wrap them on their shoulders, and swim the river. They come among our troops and try to win us over to their side. Some of them—— What are you laughing at, old fellow? They're no easy fruit to digest! They have a hundred and one methods, and that's why they're dangerous. Plenty of our men have been trapped by them."

A woman hung her head, loosened her coat, and corked her child's mouth with a ruddy breast. An elderly fellow swayed back and forth and kept patting his thigh. "What times!" he exclaimed. "What a period to be born into! Would we all be fleeing if conditions were tolerable in Szechuan?"

"Flee? Certainly nobody wanted to flee! The officials took one thing to-day and another to-morrow. When they finally get everything we have, what's there to do but go somewhere else! You're quite right; it's a bad period; it wasn't like this in the past. None of the books tell of such things. . . ." The broken voice of an old man trailed off.

"Elderly brother, you seem to be suggesting—*revolution?*" insinuated the soldier, his neck arched and his face slyly grinning.

"What! Nothing of the sort! It's a lie!"

The soldier slapped his knees and laughed heartily. Somebody in a corner whispered, "Talk less in these days." He stopped laughing and narrowed his eyes. "Don't worry, I'm not going to sell him. Ridiculous! Ask anybody, and make your questions clear, and most people will agree. . . . Hummph! Open your eyes a little bit, and you'll see what's coming."

"Do we eat or don't we?" somebody threw in, changing the subject. It at once seemed to be a matter to which everybody had been giving his greatest attention all along, but only now realized it. Some cursed the cheap quality of the food and others eagerly discussed the dishes going from the kitchen to supply the first-class cabins. A few went below to investigate whether any sign of life could be observed in their cook.

The men in the steerage kitchen seemed to share none of

the deck passengers' agitation. Oily smoke clouded the room, and the steward's eyes were squinted like two stitches in his face. He moved over to the large tub, and stirred a bamboo stick in the thin muddy-looking gruel, at the same time clearing the snivel from his growth of beard. The fat cook bent low also and inspected the tub, absently scratching himself. Near by a stoker sat on a bag of rice and looked on vacantly. Coming upon this tranquil scene, the self-appointed committee of investigation was disappointed and began to complain.

"*Wei*, steward, we're starving to death."

"He's good on his abacus. He doesn't want to waste any more than necessary on you."

The steward paused his stirring and blinked angrily at them. "Ready soon," he growled. "Keep your hands inside your throats."

"Ready soon—soon," echoed Fatty complacently, continuing his scratching. He dipped the gourd ladle into the stewing food, and, lifting up a few drops, put it carefully to his lips. Then he neatly wiped with his apron the part of the ladle that he had touched, and dutifully endeavoured to comfort the committee. "Ready soon, ready soon. A few more strokes of the flames."

"Don't hurry him. If you do he'll give us the dish-water to drink," a surly voice called out.

Fatty glanced at him indifferently. Then he yawned widely, buttressed his hands on his waist, and thrust his head through a porthole.

The wind tore at the smoke and made plumes of the spray. On shore it drove up a fine curtain of dust. Behind a nest of huts there seemed to be a crowd of people massed under brilliant red banners. A little farther on, beyond question, were some moving figures of men. The ship suddenly lurched and creaked ominously, as if the mysterious shores were curling up beneath the water and crushing it in their maw.

"Look there! What's that?" somebody cried, peering with keen eyes towards the shore.

"A meeting, simply a meeting! They're always having them, don't worry about it."

"Tickets! Get your tickets ready!" came a voice from the deck overhead. Everybody stopped talking for a minute, but soon a murmur of protest began.

"What, another look!"

"They treat us like criminals!"

"Is this false? Is it false, I ask you?" demanded a man with a bald shining pate, pulling his ticket from a tobacco-box hanging to his girdle and brandishing it in fury. "Am I afraid if he looks at it a hundred times?"

With stomachs empty of food but mouths full of words, the passengers below crowded up to the next deck in a disorderly manner, looking like refugees starved for a long time—which, more or less, they were.

Down in the smoky kitchen Fatty pulled his head in through the port and laughed. The stoker put more coal in the stove. The steward grasped some large clay bowls and laid them out on the long plank which served as table for the steerage passengers. Then he rubbed his eyes with his apron and paused thoughtfully. He went into the room adjoining his cabin, and after a moment came out, laughing. He carefully closed the door behind him.

"Be patient," he shouted, "you can eat right after the ticket inspection."

There was no answer. He picked up the gourd and dipped some bean sprouts from a tile vessel, putting a few in each of the clay bowls. The smoke thickened and every one began to cough. Spray danced through the port; now and then a big wave lashed against the ship and the bowls struck each other with a hollow tinkle.

Heavy footsteps sounded on the stair.

"Quick, they're coming down here to make another inspection."

The steward suddenly swung his head around, but just as suddenly closed his mouth. His hands fell weakly to his sides, and the ladle became a problem for him: he did not know whether to drop it or to keep it. His face lengthened and his eyes almost closed.

The cabin boys did not reveal anything by their glances, and the compradore gave no clue by his conversation, for he was speaking to the foreign captain in English, which the steward did not understand. But in a moment the compradore led two servants into the provision room from which, a little while before, the steward had emerged laughing.

He cried out now, seemingly offering some inducement to those who were making the search:

"A cup of wine! A cup or more . . ." but his tongue hardened and his voice shook. The servants beside the captain stood looking at the steward sympathetically.

Two "Yellow Fish" were dragged from the room and stood shaking before the officers. Their slender brown fingers fluttered to straighten their collars and button their shirts. A musty odour of clay and meat and fish hung in their blue cotton clothes and seemed to pour out of their yellow skin.

"Compradore, *lao-yeh*, old friend . . ." the steward stammered.

"I can't make any decisions," the compradore answered in Chinese, pointing his chin to the foreigners. He followed the others up the stairs.

"An enemy has laid this plot, I tell you," wailed the steward. "Somebody has secretly done this to ruin me."

Nobody answered him. The old man slumped wearily on to a sack and rubbed his burning eyes. Were his hopes, he wondered, to be wiped out by a single brush stroke? His job—he was not exactly in the company's employ, but worked for a contractor who fed steerage passengers at so much a head—was tiresome and unhealthy. He had endured this smoky hole always with the dream of getting together enough to return to his home and die in meagre comfort and peace. This very trip, in fact, he had determined was to be his last, and to fill out his purse a little he had taken the risk . . . stowaways.

"Don't get excited," advised Fatty. "What's the good of worrying."

Somebody called down the steps.

The steward untied his apron, hastily brushed the ashes from his clothes, and pulled himself above. "Coming, I'm coming," he announced.

"See the Captain himself," the assistant pursuer told him.

"What have I done? I say simply some one has plotted against me."

The whistle screamed steadily and the ship slowed down, as though to rest now that she had safely run the gorges, and completed her voyage beyond law. The wind had ceased, and one could clearly see the yellow shore and clustered huts, a rotten boat tied to a tree, and beyond a long glitter. That was the face of a lake.

The passengers forgot their hunger and crowded round the door of the compradore's cabin, standing on tiptoe, peering in, waiting to learn the verdict against the stowaways. They heard him explaining:

"It's not easy to reason with foreigners. . . . They have their regulations printed clearly on paper, and, worse than that, they enforce them!"

"I don't know the regulations," shouted one of the "Yellow Fish," jumping up and down with fright. "This is the first time I've been away from home. How could I know?"

"I paid money to ride," exclaimed the other. "I gave it to him."

The compradore screamed at them. "Get your baggage together, and no more talk. You're told to go ashore and go ashore you must!"

"I've never injured anybody," the steward kept repeating in a piteous voice, his eyes staring idiotically. "That's the truth! It's a plot."

The passengers moved back and began to discuss the thing among themselves, everybody talking at once. One of them shouted in a high voice above the others, "We're all Chinese; we must stand by them."

"That's right! Right!" Several others echoed.

The majority finally decided that the "Yellow Fish" were not to leave the ship, for they had paid: simply let the steward refund the money he had received by violating the rule.

But the compradore did not agree. "It's not my order, and not my responsibility. I can't do anything about it." He flung a leg over the back of the sofa, and remained with his face turned away from the others till the ship gradually settled to a stop.

A lifeboat was poised over the port side, facing the southern bank of the river. Sailors stood at the windlasses, manning the ropes, slowly letting go. They moved up and down, with bent legs, as if climbing trees.

"I'll pay the money for them, although it's only a plot against me," shrieked the steward, spraying the deck with saliva in his excitement. "I'll pay the full fare when we reach Hankow."

"What else do you want? Their lives? Isn't it enough if he pays?" demanded one of the crowd.

The whistle shrilled like an angry god. Everybody on board broke from the cabins in alarm, and the hum of voices drowned the steady chant of the ship's engines. The decks swarmed. Near the loosened boat men stood with their backs jamming the noses of others behind them, while they used their hands to protect their own chins from being jabbed by those in front.

Suddenly the shore was dotted with hurrying men carrying wooden signs bearing inscribed slogans. Columns of

figures in the background marched forward with red flags
waving. This was just the spectacle every one had been
stiffening his neck to see a few minutes ago, yet now that
it was before them none of the passengers seemed anxious
to know more about it.

"Never mind! Don't get excited, don't be afraid! They
won't attack us."

These comforting words from an officer did nothing to
still the apprehension of the bewildered passengers, upon
whom the red flags produced various reactions. Some of
them regretted that God continued to make man without
wings. But the refugees, crowded round the compradore's
cabin, grew warm with indignation as gradually they
understood the tragic possibilities of the sentence imposed
by the Captain.

"Why, it's simply sending them to death! Coming
ashore like this they're certain to be regarded as white
spies!"

"What a place to put them down, ugh! They'll be
killed."

Angry mutterings arose against the injustice of foreign
rule.

Forgetful of personal danger for a moment, several men
in the crowd cursed the compradore for allying himself with
the foreigners against Chinese. The three victims themselves verged on crying, a greenish tinge coloured their lips,
and the blood raced in their temples. "This is what comes
of setting out to seek a fortune!" thought the "Yellow Fish."

The compradore knew the temper of the Captain as a
dog knows the heart of his master, but moved by the
appeals he resolved to ask for mercy. "Well, let's try our
luck. I'll see him again."

"You won't be able to find him. He'll hide himself,"
some one shouted.

"No, no, go ahead!" others urged. "Where can a man
hide on this ship?"

The compradore did not have to tell them the result of his mission, for when he returned he was accompanied by four marines.

Some one wailed out: "What did I say? Didn't I say it would be useless?" Boldness and bravery suddenly oozed from the refugees, cowed into submissiveness. Not so much out of fear of the armed guards as out of their ancient heritage of resignation to law, regardless of the complexion of its administrators, they drew back, broke into little groups, and offered no more objections. What remained of their wrath was expressed by eloquent manipulations of their eyebrows.

The guards grunted and shouted and gesticulated to the condemned men, ordered them into the boat, and menaced them with their guns.

"Ah, this is what comes of seeking a fortune!" each of the three cried out intermittently, but with none of the submissiveness of the onlookers. They waved their hands, stamped their feet, and obstinately refused to move. They planted themselves against a bulkhead, and the foreigners prodding them seemed to be amused.

"Hey, help them off!" the compradore shouted from the deck above to some of the cabin boys. "Move yourselves a little! Can't you do anything but eat?" His face was red and the muscles bulged on his neck. They looked up at him resentfully, shrugged their shoulders, and slipped away.

Several officers came up now, grabbed the little bundles of clothes and thrust them into the stomachs of the steward and his "Yellow Fish." Then they pinioned their arms, dragged, rolled, and propelled them across the deck and lifted them, like convicted criminals, into the small boat.

Suddenly the Chinese soldier, who had been quiet for a long time, raised one hand and with the other clapped his chest and began shouting: "Why don't we all go with them? Go ahead! Their life isn't bad. . . . Those on shore won't bite. Why not?"

People glanced over the rail towards the Red Village. The columns of men had paused near the shore and now divided and began to spread out parallel with the river. At a command they took cover behind clumps of grass and bushes, or little hills of earth.

Two or three passengers started boldly to act on the soldier's suggestion, and moved towards the boat, but for some reason hesitated when they reached the upper deck. One could not tell from the look in their eyes whether their feelings were chiefly of anger or of fear. They turned back abruptly and quickly hid themselves behind the crowd.

The boat was freed and the sailors rowed slowly towards shore. In the middle of it, alternately pointing their hands to heaven and clapping themselves on the back, the trio shouted and wept and cursed. They began stamping their feet to give emphasis to their protests, but the boat rocked dangerously and they dropped down and clutched the arms of the sailors.

From behind a twist of dry grass close to the shore a man, clad in blue jacket and trousers, stood up and began waving his hands. He shouted something at the approaching boat, waited a moment, and then bent down and ran to some foliage on the left, where he disappeared from view. Watching him from beside the machine-guns on board the marines laughed shrilly, and put their fingers to triggers.

"Never mind!" Fatty yelled encouragement from above the iron gate at the stern. "Remember to show them the handcuff scars on your wrists! They'll treat you well."

"I've done nothing—to anyone!" The words seemed to drift along the hollows of the waves.

The soldier made a trumpet of his hands and shouted a piece of advice: "Tell them the truth! Just tell them—that you are poor workers." He turned to the crowd and said confidently, "No danger, I'll guarantee. Not one will be killed."

The little boat, with its cargo of despair, tumbled nearer

and had almost touched the bank when there was a sudden note of voices lifting over the bare plain, on which not a human being was to be seen. Then a louder, sharper sound —the crackling of rifle shots. The Chinese soldier sang out encouragement to them for the last time: "Don't worry, don't worry, I tell you! They're shooting in the air——" His voice was buried in an avalanche of noise from the upper deck—the *dadadat* of machine-guns fired by the marines.

Two of the three men who reached shore crumpled up immediately and lay motionless. Shooting from both sides of the river now answered the machine-guns, and a haze of smoke spread around the ship, in which the lifeboat was lost from view. Every passenger flew for cover.

Beyond the smoking river-banks the Red villages lay peaceful and serene, and on both sides were broad expanses of golden fields stretching in endless freedom. But the river churned up yellow waves, and under the jagged lines of fire shooting back and forth it seemed to come to life, to struggle, to move down, and prepare with its own weight to level everything before it. . . .

With its whistle groaning, the ship pulled rapidly out of range, driving the yellow water in ripples that ended in flowery spray against the reddened shore beside the fallen men.

Huddled into the steerage quarters the refugees listened, terrified, as the shots gradually grew faint.

"You see," said one, "it's not we Chinese who fight them but the foreigners. What country *is* this?"

"Yes, but don't forget our own officials. They fight them; they and the foreigners."

"Good!" cursed the grey old cynic. "The more people killed the better. As it is, who can do anything to improve things? There are too many of us, simply too many."

APPENDIX A

THE MODERN CHINESE LITERARY MOVEMENT

By NYM WALES

THE modern literary movement in China divides rather neatly into two well-defined periods, following closely upon shiftings in the political revolutionary movement. It began with the Literary Renaissance from 1917 to 1927, a period of pollination and assimilation under the stimulus of the translations from Western literature of the 'returned students' from abroad, which had its brief flowering in the May Fourth Movement of 1919. This decade, called by the Chinese "From Literary Revolution to Revolutionary Literature," was given over to the expression of the desperate and confused dreams of the new Chinese *bourgeoisie* for Liberty, Equality, and Fraternity, and represents their revolutionary struggle against the ancient social system. It came to an abrupt end in 1927 with the *coup d'état* of the Right Kuomintang, which marked the demise of the half-accomplished *bourgeois* revolution, and the independent development of the peasants' and workers' revolution under Communist leadership. Following the military *coup d'état* the vital body of the literary movement swung sharply to the Left in the opposite direction, expressing its bitter disillusionment with the weakness and reaction of the middle class, and its faith in the mass revolution stirring underneath. From 1928 to the present time the Leftist revolutionary literature has dominated the field.

The Literary Renaissance was important as an expression of fundamental cultural change rather than as a period of literary creativity, and its production remained immature, imitative, and artificial for the most part, revealing a basic sterility. It was a revolution in language as well as thought, however, and no one can understand the nature of the movement who does not have some idea of the tremendous difficulties inherent in the language problem alone in China.

Until 1917 there existed in mutual stalemate three fairly distinct strata of literature: (1) the ancient cult of the *literati* in the dead *wen-yen* classical written language, in literature an empty shell of formalism since the Sung Dynasty, although the classics were still the basis of education and *wen-yen* the only officially acceptable literary style; (2) the healthy parvenu *pai-hua*, 'plain speech,' literature of the people in the spoken language, ashamed of itself and despised and outcast by the *wen-yen literati*; and (3) the story-tellers' literature in the provincial dialects of the masses, unwritten as in Homeric times.

The Literary Renaissance accomplished three things. Its first act was to dispossess the old *wen-yen literati* and put the classics on the ancient history shelves; second, it enthroned the vulgar *pai-hua* vernacular language in the place of *wen-yen*, made it the legitimate literary medium, and idealized the old despised *pai-hua* literature—the novels, stories, and dramas such as *All Men are Brothers,* recently translated by Pearl S. Buck, and *The Romance of Three Kingdoms*—some of which was re-edited by Hu Shih and others as a language base for the new literary movement to develop upon; and, third, it adapted modern literary forms from abroad in the May Fourth Literary Movement begun in 1919.

The whole renaissance movement, however, took place within the small circle of modern-educated students, and became merely a new cult of the *literati*. It could not and did not touch the illiterate mass of the people, including most of the middle class. The new body of literature was grafted like a foreign shoot on the sturdy old tree of the old *pai-hua* literature. This exotic shoot, however, remained alien, colonial, and artificial like the pitiful new *bourgeoisie* which produced it, and it withered away in a very short time—as a new trunk growing from the very roots of the race stole all nourishment from it in the literature of the mass revolution. In perspective, the most useful work of this decade seems to be in its translation activities, which made available to China her heritage of the world's literature, though it was extremely valuable as a mechanical period of developing technique in creative writing.

Led by Hu Shih and Ch'ên Tu-hsiu the Literary Revolution

against *wen-yen* begun in 1917 was entirely won by 1920, and soon the whole educational system was based upon it, a reaction in favour of *wen-yen* in 1934 resulting only in a strong movement for further simplification by doing away with the ideograph and using latinization. Showing the tremendous stimulus to literary creation of the elastic new *pai-hua* form, about three hundred new student magazines came into being within four years after 1917, along with many true literary journals.

Previous to the May Fourth Movement in 1919 practically none of the new creative literature had been produced, except experimental poetry and essay-journalism. Lu Hsün was the pioneer, with his *Diary of a Mad Man,* published in Ch'ên Tu-hsiu's famous magazine *New Youth* in 1918, followed by his two short stories, *K'ung I-chi* and *Medicine.* His collection of short stories, *Na Han,* including *The Story of Ah Q,* enchanted the whole country in 1923, and even now remains the best-seller among modern fiction. He was promptly hailed as the Gorki or Chekhov of China—as one prefers one or the other.

The May Fourth Movement was the nationalist-revolutionary movement against "Imperialism and Feudalism," begun by the Peking students on that day in 1919, and the literary drive led in the struggle. At bottom it was a fight of the individual for freedom from all the fetters which bound him on every side.

The literary movement divided into two polar tendencies, Romanticism and Realism, centring around two rival literary societies. The Romantic movement gravitated around the "Creationist Society," which was intensely absorbed in 'creativity' in and for itself—this being a new term in the Chinese lexicon. It was also very much concerned with the other new problems of love between the sexes and the freedom of women. They struggled for 'art for art's sake' against the old moralism and didacticism, and also against the Realist school which tended to be absorbed with humanitarianism. One wing of the Romantics was virile and truly revolutionary, led by Kuo Mo-jo, the translator and admirer of Goethe, and curiously enough it was the Creationists who formed the nucleus of the new Left-proletarian literature in 1927. The other wing was decadent, pessimistic to the point of morbidness, or maudlin, and tended towards mere dilettantism, represented by Yü Ta-fu. The

Y

society was organized in 1920 by several students returned from Japan, though their organ, *Creation Monthly*, did not appear until 1922. The important figures were Kuo Mo-jo and Yü Ta-fu, surrounded by T'ien Han (T'ien Tso-ch'ang), Mu Mou-t'ien, Chang Tzŭ-p'ing, a sensualist, Ch'êng Po-ch'i, and later by Ch'êng Fang-wu, Li Ch'u-li, Fêng Nai-ch'ao, Wang Tu-ching, and Chou Ch'uan-p'ing. While still in Japan Kuo Mo-jo published his volume of poems, *Goddess*, in 1921, and Yü Ta-fu his novel, *Sinking*, about the same time; after this their movement had great influence upon the new youth of the period.

The opposition to the Creationists was the Realist "Literary Research Society" organized in November 1920, which included Mao Tun (Shên Yen-ping), Wang T'ung-chao, Chêng Chên-to, Lo Hua-shêng (Hsü Ti-shan), Miss Lu Yin, Ch'ien Hsüan-t'ung, essayist, and Yü P'ing-po, poet. The important writers of this group during the May Fourth period were Lu Hsün[1] (Chou Shu-jên) and his brother, Chou Tso-jên, Yeh Shao-chün, and Miss (Hsieh) Ping-hsin. Their organs were *Short Story Monthly* and *Literature* (*Wen Hsüeh*). Like the Creationists, it was a loose organization composed of diverse elements banded together for mutual help and purposes of publication. In general these writers emphasized realistic observation and stated the attitude of the group that "literature should reflect the social phenomena and disclose or discuss some problem in connexion with the life of man."

Both organizations stressed translation work very much. The "Literary Researchers" concentrated principally upon Japanese, Russian, and minor European literature. For instance, Chou Tso-jên translated from Japanese, Polish, Yiddish, and Hungarian writers; Lu Hsün from Russian, Japanese, and others; Chêng Chên-to from 'world literature' collections, German, Russian, and Indian—including Tagore; Mao Tun from Spanish and modern Yiddish writers. Of the Creationists Kuo Mo-jo, who is said to have done more translation work than any other Chinese, translated from German, English—Shelley, Galsworthy, and Upton Sinclair—and Russian writers; Mu Mou-t'ien, who

---

[1] Lu Hsün did not formally join this society, but is always included with them, along with his brother, who was the literary ideologist for the group.

ranks next to Kuo as translator, concentrated mostly upon the Russians; T'ien Han, the dramatist, translated Shakespeare's, Maeterlinck's, and Oscar Wilde's plays and various modern Japanese plays. They were all enamoured of the Russian writers.

Another group centred about the magazine *Contemporary Critic* (1924–26) and included Hu Shih, Hu Yeh-p'ing, and Hsü Chih-mo, the poet. Hsü Chih-mo was a fairly prolific translator also. He translated works of Stevenson, Voltaire's *Candide*, and some from the Italian writers. Still another magazine was *Yü Ssŭ* (1924–1928), whose contributors included Lu Hsün, Chou Tso-jên, Ch'ien Hsüan-t'ung, and Lin Yü-t'ang.

Of the whole May Fourth period only two permanent literary figures remain—Lu Hsün and Kuo Mo-jo—and their lives are epics in the development of China's revolutionary intellectuals. Yü Ta-fu was representative of his period and historically valid as such, and also Chou Tso-jên as essayist and critic. Apart from those for whom the May Fourth period was a chrysalis stage and who came into their own only in the Leftist movement later, nearly all others fade into a tapestry background and are obsolete. There was only one '*bourgeois*' literary survival—Hsü Chih-mo, leader of the "*Crescent Moon*" school of poetry. Hsü, the *pai-hua* poet of love and emotion, did not take any interest in revolution, but was killed in an aeroplane crash in 1931, in the midst of his career. Lin Yü-t'ang, essayist, and Chêng Chên-to, critic, carried on independently, but neither of these are '*bourgeois*' figures as such. Lin once edited a militant Left-wing newspaper in Hankow in 1927, but became a disillusioned satirist, and in 1932 founded a "Humorist" movement in essay and journalism. Chêng Chên-to became an outstanding liberal critic, with Left sympathies, and a general *littérateur* and scholar.

The most important of these retired writers were Yü Ta-fu, Chang Tzŭ-p'ing, Chou Tso-jên, Miss (Hsieh) Ping-hsin, Ch'ien Hsüan-t'ung, and Hu Shih as poet. Others were Lo Hua-shêng, short-story writer, Miss Lu Yin, sentimental novelist, and Yü P'ing-po, poet.

Where are these to-day? Miss (Hsieh) Ping-hsin, more important as poet than short-story writer, lives a domestic life in Peking. She wrote mostly of sentimental mother-love and filial devotion, but is still read for the beauty of her language. Miss Lu Yin is dead. All others except Yü Ta-fu, who recently joined the Fukien Government, are teaching in the universities in literary retirement. Chou Tso-jên was a critic, essayist, and poet. Ch'ien Hsüan-t'ung was an essayist and scholar. Chang Tzŭ-p'ing wrote over thirty novels and was one of the most prolific—and careless—writers. He was popular because of the erotic appeal in his love-triangle affairs, and all his writings are a hackneyed repetition of this single pattern. After the May 30th incident in 1925 Hu Shih and his followers 'became hermits,' as the Chinese say, and took up research in ancient history and the classics for the most part. Though they occupied positions in the universities by virtue of appointment from above, they had no leadership among the youth, and openly clashed with the Leftist student movement in 1935.

Of the living limb of the literary movement that went forward, Lu Hsün and Kuo Mo-jo became leaders in the Leftist movement, along with the Creationists, T'ien Han, Mu Mou-t'ien, Chêng Po-ch'i, Ch'êng Fang-wu, Li Ch'u-li, Fêng Nai-ch'ao, Wang Tu-ching, and Chou Ch'uan-p'ing, and a few of the Literary Research group, Mao Tun, Yeh Shao-chün, and Wang T'ung-chao. Hu Yeh-p'ing also joined the Left, and was executed in 1931 along with other Left writers. Mao Tun, T'ien Han, Wang T'ung-chao, and Hu Yeh-p'ing did their best work in the Left movement. Lu Hsün and Mao Tun live in hiding in Shanghai, but continue leadership of the Left movement. Kuo Mo-jo is in exile in Japan, studying archæology. T'ien Han, the best Chinese playwright, was imprisoned in 1935, and lives under surveillance in Nanking since his release. Li Ch'u-li was imprisoned in 1931 and is still confined. Fêng Nai-ch'ao 'disappeared' mysteriously. Ch'ên Tu-hsiu, essayist, became first leader of the Communist Party and is now in prison, the two young sons of this flaming spirit of the Youth Movement having been executed. Both Yü Ta-fu and Chang Tzŭ-p'ing attempted to join the Left in 1927, but were unsuccessful in this field.

The swing to the Left began after the May 30th incident in 1925. This was a signal for a tremendous upsurge of the mass movement under Soviet Russian advice, which influence had also penetrated into intellectual and school circles by that time, although the Leftist intellectual influence came mostly through the medium of Japan and Japanese translations of Marxist studies, rather than direct from Russia. The phenomenon of the rousing of the proletarian masses astounded the intellectuals, of whom some were delighted with it and some terrified. Many writers joined in the excitement of the next two years as active propagandist workers in the Revolution, and scores of young student-editors and writers were killed or executed in the 'purgation' of Communism following 1927. Others waited and did not join the Left movement until the *bourgeoisie* had 'betrayed,' which excited them to action.

After 1927 the literary centre shifted to Shanghai from Peking. The emotional volatile Creationists were tremendously stimulated by the Revolution and, led by the fiery Kuo Mo-jo (who, like Mao Tun, had actually joined the Army), entered pell-mell into the fray immediately. Three groups carried forward the banner "For a Revolutionary Proletarian Literature" and began a short violent Revolutionary Romantic period, as they fought each other on questions of theory, and attacked Lu Hsün and his *Yü Ssŭ* magazine group, who remained onlookers. These three centred about three Left magazines: *Creation* (established in 1922 and suppressed on February 7, 1929), *The Critique of Culture* (begun and suppressed in 1929), and *The Sun Monthly* (begun in 1928 and suspended in 1932). Chiang Kuang-tz'ŭ was representative of this Revolutionary Romanticism. Others were Hung Ling-fei (executed in 1934), Yang Tun-jên, Ch'ien Hsing-ts'un, Kung Pin-lu, and Fêng Nai-ch'ao (disappeared). Kuo Mo-jo at this time wrote stories idealizing workers, such as his *Only One Arm*, which told of a worker who had lost one arm to the machine, but had one left—for the Revolution.

As the proletarian writers were dominant, other groups remained mere onlookers for the most part. The *bourgeois* writers took refuge in a new magazine (begun in 1928 and suspended in 1933 for criticism of the Kuomintang) called *The Crescent Moon*, which was devoted principally to research in the arts and general cultural discussions from the liberal viewpoint, rather than creative literature, though it published such important writing as the poetry of Hsü Chih-mo. *Contemporary Critic*, established in 1924, with Hu Shih, Yü Ta-fu, Chang Tzŭ-p'ing,

Hu Yeh-p'ing, and Hsü Chih-mo as contributors, ceased publication in 1926; and *Yü Ssŭ* (*Threads of Talk*), a popular magazine with a circulation of ten thousand a week, whose contributors were Lu Hsün, Chou Tso-jên, Ch'ien Hsüan-t'ung, and Lin Yü-t'ang, which was also established in 1924, was suspended in 1928 when Lu Hsün, its leading spirit, changed his position. *Short Story Monthly*, edited by Mao Tun, Chêng Chên-to, and Keng Chi-chih (a famous Russian translator), merely followed the trend without any independent position, publishing mostly the Leftists whose works were in popular demand. There were no other important regular literary journals after this time, except the sporadic Left-wing publications, until *Short Story Monthly* was succeeded by *Literature* in 1933. *Les Contemporains* (1932–34), devoted to the "Third Kind" of writing, was suspended a few months after the Leftists decided to boycott it. Occasional quarterlies appeared including both Left and other writers.

After 1929 the modern drama developed under the leadership of T'ien Han and Hung-shên, both of whom became Leftists. Ts'ao Yü and Li Chien-wu are other important dramatists, the former a Leftist in tendency and the latter a Romantic liberal. T'ien Han popularized Ibsen and Romain Rolland.

In this period, from 1927 to 1932, the Left literature was intentionally neglectful of 'art' and concerned almost entirely with propaganda, theoretical analysis, and journalism. It had tremendous influence, though its literary value was transient. After the Right reaction in 1927 the revolutionary intellectuals took out their frustration in bitter anger against the betrayal by the *bourgeosie* and idealized the peasants and workers, along with analysing the psychology of the revolutionary students and intellectuals of the period.

Only in 1930 did the Left movement centralize, when the China League of Left Writers, of fifty initial members, was formed in Shanghai on March 2, 1930, with Lu Hsün as the key organizing figure. Lu Hsün was not won over to the new revolutionary viewpoint until by 1930 he had become convinced of its validity by the cold logic of historic necessity. This was a great triumph for the Left, and with the most important and brilliant writer in the country at their head, the Leftists had the literary world entirely at their mercy—a dictatorship equivalent to the military dictatorship of the Kuomintang in the political world. All previous sectarian Left groups dissolved and joined together in the League in solid *camaraderie*, with a broad peripheral following on the outside.

Many Left magazines appeared, such as *Sprout*, edited by Lu Hsün, and *The Great Dipper*, edited by Ting Ling, and all were periodically suppressed as soon as the police got around to doing so, though the writers used innumerable pen-names and all manner of camouflage to deceive the censors.

In 1931 and 1932 the Left movement was at its height in the intellectual and student world. The Kuomintang suddenly woke to the fact of its tremendous power and influence and began the suppression in earnest. Until this time the militarists had been too busy with wars to pay much attention to the development of the Left revolution in cultural circles; also the Kuomintang hardly dared appear so reactionary as extreme suppression of the leading intellectuals in the country would reveal. As a warning, on February 7, 1931, Hu Yeh-p'ing, aged twenty-six (husband of Ting Ling), was executed in Shanghai, along with five promising young members of the Left League: Feng Kêng, a girl-novelist, aged twenty-four; Tsung Hui, twenty-one; Yin Fu, twenty-two; Li Wei-shêng, twenty-eight; and Jou Shih, thirty-one. In 1932 a Fascist co-ordination movement began in a special "Campaign Against Cultural Banditry," with specially trained political police and Blue Shirt terrorist-spies operating.

Under this terrorism and the need for discretion the Left wing went into a New Realism movement, characterized by objective, analytical description of life and social conditions, with little obvious propaganda, but with clear indication of the revolutionary necessities involved. It is regarded by all critics as the most promising development that has yet appeared in modern Chinese literature. What the writers lost in freedom of expression they gained in intensity and insidiously persuasive technique. Mao Tun and Miss Ting Ling rose meteorically as leaders in this New Realist movement. Others are Chang T'ien-yi, short-story writer and novelist, Lao Shê, Wang T'ung-chao, and Sun Hsi-chen, novelists. The very newest crop of extremely talented young writers are Sha Ting, T'ien Chün (Hsiao Chün) and his wife, Hsiao Hung, Wu Tsu-hsiang, Yeh Tzŭ, Ai Wu, Chou Wen, Tung P'ing, O Yang-shan, T'ai Ching-nung (reported executed 1933), Wei Chih-shih, Lou Shih-yi (imprisoned 1933; fate unknown), and others such as Miss Shih Ming (who writes under several pen-names), a very young writer. Left-wing dramatists include T'ien Han, Hung Shên, and Ts'ao Yü. P'u Fêng is perhaps the most interesting Left poet.

Of the Revolutionary Romantic strain, sympathetic with the Left, there are Pa Chin, an anarchist, very popular with youth, Miss Pai Wei, Miss Hsieh Ping-ying, Tai Ping-wan, Liu Yen (Yao) P'êng-tzŭ (reported executed in 1935), and others.

During the critical period in 1932 there also arose what Lu Hsün dubbed the "Third Kind" of writer, demanding entire freedom of creation, such as Tu Hêng (Ssŭ Wên). Shih Chê-ts'un attempts the Freudian psycho-analytical approach. A curious type of Fascist literature also appeared, the product of several Leftists who found it necessary to earn their living and freedom by doing hackwork for several Kuomintang-Fascist magazines. At the same time a variety of Decadent-Sensualism, called "Cityism" by the Chinese, appeared. This describes the life in the modern cities for the amusement of readers, often with a feeling of suicidal seeking for escape. Mu Shih-ying, who turned from the Left to pessimistic description without faith in revolutionary change, is one of these, and also his follower, Hei Ying, and Liu Na-ao. A "Humorist" movement in essay and journalism, launched, as we have said, in 1932 by Lin Yu-t'ang, was very much in vogue for two years, but as the political crisis became grimmer the humorous viewpoint became less amusing.

Alongside the Left movement and its periphery there are only a few non-political and neutral writers of creative fiction in China to-day. Pure stylists and artists-for-art's-sake are out of place amid the chaotic revolutionary turmoil—and have few readers. The only important one is Shên Ts'ung-wên, who has written forty books before the age of thirty. He is a romantic, and primarily only a story-teller and stylist. Others are Fei Ming, Li Chien-wu, Miss Ling Shu-hua, Miss Su Mei, Ch'eng Hsiang-ho, Tsao Ching-tsên, Chien Hsien-ai, and Hsiung Fu-hsi.

In poetry the pure artists are relatively more successful in competing with the Left wing.

The "Crescent Moon" school of Hsü Chih-mo, which attempted to utilize Western poetic forms, has been most popular since Kuo Mo-jo, though it declined after 1932. Hsü was succeeded by Jao Mêng-kan, Ch'en Mêng-chia, Pien Chih-lin, and Chu Hsiang, a humanitarian who drowned himself in 1934. These tended to follow Les Parnassiens in Europe in style. Chang K'e-chia recently attempted to lead a movement for simplicity and clarity in opposition to an abstruse Symbolist school initiated by Li Ching-fa, whose followers were Tai Wang-shu and (Yao) Peng Tzŭ, who turned to the Left and was reported executed in Tientsin in 1935. The Leftists publish under innumerable pen-names and are difficult to follow. Most of their work tends towards Symbolism, partly because of the necessity of evading the censors.

Because of the extreme suppression levelled against the Left movement and the almost complete sterility of the bourgeois writers the literary movement has been greatly checked during the past two years or so. China is again being somewhat forced back into 'literary colonialism' because of the obstacles placed in the way of publishing the new creative writing dealing with the vital, and therefore censorable, subjects of the day. As a result a temporary renewal of translation activity and period of 'collections' and historical study has begun. The young creative writers of China have always had a desperate struggle to compete with the translations of Western masterpieces, and these translations have greatly deterred the independent development of modern Chinese literature by stealing a part of the reading public —particularly that part which seeks only entertainment.

The most interesting recent development has been the sponsoring by the Left writers of a Mass Language Movement in 1935, countering an abortive Back-to-Confucius attempt to restore the classical wen-yen as the literary medium. Latinization —doing away with the ideograph—is considered to be the only way of making true mass education possible. The intellectuals are now thwarted in their attempts even to communicate with the vast illiterate masses, and it is hoped that latinization of the language will make possible a revolutionary proletarian literature not only *about* the peasants and workers but *for* and even actually *by* them. The literary form of *pai-hua*, full of Westernized forms and innumerable new words, is almost as unintelligible to the masses as the old *wen-yen* and remains pretty much the domain of the modern intellectuals. In latinized form even the provincial dialects may be utilized as a literary medium, or—more important at present—as a means of merely being able to learn to read and write a true spoken language.

Seldom before in history have the literary intellectuals of any country put up a more gallant struggle than the present revolutionary writers of China. The sheer vitality of the Left movement is amazing. According to a list prepared by Mao Tun in 1935 the following important members of the League of Left Writers have suffered the fates mentioned: Executed together on February 7, 1931, Jou Shih, Hu Yeh-p'ing, Miss Feng Kêng, Li Wei-sheng, and Yin Fu; executed in 1928, Jen Kuo-chen, an early Leftist. Imprisoned on date given, fate uncertain but believed to be still alive in prison, Li Ch'u-li, 1931, Ku Wan-chuan, 1933, Pan Tze-nine, 1933, Lou Shih-yi, 1934, Hua Ti, 1935, Ping Shan, 1935, Ho Kuo-tien, 1935, and P'eng K'ang, an early Leftist, 1929. Imprisoned and released after a year or so, Ai Wu, February 1933–34, Miss Ts'ao Ming, June 1934—reported freed on uncertain date—and Miss Ting Ling, May 1933–35. Pan Hsün (Pan Hsien) was arrested in 1934, and starved to death in a Tientsin prison in 1935, after receiving no food for nine days. Ting Chiu was killed in escaping arrest with Ting Ling in May 1933.

From other sources it was later reported that Pan Tzŭ-nien had been secretly executed. T'ai Ching-nung was reported executed in Peking in 1933, Hung Ling-fei was executed in Tientsin in 1934, and (Yao) P'êng-tzŭ was arrested in Tientsin in 1935, and reported immediately executed as a Communist. In March 1935 four prominent Left writers were arrested— T'ien Han, Hua Han, Ling Pai-shui, and Hsü Ti-hsing. Of these only T'ien Han was "released." T'ien, like Miss Ting Ling, now lives under close observation in Nanking.

This is a very scanty report as such information is not easy to get in China because the military prisons give out no information about political prisoners. Dozens of talented young student-editors and writers have been imprisoned in various cities, these being the favourite quarry for police raids. In a four-page leaflet printed in Shanghai in 1936, entitled "A Glimpse of Contemporary Chinese Literature," Mr. P. C. Robert (a well-known Chinese literary editor and author writing under an English name) states: "The execution of some forty writers of the Left wing by the Nanking Government caused universal sympathy throughout the country. . . . Yet during the last two or three years Nanking has made many secret arrests. . . . There have been no longer any executions, but merely a mysterious 'disappearing' from time to time."

A report to the Congress of American Revolutionary Writers made by the China League of Left Writers on April 11, 1935, states that "during the past six months twenty out of a total of one hundred members of the League in Shanghai alone have been arrested or kidnapped."

Lu Hsün said in an interview that he personally knew of thirty writers arrested in Shanghai alone since 1927, who were literary figures of some distinction, and not journalists or young unknown writers. Because of the terrorist methods used against it the League was forced to dissolve in 1935, and at present there is no formal organization, although in the spring of 1936 Mao Tun was attempting to form a new Writers' Union. Previous to its dissolution, according to the above report, the Left League had branches "in almost all important cities in China, and even in Tokyo, where some forty members have gone into exile."

Lu Hsün is without question the most important modern writer China has produced. He is not only a writer of creative fiction and probably the best short-story writer, but also an active intellectual leader, and one of the best essayists and critics. As he is perhaps the most respected critic in China, it is of interest to quote some of his opinions, as expressed in a recent conversation with Edgar Snow:

> Mao Tun, Miss Ting Ling, Kuo Mo-jo, Chang T'ien-yi, Yü Ta-fu, Shên Ts'ung-wên, and T'ien Chün are probably the best writers that have yet appeared since the modern literary movement began. These names include both the best short-story writers and novelists. No novelist of real importance has yet been produced. The 'novels' of Shên Ts'ung-wên, Yü Ta-fu, Lao Shê, and others are in form really

novelettes or long short-stories, and the authors owe their fame to short-story work rather than to attempts at novel-writing.

The short story is of greater importance than any other branch of modern Chinese literary development. In technique, materials, style, in fact, in all respects, it is almost totally new to the literary tradition of China, whereas the drama, for instance, borrows considerably from the past. The best dramatists are Kuo Mo-jo, T'ien Han, Hung Shên, and a new Leftist playwright, Ts'ao Yü.

In poetry Ping Hsin, Kuo Mo-jo, and Hu Shih have done as well as others, but none of modern Chinese poetry seems to be of anything but experimental value. Our modern poetry is thus far a failure. In the essay we have done better. Important essayists include Chou Tso-jen, Lin Yü-t'ang, Ch'ên Tu-hsiu, and Liang Ch'i-chao—the famous Ch'ing scholar who antedates the present literary movement.

Our best writers are at present almost without exception Leftists. This seems to be because their writings are the only ones of sufficient vital content seriously to interest intellectuals. The best Left writers are Mao Tun, Miss Ting Ling, Sha Ting, Jou Shih, Kuo Mo-jo, Chang T'ien-yi, T'ien Chün, Yeh Tzŭ, Ai Wu, and Chou Wên. Hsiao Hung, the wife of T'ien Chün (whose real name is Hsiao Chün), is the most promising of our women writers, and shows possibilities of becoming as much in advance of Miss Ting Ling as the latter was in succeeding Miss Ping Hsin.

China cannot go through a period of true *bourgeois* literary development, any more than it can go through a period of independent *bourgeois* political development. There is no time for it, and no privilege of choice before us. The only possible culture for China to-day is Left revolutionary culture, the alternative being colonial acceptance of an invading imperialist culture, which means to have no independent or national culture at all. "While the rest of the world is using aeroplanes China cannot use sidewheel steamers—no more in art than in life. We have to leap ahead to the thing that has greatest value and meaning in the world scene to-day."

It is precisely because of that great leap from feudal social concepts into proletarian cultural concepts that the foundations of modern Chinese literature are poor. Chinese literary development is probably unique in this respect. Even in the earliest beginnings of the renaissance movement there was a strong inclination to the Left. It is a curious fact that China has produced no important *bourgeois* writer. Even Lin Yü-t'ang cannot be classed in that way, for he belongs more to the literary tradition of old scholasticism, which grew out of a feudal background, than he does to modern *bourgeois* concepts—

which in fact he satirizes. Ping Hsin did not belong to the *bourgeoisie* either: there were never any cultural problems posed in her work, which was nearly all written for children.

At the same time it is perfectly true that no genuine 'proletarian' writers have yet emerged in China from the peasants and workers. Left literature is still confined to the realm of revolutionary intellectuals and the 'petty-*bourgeoisie*.'

Best modern writers selected by other critics usually include, besides those Lu Hsün mentions, Lao Shê, Pa Chin, Wang T'ung-chao, and Hsü Chih-mo, the poet. Mao Tun and Shên Ts'ung-wên are generally considered China's best novelists. Chinese are masters of the essay. Modern drama had a phenomenal rise for a few years, but has now been greatly handicapped by censorship and terrorist practices. T'ien Han and several other Left dramatists wrote some intensely interesting scenarios, a few of which were screened, but the drastic action taken against 'dangerous thoughts' by the authorities has temporarily succeeded in destroying the originality of the new Chinese theatre.

Living China is the first comprehensive collection of representative short stories to be compiled. Selections from the most important short-story writers were submitted to the publishers, including work by Lu Hsün, Mao Tun, Ting Ling, Shên Ts'ung-wên, Yü Ta-fu, Kuo Mo-jo, Chang T'ien-yi, Jou Shih, Pa Chin, Sha Ting, T'ien Chün, and (Hsieh) Ping Hsin, along with other representative writers such as Sun Hsi-chen, Mu Shih-ying, and two examples of the very newest young writers, Miss Shih Ming, a Left New Realist (who publishes in China under several different pen-names), and Hsiao Ch'ien, a follower of Shên Ts'ung-wên's independent Romanticism. Because of space limitations all the short stories submitted could not be included in this volume, and for the same reason the writers Lao Shê, Wang T'ung-chao, and Chang Tzŭ-p'ing are not represented, their best work being their longest.

Practically all Chinese creative writers attempt every form of writing. This is not because of any special gift of versatility, perhaps, but because of failure—or often inability because of financial pressure—to concentrate on the mastery of one particular technique. There is no doubt that literature has suffered much through this dissipation of talent, without any sure

direction. Not only do they write both short stories and novels
—and poetry—but usually they are also essayists, journalists,
editors, and translators, and often dramatists and text-book
writers as well. This lack of concentration to some extent explains
why not a single monumental work has yet been produced,
such as the long, exhaustive, and powerful novels of Russia,
although the tremendous scope of the dramatic material in
China is at least the equivalent of that from which grew the
great materpieces of Russian literature.

There is no special word for 'novel' in Chinese even now.
Hsiao-shuo, literally 'small talk,' serves both to indicate long and
short stories—novels, novelettes, and short stories—and this is
reflected in the lack of clear distinction between these forms in
Chinese. *Ch'ang-p'ien hsiao-shuo*, for long story or novel, and
tuan-p'ien hsiao-shuo, for short story, are recent terms, but are
also somewhat ambiguous. Neither the novel nor the short
story has yet become a highly specialized art in China. Chinese
writers tend to produce formless works, with little emphasis
on plot, both in the novel and the short story. Many *hsiao-shuo*
are little more than essays or dialogues. At the same time the
best essays often have a distinctly narrative appeal about them—
as, for example, some of Lu Hsün's. Great emphasis is placed
on conversation, which often drags interminably.

The modern short story is a new form for China, deriving
principally from Russia, much as the modern European model.
The only other important influence is French. English-language
writers are read for interest, but seem to be alien to the Chinese
psychology, method, and general material background. The
influence of Russia upon both Japan and China is wide and
profound, in spite of the tremendous obstacles placed in the
way of this cultural trend because of political exigencies. There
are many reasons for this orientation towards Russia, but the
fundamental one is analogous revolutionary movements. From
the very beginning of the modern literary movement the Russians captured the hearts of the Chinese.

Most of the Russian influence on Chinese literature comes
through the medium of Japanese translation—in fact, the channel
through which the modern art movements in China have flowed
is Japanese adaptation of Western forms. This is particularly

true of Soviet writers and books on Communist theory. Many pre-revolutionary Russian classics were, however, translated from the English. In the same way the early Creationists and Chou Tso-jen, who introduced modern Japanese poetry and did voluminous translation work, were indebted to Japan as *Alma Mater* in their Western education. This is partly because of its proximity for study, and also the ease of translation from Japanese into Chinese. Few Chinese have been able to translate directly from the Russian, and several of these were executed for their pains, such as Jen Kuo-chen and Tzǔ Chu-p'o (executed in Fukien in 1933). Chiang Kuang-tz'ǔ, possibly the best Russian translator, who died from a broken heart in Shanghai in 1932 after being expelled from the Communist Party, referred to himself as the Demyan Bedny or Vladimir Mayakovsky of China, and was much influenced by Russian Futurism. During the Revolutionary Romantic period from 1927 to 1932, of which Chiang Kuang-tz'ǔ was the central figure, the Chinese were so enamoured of Russia that some writers even used Russian pen-names—partly in order to ensure for themselves a devoted reading public. Kêng Chi-chih, an editor of *Short Story Monthly*, was another translator from the Russian.

Previous to the *pai-hua* literary revolution in 1917 a good deal of translation work had been done in *wen-yen*, such as that by Yen Fu, who rendered Western writers on nineteenth-century philosophy and science into Chinese—Adam Smith, John Stuart Mill, and Huxley—and an extraordinary old scholar named Lin Shu. Lin Shu 'translated' and published 132 books from the English into *wen-yen* without knowing a single word of English! His collaborator was Wei I, who rendered the English into *pai-hua* Chinese for Lin. These two translated Tolstoy, Scott, Conan Doyle, Dumas, Dickens, Rider Haggard, Shakespeare, Cervantes, Defoe, Swift, and Lamb, for instance. From the American they selected only *Uncle Tom's Cabin*.

However, immediately after the May Fourth Literary Movement began in 1919 most of the popular translations were of Russian works—taken from various languages. Most of the important Russians have been translated. Of all writers Tolstoy has probably had the greatest total influence on Chinese literature. This is because he writes in a vein and uses materials not only easily understandable to the Chinese, but highly relevant to their own problems. His epics of peasant life and philosophy of peace and paternalism fit easily into the Chinese social consciousness, being quite Oriental in their implications. Tolstoy was one of the writers translated into the *wen-yen* by Lin Shu, and was popular during that reformist period. The peasant revolution is still the prime dramatic material in China, and most of the Left writers use this as theme, rather than the city worker-proletariat. Gorky was not understood by the Chinese until about 1925–27, because of his philosophy; but since his *Mother* was published in China he has been an important figure. Turgenev ranks next to Tolstoy as an influence in Chinese literature. Artzibashev is third and Chekhov fourth. Other widely read Russians are Gorky, Dostoevsky, Pushkin, Gogol, Andreyev, Bunin, Ostrovsky, Arashenko, Semonyoff, Brock, Lupshkin, and Korolenko.

Since the Communist movement gained momentum in China the newer Russian writers are much in demand, though most of them are banned and circulate secretly in dog-eared copies from friend to friend. Ognyov's *Diary of a Communist Schoolboy* and Madame Kollontai's *Red Love* are two of the most widely read modern books, along with Gladkov's *Cement* and books by Ivanov and Pilnyak. During the beginning of the Left literary movement proper, in 1928–29, about one hundred works by Russian writers were translated. Bukharin and Lunacharsky are the most influential literary critics in China.

The French influence ranks next to the Russian: Flaubert and de Maupassant. Others are Zola, Rousseau, Victor Hugo, du Maurier, Daudet, Voltaire, Gourmand, Montaigne, Merimée, Musée, Mirabeau, St Beauin, Veretillac, Loti, Gautier. Prévost's *Manon Lescaut* and Dumas's *La Dame aux Camélias* were two popular books. Romain Rolland, Henri Barbusse, and André Gide are tremendously admired by the Chinese to-day.

Ibsen, who was introduced by T'ien Han, has had great influence upon the drama. Rabindranath Tagore is the greatest single influence in poetry. Miss Hsieh Ping-hsin and Hsü Chih-mo both imitated him. Hu Shih imitated Whitman in his early *Experiments*. The French, Japanese, and Russian moderns have had considerable influence in poetry also.

The only German works which really attracted the Chinese were those of Goethe and Heine, and Remarque's *All Quiet on the Western Front*.

Upton Sinclair is the most popular American writer among Chinese, followed by Jack London and John Reed. Recently Michael Gold (especially his *Jew Without Money*) and Miss Agnes Smedley have been widely read, and also Pearl Buck's *The Good Earth*. Stories by Edgar Allan Poe and Mark Twain and *Uncle Tom's Cabin* are standard works of interest.

The only English writers who rouse much enthusiasm among the Chinese are George Bernard Shaw and Oscar Wilde. Of course, the classics, such as Shakespeare, are dutifully read. Dickens' novels, *Robinson Crusoe*, and *Gulliver's Travels* are liked. Sir James Barrie's *The Admirable Crichton* is a very popular book, possibly because of the Chinese predilection for versatility in all things. T. S. Eliot, D. H. Lawrence, and Katherine Mansfield are known in China, but James Joyce is not yet a discovery—doubtless he and Gertrude Stein will one day translate nicely into Chinese, for that language has a similar disregard for grammar. It is curious that English literature has so little real influence in China, because the whole educational system (due to missionary influence) tends to be based upon English as a medium for transmission of modern ideas, and every inducement is made to encourage the reading of these authors. In fact, English classics are forced upon the colleges and middle schools in great quantities. But it seems to be only because of the wide reading public in English and the number of students able to translate from the English that most of the English books are read and made available. Russian, for instance, is almost an unknown tongue in China, and it is very nearly impossible for any student to get the opportunity to study it.

David Willard Lyon in an article on "The Past Decade in Chinese Literature"[1] throws an interesting sidelight upon Chinese reading habits. Of the foreign books in translation most frequently called for by the patrons of the National Library of Peking in 1934 the following are listed:

Russian: Artzibashev, *Sanine*; Chekhov, *Collection of Short*

[1] *The Journal of the North China Branch of the Royal Asiatic Society,* vol. lxv, 1934.

Z

Stories; Gorki, *The Bystander*; Tolstoy, *Resurrection*; Turgenev, *First Love*. French: Dumas, *La Dame aux Camélias*; Anatole France, *Thaïs*; Rousseau, *Les Confessions*. Danish: Ibsen's plays. English: Barrie, *The Admirable Crichton*; Defoe, *Robinson Crusoe*; Shakespeare, *The Merchant of Venice*; Shaw, *Mrs Warren's Profession*; Oscar Wilde, *Lady Windermere's Fan* and *Salome*. American: Upton Sinclair, *Boston, Cement,* and *Oil* (in three different translations). German: Goethe, *Faust*; Remarque, *All Quiet on the Western Front* and *The Road Back*. Of the eleven most-called-for books on general subjects six were on Communist theory, and included Bukharin, Engels, Marx, and studies of the Five-year Plan in Russia. The five others were: C. F. Andrews, *Gandhi, His Own Story*; M. Beer, *Social Struggles in Antiquity*; the *Report of the Lytton Commission of the League of Nations* and the *Report of the Committee of Nineteen on the Sino-Japanese Dispute*; the *Tanaka Memorial*.

Lu Hsün says that the foreign literature which he remembers as having influenced him was, in his early reading, *Uncle Tom's Cabin, Robinson Crusoe,* and the novels of Dumas; later there was Sienkiewicz' *Quo Vadis*, and the works of Swift, Byron, Andreyev, and Poe, and, later still, those of Gogol, Turgenev, Chekhov, Heine, Nietzsche, and Matsume. He hates Dante as "a very evil man."

Mao Tun was influenced by Turgenev and Dickens; Ting Ling by Flaubert and de Maupassant; Pa Chin by the French sentimentalists; Yü Ta-fu by Turgenev; and Kuo Mo-jo by Goethe. Of course, a great deal of this influence comes through the Japanese Westernizations. Yü Ta-fu, Kuo Mo-jo, Chang Tzǔ-p'ing, and the Creationists owe much to the Japanese in their work.

Nearly all the early writers were bilingual 'returned students.' Many were also well educated in the Chinese classics, however. The life of Lu Hsün, for instance, runs like a fine golden thread through the period which separates the ancient *wen-yen* scholar tradition from the Communist moderns, who even demand Latinization of the language. Out of the interweaving of the various influences brought together by these writers and translators from the four corners of the globe a fairly solid ground-fabric has now been made, on which the present writing generation may pattern their work. The May Fourth period of imitation is over; and also the short years of the revolutionary Romantics enamoured of Soviet Russia for itself. The literary movement, like the Revolution, has deepened and formulated itself as an independent entity.

Most of the youngest writers, who reveal greater talent than formerly, know no foreign language at all, or have only the barest smattering necessary for the study of modern science and art. The dazzling wealth of the sudden gift of world literature to Chinese readers has lost its initial fascination. Readers are now prepared to buy native literature instead of Western masterpieces in translation, and writers are prepared to fashion it in modern art-forms and from the dramatic materials which surround them. Only the suppression of freedom of expression and of the spirit of free inquiry holds them back from creating a vital new literature comparable to that produced by any great nation in any great historic period of its development, and this suppression in itself is a dialectical force which must soon bring about its opposite in a tremendous explosion.

PEKING
June 1936

APPENDIX B
BIBLIOGRAPHY

THE complete works of the various authors included in this volume are not, of course, listed below, but the most important books of each are mentioned in the biographical notes. A list of the works of prominent Chinese authors, up to 1932, will be found in Ku Fêng-ch'êng's *Chung Wai Wên-hsüeh-chia Tzŭ-tien* (*A Dictionary of Chinese and Foreign Authors*) (Lou-hua Library, Shanghai, 1932). Some of the books and articles recommended there have been especially helpful in the preparation of this volume, and all are likely to prove useful to anyone interested in undertaking further study in the field of modern Chinese literature.

GENERAL WORKS OF REFERENCE

CHANG JO-YING: *Chung-kuo Hsin Wên-hsüeh Yün-tung, Shih Tz'ŭ-liao* (*Historical Materials of the New Chinese Literary Movement*) (Shanghai, 1932).

CHÊNG CHÊN-TO: *Chung-kuo Wên-hsüeh Shih* (*History of Chinese Literature*) (4 vols.; P'u Shê Book Company, Peiping, 1932).

HUA HAN: "The New Literary Movement in China," an article in the *Wên-yi Chang-shuo* (*Lectures on Chinese Literature*), April 10, 1930 (now suppressed).

HUANG JEN-YING (editor): *Kuo Mo-jo Lun* (*On Kuo Mo-jo*) (Kuang-yü Bookstore, Shanghai, 1934).

KU FÊNG-CH'ÊNG (editor): *Chung Wai Wên-hsüeh-chia Tzŭ-tien* (*A Dictionary of Chinese and Foreign Authors*) (Lou-hua Library, Shanghai, 1932).

KUO MO-JO: *Tzŭ-chuan* (*Autobiography*) (3 vols.; Shanghai, 1930).

LU HSÜN and sixteen others: *Ch'uang-tso-ti Ching-yen* (*Experience of Authorship*) (T'ien Ma Bookstore, Shanghai, 1932).

LU HSÜN: *Chung-kuo Hsiao-shuo Shih-liao* (*Historical Outline of Chinese Fiction*), including stories and novels to the Ch'ing Dynasty (5th edition, January 1929; Liang-yu Bookstore, Shanghai).

356

MAO TUN: "Literary Research Society," an essay in the *Hsien Tai* (or *Les Contemporains*) (Shih Chê Ts'un edition, May 1933).

MU YU: *Wu Nien* ("The Fifth Year"), an essay in the *Hsin Pao's* third issue of a special literary supplement, September 17, 1935.

SHANGHAI LOU-HUA LIBRARY COMPANY (editors): *Tang-tai Wên-yi Lun-chi* (*Essays on Contemporary Literature*) (Lou-hua Library, Shanghai, 1930).

SSŬ WÊN: *Tan Jen* ("Third Kind [of Man]"), an essay on literary disputes which appeared in *Hsien Tai*, a literary monthly (Shanghai, January 1933).

T'AI CHING-NUNG (editor): *Kuan-yü Lu Hsün Chi-ch'i Chu-tso* (*About Lu Hsün and his Works*) (Kai-ming Bookstore, Shanghai, 1933).

T'AN CHEN-PI: *Chung-kuo Wên-hsüeh Ching-hua Shih* (*History of the Development of Chinese Literature*) (Shanghai, 1932).

WANG CHÊH-FU: *Chung-kuo Hsin-wên-hsüeh Yün-tung Shih* (*History of the New Chinese Literary Movement*), with an introduction by Hu Shih (Shanghai, 1934).

SELECTIONS AND COLLECTIONS

CHANG T'IEN-YI: *Fan Kung* (*Counter-attack*), a collection of his short stories (Life Publishing Company, Shanghai, 1934).

CHINESE LITERARY YEAR BOOK SOCIETY (editors): *Chung-kuo Wên-yi Nien-chien* (*Chinese Literary Year Book*), a collection of short stories, vol. i (Modern Bookstore, Shanghai, 1933).

LU HSÜN (editor): *Chung-kuo Hsin Wên-hsüeh Ta Hsi* (*Great Series of New Chinese Literature*), contemporary Chinese short stories (2 vols.; Liang-yu Bookstore, Shanghai, 1935).

LU HSÜN: *Lu Hsün Tzǔ-hsüan Chi* (*Lu Hsün's Selected Works*) (T'ien Ma Bookstore, Shanghai, 1932).

LU HSÜN: *Na Han* (*Shouts of Encouragement*), a collection of his short stories—now an historic book (Peiping, 1923).

MAO TUN: *Mao Tun Tzǔ-hsüan Chi* (*Mao Tun's Selected Works*) (T'ien Ma Bookstore, Shanghai, 1932).

MAO TUN: *Mao Tun Tuan-p'ien Hsiao-shuo Chi* (*Selected Short Stories of Mao Tun*) (Kai-ming Bookstore, Shanghai, 1934).

MU SHIH-YING: *Nan Pei Chi* (*North Pole, South Pole*), a collection of his short stories (Hu-feng Bookstore, Shanghai, 1932).

PA CHIN: *Kuang-ming* (*Splendid*), a collection of his short stories (New China Bookstore, Peiping, 1932).

P'ENG TZǓ (editor): *Ting Ling Hsüan Chi* (*Ting Ling's Selected Works*) (T'ien Ma Bookstore, Shanghai, 1932).

SHÊN TS'UNG-WÊN: *Ju Shui Chi* (*Sproutings*), a collection of his short stories (Life Publishing Company, Shanghai, 1934).

SHÊN TS'UNG-WÊN: *Ts'ung-wên Tzŭ Chi* ([*Shên*] *Ts'ung-wên's First Collection*) (Crescent Moon Publishing Company, Shanghai, 1931).

T'IEN CHÜN: *Pa Yüeh-ti Hsiang-ts'un* (*Village in August*), a novel (Slave Series, No. 2; Shanghai, 1936).

TSAO CHIA-PI: *Chung-kuo Hsin Wên-hsüeh Chi Shu* (*New Chinese Literature Series*), a selection of modern Chinese short stories from the Literary Renaissance to 1926, with introductions by Lu Hsün and Mao Tun (2 vols.; Good Friends Book Company, Shanghai, 1935).

TU HÊN: *Huai Hsiang Chi* (*Homesick*), a collection of his stories (Shanghai, 1934).

WÊN-HSIN SOCIETY (editors): *Hsien Tai Chung-kuo Hsiao-shuo Hsüan* (*Selected Contemporary Chinese Short Stories*) (2 vols.; Chiang-nan Literary Society, Shanghai, 1933).

YANG CHING-HAO (editor): *Chung-kuo Wên-yi Nien-chien* (*Chinese Literary Year Book*), selected short stories, vol. i (Pei-hsing Bookstore, Shanghai, 1934).

YEH SHAO-CHÜN and others: *Ch'uang-tso Hsiao-shuo Hsüan* (*Selected Chinese Short Stories*) (Shanghai, 1934).

YEH TZŬ: *Feng Shou* (*Harvest*), short stories (Slave Series, No. 1; Yung-kuang Bookstore, Shanghai, 1935).

The following magazines have been found to contain material of great value on the subject of modern Chinese literature:

Hsiao-Shuo (*Short Story*), a Shanghai monthly.

Hsiao-Shuo Yüeh-pao (*Short Story Monthly*), edited by Chêng Chên-to (Shanghai).

Ho Tan (*Why No Dawn?*), vol. i, Nos. 3, 4, and 5, published by the Ho-tan Society (Peiping, 1936).

Shih-chieh Wên-hsüeh (*World Literature*), a monthly, now suppressed (Shanghai, 1934).

Shui Hsing (*Mercury*), a monthly, vol. i, No. 6 (Peiping, 1935).

Tang-tai Wên-hsüeh (*Contemporary Literature*), a monthly, now suppressed (Shanghai, 1934).

Tso-chia (*Authors*), vol. i, No. 1, edited by Mêng Shih-huan (Shanghai, 1936).

Wên-hsüeh Yueh-pao (*Literary Monthly*), edited by Chêng Chên-to, vols. iii and iv (Shanghai, 1933–34).

Wên-yi (*Literature*), a monthly, edited by the Contemporary Cultural Research Society, vol. i, Nos. 2 and 3 (Shanghai, 1934).

Wên-hsüeh Chi-k'an (*Literary Quarterly*), edited by Chêng Chên-to, vol. i (Peiping, 1934).

Wên-hsüeh Hsing Chi (*Literature—New Edition*), vol. i, No. 1 (Shanghai, 1935).

BIBLIOGRAPHY OF ENGLISH BOOKS AND ARTICLES

Nothing comprehensive has been written in English concerning the modern literary movement in China, and Nym Wales' article in this volume is the most detailed study yet made. Other references of value will, however, be found in the following books and articles:

ACTON, HAROLD: *Modern Chinese Poetry* (Duckworth, London, 1935). An introduction discusses contemporary Chinese poetry.

HU SHIH: *The Chinese Renaissance* (University of Chicago, 1934). Contains material on the 'language reform' and the so-called "Literary Renaissance."

LEAGUE OF LEFT WRITERS: *Greetings to the Congress of American Writers*, a manifesto issued on April 11, 1935, published in *China To-day*, June 1935. Contains a detailed report on 'thought-purgation' and the terror imposed on writers and artists in Kuomintang China.

LIN YÜ-T'ANG: *My Country and My People* (Heinemann, London, 1936). In a chapter on Chinese literature Mr Lin briefly comments on modern writers.

ROBERT, P. C. (HSIAO CH'IEN): *A Glimpse of Contemporary Chinese Literature*, (Shanghai, 1935). A four-page leaflet summarizing modern literary trends.

SNOW, EDGAR: "The Ways of the Chinese Censor," in *Current History* (July 1935). Reports on the suppression of Left art and literature in China.

VARGAS, PHILIP DE: "Some Elements in the Chinese Renaissance," in *New China Review* (April 1922). Discusses the *pai-hua* movement.

YAO HSIN-NUNG: "New Literary Movement, its Tendency and Future," in the *North China Daily News* (April 7, 1933). A good summary.

ZEN, SOPHIA H. CHEN (editor): *Symposium on Chinese Culture* (China Institute of Pacific Relations, Shanghai, 1931). Contains a chapter in which Hu Shih discusses the *pai-hua* language reform.

PREVIOUS TRANSLATIONS

Two very short selections from modern Chinese short stories have been translated and published in English. Mr J. B. Kyn Yn Yu (Chin Yin-yi?) has published *The Tragedy of Ah Qui* (Routledge, 1930), which contains a somewhat bowdlerized version of Lu Hsün's *Ah Q Chêng Chuan* and several other modern stories. Another version of *Ah Q Chêng Chuan* is George Kin Leung's *The True Story of Ah Q*, published by the Commercial Press (Shanghai, 1929). *Short Stories from China*, a booklet published by Martin Lawrence (London, 1934), contains six revolutionary tales, of which *Slave Mother*, by Jou Shih, is reprinted in this volume. There are no other English translations available in book form.

DATE DUE

GAYLORD   PRINTED IN U.S.A.